the smallest part

NEW YORK TI ·HOR

AMY ⟩N

Library of Congress Cataloging-in-Publication Data

Harmon, Amy
The Smallest Part — 1st edition
ISBN-13: 978-1979819503 | ISBN-10: 1979819505

In the end, only three things matter:

How much you loved,

How gently you lived,

And how gracefully you let go

Of things not meant for you.

Unknown

PROLOGUE

♀ ♂

It was a big lie. The biggest lie she'd ever told. It reverberated through her head as she said it, ringing eerily, and the girl behind her eyes—the girl who knew the truth—screamed, and her scream echoed along with the lie.

"Are you in love with Noah, Mercedes?" Cora asked. "I mean . . . I know you love him. You've been friends forever. We all have. But are you *in* love with him?"

Mercedes had wondered since if her response would have been different had she been facing Cora, looking into her big, blue eyes as she answered the question. She didn't know if she would have been able to hide the truth from her. Cora knew her too well. But Mercedes had been lying to herself for a long time, and she was good at it. She was the mighty stone-face, the tough chick, the sassy Latina, and Cora loved Noah too. She was *in* love with Noah.

So Mercedes lied.

"Ha! No. Not like that. Never like that. Noah is like my brother. No." Mercedes heard the lie in the way her accent suddenly appeared when she said "never." Her *r* curled, and curled again on "brother," underlining the falsehood. Mercedes didn't speak English at home, but she spoke it fluently, and her accent only reared its ethnic head when she wanted it to. Or when she was full of shit. Mercedes wasn't selfless. Noah had kissed her, and she had kissed him back. She thought about him constantly. Morning, noon, and night. If it had been anyone else—anyone—she would have

i

stuck out her chest, folded her skinny arms, and let her feelings be known. She would have claimed him. She would have.

But it was Cora. Brave, beautiful, broken Cora.

When Mercedes watched Noah and Cora together, they looked right. They fit. Cora had always been taller than all the boys, but she wasn't taller than Noah. Noah grew six inches his sophomore year in high school, climbing to six-foot two, and he and Cora were like slender trees, looking down on a forest of saplings, looking down on Mercedes with their lovely benevolence. Mercedes grew a few inches herself sophomore year and topped out at five-foot two. She was grateful to have reached that not-so-lofty height; her mother, Alma, was five feet on her tip-toes, and Oscar, her papi, had been five-foot six in his dreams.

Cora's willowy frame and sweet temperament complemented Noah's lean height and his introspective nature. Noah's eyes were the saddest, wisest eyes Mercedes had ever seen. His eyes had always been that way. The wavy, brown curls flopping over his forehead and coiling at his nape softened his angular face with all its sharp edges. He'd buzzed it once, the summer before eighth grade, and he'd looked so naked, so strange, that Mercedes had made him promise never to do it again. It had scared her seeing him that way, as if there were no child left inside him, as if there never had been. But when Cora was around, Noah's eyes weren't nearly so sad and nearly so wise. But then love makes fools of everyone, doesn't it?

Mercedes knew Noah first. She could have said that. She could have called dibs. They met when they were eight years old, two years before Cora moved into the Three Amigos apartment complex. He'd been leaning against the door to his unit, playing with a yo-yo. His knees were knobby and his shorts too short, as if he never grew wider, only longer, and had been wearing them since he was four.

"Hi," Mercedes had greeted him, her eyes on the bouncing string and the expert way he moved his wrist. He had such patience, such a quiet containment, even then . . .

His eyes lifted, smiling at the corners, before they dropped back to the shiny red yo-yo with the dirty string.

"Hello," he responded softly.

"I'm Mercedes. You can call me Sadie. I live over there." She pointed

at the door across the hall.

"Mercedes? Like the car?"

"Is it a cool car?" she asked.

"Expensive."

"Well then, yeah. Just like the car." Mercedes nodded seriously. Expensive was good.

"I'm Noah."

"Like the guy with the ark?" she asked.

He flipped the yo-yo up into his palm but didn't release it again. His brow furrowed as he studied her.

"What guy is that?"

"You know. He had a big ark and put the animals on it because the world was going to be flooded. The guy who's responsible for rainbows."

"I've never heard of him." His eyes were wide. "How many animals did he save?"

Mercedes laughed, bewildered. Everyone knew about Noah's ark, didn't they? She'd been raised on Noah's ark and Daniel in the lion's den and Moses and the parting of the Red Sea. She knew all the Bible stories. It was the only book her grandma—her abuela—ever read to her. They even had a picture of the pope on their living room wall and the Virgin Mary above the toilet, with little candles resting on the tank. Abuela insisted, because it was the only place there was ever any privacy for prayer.

"He saved all kinds. Two of each. A girl and a boy."

"And the rainbow?"

"God told Noah he wouldn't ever flood the earth again and gave him a rainbow as a promise.

"Huh. Cool. How long ago was that?"

"A long, long time. About 300 years or so," Mercedes mused, liking the way it felt to know the answers to his questions. Being the youngest in her family—a family that consisted of her and her parents, her maternal grandmother, an aunt, and two older cousins all crammed into a three-bedroom apartment—meant no one listened to her. It was crowded, and Mercedes was a beloved annoyance.

"Huh." Noah suddenly looked doubtful. "What if one of the animals died?"

Mercedes didn't really know what he was asking, so she shrugged.

"What if the girl tiger died? Or the boy lion?" he persisted.

Oh. Mercedes realized what he was getting at. You had to have one of each to have a baby. Abuela had explained that much.

"I guess they didn't die since we have lions and tigers now, right?"

"Hmm. Maybe that's why dinosaurs are extinct," he pondered, rubbing his chin.

"They wouldn't have fit on the ark, anyway, at least not Brontosaurus," Mercedes added wisely.

"So only two of each?" he queried.

"Yeah. Only two."

Only two.

And Cora and Noah were a pair. A beautiful pair.

So Mercedes lied.

And with that lie, she let him go.

ONE

1985

"*What is she doing?*" *Mercedes whispered. Her voice was awed, not critical, and Noah tipped his head in consternation, not sure he knew.*

"*She's talking to someone,*" *he whispered back.*

"*But there's no one there,*" *Mercedes insisted.*

They watched the girl, a wisp of pale limbs and fiery hair, as she twirled around and talked dramatically to someone they couldn't see.

"*She's so pretty,*" *Mercedes whispered.* "*She looks like a fairy who's lost her wings.*"

"*Or her marbles,*" *Noah murmured. He was working his way through a stack of library books and had borrowed* Peter Pan *by J.M. Barrie on a whim. It was better than he'd anticipated. The red-haired girl kind of reminded him of Tinker Bell, come to think of it. Tinker Bell or Tootles, the lost boy who had lost his marbles. It turned out the marbles were Tootles's happy thoughts. Maybe the girl was trying to find her happy thoughts. Noah looked down at Mercedes, standing transfixed beside him. She seemed enchanted with the red-haired girl.*

"*Her name is Cora,*" *Noah offered, hoping Mercedes wouldn't leave him behind. With a girl to play with, one of the same age, Mer wouldn't need him anymore.* "*She lives in 5B.*"

1

"Is she older than us? She looks older," Mercedes mused, wrinkling her nose.

"No. She's ten too."

"Have you talked to her?"

"No. She was crying when I saw her yesterday." Her tears had made Noah turn around and walk away, and he'd felt bad about it ever since. He'd wanted to give her privacy, but he should have asked her if she was okay.

"Was she hurt or was she sad?"

"Sad, I think. Something's wrong with her dad," Noah said.

"How do you know all of this if you haven't talked to her?" Mercedes asked, suspicious.

"My mom talked to her mom."

"Your mom . . . talked?" Mercedes gaped. Noah's mom—Shelly—rarely left the house in the daylight. She worked nights in the hospital, in the records department, all alone with rows and rows of files and a big ring of keys. Noah thought the hospital was peaceful at night. Mercedes said it sounded creepy. His mother slept during the day, she always had dark circles under her eyes, and Mercedes had never heard her say a word. Noah spoke for her when Mer was around.

"My mom probably just listened," Noah amended, but Mercedes wasn't paying attention to him anymore. She was watching the girl, Cora, with a delighted smile.

"She's playing pretend," Mercedes crowed, as if solving the puzzle. *"Maybe she'll let us play with her."*

At that moment, the girl turned and saw them watching her. She smiled, and Noah's breath caught. Her smile was like sunshine, warm and bright and welcoming. She waved eagerly, as though they'd already met, and she'd been waiting for them to join her.

"Come on, Noah," Mercedes said, slipping her hand into his and pulling him forward. *"She's going to be our friend."*

2004

Cora stood on Mercedes's doorstep looking disheveled and disorganized, her one-year old daughter, Gia, on her hip. Her hair hung to her waist in slightly tangled, crimson waves—beach hair. She wasn't made up, and her blue eyes were shadowed, her freckles dark on her pale cheeks, but she was still beautiful. Slim and tall, narrow-hipped and small-breasted, she'd thought about being a model until she realized modeling meant she would have to leave Noah and Mercedes behind. They had all been inseparable once. Shared fear. Shared uncertainty. Shared childhood. Whatever it was, it had cemented them.

Cora set Gia down and watched her walk on teetering steps across Mercedes's living room to the couch, where Gia grabbed a hold and tossed a triumphant look over her shoulder, as if to say, "Did you see that?"

Mercedes clapped and scooped her up.

"You're walking! She's walking, Cora!" Mercedes danced with Gia, who giggled and burped and giggled again.

"She just ate, Sadie. Don't jostle her or her bottle is going to end up all over your shirt," Cora warned. Mercedes set Gia down, steadying her, and backed away. "Come see me, Gia. Come to me!" Gia toddled toward her godmother, zombie-like, arms out, legs stiff.

"When did this happen?" Mercedes shrieked, swooping her up again. "She was crawling on her birthday, and now this!" Mercedes was devastated that she'd missed the transition. Gia had turned one two weeks ago. Mercedes had hosted a party with a few of their friends and so many pink balloons her living room had looked like a bubble bath commercial.

"A few days ago. Noah turned around, and she was following him," Cora reported.

"So big!" Mercedes crowed. "So smart. Such a smart girl!"

Cora shifted, hovering by the door. She looked weary. Worn.

"Well, she's eaten, but what about you and me? Where should we go for lunch?" Mercedes asked, kissing Gia's neck, only to have her squirm to be put down.

"Actually, I have a doctor's appointment. I'm sorry. I scheduled it for today, thinking I could ask you to watch her, and then forgot all about it. Can she stay here for an hour or two? That's not as fun as going to lunch, but honestly . . . Gia's a handful, and we'd be chasing her all over the restaurant."

"Sure. No problem. Are you okay, Cora?"

"Yeah. Fine. Just a one-year, post-baby exam. Nothing to worry about. I could bring her with me, but . . . she's into everything . . . and . . ." There was something about her tone, her listlessness, that made Mercedes not believe her. Cora wasn't simple. She was deeply complex, but she hid from her complexities by smiling banally at the world and making everyone believe nothing flickered behind her eyes.

"I'll come with you. I'll stay in the waiting room with Gia while you have your check-up. And when you're done, we'll go out. Or we can come back here and eat. I'll trim your ends and wax all your unwanted hair," Mercedes offered, waggling her eyebrows. Beautifying humanity was her gift and her goal.

"Wow. Waxing. That's really tempting, Sadie," Cora deadpanned. "I'll pass."

"I'll give you a pedicure too. You'll feel like a new woman when I'm done. Nothing feels as good as being pretty from head to toe."

"That would be nice. I don't feel very pretty lately." Cora's smile was wan. "But there's no reason to go with me to the doctor. You and Gia will be much happier here. I'll come back when I'm done, and I'll let you have your way with me. I know you. You'll pester me until I give in."

"Yes. I will. And Cora?"

Cora's eyes skittered away. "Yes?"

"You would tell me if something was wrong, wouldn't you?" Mercedes pressed.

Cora looked out the open door as though she needed to get going.

"Are you late?" Mercedes asked. Cora tended to be very late or very early, like her internal clock was always off.

"No. No, I have time," she said. But she stayed near the door, her eyes focused on the light streaming in from outside. "If something were to happen to me . . . you would take care of them, wouldn't you, Sadie?" she asked.

"What are you talking about?" Mercedes gasped, gaping at her friend.

"Nothing. Just thinking out loud. It's hormones. Ignore me." Cora tried to smile.

"Hormones or not . . . you're scaring me."

Cora waved her hand, dismissing the words. "I'm okay. Just really tired. I haven't slept through the night for so long, I can't remember what a good night's rest feels like. I'm in a fog most days."

"Are you still nursing Gia at night?"

"No. I weaned her." Her mouth trembled, and Mercedes's unease ratcheted up another notch.

"That's good, right?" Mercedes said softly. "You'll sleep better if you're not getting up to feed her. And she's over a year old now."

Cora's eyes filled up with tears, and she nodded rapidly, wiping her eyes. "It's good. I can go back on my medication, I'll have my body back, and maybe Noah will get his wife back. I haven't been a very good wife. But I'm sad that it's over. I loved nursing her."

Mercedes nodded, not knowing what to say. She'd never been a mother, never nursed a child, never experienced the cycle of emotions she was sure were typical of the first year.

"I better go." Cora leaned down until her face hovered above her daughter's head. She kissed Gia's downy crown and said, "I love you, Gia bug." Gia smiled and instantly latched on to her mother's curtain of red hair. Cora patiently unclamped the little hands from her long locks and straightened.

"I'll be back soon, Sadie. Thank you." Cora hesitated for a heartbeat, and turning, wrapped Mercedes in a fierce hug. She had to stoop to enfold her shorter friend, but laid her head against Mercedes's dark hair the way she'd done when they were younger.

"I love you, Sadie. So much," Cora murmured.

"I love you too, *mama*." Mercedes hugged her back. Cora was affectionate and emotional; she always had been. But it had been a while—years —since she'd told Mercedes she loved her so earnestly, without it being tossed out in passing or parting. She released Mercedes abruptly and walked out the door without a backward glance.

Hours passed, but Cora didn't come home. Gia fell asleep just after her mother left but woke an hour and a half later, fussy and hungry. Mercedes fed her a mashed banana and a few bites of the baked potato she'd made herself for lunch. Gia ate happily, and afterward they went for a walk, babbling to each other—Gia in an unknown tongue, Mercedes in Spanish, determined to make her goddaughter bilingual. It was a rare day for April. The sun was shining off the snow and no wind rustled the brittle branches above their heads or nipped at their cheeks. Mercedes was sure when they returned, Cora would be waiting for them. But she wasn't.

Mercedes changed Gia's diaper and coaxed her to walk a few more times before settling her with a pile of toys in the middle of the living room. Doctors were notoriously unreliable—especially OBGYNs. All it took was one patient going into labor to screw up the day's schedule.

When Gia began to fuss and rub her eyes, Mercedes gave her a bottle of baby formula Cora left, and when she was finished, laid her back down amid the pillows and toys. Gia fell asleep again, her little bottom in the air, her arms tucked beneath her. Cora had been gone since noon. It was five o'clock. Mercedes called Noah, but the secretary at the Montlake Clinic reported that he was in a counseling session, and she would have him call her back when he was through. The salon where Mercedes worked was closed on Mondays, making it the day she caught up with her life. She typically cleaned, ran errands, watched TV, and baked, but she was too anxious to sit still and watch television. Her house was clean, and any errands would have to wait until Cora came back, so she resorted to her old standby, cooking. She'd just started frying her first batch of empañadas when her phone peeled. She ran to it, certain it was Cora.

Noah's name lit up the screen.

"Hey," she answered.

"Is Gia with you?" He sounded panicked, odd, and Mercedes could tell from the sounds bleeding through the receiver, that he was outside or in his car. A horn blared, muted and distant in her ear, and Noah cursed.

"Yes. She is. But Cora should have been here hours ago, Noah. She had a doctor's appointment, and she hasn't come back. Have you heard from her?"

"Gia's with you. Gia's okay," he panted. "I thought . . . I was afraid . . ."

"Noah? What's going on?" Mercedes interrupted.

"I thought Gia was with Cora. They said the car seat was empty—" He stopped. "Cora's been in an accident. I'll call you when I know more.

They won't tell me anything else."

"What? Where is she? Tell me where you are."

"She's at the hospital—at Uni. I'm heading there now. I don't know anything else."

"I'll be there as soon as I can."

The phone went silent in her hands, and she raced through the house, turning off the oven, gathering her purse and her keys, and banging out the door before remembering the child sleeping in a circle of pillows on her living room floor. She didn't have Gia's car seat.

"Crap. Okay. That's cool. I'll strap her in." It wasn't cool. It wasn't okay. It wasn't safe, and if she got pulled over, she'd get a ticket the size of Texas. But she didn't have much choice.

Mercedes bundled Gia up, snagging her diaper bag and a blanket from the floor as she hurried from the house, her mind a tumble, aware of only the next breath and the next step, refusing to tarry on one thought or fear for too long. She wouldn't think. She would simply do. And all would be well. It would be okay. Everything would be fine.

Gia didn't wake on the way to the hospital. Mercedes had decided to lay her in the footwell on the passenger side, tucking her blanket around her and making her as comfortable as possible; she was safer there than rolling around on the seat. Mercedes drove like she had a wedding cake in the trunk, her hands gripping the wheel, her eyes scanning the road and flickering back and forth between the sleeping child and the traffic ahead like a metronome. Tick, tock, tick, tock. She didn't turn on the radio. She breathed. She drove. And her eyes swung back and forth.

The afternoon was vibrant and bold, detailed and undeniable. Not surreal. Not separate. She was living it. Wholly. Irrefutably. And her fear burned every scene and segment into her memory. When it was all over, she remembered exactly where she parked in the crowded lot, grateful she'd found a spot. She remembered breathing a prayer of thanks to the Madonna that she'd arrived without Gia waking. She remembered staring down at her feet, realizing she was wearing stilettos. Red stilettos and socks. They'd been right next to her front door, and she'd shoved her feet into them before running to her car. Red stilettos, jeggings, and a bright purple top. Purple and red. Not a great combination. She kicked off the shoes, pulled off her socks, and then put the heels back on. Her hair was in a tight knot on the top of her head, and she was wearing the earrings she'd made herself—dangling hoops strung with beads in a dozen colors. The earrings made the red and purple work. *Why was she thinking about her outfit?*

Her makeup was done—it was always done—and when she pulled the mirrored visor down, searching for her sunglasses, her face looked the same as it always did. She needed sunglasses. She needed to cover her eyes. She needed to shield herself from what was coming. Something terrible was coming. She was suddenly shaking, so afraid that she considered not going inside at all. She hated hospitals. She would wait with Gia in the parking lot until Noah called her again or until the baby woke. She slid the glasses over her nose and felt for her lipstick in her purse. She found it, the tube sleek and small in her hand. She uncapped it and tried to slick it over her lips, but it fell from her trembling fingers and rolled beneath the seat. She opened the car door and stepped out, so she could more easily retrieve it. Crouching down, she felt for it, found it, and pulled it free. A long crimson hair clung to the waxy stick.

Mercedes stared at the red strand. It wasn't her hair. It was Cora's, and Cora was inside. Cora needed her. She pulled the hair free and recapped the lipstick, resolute. Without allowing herself to hesitate a moment longer, she collected her things, walked around to the passenger side of her old Corolla, and lifted Gia into her arms. Locking the door from the fob in her hand, she strode toward the hospital, eyes covered, lips painted, arms full.

Everything would be all right. Everything would be fine. She would make it okay.

She called Noah. He didn't answer. The phone buzzed and buzzed in her hand until his voice mail picked up. She left a message and told him she was in the ER waiting room.

She found a seat in a quiet corner, easing her purse and Gia's bag to the ground, her eyes scanning the area for Noah. Gia stared up at her, bleary-eyed, her pale hair standing up in a tufty halo around her head.

"Hi, baby girl. You're awake. We're going to see Daddy," Mercedes murmured feebly. Gia didn't cry or seem alarmed to find herself in a strange place. She sat on Mercedes's lap, looking around the crowded waiting room with calm curiosity. Mercedes called Noah again. And again.

After fifteen minutes of waiting, Mercedes walked to Admitting and asked the woman behind the desk for help.

"My friend was brought here. She was in an accident. This is her daughter. Her husband was on his way. Can you page him or . . . direct me to her?" Mercedes asked.

"What's her name?"

"Cora Andelin."

The woman's hands froze for a half second before she typed the name into the computer. She didn't verify the spelling or ask Mercedes anything else. She picked up the phone and made a call, not looking up.

"Has Dr. Andelin arrived?" she said into the receiver. Mercedes realized the woman must know Noah. He'd practically grown up there, and a hospital was like a small town. Noah said everyone knew everyone else, and gossip was served daily—hot, cold, or leftover from the day before. "I have a woman here . . . a friend of the family. With his little girl." The woman pressed her fingers to her mouth, like she didn't want to speak in front of Mercedes. She nodded, said "Okay," to the person on the other end of the call, and nodded again.

"Have a seat. Dr. Andelin's on his way out," she said, setting the phone in its cradle. She spoke matter-of-factly but didn't quite meet Mercedes's gaze.

"Thank you for your help," Mercedes said and turned away.

She felt the woman watching her as she retreated, but forgot all about her when she saw Noah push through a pair of swinging doors. He walked like he wasn't aware he was moving, like his legs had been programmed to propel him forward, but his mind was standing still. And she knew then, without him saying a word, what she'd known the night Papi died.

"Noah?" Mercedes asked as he neared. "Where's Cora?"

He started to shake, and his legs buckled. Mercedes grabbed his arm and pushed him toward a chair. People were watching them, their faces full of curiosity and concern. Noah sat for a millisecond then rose again, like movement kept his anguish from settling. He took Gia from Mercedes and began striding toward the entrance doors, his long legs eating up the distance.

"Noah?" Mercedes scrambled after him, expecting him to take her to Cora, wherever she was. But once he was outside, facing the brilliant sunset that infused his pale face with false hope, he halted abruptly. Turning blindly, he began walking this way and that, searching for an escape hatch, a sink hole to swallow him up. He held Gia like a newborn, cradling her like he was holding her for the first time, and Gia let him, staring up at him, happy and content. She smiled and reached for his beard.

"Da da da da," she gurgled.

"Where is Cora, Noah?" Mercedes demanded. She was inexplicably angry with him. He wouldn't dare tell her something she didn't want to hear. He wouldn't dare. But Mercedes knew, and each breath was laced with arsenic.

"She's gone," he choked. Mercedes watched his countenance crack, his eyes flutter closed, and his arms tighten around Gia as he sank down on an empty bench. Noah cried the day he and Cora were married. He'd waited at the end of the aisle in his dress blues, the jacket a little too small in the shoulders and the sleeves, the trousers an inch too short. He'd grown since he was fitted for the uniform. Tears had streamed down his face as Cora had walked toward him on the arm of her mother.

The tears he cried now were very different. They scurried down his cheeks and hid in his beard, terrified and heavy, desperate to escape the deluge.

"What do you mean . . . gone?" Mercedes gasped.

"She's . . . dead, Mer," he cried.

She reeled back, swinging her purse and the diaper bag in a wide arc, attempting to protect herself—too little, too late—from a direct hit.

It was freshman year again. Third period PE. The only one left in a game of dodge ball. She hated getting hit. She avoided it at all cost. She would slide and shimmy and squirm away. But she was the only available target, and there were too many balls coming at her to avoid them all. She tried to catch one only to have another hit her in the face. She staggered, the sting and the insult of the impact almost as great as the pain. Chest burning, face screaming, she'd been too stunned to react.

Mercedes stood, looking down at Noah, and felt the same affront, the same agony, the same biting disbelief as she struggled to draw breath through seizing lungs.

Gia began to wail, her father's distress scaring her, and Noah attempted to hide his tears, running his large hand over his face, his shoulders shaking as he wept.

"Someone saw her go over the edge and called it in. They found her c-car at the bottom of a ravine in Emigration Canyon, up-s-side down in the c-creek," he stammered, choking back sobs. "The water's high—higher than it's been in years. They don't know if she drowned . . . or if she was d-dead before her car stopped."

"Why was she in the canyon? She had a doctor's appointment," Mercedes whispered, still standing. Still stunned. But a scream was growing in her belly and bubbling in her chest. Her hands were hot. Her chest was cold. Noah said something about the sun glaring off the snow that still lined the roads and covered the mountains, about the heavy run-off from the spring melt. Emigration Canyon was ten minutes away, if that. They lived at the base of the foothills on Salt Lake City's east bench. But Mercedes could only see Cora's face, the way she looked standing in her living room, weary and worn.

You'll take care of them if something happens to me, won't you Sadie?

Mercedes wanted to go to Cora, but Noah didn't want Gia to see her lifeless mother. He stood outside the enclosure where his wife was pronounced dead, clutching his child, giving Mercedes a moment. His tears had not abated. He was walking and talking on the phone, bouncing his daughter, trying to soothe his mother-in-law, who was en route, while tears continued to collect in his beard. Mercedes stepped through the curtain that created a partition between Cora and the rest of the emergency room.

A sheet covered Cora from her shoulders to her feet, but she was missing one shoe, and a slim foot in a heavily-soiled striped sock peeked out at the very bottom. There was no blood or visible trauma. Her hair was a stringy, damp mass around her face. Mercedes smoothed it back, combing out the tangles with her fingers while she stared down at her long-time friend in disbelief. The woman on the gurney looked like Cora. But it wasn't Cora. Cora of the ephemeral smile and the little-girl-lost appeal was no longer there, and Mercedes withdrew her hand, frightened. There were tears in her chest, but her heart was so heavy and horrified that she couldn't release them. She was angry. Outraged. And she could not cry.

A scream tore through the ER, and Mercedes flinched, backing away from Cora's body. She'd heard that sound once before. It made the hair rise on her neck and a shudder steal down her back beneath her clothes. Cora's mother had arrived.

"Noah! Oh no, no, no. Where is she?" Heather McKinney mourned, already crying, already hysterical. Heather McKinney had lost her husband to suicide. Now her daughter was gone too.

Mercedes walked out of the partition and wrapped Heather in her arms as Noah was forced to repeat the story all over again. The nurse that had escorted Heather shot an apologetic look at Noah's face before informing him quietly that he should tell her when they were through so Cora could be moved from the ER. Noah blanched, as though the next steps had not even occurred to him. He wasn't a medical doctor. He was a psychologist. He didn't heal bodies, he eased hearts and untangled emotions. He unraveled dangerous thoughts and unscrambled psychoses. What happened next? Where would they take Cora? What arrangements would need to be made? For a moment, Mercedes thought she would be sick but bore down against it, willing her stomach to settle and her head to clear.

Heather was distraught and unwilling to part the curtain and face what was on the other side by herself. Gia began fussing, and Mercedes reached for her, taking her from Noah so he could take Heather in to see her daughter before they took her away. Gia had to be hungry, and her diaper was soaked. Mercedes slipped into a nearby bathroom, the space almost comforting in its silent sterility. No messy emotions, no death, nothing to do but see to the immediate needs of a small child. Long bars bracketed the walls so the sick or unsteady could cling to them as they navigated the room. There was no changing table, and Mercedes reached out and grasped one of the bars as she eased herself down, wishing something as simple as an iron rod could restore her emotional equilibrium. She spread Gia's blanket on the tile and laid her down, changing her pants with numb efficiency. In the diaper bag, she found a package of raisins and one of the long, thick teething cookies that Gia loved and that made such a mess. Gia squealed with delight when she saw it, and her innocent oblivion anchored Mercedes. The child was not suffering—not yet. Mercedes washed and dried her hands before unwrapping the cookie and handing it to Gia. Then she picked up the child, rose to her feet, and left the small bathroom for the horror beyond.

Mercedes knew there was something wrong with her. She couldn't grieve. She couldn't sleep either. But it was the lack of tears that worried her. The days after Cora's death were a strange blend of muted colors and black emotions. People repeated the same things—there were only so many things to say—and everyone cried. Everyone cried but Mercedes.

She spoke at Cora's funeral service, recounting the days of their lives and the nights of their days. She spoke honestly of her love for her friend, of Cora's love for her family, and the ways she had made the world a better place. The small congregation regarded her with tear-stained cheeks and smeary eyes when Mercedes told them about the time Cora had protected her during a dog attack. Cora had wrapped her arms around Mercedes and screamed until Noah and Papi came running. Cora had shallow bites and scratches all over her back, but Mercedes had survived unscathed. When Mercedes asked Cora why she'd done it, Cora had looked at her oddly and said, "Because you're smaller than me. And I love you."

Mercedes recalled the way Cora never said an unkind word—which was good because Mercedes said enough for both of them. The people laughed—the sound a hiccuping chorus of relief—and Mercedes smiled too. But her smile was false, even if her words were not. She didn't tell the mourners how Cora had stood in her living room, tired and depressed, and how Cora had walked out of Mercedes's house and drove her car off a cliff. Mercedes didn't tell them that. She didn't tell anyone that. She didn't know for sure if it was true, but in her heart, she believed it.

Noah had stopped crying too. At the service, his face was pale granite, his eyes cratered with misery and missed sleep. Heather cried more than everyone else put together. Alma said mothers had more tears, though her own eyes had remained dry. Mercedes had done Heather's hair before the funeral, but Heather had done her own makeup, and mascara was streaked down Heather's prematurely wrinkled cheeks like streamers at a Halloween dance.

Alma took Gia during the funeral service and entertained her in the church foyer. Alma said she wouldn't understand what was being said anyway. Her English wasn't great, but Mercedes knew she understood much more than she let on. It was her way of serving while avoiding her feelings. Mercedes was like her mother. They kept busy so they wouldn't go crazy. They stayed busy so grief couldn't catch them.

At the cemetery, they all stood around the casket suspended over the gaping hole. The ground was wet, and the leaves were just beginning to bud on skeletal limbs. The sun was bright, the day mild. April was a bitch in Utah—moody and hormonal. Some days she moaned, some days she turned a cold shoulder on her citizens, some days she teased them with rays of hope-filled warmth. The day Cora was buried she beamed psychotically, and as the casket was lowered into the ground, she wrapped the onlookers in a gentle breeze.

Noah played a song on his guitar. It was the silly tune he'd written to ask Cora to marry him. Mercedes had never had the heart to tell him it was terrible. But as she listened to his quiet voice and the awkward strumming of his long fingers, not quite holding the chord, she realized how wrong she'd been. It was a song about all the little things he loved about her, all the parts that made up the whole. He'd rhymed words like button and glutton, like boring and snoring, and when he'd played it for Cora the first time, before he popped the question, she'd hardly been able to keep a straight face.

But between the silly verses and his bashful delivery, there was love and devotion, there was commitment and promise, and there was hope. It wasn't terrible at all. It was perfect, and it was painful. It was all Mercedes could do not to cover her ears until it was over. Noah's voice broke as he sang the last line, and the small group gathered around him smiled at the song's whimsy, at his heartfelt sentiments, and their tears fell again. But Mercedes didn't cry.

TWO

1985

"What do you want to do when you grow-up?" Noah asked.
"I don't want to grow up," Cora said.

They were sitting on the hot sidewalk, shivering, trying to get dry. A delivery truck had smashed into a hydrant in front of their apartment complex shooting water into the air and spilling it down the streets. It had been over one hundred degrees every day since the Fourth of July, and the water had felt like a fountain from heaven. Noah, Mercedes, and Cora hadn't wasted time getting in their suits, afraid the fire truck would arrive and shut the water down before they could change. Their shorts and T-shirts were drenched, their legs stretched out in front of them, highlighting the differences in their skin tones. Brown, white, and red—Cora burned so easily her nose was perpetually peeling. Noah didn't burn, but his legs were white compared to Mercedes. Mercedes was normally golden, but in the summertime, she was downright chocolatey. Their legs looked like Neapolitan ice cream.

"I want to own a beauty salon when I'm older," Mercedes said. She already had a name for it. MeLo—pronounced mellow—for the first two letters of her first and last names. Mercedes Lopez. MeLo. She thought it was the perfect name for a place where people went to relax and turn into butterflies.

"Why do you want to do that?" Noah asked.

"Because I like making people look beautiful. I love makeup. I love hair. I love clothes." Mercedes shrugged. "And I like bossing people around, so I need to own it. Not just work there. What do you want to do?"

"I want to be a doctor," Noah said, lying back, his eyes on the sky, his skinny arms folded behind his head. Cora and Mercedes immediately lay back beside him.

"I couldn't be a doctor. I couldn't look at blood all day." Mercedes grimaced.

Cora shuddered. "Or bones. Or vomit."

"I don't want to be that kind of doctor," Noah said. "I want to be a doctor who helps people with mental illness."

"We're eleven, Noah. What in the hell is mental illness?" Swearing made Mercedes laugh, so she swore often.

"Noah wants to help people who are sad. Like my dad," Cora explained.

"And my mom," Noah added. He turned his head and gave Mercedes a smile. "You make them look good on the outside, Mer. I'll fix 'em up on the inside."

"Maybe I should go to beauty school too," Cora mused. "Then I could work at your salon with you, Sadie."

Mercedes shrugged. Cora forgot to brush her own hair half the time. Mer couldn't imagine her styling someone else's hair and being happy doing it. "If you want, sure. Wouldn't you rather do something else, though?"

"I told you, I don't want to grow up. It scares me," Cora murmured.

"That's because every grown-up you know needs a doctor like Noah," Mercedes said. The Three Amigos Apartments were full of crazies.

"Your mom and dad don't, Mer," Noah argued.

"That's because we're Mexican. Papi says Mexicans are tough," Mercedes said proudly, jutting out her chin.

"Then maybe when I grow up, I'll be a Mexican," Cora said. Noah and Mercedes laughed uproariously, and Mercedes sat up and looked down at her friend. Cora's hands were folded over her chest, and her eyes were closed. Her red hair fanned out around her head and shoulders on the concrete, fiery in the sun, reminding Mercedes of the painting Abuela

kept over her bed, the one of Our Lady of Guadalupe, her body surrounded by a holy glow. Cora wasn't laughing, and suddenly, neither was Mercedes.

Noah read Viktor Frankl's book, *Man's Search for Meaning* when he was sixteen. He read it so many times the cover fell off and the pages came loose. The first half of the book chronicled Frankl's experiences in a concentration camp, but the part that impacted Noah most was when Viktor described laboring in the forest near Auschwitz, believing his wife was still alive across the way in the women's camp.

She wasn't. But there was a moment when Viktor looked up into the sky and out into the cold beauty of the world around him, thinking of his wife, and he realized that the soul itself could not be incarcerated. He still had the liberty to love. He still had the freedom to hope, to experience joy and gratitude, even amid all the horror around him. The knowledge liberated him and kept him alive.

Noah thought of Viktor Frankl more in the weeks following Cora's death than he'd thought about him in years. How ironic that he, too, would long for his wife, taken from him too soon, whisked into a Neverland where only God and his angels could see her face. He had not yet experienced his own liberation; his soul was chained to the earth by regret, and Cora was in the clouds. He was the same man, but his chest had been cracked open, his skin peeled back, and in the wake of Cora's passing, he walked around with everyone staring at his gruesome, exposed heart, unable to help him, secretly wishing he'd go away until it healed.

He didn't go back to work immediately; better not to subject the staff at Montlake to his chest wound. He would have to go back soon. Cora had a sizeable life insurance policy, but there was a suicide clause, and an investigation was being done. The person who saw her car go over the edge said she hadn't even slowed. Noah didn't want the money—it made him sick and sad—but he needed it, if only to buy him some time to figure out how to negotiate fatherhood without help. Maybe that wasn't fair. He had help, though his helpers were sporting hearts almost as bruised and battered as his.

Cora's mom, Heather, cried whenever she talked to him, and Noah was grateful for her preoccupation with her own bloody scars. It kept her from seeing his. Mercedes didn't cry; her pain was more like an abscess, invisible to everyone else, but patently obvious to him. It would have to be lanced eventually, but she wasn't letting anyone near her. She cooked and cleaned and made sure Noah didn't run out of diapers and that his cupboards were stocked. She didn't ask him how he was. She knew. They moved silently in each other's orbits, solitary planets in a lonely galaxy.

Gia, in all her innocent oblivion, was his saving grace. It was only when he looked down into his daughter's sleeping face, when he held her in his arms or saw her smile, that, like Viktor, he realized joy was possible amid terrible pain. Viktor had searched for meaning in his life. Noah didn't have to look very far. Gia gave him purpose. She was his why when every day he woke up thinking, "what the hell do I get up for?"

Grief was greedy and depleting, and he could not take care of Gia if he allowed himself to wallow in it. His mother had done that. Wallow and wade, making the hole deeper and darker, until her grief became a warm cloak of excuses. Noah had been forced to grow up the moment Shelly expelled him from her womb. Her sadness had aged him.

He didn't want that for Gia. So he bandaged up his oozing flesh and put his grief in the room where he kept bad memories and useless truths. He didn't ignore it. He just didn't change his dressings or open the door very often. When he did, he barely cracked it, reaching in for the bare minimum before ducking out again and pulling the door shut behind him. He kept his eyes averted from his mangled chest and faced each day in pieces and small parts, conquering the essentials one by one, and trying not to worry about anything unnecessary. He had to feed, change, clothe, and comfort, and he focused his efforts there.

He wasn't especially skilled at diaper changing. He was ashamed to admit he hadn't changed many in the first year of Gia's life. He'd never gotten up with Gia in the night to feed her. The most he'd done was rise, take Gia from her crib, and pass her to Cora. He didn't have the necessary equipment for breast-feeding, and Cora had been adamant about the ritual.

But a month after Cora died, Noah could change a diaper and make a bottle and barely wake up to do it. No saggy bottoms and loose tabs. He diapered the way he'd learned to make his bed in boot camp. Tight corners, straight lines, everything tucked and smooth. It didn't take long before he knew what temperature Gia liked her formula, before he knew what foods she would eat—mashed potatoes were always welcome—and which ones made her shudder.

Gia's hair was another issue. It stood on end when it didn't hang in her eyes. He found a little, pink barrette in the bathroom drawer, but she immediately yanked it out along with a handful of hair, and howled in pain. Noah fell back on what he knew. He got Gia's hair wet, slicked it down with pomade, and called it good. Her hair didn't move. Problem solved. That is, until Mercedes stopped by to check on them, took one look at Gia, and crossed herself like her abuela used to do. Mercedes sat them down in the kitchen, Gia in her high chair, Noah on a stool, and gave them both haircuts.

"If we cut Gia's hair short, it will grow in better—no long pieces and bald spots. I told Cora a hundred times, but she wouldn't let me do it. She couldn't bear to cut it." Mercedes stopped talking abruptly, Cora's name dripping from the shears she held in her hands. With a deep breath, she began snipping, and Cora's wishes fell to the floor with Gia's baby hair.

When she was done, Gia's hair was an inch long on the sides and maybe two inches long on top. Mercedes wetted it down and parted it neatly like Gia was going to the office. All she needed was a tiny suit and tie.

"She looks like a businessman.," Noah murmured.

Mercedes rolled her eyes. "Like you can talk. The way you had her hair slicked back, she looked like Gordon Gekko from *Wall Street*."

It was true, and Noah laughed. Mercedes's head shot up like she'd missed the sound, and she flashed him a grin. A jolt of misery and guilt lanced his heart, and his smile fell away. Mercedes pretended not to notice.

"She looks chic. Like Twiggy," Mercedes huffed. "We'll pierce her ears if you want to make her look a little more girly."

"And what was Cora's opinion on that?" Noah asked.

Mercedes didn't answer, though he guessed she knew. She swept up the wisps of blond hair from the tile and handed Gia her sippy cup and a teething biscuit, ignoring his question. Knowing Cora, earrings were a thumbs-down. Cora cried when Gia got her shots—every time—and Noah couldn't imagine her wanting to poke holes in her baby's ears unless it was absolutely necessary.

"Your turn, cave man," Mercedes changed the subject. "That beard is only attractive if you can't hide small, woodland creatures in it."

He closed his eyes and let her have her way. She trimmed and snipped the hair on his head and the growth on his face, talking about this and that, about a new line of hair color she was selling in the shop, about the rising temperatures—finally—in Salt Lake City, and he just listened, letting her voice fill the quiet, answering only when necessary, growing drowsy in the safety of her hands.

"I've put you both to sleep," she murmured. Noah opened his eyes and peered at Gia. Her head was drooping. Mercedes set her scissors down and tucked a stack of dish towels between Gia's left cheek and the tray on her high chair, easing her to a more comfortable position. Mercedes resumed her ministrations, and his eyes grew heavy again.

"I'm leaving on Thursday, Noah. I'm taking that course I told you about—all the new innovations in beauty care, products, services, stuff like that. It's in LA . . . remember? I get to work with industry experts—Hollywood hair and makeup artists—and I will be working on the set of that period movie. I hate to leave you and Gia right now, just when you're going back to work. But I've been preparing for this for a year. I've got to go."

Noah was suddenly alert. He stared at her blankly.

"How long will you be gone?" he asked.

"It's a two-week course and another four weeks on set."

Noah had no memory whatsoever of Mercedes planning to be in Los Angeles for six weeks. Panic bubbled in his healing chest. Cora had been gone for six weeks. Six weeks was a millennium.

"Who's running the salon while you're gone?" he asked. What he wanted to ask was, "Who will run my life?"

"Keegan," she said, drawing his name out, as if trying to stimulate Noah's memory.

"Who's Keegan?" An image of a too-pretty, male stylist with white teeth and perfect hair flickered through his muddled brain. He didn't like Keegan. But Mer seemed to get along with him well enough. She and Keegan were chummy. Keegan wanted to be more than just chums. It was obvious. So far, Noah didn't think Mer had taken him up on it, but Cora had been convinced Mercedes would give in eventually. Noah hoped she wouldn't. She deserved better than a pretty face and a hollow head.

"Noah!" Mercedes lowered her brow and pursed her lips, not sure if he was teasing. He was too morose, and his comedic timing was shot to hell. "You know Keegan Tate. He's been a stylist at Maven for three years. I started training him to help me manage six months ago."

"Sure. Yeah. Keegan Tate."

"I'll call. Heather will be here, and you know you can call Mami if you need anything too."

Noah nodded woodenly. Mercedes had been training Keegan to help her manage the salon, but no one had had trained Noah to manage without Cora.

"I'm proud of you," Mercedes whispered.

"Why?" he whispered back.

"You're so strong. You're such a good daddy, and you never complain."

"What choice do I have?" he said. He sounded bitter, and he reached out a hand to his daughter's freshly-shorn head and touched her hair in silent apology.

When Cora told him she was pregnant, he took a two-day furlough and got drunk. He wasn't happy. He wasn't excited. He was scared and angry. They'd talked about kids, sure, but it had always been something a long way down the road. He'd earned his associate's degree when he was still in high school. It was cheaper that way. Four years after he graduated high school, he got his Bachelor's degree in psychology. It would have been only two years, but he joined the Air Force reserves. Between Basic Training, Tech School, and a year in Kuwait, he lost a little ground. Marrying Cora at twenty-two had been a luxury he really hadn't been able to afford. She'd just graduated and had her first teaching job, and between school, one weekend a month at Hill Air Force Base, a part-time psych tech job at the Montlake Psychiatric Clinic, and medical transcription jobs at all hours of the night, he'd had no time to do anything but breathe. He'd married her anyway.

Two years into his doctorate program in psychology, he'd picked up his Master's degree. Two and a half years after that—at twenty-seven—he became Dr. Andelin. He'd worked his ass off to get there. Cora had worked *her* ass off to get him there. For seven years, he'd gone non-stop.

Then 9/11 happened. Noah had just finished his post-doctorate internship at Hill Air Force Base—a condition of his enlistment and his doctoral program—when he was deployed. A nine-month tour in Afghanistan at the National Military Hospital in Kabul.

One month after arriving in Kabul, he found out he was going to be a father. An email from Cora—Surprise!—had triggered a meltdown. He would miss Cora's entire pregnancy. He would miss his child's birth. Of all the things he'd expected during his deployment, Cora telling him she was pregnant was not one of them. He'd thought she was going to leave him. He'd braced himself for it. The deployment couldn't have come at a worse—or better—time for their marriage. He figured the time apart would make or break them.

"Remember when you left for boot camp?" Mercedes asked, shaking him out of his private thoughts. She stepped back to view her handiwork, and something flickered in her eyes when she met his gaze. They both swiftly looked away.

"I remember."

"Well, this course is boot camp for me. I'm not looking forward to it, but I'm committed. Thankfully, it's only six weeks instead of nine, and there will be no running and weapons involved. I will also be able to call you every day—no letters required—okay?"

Noah saluted her, and she scooped pomade into her hands, rubbed them together, and styled his hair with the confidence and comfort of long companionship. Funny, he hadn't thought about boot camp—or the day he left—in forever.

He and Mercedes had never talked about that kiss. It was the only time he'd ever kissed her, the only time she'd acted like she *wanted* him to kiss her, the only time she gave him hope. It was the kiss that came before Cora. Before he'd made a choice. Before Mercedes made the choice for him.

Mercedes wrote to him at boot camp, like she promised she would. But she didn't ever mention the way they said goodbye, and how right that kiss felt. How good it was. How perfect. Mer, in her letters, was the same girl he knew at ten. The girl he knew at twelve and fourteen and sixteen. The girl who was as much a part of him as the palms of his hands or the heart in his chest. Something changed between them that night, no doubt about it. But Mer had hesitated. She'd turned back. She stepped away from the edge, and Noah didn't want to fall in love by himself. So he climbed, hand over hand, back to the way things were before, and joined her on familiar ground.

Cora wrote to him too, long, lovely letters about philosophical things, and Noah discovered that he adored Cora on paper. He'd never been able to talk to Cora like he talked to Mercedes, but when she wrote, another woman emerged, and he saw her in a whole new light. Cora was a chameleon—colorful and quiet—becoming the girl she needed to be when the curtain rose. She wasn't false; to say so would have been an injustice. She was adaptable and amenable. Sweet. Smart. And she wrote beautiful letters. She was convinced she loved him. He saw it in the curling words and the flowing phrases that filled her pages, and he began to feel things he hadn't felt before.

He fell in love with Cora when they were apart.

Oddly enough, when he was deployed to Afghanistan ten years later, after six years of marriage, the phenomenon did not repeat itself. Mercedes was as constant as always. She sent chatty letters that made him laugh and packages filled with treats and silly gifts to pass the time—a joke book with the stupidest jokes ever written, boxes of trivia questions, a yo-yo, card games, and fake dog poop. He hadn't had a yo-yo in years, but Mer reminded him that he'd been playing with one the day they met. Her letters were light and unchanging. The same Mer. His buddy. His pal.

Cora rarely wrote, and when she did, Noah didn't recognize his wife. They weren't letters from the girl who'd once captured him with her words.

Special arrangements were made for them to Skype right after Gia was born. Mer and Heather were there with Cora, who smiled weakly and asked Mer to hold Gia up to the camera so he could get a better look at his tiny, newborn daughter with her pink skin, downy fuzz, and fat cheeks. Gia's cheeks were bigger than her whole head, and he'd laughed and cried, feeling the awe and the responsibility that fatherhood brings. He told Cora he loved her, and he'd meant it, convinced Gia would be the new start they needed. She said she loved him too, but he could tell something was wrong, and he felt it, even half a world away. He blamed it on distance and the trials of giving birth alone during a long deployment. They weren't the first couple to go through it. They wouldn't be the last.

He was home again two months after Gia was born, but Cora was struggling, and he didn't know how to help her. She cried often and slept rarely. Her milk was plentiful, and Gia was content, but his wife was troubled. He asked a colleague—Dr. June from Montlake—to see her, thinking it would be easier for Cora to take advice and receive care from someone other than him, and Dr. June prescribed a mild anti-depressant. Cora was convinced it would be bad for Gia and refused to take it. Noah suggested a mother's health was key to a child's health, and that breast milk was important, but formula would do just fine if it meant Cora felt better.

"You're a psychologist, not a pediatrician, Noah. You don't have a medical degree. What do you know about it?" Her tone was weary, not angry, and he didn't push it. Maybe he should have said he knew a lot about it. He'd had a mother who was clinically depressed, who suffered from debilitating anxiety, who rarely left the house in the daylight, and who died in her sleep a week after he turned nineteen. But hey, what did he know?

He sighed, rubbing his hands over his face, and watched Mercedes sweep up his hair clippings and tidy the kitchen. Mer never stopped moving, never stopped doing, and he wanted to beg her to stay, to cancel her trip, so he didn't have to be alone. He was so damn lonely. So damn tired.

He rose and carefully removed the tray from Gia's high chair. He needed to change her pants and put her pajamas on. It was bedtime—or close enough—but he was afraid he would wake her and be unable to get her back to sleep.

He unlatched the little seatbelt that kept her from slipping out of her chair and eased her up into his arms. Her diaper felt dry and maybe pajamas weren't that important. A few golden clumps of hair were stuck to her back, and he felt a flash of panic. *It was her first haircut. Was he supposed to save her hair? Didn't some parents do that? And where did he put hair clippings if he saved them? Oh God, was he supposed to make a baby book?*

"Feed, clothe, comfort," he chanted softly. "Stick to the basics, let the other shit go."

"Words to live by," Mercedes said, drying her hands. She brushed a kiss on Gia's soft head and, standing on her tiptoes to reach his scruffy face, pressed a sisterly kiss on his cheek.

"If you need me, I will come home. You know that, right?"

"I know that." But he wouldn't ever ask her to come home.

"I love you, Noah," she said quietly.

"I love you too."

"It won't always hurt like this, will it?"

"You know the answer to that, Mer. We both do."

"Yeah. I guess we do."

She kissed his cheek again and let herself out. Noah climbed the stairs, put Gia in her crib, covered her gently, and tiptoed out. He showered quickly and fell across his bed, exhausted. But he didn't sleep. Like he'd done every night since Cora died, he pulled a blanket and a pillow from his bed and slept on the floor near Gia's crib, afraid he would sleep so hard he wouldn't hear her, afraid she would cry and no one would come.

THREE

1986

"**W**hat are you making?" Mercedes asked.

"Paper dolls," Cora answered.

Mercedes watched as Cora folded the paper and snipped away, cutting a little here, a little there. Then, her tongue sticking out between pink lips, she pulled the paper apart. Cora held a row of paper people—hands joined, feet touching—between her fingers.

"Now you color them, so they don't all look the same." She reached behind her. "I made this one earlier. I messed up and accidentally cut too deep, so this one only has three instead of six. But I liked it. It's us, see?"

She'd given the middle figure short brown curls and blue eyes.

"Is that Noah?"

"Yes. And that's you and me." The figure on Noah's left had long red hair, the figure on his right, tan skin and black braids. She'd given them all radiant smiles and colorful clothes. Mercedes recognized the striped red shirt and the jean skirt she'd worn on the first day of school. Noah was wearing the Karl Malone jersey he got for his birthday, and Cora's paper doll was colored entirely in purple—one of the colors of the Utah Jazz—indicating her new obsession. Noah liked Jazz basketball, so Cora did too. Mercedes pretended she liked the Lakers, just to be contrary, but she had a poster of the Jazz point guard, John Stockton, on the inside of her closet

27

door. Her favorite number was 12, like the number on his jersey. John Stockton was the little guy on the floor. He handled the ball and made everyone else look good. Mercedes liked that.

"What do you think?" Cora said, dangling the paper trio in front of her.

"Cute." Mercedes still played with her Barbie dolls when she was alone. Twelve was a little too old for play-acting, but she liked to dress them and experiment with their hair. Paper dolls would be fun to decorate.

"You can have these. There's six of them, just like your family," Cora offered.

Abuela, Mami, Papi, Mercedes, and her two older cousins, Jose and Angel, did indeed make six. Tia Luisa had gone back to Mexico, and Mercedes had big news. "Jose and Angel are moving out. I won't have to share a room with Abuela anymore. I will have my own room. Just like you and Noah."

"That's easy to fix." Cora promptly cut two figures off the end of the row of dolls, making a family of four, and the detached figures fluttered to the ground.

"Adios, Angel and Jose," Mercedes said. She and Cora laughed, and Mercedes began to decorate her paper family with Cora's markers. Cora retrieved the severed couple—Angel and Jose—from the floor. She held it, studying the faceless figures.

"My dad wants to leave too," she murmured. Slowly, she separated one paper doll from the other and watched as it fell. "Bye, Daddy."

"Noah?"

The blinds were all closed, and the house was so dark Mercedes stood just inside the door, blindly feeling along the wall to locate the switch. Finding it, she flipped it and gasped as the living room was flooded with light. Noah had always been obnoxiously tidy, but the living room was a wreck. It smelled like sour milk, moldy takeout, and wet dog. Noah didn't

even have a dog. A small trashcan, overflowing with tightly wrapped diapers stood near the door as if Noah had intended to take it out and gotten
distracted. A mountain of laundry that seemed to be clean but hadn't been
folded spilled from the couch. Mercedes walked slowly through the mess,
flipping on lights and breathing through her mouth, her alarm growing with
each step.

"Noah?" she called again, louder. His kitchen looked like a scene
from that Bruce Willis movie where the kid sees dead people. Every cupboard was open but half-empty. Most of the dishes were in the sink and
piled on the table. The refrigerator was ajar, emitting a tired light and a
foul odor. A box of Raisin Bran spilled its contents across the counter, and
a half-full carton of milk sat beside it, the cap missing. Something squished
beneath her left shoe, and she did a shimmying side step to avoid the long
row of ants surrounding the crushed banana skewered by her stiletto heel.

"Noah!" Mercedes hollered, more worried than angry, but a little
pissed too. He should have called her. From the looks of the house, the last
six weeks had not gone well. She balanced on one foot and freed her shoe
from the gooey ant feast.

Her shoe restored, Mercedes climbed the stairs to the two small bed-
rooms, stomping so that if Noah was naked, he had plenty of time to pull
on some pants.

The lamp by the bed was on, but they were asleep, Gia sprawled
across Noah's chest. Drool dribbled from her mouth and onto his white
undershirt. He'd pulled a pink blanket over her back, and his arms cradled
her, but they were out. Mercedes studied them for a moment, father and
daughter, and felt a rush of tenderness and despair. For months he'd been
juggling everything alone, and he'd obviously hit a wall. She felt bad for
yelling when she'd entered the house. It had been so quiet—and so filthy—
she'd overlooked the obvious. Mercedes backed out of the bedroom and
softly shut the door behind her.

Mercedes kicked off her heels, dug through the pile of clean laundry
in the living room and found a pair of Noah's boxer shorts, one of his T-
shirts, and a pair of socks, because walking around barefoot in the apartment in its current state gave her the heebie jeebies, and she wasn't going
to scrub floors in a pencil skirt. She flipped on the lights and got to work,
making a grocery list as she went; the refrigerator was so empty it wasn't

hard to clean. It appeared Noah and Gia were living on mashed potatoes and baby food, and there wasn't much else in the house. She scrubbed the bathroom, walls and all, taking off a little paint in the process, and added paint to her list. She'd give the bathroom a facelift when she had a minute.

Bug spray, toilet paper, trash bags, dish soap, laundry detergent, eggs, milk, cheese . . . the list kept growing. Three hours, three loads of laundry, and three garbage bags later, Mercedes had the place whipped into shape, and still silence from upstairs. She changed out of Noah's clothes and donned her pencil skirt and heels once more, slipping out to make a much-needed trip to the grocery store.

She was unloading groceries into Noah's clean refrigerator when she heard footsteps overhead, the sound of the bathroom door opening and closing, and the shower turning on. She finished putting her purchases away and started a pot of coffee. If Noah was up, she was going to run the vacuum. It would alert him that she was there if his clean bathroom hadn't already clued him in.

Ten minutes later, he descended the stairs, and Mercedes called out to him.

"I'm in here, Noah, declaring war on the thousands of ants living in your kitchen."

He walked in, wearing sweats and a grey, Jazz Basketball T-shirt. He opened the refrigerator, took stock of its contents, and removed the orange juice, pouring a glass and drinking it before rinsing it, drying it, and putting the glass back in the cupboard. That was the Noah she was used to. He moved to the kitchen table and sat down wearily.

"You're back."

"I am."

"You didn't have to do this," he muttered.

"I did. The place was a mess, Noah."

He nodded slowly, but he didn't defend himself. His eyes were darkly rimmed, and his wet hair stood on end, like he'd run the towel over it and forgotten about it. She smoothed it down so it wouldn't dry that way. He bowed his head beneath her hands, submissive.

"Are you growing out your hair?" It clearly hadn't been cut since she saw him last. He always wore it in a severe crop and it was now curling over his forehead, reminding her of his boyhood days.

"No. Not on purpose. It's just another thing I haven't had time to do."

"How are you?" she asked, needing to know, hoping he would tell her.

"I'm tired, Mer." He was the only one in the whole world who called her Mer. Everyone else called her Mercedes or Sadie.

"Why haven't you called me?" she asked quietly. She'd only been back for two days, but all the time she'd been gone, she hadn't heard a word. He hadn't answered her emails or returned her calls. She'd called Heather several times just to make sure everything was okay.

"And said what? Come home from LA and clean my house and buy me groceries? I'm a grown man with one small child. I'm handling it. Not always well, but I'm doing the best I can. Gia's been sick, and it's thrown the schedule off."

"Sick how?"

"She got a cold. Then she got an ear infection. We went to Instacare yesterday and got some antibiotics. She should start feeling better soon. No fever today."

"Why don't you go back to bed? Gia's asleep now. You should be too."

"I have to go to work."

"Tonight?" It was almost ten o'clock on a Sunday night.

"Mondays and Saturdays, I work days. On Saturdays, Heather takes Gia. Tuesdays and Thursdays, and every other Sunday, I work graves. Mrs. Greer comes over and sleeps here and takes Gia to Day Care in the morning when I work nights."

"Mrs. Greer is a hundred years old," Mercedes gasped.

"Eighty. And she's raised four kids and two grandkids. All she has to do is get Gia up in the morning, change her diaper, dress her, and take her across the street to Sunnypatch. They feed Gia breakfast when she gets there. Mrs. Greer makes a little money, and she's a sweet old lady." He rubbed at his face. "I pick Gia up when I get home around 12:30 so she's only there for four hours on Wednesdays and Fridays."

"When do you sleep?"

"I sleep Monday, Wednesday, and Saturday nights."

"Don't forget every other Sunday."

"Right." He sighed.

"And Gia's at Sunnycrap for twelve hours on Mondays—every Monday?"

"Eight. I get off at five on Mondays. Please don't call it Sunnycrap. I feel guilty enough already."

"The salon isn't open on Mondays, Noah. You know that."

He nodded wearily.

"So why the hell haven't you asked me to watch Gia?"

"Because I knew you would say yes, and you have your own life."

"I'm going to pretend you didn't just say that to me."

His eyebrows rose over his bloodshot, blue eyes. "Say what?"

"I loved her too, Noah. And I love you. You are *part* of my life. I want to help. I need to help." She felt the tears that would never reach her eyes fill her throat. She cleared it, swallowing them back down. The silence swelled between them, the drip from the faucet, the hum of the refrigerator, the murmur of a passing car.

"It's been three months," he whispered.

"It feels like three years," Mercedes answered.

The silence grew again, Cora filling the space around them and between them. She sat in an empty chair, watching them miss her. Mercedes shook her head, and Cora was gone.

"I don't feel anything at all most of the time, Mer," Noah confided. His voice was hollow, and it rattled around in her head. She waited for him to continue.

"I know all the stages of grief. I know the clinical terms and the right things to say. I know how to listen and advise. But I'm numb. I keep waiting to feel something. I'm supposed to help people—sad, suicidal, dangerous, depraved. But I'm struggling to remember their names. The last few months are a blur. I've always been great at the details . . . the little things . . . the stuff most people don't see . . . I see those things. It's made me a good therapist. A good doctor. But right now . . . it's all a blur, and I'm not good at anything. I'm not a good husband." He flinched, as if remembering that he wasn't a husband at all anymore. "I'm not a good father. I'm not a good therapist. I'm a collection of parts."

Mercedes studied him, and after a moment, pulled out the chair and sat down beside him at the table, resting her chin on her hands.

"Dem bones, dem bones, dem dry bones," she sang softly.

"What?" Noah asked, confused.

"I don't remember if I read it in a book or saw it in a movie, but I heard once that we're more than just the sum of our parts, and it stuck with me," Mercedes mused. "I'm sure it was meant to be motivational, and I understood the sentiment. We're more than male or female. More than our lips and tongues, more than our hearts and our lungs, more than the muscles that move beneath our skin and the blood that runs through our veins. We're more than our arms and legs. More than our eyes. More than our feet and hands. We're more than just a collection of bones, cobbled together by God or eons of evolution. We have souls. We have purpose. We're more."

"'The whole is greater than the sum of its parts.' It's a quote by Aristotle," Noah murmured. "I believe that. But right now . . . I'm dry bones. God, what an awful song."

Mercedes laughed. "I knew you'd put it together. Motivational or not, that quote made me think of that day we spent at Bible Camp—dem bones, dem bones, dem dry bones—and how the toe bone's connected to the foot bone, the foot bone's connected to the ankle bone, and so on, all the way up to the head bone. All those bones, all those parts, working together and infused with life. *Dem bones, dem bones, dem dry bones. Now hear the word of the Lord!*" Mercedes sang.

"That song made me think of Cora's dad. It haunted me. Gave me nightmares," Noah murmured.

Cora's dad was a Marine, a member of the 1st Battalion 8th Marine Corp stationed in Beirut in 1983 when the USMC barracks were blown up by a suicide bomber. Two hundred twenty marines, eighteen sailors, and three soldiers died in the blast and the collapse of the building they were housed in. Cora's dad didn't die. Not then. He was one of the one hundred twenty-eight Americans who were wounded. His legs were crushed, and they had to amputate what was left of them at the top of his thighs. Then they sent him home with a purple heart, no legs, and no will to live.

"The truth is we're more than just the sum of our parts until something breaks down and triggers a full-system failure. One missing piece, one faulty part, and it's over," Noah muttered. "When Cora's dad lost his legs, it didn't matter that he still had his arms and hands, his mind and his heart. It didn't matter that he still had Cora and her mom."

"Cora and I overheard Heather telling him not long after he came home that they could still make love. Her voice was all hopeful and sweet, and Cora and I covered our mouths so they wouldn't hear us giggling," Mercedes said, and cleared her throat. "We didn't get how sad it was. How incredibly sad. We knew what she was talking about, even at ten years old, and we didn't want to hear about her mom and dad kissing and making babies, which was what making love meant to us. Cora's dad didn't want to hear it either. He didn't want to hear that there was life beyond his legs. He just wanted all his parts back."

"Yeah. He did. And that wasn't going to happen, so he killed himself. Cora found him. And now eighteen years later, she's gone too. And I'm numb." Noah stared at the table top, tracing a long scratch in the wood surface until it disappeared over the edge. "Maybe being numb is better than having phantom limb syndrome, or phantom wife syndrome. I forget that she's gone sometimes. Just for a minute, and then I remember, and in those moments, I'm not numb. I'm in agony. So I guess the numb isn't so bad."

"You have doctor friends, right? People you can talk to? People who can guide you through this?" Mercedes asked, her eyes on his face.

"I don't want to talk to anyone. I know that's cliché. And if one of my patients said that to me, I know exactly what my response would be. But I don't want to talk."

"You're talking to me right now."

"You've always been good at making me talk," he admitted.

"So tell *me* then. If you were diagnosing yourself, what would you say?"

"I'm numb because it's easier to be numb than to feel. Numb keeps me moving forward. Numb keeps me going to work and taking care of my daughter. Numb is functional. So I'm numb."

"Sounds reasonable. And that's all? Just numb? Are you numb when you're with Gia?"

His lips trembled. Not so numb then.

"Sometimes," he admitted.

"And when you're numb . . . do you still take care of her?"

His eyes shot to hers, indignant, flashing.

"When have I ever—ever—not taken care of my responsibilities?"

"Ha! Mad isn't numb. I made you mad. I'm good at that too," Mercedes said, smiling a little.

"True." His mouth twitched. Another success.

"Noah?"

"Yeah?"

"I'm numb too. When I'm not numb, I'm pissed. When I'm not pissed . . . I feel guilty."

"About what?"

"I feel guilty that I'm pissed."

"Okay. Why are you angry?"

"Are you being my friend or are you being a therapist?" she asked.

"Which do you need?"

Mercedes snorted. "Probably the therapist."

"Okay. Why are you angry, Mercedes?" He donned his doctor face and his professional voice. She smirked at him for a moment before she sighed and told him the truth.

"Well, Dr. Andelin. My best friend is dead. Her mother is devastated. Her little girl won't remember her when she grows up. And my friend's husband, who is *also* my best friend, won't return my calls and allow me to help him."

"And is he the only one you are pissed at?" he asked.

"Do you say pissed when you are talking to your other patients?"

"Yes. I use their words. Those are your words."

"Ah. I see." She nodded.

"Am I the only one you are pissed at, Mer?" he repeated gently.

"I'm not pissed at you. I'm pissed at life. And I'm pissed at Cora, Noah. I am really, really, angry at Cora. How messed up is that?"

He was silent, and his eyes clung to hers. "Are you angry because you think she left us on purpose? Like her dad?"

"Do you?" Mercedes whispered.

"I don't know for sure. But it's possible."

"She seemed tired, Noah. And distracted."

He nodded. "She couldn't sleep. She couldn't relax. Didn't want to take medicine because she was breastfeeding. She was . . . pretty wrung out. I shouldn't have left her alone. I knew better. But I didn't think . . . I didn't want to believe . . ." his voice faded off.

"I shouldn't have let her go to the doctor by herself," Mercedes said, seeking to shoulder her own share of the blame. "She didn't want me to come. But I should have insisted."

"She didn't go to the doctor. Dr. Wynn's office called to remind her of her appointment for the Monday after she died. When I asked, they told me she didn't have an appointment for April 5."

"She lied?" Mercedes felt a flash of hot fury followed by new guilt. She was going to have to tell him. It wasn't right not to tell him.

"Or she got the days mixed up. I know she swung by the school and talked to Janna Gregory. At the funeral, Janna said Cora was acting off, that her visit was a surprise. Cora gave her a hug and told her how much she appreciated her." Cora had taught music for six years at Little Oak Elementary School, and planned to go back when Gia was older. Janna Gregory was the principal, and she and Cora were close.

"She left a message on my phone, Mer. She told me she loved me. Told me how lucky she was to be my wife. I thought it was because she'd missed our anniversary a few days before. She felt bad about that. I didn't care. It didn't matter. But she was devastated, like she'd betrayed me."

"Before she left my house that day, she asked me if I would take care of you and Gia if something happened to her," Mercedes confessed in a rush. Such a huge, black confession. And still she didn't cry. She sat frozen, jaw clenched, hands fisted. She looked around for something to do, something to fix, something to clean or care for, but it was all done. Noah was the only one who needed care, and she couldn't meet his eyes.

"I should never have let her leave. I blame myself. I let her leave, and now she's gone. It's my fault," Mercedes finished. "I didn't want to tell you because . . . because . . . I thought it would make things harder for you. But it's my fault." Her hands began to shake, and she stood slowly and pushed her chair in, clinging to the top rung.

"I have scissors in my purse. I can cut your hair . . . if you want me to. Or I can go. If I were you, I'd want me to go."

Noah reached out and grabbed her hand, pulling it from the chair, rising beside her when she tried to let go.

Noah's eyes were a blue so dark they often looked black. But now, filled with forgiveness, they were a navy that made her knees weak and her grip strong. She clung to his hand, and willed the pain in her chest to recede.

"It's not your fault, Mer," he said, his voice firm.

She nodded, but she wasn't sure she believed him.

"You don't get to shoulder this one. I forbid it," he insisted.

"I didn't save her, Noah."

"I didn't save her either."

For a moment they were quiet, their hands clasped, lost in their own remorse and their shared loss. Then Mercedes pulled away, straightened her shoulders, and looked at her watch. She'd had all the intimacy she could bear. Noah almost smiled, watching her. He was drained, yet the emptiness was almost blissful. It was good to have her back.

"Call Mrs. Greer. Tell her no more Sunday nights. I'll make you something to eat, and I'll stay with Gia tonight and watch her tomorrow. And *every* Monday. I bet she's grown in the last six weeks! I have to clean that pigsty you two are sleeping in. I never thought I'd see the day when Noah Andelin didn't have his shit together. It's a sure sign that you are human. Take heart. You may be numb, but you aren't perfect."

He laughed. "I missed you, Mer. Thanks for being mean to me. It makes me feel almost normal."

FOUR

1986

"*Stockton, at the top of the key. He hippity-hops left, finds Malone, Malone fakes and spins. It's up, it's good!" Mercedes did her best Hot Rod Hundley—color commentator for the Utah Jazz—impersonation as Noah buried the shot. Her impersonation sucked, but Noah didn't seem to mind. He gave her a high five and passed her the ball so they could do it again. She dribbled this way and that, avoiding the cracks in the concrete, and instead of passing him the ball, she took the shot. He tried to block it, but Mercedes was used to that. The ball sailed over his outstretched hands and swished through the hoop.*

"Stockton scores!" Mercedes shouted. "Nothin' but net."

"We're on the same team, Mer," Noah complained.

"So why did you try to block my shot, Karl?" she countered.

"Why do you two always get to be Karl Malone and John Stockton?" Cora grumbled. "And why don't you ever pass me the ball?"

"Mark Eaton's cool, Corey. And he has red hair, just like you," Noah soothed.

"He's a giant!" Cora whined. "And he has a beard!"

"I like beards," Mercedes said.

"You do?' Noah asked, wide-eyed.

Mercedes ignored him, turning to Cora who stood beneath the bas-

38

ketball hoop, her arms folded, her face glum. "Eaton is the center of the team, Cora. There are two guards, two forwards, but only one center. That means you're very important," she explained.

Cora wasn't convinced, so Mercedes began her play-by-play once more. "Eaton's right under the basket. He's wide open. Malone sets a pick, Stockton glides by, finds the big man in the middle." She tossed Cora the ball. "Eaton puts that baby to bed!"

Cora, her smile wide, caught the ball and banked it off the backboard, her touch light, her head back. The ball rattled around the rim and fell through the net.

They all cheered wildly, circling the concrete pad with their hands in the air like they'd just won the NBA championship. They practiced their free throws until it was too dark to see the net and planned to meet up after school to play again.

But Cora didn't show the next day. She wasn't at school and no one answered her door when Noah and Mercedes rang the doorbell and tried to peer through the front window. They went to the small court and began playing HORSE without her, certain she would join them when she could.

It wasn't until Mercedes missed a shot, the ball sailing over the backboard and disappearing behind the rusted metal dumpster that they found her. Trash days were Mondays, and it was Tuesday, so the bin was relatively empty. Mercedes was grateful the ball hadn't dropped inside, and she chased it down, coming to a horrified halt when she saw Cora lying in a heap between the back of the dumpster and the fence.

Mercedes must have called for Noah—she didn't remember doing so —but he was suddenly beside her, standing over Cora. They didn't scream for help, and they didn't run away. The thought never occurred to either of them.

Noah said Cora's name, and she opened her eyes. She wore jeans and a black turtleneck, and her face was so pale it appeared to float, separate from her body, like the moon in a dark sky. Her matted, red hair reminded Mercedes of the clown mask Noah had worn the Halloween before last, lank and garish, falling in her face. She lay with her arms wrapped around her midsection, and her hands were smeared with blood.

"Corey?" Noah said again, kneeling beside her.

Cora began to cry, a deep, keening wail that reverberated in Mer-

cedes's belly—like riding a roller coaster and leaving your stomach behind. But it didn't feel good, and her stomach didn't settle or flip in excitement. It stayed, floating somewhere at the base of her throat, and she
gagged on her fear.

"Are you hurt, Cora?" Mercedes whispered, squatting down beside
Noah. "Where have you been?" Mercedes touched Cora's arm—her skin
was so hot—and Cora jerked and sat up abruptly, shuddering and whim-
pering.

"Can you walk?" Noah asked.

"Tell me what hurts," Mercedes said and patted Cora's knee, mutter-
ing the way her abuela did when she was trying to give comfort, using soft
words and random observations that took Mercedes's mind away from her
troubles. Abuela would bandage scraped knees or wipe away tears while
she said things like, "I made tamales this morning. I think they are the best
I've ever made. I wrapped them up so tight and safe. They are happy tamales. And when we eat them, they will make us happy too." Or, "When I
walked home from the store today, the clouds above were in the shape of
Our Lady—she was looking down on me—and I felt loved." Even Abuela's
ailments were turned into cause for gratitude. "I have a tickle in my throat
today. I think it is because you made me laugh so hard last night. We are
so lucky to laugh together, don't you think?" They were words that meant
nothing and everything. Words that made Mercedes feel safe and reminded
her that life would go on beyond a temporary pain. Mercedes tried to give
the same kind of words to Cora, hopeful that she would be soothed by the
inanities and anchored by their normalcy.

"We looked for you, Cora. You didn't come to school and no one answered the door when we got home. We thought maybe you had a new
book and wanted to read instead of shooting hoops. Noah said it must be a
romance because you were nowhere to be found, and that's your favorite
kind. I read a new book last week, for English class. Did I tell you about
it? I thought I wouldn't like it, but I did. There was no romance, but I fell
in love anyway. It was called The Outsiders. It reminded me of us. There
were characters with names like Soda Pop and Pony Boy. Should we call
Noah Pony Boy?"

This time, Cora didn't jerk away, but her tears came faster.

"I can't go home," she moaned.

"Can you stand?" Noah asked.

She tried, but her legs trembled. Mercedes pulled Cora's arm around her shoulders and wrapped her arm around Cora's waist. Noah did the same, and they eased her to her feet. Cora was shaky but didn't appear to be injured, despite the blood.

"What time is it?" Cora whispered. "What . . . day?"

Noah and Mercedes exchanged a worried look over Cora's drooping head.

"It's Tuesday," Noah offered.

"It's still Tuesday?" Cora said in wonder.

"Where were you, Cora?" Mercedes asked again.

"I was sick. Mom let me stay home from school. I don't think Daddy knew I was there," Cora stammered.

"Why is there blood on your hands?" Noah asked.

"Daddy left me, and I tried to bring him back," she whispered.

"Open it," Mercedes demanded, pushing the package into Noah's hands. It was his birthday—October 14th—and she was making sure he celebrated being thirty years old. He had a tired look that he hadn't worn on his twenty-ninth birthday, but that was to be expected after the last six months. She'd made him a cake, three chocolate layers, vanilla buttercream frosting, and candy bar shavings, got a babysitter, and was making him open his presents.

He was being a good sport about it, shaking each box and making ridiculous guesses—a hula hoop, a Subway sandwich, a new car—before opening each one, careful not to rip the paper. It was an old habit from being a kid with nothing. Everything got re-used.

The first gift was a picture of the three of them, skinny-limbed and tousled hair, their shoelaces untied, teetering on the edge of childhood. Mercedes had budding breasts and scabbed knees, Noah wore a backwards ball cap and sported little biceps, and Cora was a head taller than both of them, looking like the big sister, her arms folded in front of her, her smile shy. Noah clutched a basketball against his left side and had his other arm slung over Mercedes's shoulders. Mercedes had an arm around Noah on her left, Cora on her right, a cheesy, squinty-eyed grin on her face.

"I remember the day this was taken," Noah said, softly smiling.

"Me too. But was it . . . before?" Mercedes asked. "I couldn't remember."

"Yeah. It was."

"It was a good day. We got to go to a pre-season Jazz game, remember? Papi got four free tickets on a job he did, and he took us."

Noah nodded. "The Jazz against the Clippers. The Jazz killed 'em."

"I got sick—"

"And threw up in my collectible cup," Noah finished.

"You didn't even get mad at me. You carried it away like it was no big deal. What thirteen-year-old boy does that?"

"I was afraid if I didn't get rid of it, Cora was going to puke too, and I didn't have another cup."

"Open the other present," she said.

"You got me two?"

"I got you more than two. Open it!" Mercedes insisted.

He tore off the wrapping and pulled out a collectible, 32-ounce mug with a screw-on lid and Karl Malone and John Stockton on the side, the old Jazz logo rimming the top.

"Where did you find this?" he cried.

"I have my ways. It's not exactly the same as the one you had . . . but close. And bonus, there's no vomit inside. However, there *is* something else." Noah screwed off the cap and tipped it over. Two Jazz tickets slid out into his hand.

"They're for tonight, which is why I asked Heather to watch Gia. And —" Mercedes picked up the final box. "You can wear this."

"There's a definite theme going on here," he mused, but pulled the ribbon from the remaining box. When he removed the folded, purple jersey, shaking it out so he could see it, his eyes widened and swung to hers.

"Eaton?"

She shrugged, worried that maybe she'd messed up. "I was going to get you a Malone, #32 jersey, but then I saw that. And it felt right. I got one for myself too. It made me laugh. It's like Cora's going with us that way."

His throat worked for a moment, his eyes clinging to the jersey. "I love it," he whispered. "Cora would get a kick out of it." His eyes rose to hers. "Thank you, Mer."

"You're welcome. Your final gift is hotdogs at the Delta Center, so go change. We're gonna be late."

They weren't late, but the skies were dark and cold as they walked hand in hand from the crowded parking lot, hurrying against the sharp wind. The leaves scattered like flocks of starlings, rushing, lifting, and twirling away. Mercedes's legs were so cold in her ripped jeans she couldn't feel them, and her toes felt like foreign objects on the end of her four-inch heels.

"It's basketball, Mer. Not fashion week. What happened to the days of sneakers and basketball shorts?"

"I still own some sneakers. But they have heels too."

Noah laughed and pulled on her long ponytail. She'd threaded it through the opening of her cap, but it still swung halfway down her back. "High heels, ripped jeans, and a baseball cap," he catalogued.

"And hoops," she said, flicking the huge, gold hoops hanging from her ears. "Ya gotta wear hoops when you're watchin' hoop." She sounded like Rosie Perez from *White Men Can't Jump*.

"It works for you."

"I know." She winked. "Heels make me tall."

"You're still not tall, sweetheart," Noah said.

"They make me feel tall on the inside." She knew the endearment was an afterthought, but she liked the sound of it. When most men called her sweetheart, it was dismissive. When Noah called her sweetheart, she felt his affection.

"It won't be the same without Karl," Mercedes mourned, changing the subject. "Who are we going to cheer for now? The traitor."

"I can't believe he went to the Lakers," Noah said, sounding like his younger self. He'd always despised the Lakers. When she'd asked him why, he told her it was because they were always winning. He liked rooting for the underdog.

"I never used to miss a game, now I don't even know half the Jazz players," he confessed.

"Maybe it's time we restart our fandom," she suggested.

"Maybe so."

The arena was bright and raucous, and it smelled like salt and nacho cheese. A beat thumped across the ceiling, down the rows, and gathered on the floor where the players were warming up. It was like Disneyland, where no troubles existed, and nothing mattered but the next few hours. They found their seats, pulled their jackets off, and Noah left to get them some drinks and snacks before the opening tip. When he returned, his arms full, he handed Mercedes a cup and folded himself into the seat beside her.

"These tickets had to cost you an arm and a leg, Mer."

"Don't worry. I slept with a client. Got 'em for free."

"Oh yeah? Good. I was feeling guilty."

She snickered and took a big swig from her Diet Coke.

They spent the first half getting acquainted with who was who, getting used to a new lineup, and talking about the old days.

"Ostertag's still here!" Mercedes crowed, and she and Noah threw their heads back and called his name, "Oooooooosterrrrtaaaag," the way Hot Rod Hundley did whenever the big, bald center scored.

It wasn't until the time out at the beginning of the fourth quarter that everything went bad. The huge jumbotron hanging in the center of the arena lit up with the Kissing Cam. It took a moment for the crowd to get in on the action, but it wasn't long before the whole arena was laughing and pointing as the camera swung from couple to couple, everyone participating with good natured pecks and the occasional passionate lip-lock. It wasn't until the people around them started to scream and point, that Mercedes recognized herself, larger than life, sitting beside Noah, and realized what was happening. The words KISS HER lit up the screen around their faces, pulsing bigger and bigger.

"*Por que?*" Mercedes groaned.

Noah's face was tight and his shoulders stiff, but he leaned toward her, sliding his hand around her neck and pulling her close. His kiss was light and soft, his eyes open and holding hers. His beard tickled her chin and the crowd clapped and hollered until another couple lit up the jumbotron, closing the curtain on their performance.

Like that, their laughter was gone, taking with it the carefree teasing and the window of peace and forgetfulness. For several minutes, they sat in awkward silence, aware of each other in a way they weren't before, uncomfortable with each other in a way they'd never been. Mercedes reached over and laced her fingers through his.

"I'm sorry, Noah."

He didn't ask her for what. He didn't brush away the apology. He just squeezed her hand once and let it go, keeping his eyes trained on the court. He watched the game, though from his bleak expression and faraway eyes, Mer knew he wasn't following the action. The game wasn't fun anymore. Being with him wasn't fun. It hurt. All of it. And it was way too soon.

"Let's go home," she said, and pulled on her coat.

His eyes found hers. "Are you sure?"

"Yeah." She nodded. "If we leave now, we won't have to fight the crowds."

He stood immediately, snagging his own coat, and followed her up the stairs toward the exit. Noah didn't take her hand like he had on the way in. He walked with his hands stuffed in his pockets and his eyes on the ground. When they made it out the main entrance doors and started down the sidewalk to the huge parking lot, he picked up speed, and Mercedes struggled to keep up with his long stride. He was at least two lengths in front of her when he suddenly realized she wasn't beside him. He turned and cursed quietly, stopped, and waited for her to catch up. But he didn't resume walking when she reached him.

"I haven't kissed anyone but Cora in ten years," he blurted.

"I'm not *anyone*. Kissing me is like kissing Gia. Right? Like kissing your mom."

He scoffed. "I never kissed my mom. *Your* mom kissed me more than my mom did."

The odd twisting in her chest came again, causing her to press a hand between her breasts to ease the pain.

"Mami kissed you because it was easier than telling you she loved you," she explained, knowing the reason wasn't important, but needing something to say.

"Yeah. I know." Noah was silent for a moment, standing hunched against the cold, one hand in his pocket, one hand clamped around the back of his neck.

"The thing is . . . kissing you isn't like kissing Gia, Mer. Kissing you . . . feels like I'm betraying Cora. And even though she's gone, I'm not ready to go there yet. Not even with my best friend. Not even for the Kissing Cam."

Mercedes didn't trust herself to speak or even meet his gaze. She just nodded and began walking again, desperate to escape the sense that her six-month sabbatical from crying was about to end in very noisy, painful tears. She hadn't cried for Cora. She hadn't cried for Noah or Gia. She hadn't cried for herself.

"I'm sorry, Noah. This was a terrible mistake," she gasped, walking so fast she was almost running, her arms folded across her chest. "I thought it would be good. I thought it would be okay. I thought we would laugh, and we could forget for a while. That's all."

He was easily keeping stride with her, but she could hear his frustration when he reached out and grabbed her arm, forcing her to slow down. "I don't want to forget, Mer. That's what I'm trying to tell you. If I forget her . . . then she will truly be gone."

It was like a dam burst in her chest, a rush of water and grief so torrential, she couldn't see her shoes. And she couldn't take another step. She sank to her haunches in the middle of the sidewalk and covered her face with her hands.

"Mer?" Noah whispered, sinking down beside her. He tried to lift her chin, to pull her hands from her face, but she yanked her head away, the momentum sending her falling back so she sat down hard on the concrete.

"I've hurt your feelings. That's not what I wanted. I just needed to explain," Noah said, aghast.

"Let's just g-go home, ok-kay?" she sobbed. "I'm all right. I'm j-just t-tired. N-no b-big d-deal."

He helped her to her feet, looping his arm around her waist, and she walked the final stretch to the parking lot, staggering like she'd had too much to drink. She wished she had. The lot was packed with cars of every make and color, but there wasn't a soul in sight, and they slipped in between the sleeping vehicles until they found her Corolla.

"I'm driving," Noah said when she began digging in her purse for her keys. She surrendered her purse without a fight and let him tuck her into the passenger seat and pull the belt across her lap and click it home. But he didn't move away. He wiped the tears from her cheeks, peering under the brim of her baseball cap, his own eyes wet in the weak light.

"I forget sometimes that you loved Cora for as long as I did. I forget that you lost her too. I didn't mean to be an asshole. It was just a silly kiss, and I freaked out."

"N-no. Y-you weren't . . . an asshole." Mercedes couldn't catch her breath, and she couldn't stop crying. She gritted her teeth, willing control, commanding her teeth to stop chattering and her tears to stop falling.

"I miss her too, and I loved her too, but it's not the same kind of loss. Let's not pretend it is," she said slowly, breathing with each word so she wouldn't stammer. Noah unclicked the seatbelt and gathered her into his arms, holding her so tight she could feel his heartbeat against her ear.

"Want to hear something cool?" he whispered.

"Always."

"A common, American field ant can carry up to 5000 times its own body weight."

"Nerd alert. You've told me that one before," she whispered back, sniffling.

"Yeah . . . and do you remember what you said?"

"I asked you how much a Mexican ant could carry, because I was sure it was more."

"Such a smart ass," he said softly, a smile in his voice.

"Smart ant," she hiccuped. "I think those were lazy American field ants in your kitchen, thinking they owned the place."

Noah released her and pulled her seatbelt on again. Then he walked around the car and slid behind the wheel. He started the Corolla and maneuvered his way out of the crowded lot and onto the busy streets surrounding the Delta Center.

"Any reason you're thinking about ants while I'm losing my shit?" Mercedes said, wondering if she dared look at her reflection in the visor mirror. Her eyes felt scratchy and hot.

"You are a tiny, worker ant. You never stop. Never take a break. You work harder than anyone I know. And you carry everyone else's weight. You always have. But you can't be strong all the time. I forget that too."

"The numb just finally wore off," she murmured.

"Yeah. It happens. Mine still comes and goes."

"I should have just flipped the jumbotron the bird," Mercedes said, suddenly angry. "I mean, we're not circus clowns, there to entertain the crowd. Kissing Cam! That Kissing Cam can kiss my ass." Her indignation felt good, and she wiped at her eyes, confident she'd found her control.

"I ruined tonight. I'm sorry," Noah said. Mercedes felt her lips tremble, and her eyes filled again. Damn.

"You didn't ruin it. It was too soon," she said firmly, looking out the window so he wouldn't see the tears streaming down her cheeks all over again.

"It'll be easier next time," he soothed.

"Next time?"

"Next game. We have a fandom to rebuild, remember? I'll bring the beer . . . actually, I won't. I'll bring the baby, so no beer. And you can't hold your liquor, from what I remember."

Mercedes swiped at her cheeks, but there was no end in sight. "Can I be Deron Williams? He's a pretty good point guard. Not John Stockton, but nobody's John Stockton," she muttered, keeping her voice steady.

"Only if I can be Carlos Boozer. He kinda reminds me of Malone." Noah reached into her purse and pulled out a package of tissues and set it on her knee.

"Boozer and Williams. It has a ring. I think I'm going to start calling you Boozer. Gia can be Ostertag," Mercedes said, crying softly as she ripped a tissue from the package.

"Gia can be Coach Sloan. God knows she calls the shots."

Mercedes scrubbed at her face, and Noah let the conversation slip into silence. They were almost to his townhome when he spoke again, his voice gentle.

"Believe it or not, you'll feel better tomorrow."

Mercedes nodded, still crying. Maybe she would. Maybe the vise would be gone, or maybe it would just be easier to endure.

"Will *you* feel better tomorrow?" she whispered.

He stared at the road for so long, Mercedes thought he wasn't going to answer.

"Honestly, you make me feel better, Mer. You make me laugh. You make me talk. And . . . I struggle with that, like feeling better is wrong too."

"You feel bad when you laugh?" she asked, her heart aching for him.

"I feel bad that it's *you* who makes me laugh. I know what I'm feeling is pretty typical. I counsel patients struggling with this kind of guilt all the time. They almost beg me for permission to feel good again. The truth is, I sympathized before. Now I understand. When is it okay to move on?" He shrugged. "I don't know the answer to that. I just know . . . not . . . yet."

They turned into his driveway, and he turned off the key.

"Come inside for a minute. We can check the score."

Mercedes nodded. Her head was throbbing, and she needed a glass of water. "Don't forget there's cake in the fridge." She blew her nose, not caring if it was gross.

Noah pumped the air with his fist. "That's right!" he hissed. "Chocolate layers. Buttercream frosting. And it's all mine."

"Well . . . mostly yours. I had a piece while you were changing Gia's diaper before she and Heather left. I had to test it for you."

"You cut my birthday cake?" he said in mock outrage.

"An ant's gotta eat," she muttered. "And I could use another piece."

FIVE

1987

*N*oah slipped away from the records room when his mother dozed off at her desk. The halls were dimmed in some areas of the hospital after midnight. He wasn't afraid, but he should have been. He pushed the big, metal button that made the doors swing wide and traipsed through, easy as you please. A kid wandering the halls shouldn't have been so easily overlooked. But there were so few people around. In fact, there was only one, standing just beyond the doors, and Noah jumped, startled to have company after all.

The man crouched down in front of Noah, putting their eyes on the same level. He was thin, and the bones of his wrists protruded like the bolts on bike wheels, his collar bones like handle bars, his eyes spinning like the spokes.

"What's your name, kid?"

"Noah. What's yours?"

"Noah, huh? When's the flood comin?" he cackled.

Mer had told him about the man named Noah and his ark with all the animals, so he knew what the man was talking about.

"The flood already came and went," Noah said. "You're safe."

The man looked at Noah, dumbfounded, and then he began to weep. "I'm not safe, Noah. I've never been safe. Nobody is safe."

"You're safe here. It's a good place."

"But they're gonna kick me out. Eventually, they're going to make me leave. I'll drown. I'll drown, Noah! You gotta help me."

"How?" Noah squeaked.

"Take me home with you," he begged. "I don't eat much. And I'll tell you when there's ghosts in your room, and ask 'em to leave."

"You see ghosts?"

"Yeah. They're all over. They show me things." The man cocked his head to the side, and his pinwheel eyes seemed to focus beyond Noah's head. "Did your daddy die, Noah?"

"No. I don't think so. He's just gone."

"Huh. Somebody's daddy died. He's missin' the back of his head . . . and his legs. Why's he missin' his legs, Noah? He a soldier or something?"

Suddenly there was a shout, and an orderly as black as coal and as big as a grizzly bear came rumbling down the adjacent hallway, moving surprisingly fast. A doctor and a blond nurse were coming from the other direction. The man of sharp bones and whirling eyes was gone in a flash, running toward the doctor and the nurse at full speed, his narrow butt flashing through the gap in his gown with every step. Noah would have run away from the big man too. The odds were better with the doctor and the nurse.

"John?" The doctor called out to the skinny man. "John, we need you to come with us."

The man named John ran through the doctor and the nurse like it was a game of Red Rover on the playground. The man and woman toppled like bowling pins, and John staggered and almost fell. A policeman appeared at the intersection of another hallway, and without hesitation, zapped the fleeing John with a bolt of electricity. John jerked and fell, lassoed by lightning, and Noah backed away, ducking down another hallway, and slipping into the elevator, back to the records department and the relative safety of his mother.

Noah's mother said John Davis Cutler had killed someone. A few someones. The fact that he'd gotten loose inside a hospital was a big deal. They called him Houdini because he was so skilled at slipping away.

"Who did he kill?" Noah asked his mother, shocked. John of the tears

and bad jokes didn't seem like a killer. Killers carried machetes and machine guns. Killers wore sunglasses and chewed on toothpicks. Killers had long, greasy ponytails and rode motorcycles with spurs on their boots.

"He killed two women. His file says he thought they were already dead. Drugs fried his brain, Noah. Don't ever take drugs." Shelly Andelin nodded like she'd done her duty, enough said.

"He said if they made him leave, he was going to drown. Who's gonna make him leave? Are they gonna put him in jail? Why would he drown in jail?"

"You talked to him?" she gasped.

"Yeah."

For a moment, Noah saw her love for him in the fear that widened her eyes and slackened her jaw. Then she clamped her teeth closed and squeezed her lids tight, pushing out the fear and the love and finding that old cloak of self-pity that kept her safe from caring too much about him or anyone else.

"I can't bring you anymore, Noah. I could have lost my job last night. If everyone wasn't so upset about Houdini breaking out of Psych, they woulda fired my ass."

Noah thought of the rows of records detailing the workings of the minds and bodies of so many damaged people. And he mourned. He was fourteen, and he wasn't afraid to stay at home alone. He'd done it more often than not. Mer wasn't far, and Alma, Oscar and Abuela would let him sleep on the couch if he didn't want to be by himself. But he wanted to read the files. He wanted to learn. He was going to be a doctor someday. He was going to help people like John.

"Who's going to help you? I make the work go faster. You said so yourself," Noah pressed.

His mother bit her lip and wrung her hands. "Maybe you can come with me here and there, just so I don't get behind. But you've got to promise me you won't wander. Ever again."

"I promise," he said. The shelves of files would have to be enough.

Little ghosts and bats hung from the trees lining his street and carved pumpkins adorned every doorstep, but Noah still forgot all about Halloween. He hadn't cared about Halloween for so long, it didn't even register anymore. The year before, Cora had dressed Gia in orange foot pajamas and a stocking cap that looked like a green stem, and they sat out on the front stoop with a huge bowl of candy, greeting the trick-or-treaters as they approached. Gia had been too little to know what was going on, and it was cold. Cora came inside and handed the bowl to Noah, who had put up with the doorbell ringing for about an hour before he turned off the porch light and called it a night.

Halloween fell on a Sunday that year, and Utah, with its high-density Mormon population, didn't do Halloween on the Sabbath. So Saturday was the designated day, and Noah realized in the middle of his twelve-hour shift, when a psych tech asked him if he had Halloween plans, that he should have purchased a costume for Gia and bought some candy for the trick-or-treaters. He hadn't done either.

On his way home from work, he stopped at Walgreen's and bought a plastic pumpkin bucket and all the Halloween candy left on the shelves, which wasn't much. Kids who came to his house were getting the crap no one else wanted. Unfortunately, the only costumes remaining at Walgreen's were way too big for an eighteen-month-old toddler. There was a clown mask that might have worked, but he didn't like clowns, and the rubber stunk. Heather had completely forgotten about Halloween too, and she stared at him blankly when he stopped to pick up Gia. Heather begged a bag of cheap candy off him, but wasn't any help with a costume.

While Gia ate her supper, watching him from her high chair as she pinched peas and carrots between her tiny fingers, Noah cut holes into an old, white pillowcase—two holes on the sides for two small arms, two more for eyes, and one for the mouth.

"We're going old school, Gia Bug," he warned. "Your old man was a ghost several years in a row." He felt like a ghost now, flitting quietly through his life.

When he pulled the case over Gia's head, she peered out at him in wonder, reminding him of a tiny ET, and miraculously, she didn't try to tug it off again. She kept the costume on as they traipsed around his neighborhood with the pumpkin bucket and a gaggle of costumed kiddos and their parents. He even taught her to say BOO! when people answered their doors. She loved every minute of it, especially handing out tiny handfuls of Tootsie Rolls and Dum Dum Suckers—his candy really was crap—to the endless stream of trick-or-treaters that came to their door.

She fell asleep at nine o'clock, still wearing the pillowcase. When he carried her up to her crib and removed his homemade costume, he realized she had somehow managed to get a sucker stuck in her hair and chocolate all over her face. Regardless, he considered the night a total parenting win. She didn't stir when he used a warm washcloth on her face and hands, changed her diaper, and cut the sucker from her hair. Halloween had worn her right out. He pulled a pink nightgown—a gift from Mercedes—over her head, threaded her limp arms through the sleeves and covered her carefully before slipping out and closing the door.

For the first time since Cora died, Noah slept in his bed instead of on the floor next to her crib. He kept the baby monitor beside his pillow, turned up as loud as it would go, but it was progress, and before he went to sleep, he sent a picture of Gia in her homemade costume to Mercedes's email. She replied a half hour later with a picture of Cora, Noah, and Mercedes from a Halloween almost two decades before, a Halloween he'd completely forgotten about. They were all in ghostly sheets and sneakers, with pillowcases filled with candy clutched in their hands. When it came to candy, there was no messing around. They had trick-or-treated for hours that year. It was obvious who was who by their height and the shoes on their feet. Funny how you could forget something so completely, and a snapshot brought it all back, worn sneakers and all.

On the memo line of the email Mercedes wrote, "Gia Andelin, carrying on the Three Amigos tradition," and Noah went to bed with a smile on his face and a sentimental ache in his chest.

It was circle. That's what they called it. It was common in group sessions because it was effective. No corners. No sharp edges. Everyone facing everyone else, unable to hide, even the therapists. Noah was still the newest doctor in rotation at Montlake since returning from Afghanistan. The other doctors preferred one-on-one consultation and left the group sessions to the therapists and psych techs. The circle could be taxing, but Noah liked to watch the interaction between patients. Most of the time, it told him things a private consult couldn't. But that night, Noah wasn't ready for circle. It had been a long month, and he was weary and emotionally spent, and he hoped for an uneventful, peaceful group session.

He didn't get one.

David—Tag—Taggert was vibrating like a junkie, though he was clean as a whistle and had been for weeks. He drank too much before he arrived at Montlake, but that wasn't his problem now. Moses Wright was eyeing him, eyeing everyone, but his eyes had taken on the faraway gleam that made Noah think of pinwheels and John Davis Cutler. He'd been on duty the night they brought Moses Wright in, heavily sedated, and again a few nights later when Tag Taggert had been brought in, shouting and crying. It was an oddly accurate first impression of both.

They were both eighteen and too young for the adult ward, in Noah's opinion. But that was the law, and they weren't little boys. In fact, they were both powerfully built and majorly troubled. But the similarities ended there.

Tag was a white, shaggy-headed cowboy, and he wanted to talk. He was *all* talk. Moses was mixed-race and quiet. He listened. Maybe he didn't talk much because nobody *believed* what he said. Noah had read his file, but he hadn't spent much time with him. All he knew was Moses claimed he could see ghosts, and he drew the things they showed him.

Noah had never had a patient like him. But he'd known someone, a long time ago, someone who'd seen ghosts and overdosed to make them go away. John Davis Cutler, who confused the living with the dead and the dead with the living. Who killed a woman at a rest stop because he was convinced she was a demon. Noah didn't want Moses to end up like John Davis Cutler.

They were ten minutes into the group session when Moses decided he was through listening.

"Who here knows a girl named Molly?" he blurted out, interrupting a woman weeping for the children she hadn't seen in two years. The woman stopped, sniffled, and forgot about her children all over again.

"What did you say?" Tag hissed, his arms hanging loosely between his knees. To the casual observer he was relaxed. Noah knew better; Tag's head was about to explode.

"Molly. Do you know a girl named Molly? A dead girl named Molly?" Moses threw the words at Tag, and Noah was a heartbeat too slow. Blame it on fatigue. Blame it on his reluctance to get between two troubled, young men.

"You son of a bitch," Tag shouted, and was across the circle before Moses could blink. Whatever Moses had intended, it wasn't combat, and his face registered shock as Tag hurtled into him, knocking him back in his chair. Moses recovered quickly, and his fists were flying before he hit the ground. Tag was raining blows as he bellowed something about his sister, and it took Noah, Chaz, and three others to pull them apart. Noah had Moses face down, shoving his face into the floor, and Tag was still running his mouth, outrage pouring from his lips, his body vibrating beneath Chaz, who had him in an identical position.

"How did you know?" Tag gasped. "How did you know about my sister?"

"Tag. No more!" Noah snapped, and traded positions with an orderly who, unlike Noah, was not bleeding.

"My sister's been missing for over a year, and this son of a bitch acts like he knows something about it?" Tag raged. "You think I'm gonna shut up? Think again, Doc."

Noah put three chairs together and cleared the room, instructing Chaz and the other orderly to stay to ensure nobody got killed. They helped Moses and Tag rise from the floor, and pushed them down into two of the seats. Noah took the seat at the top of the triangle, equidistant between Tag and Moses, and swiped at his bloody lip. Chaz handed him a tissue, his eyes apologetic. Chaz was the muscle in the room and would consider it his fault Noah had gotten hurt. But Noah hadn't let Chaz protect him. Noah gave the orderly a small smile and then regarded Moses and Tag, who didn't seem any the worse for wear.

"Moses, do you want to explain to Tag what you meant when you asked about a girl named Molly?" Noah instructed quietly.

"A dead girl named Molly!" Tag hissed. Chaz patted his shoulder, a reminder to calm down, and Tag swore violently.

"I don't know if she's his sister. I don't know *him*. But I've been seeing a girl named Molly off and on for almost five months," Moses said.

Noah studied him, perplexed. "Seeing her? Do you mean you have a relationship with Molly?"

"I mean she's *dead*, and I know she's dead because for the last five months I've been able to *see* her," Moses repeated patiently.

Tag's face was almost comical in its fury. Noah caught his eye and breathed slowly, in and out, urging him to do the same. Then he turned back to Moses.

"You see her . . . how?" He really didn't want Moses to be a John Davis Cutler.

"The same way I can see your dead wife, Doc. She keeps showing me a car visor and snow and pebbles at the bottom of a river. I don't know why. But you can probably tell me."

Noah felt his jaw tighten and his heart stop. "What are you talking about?" His voice was calm, but his head was spinning. Moses continued, forcing Noah to mentally stumble after him.

"She follows you around the joint. She messed you up. She knows it, and she's worried about you. I know she's your wife because she shows you waiting for her at the end of the aisle. Your wedding day. Your uniform is a little too short in the sleeves." Moses said this all flippantly, as if it wasn't real life. As if it wasn't Noah's wife. As if his knowledge was common and Noah's grief, all too public. Noah glanced at Tag and saw that he'd lost his fury. Tag stared back in confusion and compassion. And Noah went with it. He showed them his scars so they would trust him with theirs.

"My wife, Cora, was driving home from . . . work. They think she was blinded—temporarily—by the sun reflecting off the snow. It's like that sometimes up here on the bench, you know. She drifted into the guardrail.

Her car landed upside down in the creek bed. She . . . drowned."

Noah supplied the information matter-of-factly, giving a sterilized version of a blood-spattered memory, but his hands shook when he touched his beard. Mer would say the beard stroke was his tell, a sign that he hadn't told the whole truth. But only Mer would know, and she wasn't there.

But Moses wasn't done, and Noah's scars were still the only ones being exposed.

"Peanut butter, Downey fabric softener, Harry Connick, Jr., umbrellas." He paused with obvious discomfort and then continued in a rush. "Your beard. She loved the way it felt, when you . . .when you . . ." His voice trailed off.

When he made love to her.

Cora liked his beard. Noah shaved it and grew it back every time duty demanded. The military didn't allow facial hair among the rank and file. In her own perverse way, he thought that was why Cora loved it. The beard reassured her that he would get out, that he would not end up like her father, that he wouldn't be a casualty of war. Cora was a casualty instead.

Noah hadn't thought about making love to Cora for a long time. When he'd returned from Afghanistan, she was still recovering from delivering Gia. And after that, even when her doctor gave the all clear, she was tired and self-conscious, and she didn't seem to want him to touch her. The few times they came together had them scurrying apart when they were done, turning away to hide their despair and their disappointment in each other.

Moses's words were a reminder that it hadn't always been that way.

Somehow, Noah found his voice. "Those were some of her favorite things. She walked down the aisle on our wedding day to a Harry Connick song. And yeah. I'd grown out of my uniform. She always laughed about that and said it was just like me to try and make it work. And her umbrella collection was out of control." Noah's voice broke, and he stroked his beard again, trying to soothe himself, trying to rein in the emotion threatening to break free. He'd lost control of the session—if he was honest, he'd never had control—and he needed to end it now before Moses reduced him to a quivering mess in the corner.

"If you know all that—about Dr. Andelin's wife—then I want you to tell me about Molly," Tag said, straightening in his chair and swinging his gaze from Moses back to Noah.

Noah rose to his feet.

"Tag, I promise we'll revisit this. But not now. Not tonight." And with a nod to the orderlies, who seemed as shaken as he was, Noah ushered everyone out of the room.

"You aren't as calm and gentle as you want us all to believe, are you, Dr. Noah? You know how to handle yourself," Moses said when Noah pulled out a chair and sat down beside him. Noah hadn't seen Moses since Tuesday night. It was Thursday now. He'd had some time to recover.

"I spent some time in the military." Noah shrugged.

"That makes sense. You didn't mind wading in with Chaz."

"I like Chaz, and he was outnumbered."

"I like him too. I wouldn't hurt Chaz."

"I know. But sometimes people get hurt, even when we don't mean it."

"Those for me?" Moses's eyes were on the stacks of drawing paper and the Styrofoam cup of grease pencils.

"Yes."

"Can I have 'em now?"

"You can." Noah pushed the supplies toward him.

"You lost your wife."

"I did." Noah wondered who was helping who. "But you said she was okay."

"She is."

"That is a great comfort to me."

Moses shrugged. "It's true."

Noah nodded, acknowledging, even if he wasn't completely sure he believed. And he changed the subject.

"Who have you lost, Moses?"

"Nobody," Moses said, derisive.

The word hung between them, painting the air with false disdain. Noah didn't correct Moses or tell him he knew different. He just handed him a pencil and sat back.

"I lost GiGi," Moses whispered, almost remorseful. "GiGi wasn't nobody." He said the name with hard g's—gee gee—and Noah waited for him to explain her significance. Noah knew who she was. He'd read the file. But he waited. Moses's knee started to bounce, and his shoulders twitched. His hand started moving across the page, and a woman with a thousand lines and flyaway hair was brought to life.

"Is that GiGi?"

"Yes," Moses grunted.

"She looks a little like Abuela," Noah commented. Moses looked up, surprised.

"You don't look Hispanic, but . . . I guess how we look doesn't tell the whole story, does it?"

"No. Not even close. It doesn't tell the best parts," Noah murmured. "But I don't think I'm Hispanic. I guess I could be. I don't know who my dad was."

Moses hesitated, his hand pausing over the paper. "You don't?"

"No. I don't even know his name."

"Me neither," Moses muttered. "But to be fair, I'm guessin' he never knew I existed."

Noah didn't respond. He just watched Moses move onto another piece of paper, setting the picture of his grandmother aside.

"So who's Abuela?" Moses asked, his eyes on the paper. Noah was surprised at his interest.

"My friend's grandmother. She made me feel loved. She was good to me," Noah said.

"She gone?"

"She is. She died when I was serving in Afghanistan two years ago. I didn't get to say goodbye. I miss her."

"I didn't get to say goodbye to GiGi either."

"You can't see her?" Noah asked.

"No. I don't ever see the dead I want to see."

"What about right now? Are you seeing anyone you don't want to see?

"Besides you, Doc?" Moses shot back, a smile in his voice.

"Besides me."

"Nah. Right now the dead are quiet. It's nice."

Noah nodded. "That's good. I could use a little quiet myself. Will you let me sit here while you draw?"

"As long as you don't stare at me and write a bunch of notes in my file that I can't read."

"I'll show you everything I write if you show me everything you draw."

"I don't really want to know what you think about me, Doc."

Noah laughed. "I understand that. Sometimes it's better that way. But you might be surprised what I think."

"You sure you're a doctor? You aren't very old."

"Neither are you. But look what you can do." Noah nodded toward the drawings.

Moses smiled. "I feel ancient."

"Me too," Noah murmured.

Moses looked down at the page and his hand began to sail again. Noah didn't ask him for an explanation. He just sat, watching him create, watching a face emerge from the lines.

It was Cora. Her hair whipping around her face, her eyes so alive his heart seized in his chest. Moses had drawn her smiling, as though that was what he saw, and Noah took the portrait from his outstretched hands.

"She's okay, Doc."

"I believe you, Moses."

"Are *you* okay?"

"Right now, I feel better than I've felt in a long time."

SIX

1988

*T*here are places where Christmas should never be spent. McDonalds, the laundromat, a gas station, or stranded on the side of the road, just to name a few. Mercedes was sure there were hundreds of terrible places, but the hospital ranked up there with the very worst.

Oscar had been sick for weeks. Every night his coughing kept her awake. It kept them all awake. Yet morning would come, and Oscar would get up and head out the door; he never missed a day of work. Alma grew quiet, Abuela prayed, but Mercedes assumed that if Papi was okay to go to work he must be okay. But he wasn't.

He didn't go to midnight mass on Nochebuena and on Christmas day —his only day off—he didn't get out of bed. They opened presents sitting around him, trying to coax him to eat some of Abuela's pozole, but he smiled and shooed them away, apologizing for his fatigue and his lack of spirit. By Christmas night, his fever had spiked, he couldn't breathe, and when Alma tried to get him out to the car so she could take him to the hospital, he collapsed before he reached the door.

Alma made Mercedes call 911 because she spoke the best English, and when the ambulance came and took Oscar, Alma rode with him, leaving Abuela and Mercedes to watch helplessly as the ambulance sped away, leaving them behind. Mercedes scrambled up the stairs to Noah's apartment, determined to find them a ride.

"Noah!" Mercedes pounded on his door with both hands. She knew he was home. Cora and her mother had gone south to Heather's family for Christmas, but Noah and his mother didn't have anywhere to go, and it wasn't late enough for Shelly to leave for work.

Noah came to the door, but stepped out into the hallway, pulling it closed behind him.

"What's wrong, Mer?"

"Papi's sick. The ambulance came. The lights were flashing and everything, didn't you see?" She didn't give him a chance to answer. "Mami went with Papi in the ambulance, but Abuela can't drive, and we can't wait here. Can your mother take us? They said they were taking him to U of U. That's her hospital, right?"

"She can't take you," he said, shaking his head. "She's not working tonight and she's . . . asleep."

Mercedes knew what that meant. Shelly was in a chemically induced sleep and wouldn't be waking any time soon.

"But I can take you," Noah said firmly.

"No, you can't!" Mercedes said, trying not to cry. "You're only fourteen, Noah!"

"I drive all the time, Mer. Don't worry. Give me a minute to grab the keys."

He was outside seconds later, wearing his puffy new coat and dangling a set of keys from his fingers, locking the apartment door behind him. That morning, Mercedes had delivered a plate of tamales and cinnamon sugar tortillas that Abuela made and made Noah open his present, a jacket she'd scrimped and saved for. He'd worn the same coat three years in a row, and the sleeves stopped two inches above his wrists and the zipper was broken. Noah had been thrilled with the gift, but the morning's happiness felt like a lifetime ago.

Noah handled his mother's rusty blue Impala with the confidence and care of a sixty-year-old man. He drove with both hands on the wheel, traveling at the speed limit, stopping at the lights, signaling when he turned, and eventually pulling into the hospital parking lot like he'd driven the route a hundred times. Maybe he had. Abuela hadn't questioned Noah when he slid behind the wheel. She'd simply climbed in the backseat and *folded her hands across her lap, waiting to be delivered to her destination. Mer sat in the front by Noah, heart in her throat, hands braced against the dashboard, prepared to die, and praying Papi wouldn't be in heaven when she arrived.*

Now they sat in the Emergency Room next to a crooked Christmas tree with cheap gold tinsel and red and green bows, waiting for news. They'd gotten word to Alma that they were in the waiting room, but hadn't heard anything since arriving an hour before. Noah sat beside Mercedes wearing his new coat, his elbows on his knobby knees, his big feet in his worn, no-brand sneakers tapping a nervous rhythm on the industrial floor.

"I hate it here," Mercedes whispered, resorting to anger instead of grief.

"I don't," Noah said.

"Why?" she gasped. How could anyone like a hospital waiting room?

He shrugged. "It makes me hopeful. If people are here, they're getting help."

"But people come here to die. People are sick. And scared." Mercedes was sick and scared. She stood abruptly, unable to sit still a second longer.

"Let's go for a walk," Noah suggested, rising beside her. "Come on. I'll show Abuela the chapel. She can pray while we get some fresh air."

"What if Mami needs us?"

"We won't be long. And I'll tell Agnes to page us if there's news."

"Agnes?"

"Agnes always works the ER desk at night. She's nice," Noah explained.

Noah knew his way around, and Abuela seemed grateful for the opportunity to light a candle and say a prayer for her son-in-law, so Noah and Mer left her alone in the shadowy room with the stained-glass windows and made their way outside, seeking space and a quiet not interspersed with swishing doors and canned Christmas music. The red emergency room sign above their heads gave the pale fog a pink cast, like cotton candy at a winter carnival.

"Look!" Noah said.

A fat flake, furry with ice, meandered through the air and landed in Noah's dark hair. Another one chased it down, and he caught it in his *hand. He raised his face in anticipation of more.*

"We might get a white Christmas after all," he said, trying to lift her spirits. "People wish on the first stars in the sky. Maybe we can wish on the first snowflakes of the season."

Mercedes closed her eyes and wished with all her might, a wish that was part prayer, part pleading, part angry ultimatum. But her dread continued to mushroom.

"I have a very bad feeling, Noah," Mercedes whispered, her chest so tight she could hardly draw breath.

Noah reached out and took her hand, threading his icy fingers through her much smaller ones.

"It's going to be okay, Mer. It has to be. It's Christmas."

When your father dies on Christmas day, it tends to ruin the holiday, and Mercedes always breathed a sigh of relief when the new year rolled around, grateful another anniversary had passed. But with Cora's passing, the memory of Papi's death took a backseat to fresher pain. Alma, who usually struggled with the holiday as much as Mercedes, set out the *nacimiento* she'd had for longer than Mercedes had been alive and decorated the duplex with poinsettias inside and twinkle lights around the windows. She even bought a little tree and put it on the table in front of the windows, declaring that they needed to make a special effort this year.

"Noah and the *bebe'* should spend Christmas here," Alma insisted. "We'll go to Mass and have dinner on *Nochebuena,* and open presents Christmas morning with Gia. This will be a hard year for Noah. He shouldn't be alone."

"Noah isn't Catholic, and I don't think Gia will make it through Mass, Mami," Mercedes protested, although she was relieved her mother had suggested it. When she broached the subject with Noah, he seemed equally relieved.

"I'll invite Heather too. She can have the guest room, you and Gia can have my bed, I'll sleep with Mami, and we'll all get through Christmas together," Mercedes promised.

Mercedes liked to make the distinction that at almost thirty years old, she didn't live with her mother, her mother lived with *her*. For a while after Papi died, Mercedes had worried that she, Abuela, and Mami would have to go back to Mexico. Abuela had a sister in Mexico City, and Papi had brothers in Veracruz who Mercedes had never met. But Mami had insisted there was nothing to go back to, and they would find a way to make ends meet without Papi's income. They downsized to a two-bedroom apartment at The Three Amigos, and Alma took on full-time housekeeping work at the same hospital where her husband died and Shelly Andelin's fourteen-year-old son practically ran the records department. Abuela continued making homemade tamales for the restaurants she and her daughter had been servicing for years, and Mercedes got a job cleaning a salon called Maven on Union Boulevard after school. It took her two hours every night, six nights a week, and the owner—Gloria Maven—paid her $200 a month, not terrible wages for a fourteen-year-old girl in 1989, but Mercedes made sure Mrs. Maven got more than she paid for.

At sixteen, Mercedes began doing pedicures too, bringing home another $400 on top of her cleaning job, making enough to cover the rent and a little extra all by herself. Gloria Maven liked her passion and her work ethic, and promised Mercedes a stylist position when she finished hair school, which Mercedes did—attending classes on nights and weekends—before she'd even graduated from high school.

Mercedes left the Three Amigos Apartments behind when Noah and Cora got married, but Abuela and Alma had still needed her income, so she took them with her, saving the expense of two households. She'd chafed a little at her lack of privacy and independence, but when Abuela had died five years later, she'd been grateful for the time they'd had together.

She and her mother had remained in the duplex, conveniently located a mile from the salon, three miles from the hospital, and two miles from Noah and Cora's townhome. And though she could have afforded something newer and much nicer, Mercedes still drove the Toyota Corolla she'd driven for ten years, and she still bought her clothes at the Goodwill. She might pride herself on looking like she shopped at Dillard's, but the money she saved on clothes and cars was put away for a bigger dream. She had single-handedly turned Maven into a high-end spa and boutique, and when Gloria Maven was ready to sell, Mercedes had every intention of buying. Gloria had been hinting that 2005 might be the year, and Mercedes was ready. In her opinion, the sooner Christmas was wrapped up, the better.

It was Gia who made the season bearable. She made everyone try a little harder when it would have been so easy to just ignore the holiday altogether. She had begun babbling in recognizable words—mimicking sounds and syllables, scolding her father and reading stories in enthusiastic gibberish—and making them laugh at her antics. Nothing was safe from her busy hands or mouth, and Noah was stringing lights and hanging ornaments starting halfway up his Christmas tree to keep her from stripping it bare and biting the bulbs.

"If you squint your eyes, your tree looks like it's wearing an ugly Christmas sweater," Mercedes said, looking at the half-dressed tree through her eyelashes.

"It looks like the Grinch in his Santa suit, with his green belly sticking out below it," Noah mused, standing beside her, a star in his hands, his eyes narrowed to slits.

"It does!" Mercedes chortled. She pulled the drooping Santa hat from her head and waved it excitedly. "Let's put this Santa hat on the top, instead of that star. Then it'll really look like the Grinch. Give me a boost."

Noah lifted her up, his arms bracketed around her thighs, so she could reach the top of the tree, and Gia chose that moment to wrap herself around his leg, tripping him up and sending them all crashing into the branches. Fortunately, nobody was injured. Gia cried but Noah and Mercedes couldn't stop laughing.

Noah didn't even bother putting gifts beneath his tree. Gia unwrapped everything immediately, and he ended up turning everything he purchased over to Mercedes for safekeeping. Christmas morning at Mercedes's house was a free-for-all, trying to keep Gia focused on one gift at a time. Mercedes bought Gia too many presents; they all did. Gia had more clothes and toys under the tiny tree than any little girl could ever want. And she didn't really want them. She pulled the paper from every box and then retrieved her old red ball from Mercedes's bin of toys, leaving the adults to exchange their gifts.

Noah bought Mercedes some heated seat covers for the Corolla and magnetized window coverings, so Mer wouldn't have to scrape her windshield when it snowed. He also bought her a vintage record player and a stack of vinyls he knew she liked—Nina Simone, Al Green, Donny Hathaway, and The Jackson 5. She squealed like a little girl and insisted on playing the latter immediately so she could dance to "I Want You Back." Noah refused to dance but laid on the floor, his hands folded beneath his head, laughing as she shimmied and shook and mouthed every word. Gia loved it too and joined in, her stance wide, her head bobbing, hips and arms swinging. Alma and Heather clapped and laughed at the baby and egged Mercedes on.

Mercedes presented Noah with three new shirts, two new pairs of slacks, a deep purple tie with tiny white polka dots that on closer inspection were basketballs, and a navy blue coat that was similar to the coat she'd bought him the year Papi died. The eighties style had come back in fashion, and she'd noticed Noah had a dress coat, but nothing casual to wear in the cold. She'd seen the coat in the Orvis store window, and it had immediately taken her back to the night he'd driven her and Abuela to the hospital, cruising down the dark streets with all the confidence of an old soul.

She'd thought a great deal about that night in recent days—his concern, his companionship, and his endearing belief that nothing would go wrong because it was Christmas. Mercedes had known, even then, that fate had a fatalistic sense of timing, and that Christmas miracles only happened in Hallmark movies. He should have known it too; Noah was not a stranger to disappointment. But he had still believed. Or maybe he'd believed because she'd needed him to.

He'd driven them all back home—Mercedes, Mami and Abuela—without Papi in the early hours before dawn, three distraught women who had no idea how they would go on. For years, Mercedes had been unable to reflect on those hours. Now, sixteen years later, sitting by his side with memories of her father in her head, she marveled at the boy who'd taken care of them all that day and in the days to come too. Noah was already the man of his own house, and he temporarily became the man of theirs.

"You look very handsome, Noah," Heather said. "That coat fits you perfectly."

Noah ran his hand down the quilted sleeves. "It does. It looks like the coat you gave me when we were kids, Mer."

"I know. It reminded me how you took care of us that year, and I thought it was time I said thank you." Noah's eyes rose and caught hers, and grief shimmered in the air, tempered by the knowledge that they'd all made it through heartache before.

"And now you are taking care of him," Heather said, her voice soft, her eyes bright.

"We are all taking care of each other, Heather," Mercedes said as Noah leaned over and dropped a kiss on the top of her head.

Heather nodded, and Alma patted her hand. Alma pointed at the last gift beneath the tree.

"For you, Heather," she said in accented English.

"That one is from me and Gia, Heather," Noah said, and Mercedes heard the nerves in his voice.

Heather pulled the wrapping off a large canvas painting and stared, transfixed. Cora was captured in swirls of color—vivid reds and bold blues, blushing pinks and shades of gold and bits of shadow glowing from the page. It was magnificent.

"I thought you should have it," Noah said, his eyes on his mother-in-law. Her red hair was faded and her eyes worn, but the resemblance was unmistakable between mother and daughter, and when she covered her mouth on a sob, they all cried with her.

"Gia should have it," she choked.

"I had a color copy made for Gia, to hang in her room. That's the original, and it's yours. Someday, if you want Gia to have it, then you can give it to her."

"Who did this?" Heather cried.

"There's a patient at Montlake. An artist. I asked him—commissioned him—to paint her."

"He captured her—all the best parts—how did he do that?" Heather marveled, tears running down her cheeks.

"He has an amazing gift," Noah said, and Mercedes knew there was more, but didn't press.

Later, when breakfast was cleaned up, Heather was napping, and Alma had left for Christmas Mass, Mercedes handed Noah a cup of coffee, sank down beside him on the sofa, and urged the full story behind the painting.

"Tell me about the picture, Noah. Tell me about the artist."

"The police brought him in a month ago. He found his grandmother dead in the kitchen. Instead of going for help, he had a psychotic break of sorts. They found him covered with paint, drawing murals on her living room walls. Brilliant kid. He's a genius. A . . . savant. His art is unbelievably realistic and . . . beautiful . . . and terrifying. He got hold of a can of pencil nubs and covered the walls of his room in the oddest things," Noah said.

"Like what?" Mercedes asked.

"He claims that . . . dead people . . . show him things. And if he paints what they show him, they leave him alone."

"He's delusional?"

"No. I don't think he is. He knows things that nobody could possibly know. Dr. June's twin sister died when she was just a little kid. Moses brought it up in a counseling session. None of the staff even knew about it; I didn't know. We have an orderly—great big guy named Chaz—Moses told him his grandfather wanted him to find something. Gave him instructions. It all checked out."

Mercedes was silent, considering. Abuela had always believed in things she couldn't see, in gifts and special abilities. Maybe it was her influence, but Mercedes had no trouble believing there was a whole host of things she didn't understand about life and death. She'd always had good instincts and she trusted them. Noah was no pushover either. If he said the artist saw dead people, the artist saw dead people. End of subject.

"He saw Cora. He said sometimes . . . she follows me around. He told me . . . he told me she's fine. She's good. But she worries about me," Noah murmured.

"He said she follows you around?" Mercedes didn't like the sound of that.

"He listed all her favorite things. Umbrellas. Harry Connick, stuff like that. No one would know that, Mer. He drew her face without ever seeing a picture of her."

"Unbelievable."

"Yeah. Unbelievable. But . . . I *do* believe him. I think Moses sees the dead."

"And he said she was all right? She's . . . okay?"

"Yeah." Noah smiled, the grin quivering on his lips for a moment before he ducked his head and took a deep breath.

"Do you think . . . he would talk to me?" Mercedes whispered.

"Why?"

"He made you feel better." It was obvious. Noah had a peace about him he hadn't had even a month before.

"He did."

"I want to feel better too."

Noah took her hand. "I'll ask him, Mer. I can't start running a side operation from Montlake, but I'll ask him if he wouldn't mind talking to you."

Gia, playing at their feet, toddled toward the tree and placed her red ball on a branch as though she wanted it to hang there with the rest of the ornaments. The ball rolled off and she growled.

"No, bah," she ordered, and placed the ball back on the branch. It rolled off again.

"No, bah!" Gia was getting frustrated with the uncooperative ball.

Mercedes set her coffee aside and crawled to Gia, taking the ball from her hands.

"Here. I'll help." She wedged it near the trunk, so the branches embraced it, keeping it from falling.

"There," Mercedes said.

"Meh," Gia said happily, pointing at the ball and clapping. She then tried to reach the ball, but the branches poked at her, and she pointed again, imperious, looking from the ball to Mercedes like Mercedes had tricked her by pushing the ball back so far.

"Meh!" Gia repeated.

"What is she saying? She kept saying that last Monday—meh, meh, meh. She sounds like a little goat, and I don't know what she wants."

"Meh," Gia bleated again and pointed a small finger toward Mercedes, clearly irritated by her lack of understanding.

Noah started to laugh. "She's saying Mer."

"Meh," Gia said, nodding.

"Oh," Mercedes cried.

"She just can't say her *r's*," Noah said.

"Meh? Doesn't it just figure. She calls me Meh, the word everyone uses when they feel ambivalent about something. Meh." Mercedes laughed.

"I've never heard that," Noah said.

"Yeah, you know. How was that movie?" She shrugged her shoulders. "It was just . . . meh. Do you like this shirt? Meh."

"Gia doesn't feel ambivalent about you."

"No. She doesn't. And I love it." Mercedes grabbed Gia and nuzzled her, kissing her fat cheeks and nibbling on her neck.

"Meh." Gia giggled.

"Gia," Mercedes crooned. "Can you say Gia? Say Gia."

Gia scrunched up her entire face and said, "DEE-UH." All vowels, wrong consonant.

"Gee-uh," Mercedes repeated.

Gia clapped for her, and Mercedes and Noah both laughed.

"Meh." Gia patted Mer's cheek.

"Yep. That's me. Meh," Mercedes agreed.

"Noah," Gia called, turning toward her father. Mercedes hooted. Noah had forgotten to mention Gia's new word.

"She's not even two years old, and she's already calling me by my first name. I want to be Daddy," Noah grumbled.

"Well . . . she's calling you Noah because everyone else does. Maybe I'll start calling you Big Papa," she quipped, enjoying the flirtation.

"Yeah . . . I'm thinking you better not."

Noah and Mercedes agreed to accompany each other to their obligatory New Year's Eve work parties, first to Noah's, then Mercedes's, with plans to be home shortly after midnight. Heather had taken Gia home for the evening and would keep her through the next day, but New Year's fell on a Saturday, which was Noah's longest shift, and he had no desire to party late into the night and work all the next day. He had no desire to party at all, but pulled on a pair of grey slacks and a black dress shirt, trimmed his beard and slicked back his hair, and did his best to put on a happy face for a few hours.

Mercedes wore a red dress with little capped sleeves, a sweetheart neckline, and a full skirt, and she fixed her hair in Veronica Lake waves. With glossy, red lips and high, red heels, the whole look screamed, "Look at me," but Mercedes had always considered herself a walking advertisement of her profession. If she looked good, people would come to her to make them look good. She had business cards in her clutch.

Noah just smiled and shook his head when he picked her up. "How will I explain you, Mer?"

"No one will think we're together, Noah." She patted his cheek. "Don't worry."

"Why won't they think we're together if we arrive together?"

She shrugged. "No one ever has. How long have we been friends? Everyone knows we aren't a couple. From the very beginning, I've always been the sidekick."

Noah didn't argue with her, and when they arrived, he introduced her as his oldest friend, just like he always had. Everyone nodded and smiled kindly—if a little curiously—and made stilted small talk until Noah whisked her away to someone new. He kept her hand in his and moved through the clustered couples and hospital administrators with purpose, stopping, greeting, and engaging in one minute of conversation before moving along and repeating the same steps.

"You can drink, Mer. Don't abstain on my behalf," he said, when he noticed she hadn't eaten or sipped a single thing.

"I don't think I have time."

"Why?"

"Because when you've given every person here exactly sixty seconds, we're going to leave."

"Am I that obvious?" He winced.

"Yes. Are you timing yourself every time you stop to talk?"

"There's a ticking time bomb in my head, if that's what you mean. Everyone is making those mournful eyes at me, wondering how I'm really doing, or speculating if I've already moved on. It feels . . . weird. Cora's been gone for almost nine months, and this is the first time anyone has seen me with someone else. And for your information . . . you don't look like a sidekick."

She smiled and winked at him. "Always have been, always will be. So . . . are you ready for round two?" she suggested.

"Yes, please. Your coworkers don't know me as well."

"True. And my party is eighties themed."

Noah groaned. "Please, no."

But at the Maven staff and client bash, no one looked twice at Noah, except to say hello, before turning to Mercedes and talking shop. Noah relaxed as the evening wore on, his fear and discomfort falling away into the easy warmth of being with Mercedes and a group of people who hadn't known Cora and who didn't especially care to know him. It was nice. Mercedes even got him to dance. It was like being thirteen again, 1987, listening to the boombox while shooting hoops, Mercedes dancing while she dribbled. Every song reminded him of The Three Amigos, and for a little while he set aside the weight on his shoulders and just *was*.

Keegan Tate cut in once, whisking Mer away and holding her too close as Night Ranger moaned about Sister Christian, but Mer whirled back to Noah on the next song, laughing and leaving Keegan to find another partner. Noah made sure it didn't happen twice, shooting a warning look at anyone who approached and dancing to every song, just so Mer wouldn't leave him again.

When the countdown to midnight began, the DJ warning the crowd and pausing the music, Noah realized suddenly that he'd made it. He'd survived the worst year of his life, and considering his life, that was saying something. There were days when he hadn't been able to do anything but exist in the moment, where the thought of the future almost shut him down. He still wasn't whole, and life wasn't easy. Thinking of Cora still made his heart ache and his stomach clench, but he'd made it. Gia was growing. Gia was happy. And it was going to be okay. Eventually.

". . . Three, Two, One. Happy New Year!" the DJ blared. Balloons fell, and noisemakers blasted.

"Happy New Year, Noah!" Mercedes cried, catching a balloon and tossing it up again. Noah looked down into her laughing eyes and around at the kissing couples crowding the floor, finding himself in the same situation he'd been in months before when he was pinned by the kissing cam.

"There's no jumbotron, Noah," Mercedes protested, standing on her toes so she could speak into his ear, clearly wanting him to hear her amid the noise and the merriment, but he didn't pull away. He knew Mer had no expectations of a kiss at midnight. In fact, she probably expected a hug and a high five. The knowledge freed him, and he turned his face and brushed his lips across her cheek.

"Happy New Year, Mer." Then his lips captured hers, a gentle acknowledgement, a nod to the new year, and her hands rose to his chest in surprise. For a moment it was simply the quiet kiss of true affection, the soft exchange of warm thoughts and well wishes. But someone shoved past them, and Mercedes teetered, losing her balance. Noah's arms tightened to steady her, bringing her body more fully against his, and suddenly their mouths weren't pressed together in cautious greeting but in growing wonder. Their lips lingered, tasting and teasing, shifting and re-shaping, a kaleidoscope kiss that formed only to fall away and reconfigure.

It wasn't until the lights flickered and the eighties tunes resumed— "Auld Lang Syne" becoming UB40's "Red Red Wine"—that Noah lifted his head and Mer lowered her eyes, catching her breath and letting him go.

"I hate this song," he said.

"I know you do."

"It's going to be stuck in my head for a week."

"We better go before you start singing along then."

"Good idea."

It was so easy to slide back into the old banter, into the comfortable give and take of camaraderie, but when Noah turned off the car in Mer's driveway and sat staring at the steering wheel for a heartbeat too long, Mer reached out and pinched his arm, hard.

"Don't overthink it, Boozer," she warned.

"Huh?"

"Step away from the ledge," she demanded, monotone.

"Mer . . ."

"Turn off the fart factory," she droned.

"The fart factory?"

"I can hear your brain farting all the way over here, and it stinks."

"Oh. Gotcha," he said, a smile making the word lift at the end. "I adore you," he confessed.

"And I adore you, Boozer."

"Red, red wine, I love you right from the start," Noah clipped in reggae rhythm.

"Right from the start, with all of my heart." Mercedes answered, mimicking the cadence.

"Goodnight, Mer."

"Goodnight, Noah." She climbed out and shut the door, and he could hear her singing all the way up the walk, waving as she went.

"I really hate that song," Noah sighed to himself, but he was smiling as he pulled away, the fart factory extinguished.

SEVEN

1989

"*I*n the end, only three things matter," Abuela said. "Who He is." She pointed at the sky. "Who you are, and who your friends are."

"Why does it matter who your friends are?" What Mercedes really wanted to ask was why any of it mattered, but she didn't want to hurt her abuela's feelings.

"Our friends shape the course of our lives. You have to choose them very carefully. But if you know who He is, then He will help you know who you are. And if you know who you are, you will know who your true friends are. One thing leads to another, you see."

Mercedes didn't see, but she nodded. "Noah is my true friend."

"Yes. He is. He's a good boy."

"Cora is my true friend."

Abuela nodded, but a little more slowly this time. "You are her true friend. And that is important too. But Cora doesn't know who she is."

"Does she know who He is?" Mercedes pointed at the sky. Abuela loved to talk in mystic riddles, and Mercedes liked to tease.

Abuela narrowed her eyes, suspecting Mercedes was trying to talk circles around her.

"Only three things matter, niña," Abuela said, shaking her finger.

"Who He is, who I am, and who my friends are," Mercedes supplied, *trying not to smile.*

"If you don't know who you are, you won't see the world clearly, you understand?" Abuela was getting frustrated.

"Who am I, Abuela?"

"You are a child of God."

"And who is Cora? Maybe I can tell her who she is, so she will know."

"Mercedes—you are laughing at me." Abuela sighed.

Mercedes was immediately contrite. *"I'm sorry, Abuela. I do know who I am. I am your granddaughter, and I love you very much. I am also a tease, and sometimes I laugh when I should listen."*

"Sí. You should listen. But it is okay to laugh too."

"So tell me . . . who is Cora?" Mercedes asked, contrite.

"She is a child of God too. We all are. But she doesn't know it. When she looks at herself in the mirror, she sees you. And she sees Noah. And she sees her mother and her father, and everyone who has loved her and everyone who has let her down. But she doesn't see Cora because she doesn't know who Cora is."

"I'll tell her, Abuela." Mercedes patted her grandmother's hand. She didn't feel like laughing anymore. She felt melancholy. Sad. Like she'd just learned her friend was suffering from an illness she knew nothing about.

"I know you will, Mercedes. You are a true friend. I will tell her too. Maybe we can save her."

Moses was lean with youth but muscled like a man—eighteen going on thirty—and as tall as Noah, with chocolate milk skin and odd hazel eyes that made Mercedes want to twitch and look away. His hair was cut so close to his scalp that only a suggestion of hair remained, and he ran his hands over his head before dropping them into his lap. He stared at Mercedes quietly for a moment, and she didn't fill the silence. Noah had excused himself with a soft reminder that he would check back soon. Other visitors sat in similar rooms, all of them lining a long hallway. Moses wore the standard attire of a Montlake inmate. Pale yellow scrubs and tan socks with little rubber circles on the bottoms to prevent slipping on the linoleum floors. He should have looked harmless in the odd clothing. He didn't. A stack of drawing paper and several grease pencils lay on the table, and he picked one up, rotating it between his fingers like a drummer in a heavy metal band.

"Noah says you're done. He said you're getting out of Montlake. Where are you going to go?" Mercedes asked.

"Everywhere. Nowhere," he clipped.

"Huh. Never been." Mercedes shrugged.

A smile flickered in his eyes but didn't touch his lips.

"You Dr. Andelin's girl?" he asked, his voice a smoky rumble.

"Do I look like a girl to you, Moses?"

He smiled, his beautiful lips revealing straight white teeth. Mercedes got the feeling he didn't smile often and felt honored to have witnessed it.

"You ain't very big," he muttered. "But no, you're a woman. Still, that doesn't really answer my question."

"I'm not Noah's girl. I'm his friend. I was his wife's friend too. We grew up together."

"Cora," he supplied.

"Yes. Cora."

He shifted, his eyes straying out the window.

"Dr. Noah didn't tell me your name. I don't know what to call you."

She reached out a hand. "I'm Mercedes Lopez. Nice to meet you."

He didn't take it, and she wondered belatedly if there were rules about contact. Noah had left her alone with him, so she wasn't worried about her safety. She lowered her hands to her lap.

"Moses Wright. What do you want, Miss Lopez?" he said, his eyes coming back to hers.

"I don't know, Moses," she confessed. "You helped Noah. I thought maybe you could help me."

"Did he tell you I helped him?" Moses seemed surprised. Pleased.

"Yes."

"He doesn't think I'm crazy?"

"No. He doesn't."

"Huh. Dr. Noah . . . he's all right," Moses said softly. "I like him. And I don't like very many people."

"I like him too. And I don't like most people either."

"I kinda got that vibe." Moses smirked. "You're tough. Cora—Dr. Noah's wife—wasn't . . . tough, was she?"

"In her own way, she was."

He didn't seek to fill the silence between them, but waited for her to move the conversation forward.

"You told Noah that Cora was okay. How do you know?" she asked.

"They all are. The dead, I mean. The ones I see, anyway. Maybe the ones who aren't okay don't get to visit."

"They don't scare you?"

"They scare the shit outta me," he grunted. "But not for the reasons you think. It's . . . unsettling . . . to never be alone." He smirked as though the word was an understatement. "I don't want to see them. But some things . . . we don't get to choose. This is one of those things."

"Most things we don't get to choose . . . that's why I love clothes and makeup and hair. A million choices and nobody gets hurt."

His mouth quirked, but the half-smile faded, and his eyes shifted, growing distant. "You lose someone, Lopez? A grandma or something?"

"Yes." Mercedes watched as he turned inward, seeing something that was hidden from her.

"She looks like you. Feels like you too. Smart. Pushy. She didn't wait for me to acknowledge her," he said.

Mercedes's mouth grew dry, and her eyes were instantly wet. "You can see Abuela?"

"Abuela?" He sounded surprised. "So that's Abuela, huh? Dr. Noah mentioned her."

Mercedes waited, desperate to hear more.

"She's showing me a picture. One of those creepy Catholic paintings." He held his hand up, palm out and cupped. "Why the hell do they always have their hands like that?" he muttered.

Mercedes stared at him, perplexed.

"The woman in the picture is standing like that. There are reddish-gold sunbeams all around her, and she has a veil over her hair," Moses expounded.

Realization struck. "She's showing you Our Lady Guadalupe. The patron saint of Mexico. Abuela loved her. She had her picture over her bed."

"I think . . . she wants you to know she's seen her. Your grandma. She's seen . . . Guadalupe."

Mercedes gasped. "Dios mío. Abuela must be in heaven."

"Well . . . yeah. That's kinda the idea."

Mercedes laughed and swiped at her eyes.

"Shit," he whispered, eyes on her face.

"What?"

"I hoped she was gone." He rubbed at his head wearily and shot Mercedes an accusing look. "Your grandma is with her."

"Who?"

"Dr. Andelin's wife."

It was all Mercedes could do not to spin in her seat, looking for them, desperate to see for herself. Her skin prickled and her stomach dropped, and if it wasn't for Moses's complete lack of pretension and his own discomfort, she wouldn't have believed him. But he had nothing to gain, and Mercedes had nothing to give him but her faith.

"Cora? Cora is with Abuela?" she asked.

"Yeah." His grease pencil began to move over the paper as they talked, as though the motion calmed him. He sketched a simple row of figures connected at the feet and the hands. Paper dolls. He was drawing paper dolls, linked yet individualized. It didn't take long for the details to emerge. Noah and Cora, tall and thin, stood on each end. Mercedes stood between them, smaller, shaded, holding the three of them together. Moses shoved the paper aside. Mercedes stared at it, gazing down at their unmistakable faces.

But Moses wasn't done. He pulled a new sheet toward him and continued, the image rising from the page like a monster from the deep. Mercedes could only watch in fascinated horror as another trio of paper dolls appeared beneath his flying hand. When he was finished he flung his grease pencil, and stuck his fingers in his mouth.

"The pencil gets hot sometimes," he explained.

He slid the sketch toward Mercedes with his free hand. The drawing was eerie. One dimensional bodies—cartoonish and simple—topped with three dimensional faces, each figure smaller than the next. Noah first. Then Mercedes, and clinging to her hand, a tiny figure with floating curls. Gia.

"What does that mean?" Mercedes whispered.

"I draw what I see. That's all," Moses said, but his eyes lifted to hers, golden-green and carefully blank. "But she knows."

"She knows what?"

"You love Dr. Andelin, right? She knows."

"I've always loved him. Of course she knows. I loved her too."

He scratched his head. "Shit,' he sighed again. "And she loves you."

Mercedes nodded, stunned, and grief thrummed in her chest like a sore tooth.

"Can I have these?" she whispered.

"I don't want 'em," Moses grunted.

Mercedes stacked one picture on top of the other. It hurt to look at them. She folded them instead, hiding the images.

"Is that all?" she whispered.

His eyebrows rose, incredulous. "That isn't enough?"

"I want to understand what happened to her . . . and I still don't know."

He sighed heavily. He picked up another pencil and began drawing circles. The circles became rocks at the bottom of a creek bed. "She's showing me stones. Five of them. Smooth. Like river rocks."

"Her car was upside down in the creek," Mercedes whispered.

He nodded and continued drawing. A flag-draped coffin, haunting and unmistakable, emerged beneath his pencil. A pair of dog tags on a long chain framed the picture.

"Her dad was a marine. He lost his legs in a bombing. Came home. And killed himself," Mercedes explained.

Moses nodded again.

"Did Cora kill herself too? Is that what she's trying to tell me?"

His eyes flared, and his hands stilled. "I'm just drawing, Lopez. I don't ask questions. It's not like that. I'm not running the show. They are. They show me what they show me. I don't talk back."

"Have you ever tried?" Mercedes pressed.

"I don't want to!" he snapped.

"Cora?" Mercedes said, taking matters into her own hands. Her heart was in her throat, her lungs on fire, and she stared at Moses as she spoke. "Cora, can you hear me?"

He ground his palms into his eyes. "She hears, all right," he grumbled.

"I love you Cora. Always have. Always will. But I need to know why."

"Shit," Moses mumbled again, but he began to draw once more.

Three figures took shape, connected like the figures Moses had already drawn, with a tiny doll on the end. She recognized Cora and Gia. And she recognized the man.

"That isn't Noah," she hissed.

"No . . . it ain't," Moses whispered.

"How did it go?" Noah asked, walking Mercedes out to her car. She'd tried to slip away from Montlake without him knowing she'd gone, but Noah was waiting outside the door when she left the room. Maybe he didn't trust Moses as much as she thought. She had the pictures clenched in her hands —all except that last one—and it was all she could do to not run screaming from the facility. She'd shoved the last one in her pocket before she even left the room.

"You seem shaken," Noah said gently. "Moses is a lot to take. I tried to warn you."

"My mind is just a little blown. He's something else," she said, glad they were talking about Moses and not Cora.

"He is. He's going to be released tomorrow. I gave him my number. I told him to call me whenever he needs to. I doubt he'll take me up on it, but I hope he will. He's solid. Special. There isn't a thing wrong with Moses Wright that time, friendship, and a little freedom won't fix. He just needs to stop fighting so hard. He and David Taggert—I told you about him—have big plans. They'll either save each other or they'll get each other killed."

Mercedes didn't respond. She just wanted to get away, far away, where she could think. And rage.

"Can I see the pictures?" Noah asked.

"What?" she snapped, pulling them close.

"The pictures, Mer. Can I see them?"

"Oh. Um. Yes. They're fascinating. He was fascinating." She handed him the pictures Moses had drawn and unlocked her car, trying not to watch Noah's face as he thumbed through each one.

"He signed them?" He laughed, incredulous, but he didn't look up from the draped coffin. Mercedes watched as he moved onto the next picture.

"I asked him to. Someday Moses Wright is going to be famous. Mark my words. These are going to be worth a mint."

"I wish I'd thought of that," Noah said, but his eyes were riveted on the drawing of the paper dolls. It was the one with the three of them. Noah, Mercedes, and Gia. Mercedes didn't know what to make of it, but she didn't hide it from him. Not that one.

"Is this why you're upset?" he asked softly.

"She asked me to take care of you and Gia. I'm guessing that's what that picture means."

"Yeah. Could be. But it doesn't explain why you're upset."

"Do you do this to your patients?" she asked, her voice sharp.

"What?"

"Grill them?"

"Is that what I'm doing?" he wrinkled his brow, staring down at her. The February wind felt like tiny icepicks on her cheeks, but her heart was hot and her breaths shallow. She just needed a chance to think, and she didn't want to answer Noah's questions. She just needed to think.

"You are her husband. Gia is *her* child. And she's gone. That picture doesn't make me have the warm fuzzies. It makes me feel like a . . . thief. Like an imposter." It was the truth, but she was still lying. She wasn't upset for herself. She was scared to death for Noah.

Noah tipped his head to the side, waiting for her to elucidate. He was good at that. Waiting. Listening. Unraveling. When she said nothing, he handed her the pictures.

"You aren't an imposter, Mer. You're a life-saver."

"I've got to go, Noah. I'm running late. I'll call you," she whispered.

Rising on her toes, she kissed his cheek, just above the line of his beard. His cheek was cold, but his eyes were warm on her face when she pulled away.

"You're overthinking this, Boozer," he teased, repeating the line she'd used on him on New Year's Eve.

She tried to smile and slid into her car, waving at him as she drove away. Maybe she *was* overthinking it. Maybe she was letting her mind conjure scenarios that had no basis in reality. But she didn't think so. Her gut had never been wrong.

Mercedes didn't go back to work. The sky was grey, and snow rose in great walls along the roads, but the roads themselves were clear, and she called the reception desk at Maven and told Briana to reschedule her afternoon appointments. She drove aimlessly, her thoughts scampering back across the years, trying to make sense of something she didn't understand, something she'd *never* understood.

Cora fell in and out of love a dozen times before she married Noah. She was always looking for something that she never seemed to find. Mercedes assumed Cora was just waiting for Noah to fall in love with her too, and when he finally did, she would stop searching. But apparently, she hadn't.

Cora was the first of the three of them to lose her virginity—Ryan Wilcox, sophomore year. Cora was crazy about him until she slept with him. Then she couldn't get away fast enough. Ryan Wilcox had been interested in Mercedes first, but when Cora said she liked him, Mercedes hadn't minded stepping aside. She wasn't interested in love triangles or burning bridges over a romance that wouldn't last much longer than a week.

Whether it was her cousins and their girlfriends or her friends at school, sex seemed to ruin everything, and she, Noah, and Cora had sworn they wouldn't let boys—or girls—get in the way of their friendship. But when Noah grew up sophomore year, and suddenly all of his goodness was wrapped in a tall, handsome package, it was hard not to notice. Cora had definitely noticed.

But true to her word, Cora never made a move on Noah or attempted to change their relationship. Maybe she was reluctant to actually catch him. Maybe she valued him too much, just the way he was. Just the way *they* were. But everything changed when Noah enlisted. Mercedes had backed away and Cora had stepped forward.

"Will you forget me when I'm gone?" Noah asked.

"Of course not. How could I forget my best friend in the whole world?" Mercedes laughed.

Noah didn't say anything, but kept his eyes on her face, as if he were trying to unpeel her.

"You were outside with Kurt for a long time." He'd been sitting with Abuela for an hour, waiting for her to come inside. When he'd heard her at the door, he'd met her in the foyer and Abuela had gone to bed.

"We were making out," she answered simply.

Noah rubbed the back of his neck and laughed, incredulous. "How can I be mad at you when you are so honest?"

"Why would you be mad at me?" Mercedes asked, flummoxed.

"You're too good for Kurt Jespersen."

"Of course I am. But he's hot. And he's a good kisser. I'm eighteen, Noah. I plan to kiss a lot of guys before I settle down with one. I'm not like Cora. She's got her heart set on you." She was teasing him with the truth. Cora did have her heart set on Noah, even if none of them talked about it.

"I see." He sounded tired. "Cora is my friend, Mer. That's all."

"I know. But she would like to be more. You know it, and I know it."

"What would you do if I kissed you?" Noah asked softly. He took several steps toward her and looked down into her face.

"Don't." Her heart was racing but her voice was firm. Calm.

"Why?"

"Remember Bob?" she said.

"Huh?" Noah wasn't following.

"Remember how he and Heather used to smoke together out on her balcony?"

"Yeah?" he drew the word out, curious.

"She talked to him. They were friends. And then—"

"He wanted more," Noah finished, his tone flat.

"Yep. And do you see Bob anymore?" she asked.

"Bob's gone."

"Exactly."

Noah's shoulders slumped in dejection.

"We keep our friends. But girlfriends and boyfriends . . . we exchange those, we cut them loose. I want to keep you, Noah. The only way I can do that—keep you forever—is if you and I stay friends."

"I don't know if I can do that, Mer."

"Why?" she gasped.

"I like you too much."

Without asking, without warning, he leaned in and kissed her.

His lips were soft, his breath sweet, and the tips of his fingers were light on her cheeks. But it wasn't a kiss between friends. It wasn't a kiss goodbye. It was a desperate hello. Her heart grew and grew, filling her chest with both terror and triumph. But she didn't push him back or pull away. In the darkness, she returned the press of his lips, and when he deepened the kiss, she opened her mouth to him without hesitation.

She knew kissing him was a mistake. She knew it would make every-thing harder. But she couldn't stop. She couldn't turn away, and when his arms wrapped around her, lifting her so he could straighten his back and hold her against him, something snapped inside her. She kissed him with a fury and a fervor that had him pulling back and panting her name, before they were lost again in the sweet slide of their lips, the tangle of their tongues, and the shared sighs that kept them coming back again and again.

They clung to each other, her arms wrapped around his shoulders, his arms wrapped around her waist. His hands didn't roam, and they didn't sink to the floor. They stood in the darkened alcove, kissing like they would never get another chance, like kissing was life itself, and the moment they stopped, the world would stop too.

And stop it did.

"Will you write, Mer? Please," Noah panted.

"Of course I'll write," she whispered.

"And take care of Cora. She's not as strong as you are."

Cora's name was like cold water down her back. Mercedes pulled away. Staggered away. Noah's hand shot out to steady her, but she stepped out of reach.

She'd tried to take care of Cora. When Noah was gone the first time, it wasn't so hard. They were all still friends, still unattached, still equally connected. Noah came home when his mother died but left soon after for

Kuwait. Mercedes had asked him if he was running away. He told her he was just trying to figure out where he was going, but he'd left her and Cora behind. He'd left the Three Amigos behind.

Mercedes had just finished hair school, Cora was in college, and with Noah gone and high school over, the three of them became separate islands in their own seas. Or so she thought. In actuality, she'd been the only one adrift. Cora and Noah grew closer during the time they spent apart, and Cora didn't need Mer to take care of her.

When Noah was deployed to Afghanistan in 2002, he'd made the same request of his oldest friend. "Take care of Cora, Mer."

It was harder the second time.

Cora had been distant and dissatisfied. She was excited about her pregnancy one day, despondent and disinterested the next. Cora started avoiding Mercedes only to show up at the salon out of the blue, crying and asking her why she'd abandoned her when she needed her most. Cora was either high as a kite, full of energy and glowing with life, or completely bottomed out, struggling to brush her hair and teeth. Mercedes went over several times during Noah's nine-month deployment just to make sure Cora made it to work. When she was going to work, sticking to a routine, she did better. Toward the end of her pregnancy, she leveled out only to plummet again after Gia was born. When Noah came home he stepped right back into his old role of caretaker. It was like his mother died, and he replaced her with someone who needed him in exactly the same way.

The thought made Mercedes wince.

"I'm sorry, Cora," she whispered to herself. "That isn't fair. But I don't know what you're trying to tell me. If it is what I think it is, then I don't want to know."

If something happens to me, you'll take care of them, won't you?

Mercedes pulled into a gas station and filled up the Corolla's tank, standing in the cold, her hands shoved into her pockets. She felt the drawing she'd hastily folded and tucked away at Montlake. She pulled it out and opened it, smoothing the lines that marred the faces staring up at her from the page. Keegan Tate. She'd recognized him immediately. Why had Moses drawn a picture of Keegan Tate with Cora and Gia? It could only mean one thing.

If something happens to me, you'll take care of them, won't you?

"I'm trying Cora," Mercedes murmured. "But I can't take care of them if I'm covering for you."

EIGHT

1989

S*he'd noticed him. He smoked on his balcony—like everyone else did —but he liked to watch the kids. He watched Mercedes sometimes. She stared back once, jutting out her chin and putting her hands on her hips. She even swore in Spanish, a whole string of filthy words that she was certain he didn't understand. He understood. She heard him chuckle and blow out a long ribbon of smoke that curled back around him like a pet snake.*

"He thinks you're pretty Sadie." Cora said one day, watching the man as he watched them. From his balcony he had a straight view of the basketball court, and Mercedes didn't think he could hear them, but she wished he would go inside. She couldn't concentrate on the game, and he made her skin crawl.

"Gross, Cora," Mercedes growled.

"He watches you."

"He watches you too," Mercedes huffed. She didn't want to be the only one.

"He looks a little like my dad."

"No he doesn't, Cora."

"He's probably lonely. I think I'm going to go talk to him."

"Don't you dare. Cora, he's probably a child molester."

"We're not children anymore, Sadie."

"We sure as hell are!"

"You don't have to come with me."

Mercedes wasn't letting Cora go alone, and Cora seemed determined to talk to the man. She marched across the grass and stood beneath his balcony, shading her eyes as she smiled up at him.

"Hi," Cora called. The man smiled.

"Hi there, Red." He snuffed out his cigarette and smoothed his hair.

"What's your name?" Cora asked.

"Payton," he said, smirking around his cigarette.

"Well . . . Mr. Payton. How long have you lived here?" Cora asked.

"Just Payton. You know how long. You been watching me, girl."

"You have?" Mercedes hissed, staring at her friend.

"You look like my dad, Mr. Payton. He died," Cora explained.

"You don't look anything like her dad," Mercedes scoffed.

"That's too bad about your dad, Red." Payton ignored Mercedes. "What's your name?"

"I'm Cora."

"And my friends call me Nunya Damn Business," Mercedes interjected. She pulled on Cora's arm as the man laughed.

"Come up, Cora," the man said. "We'll talk about your dad. I'll get you a soda. You been playing ball so you're probably thirsty."

"We don't want a soda." Mercedes shook her head and folded her arms.

"Okay," Cora said, eager. The man's balcony was two levels up, and Cora trotted toward the stairs that would lead her up to the second-floor apartments.

"Cora!" Mercedes yelled, incensed.

"I want to talk to him, Sadie. I told you, you don't have to come."

"The hell I don't."

Payton was waiting for them, his door open wide, sodas in hand. He stepped aside and bid them enter, and Cora pranced inside like she'd known him all her life. Mercedes stood in the doorway and kept one hand on the frame, one hand on the door. Cora took the grape Fantas from Payton's hand and handed one to Mercedes. Mercedes took it, ready to chuck it at Payton's face if he made a wrong move. It was cold and slick, and

Cora immediately popped the tab on her can and took a long pull.

"You look kinda like my little girl too, you know that? She had the same red curls." Payton reached out and touched the lock of hair laying against Cora's left breast. She stepped back, and Mercedes stepped forward. Payton stepped between them.

"You have a little girl?" Cora whispered, and Mercedes groaned.

Payton made a sorrowful face. "She died. I miss her."

"Bullshit," Mercedes hissed. She was truly afraid. Cora was acting as though she were in a play, as though someone was about to yell "cut!" and she had to sell the scene.

"Now that's not nice, Nunya," Payton said, sly. It took Mercedes a minute to realize he was talking to her. "Cora and I are gonna talk for a minute. You go on home." He tried to push Mercedes out the door.

"Cora!" Mercedes clung to the frame, refusing to leave without her friend. Payton picked her up, but not before his hands cupped her bottom and slid up her sides. He plopped her down in the hallway beyond.

"Go home, Nunya," he said.

Suddenly Cora was shoving past Payton, wrapping her arms around Mercedes and wrenching her from Payton's grasp. Mercedes's grape soda smashed against the pavement and burst, spraying their feet and legs with sudsy purple, and Payton swore and made a grab for Cora's arm. Her cheeks were pink and her eyes wide, like she'd suddenly woken up to the danger she'd placed them in, and she wriggled free, pulling Mercedes with her. Then they were running, streaking down the stairs and across the stretch of grass that led past the concrete slab and basketball hoop to the apartments on the other side.

"I'm sorry, Sadie," Cora panted as they reached the hallway that spanned their front doors.

"What in the hell were you thinking?" Mercedes cried. She wanted to shake her friend, to slap her, to open up her head and look inside. Her stomach hurt, and she thought she might throw up.

"I don't know," Cora stammered. "I really don't know."

For three weeks, Mercedes stewed and worried. The picture Moses had drawn was burned into her mind—three paper dolls with familiar faces, mocking her when she closed her eyes. She didn't know what to do. Keegan had never said anything to her about Cora, and Mercedes had never noticed anything between them. When Cora died, Keegan came to the funeral; everyone from Maven had come to the funeral. Keegan had hugged her tightly, expressing his condolences, but that was all. They'd never talked about Cora's passing, and Keegan had never seemed personally affected. Mercedes kept talking herself out of confronting him, but the proverbial can of worms had been opened, and try as she might, Mercedes could not bring herself to touch them. Now they were crawling, dirt clinging to their writhing flesh, in and out of her thoughts, making her miserable, robbing her sleep, and stealing her peace.

She and Keegan were alone, shutting down the shop, when the opportunity arose. They usually staggered their shifts, one opening, one closing, but that Saturday night, they found themselves together as the last customer left and the door was locked.

"Do you want to grab a bite, Mercedes?" Keegan asked, not looking up from the till. "It's been a while. We could catch up."

She studied him, trying to see him the way Cora must have seen him, the way others saw him, and couldn't because she saw right through him. He had no substance. No weight. And she had no interest in being one of many as he flitted through life. He wasn't as tall as Noah, maybe six feet in his heeled boots, but he was pretty, with perfect hair and a great jawline. He had bright blue eyes that he liked to narrow and pouting lips that he liked to purse, as if he were deep in thought over his next move. Women loved it. He would stare at them in the mirror for several minutes, as if pondering how he could best turn them into their most beautiful selves. He would touch their hair and run his fingers through it, tipping his head this way and that. He would make comments like, "God, you've got great eyes. Let's give your hair a little color to make them pop. You're going to look amazing," or "Look at this bone structure. Fabulous. No matter what I do, you'll be beautiful. You make my job so easy."

His clients would giggle and let him do whatever he wanted. And he did *whatever the hell* he wanted. The women who saw him were almost always on a high when they left the salon. His attention was an aphrodisiac, and he had a waiting list three months long. Gloria Maven loved him because he was a huge draw.

But when the aphrodisiac wore off, some women came back crying. Second thoughts and extreme haircuts weren't always the best combination. Luckily, Keegan was quite skilled at his craft, and even when a woman was regretful, he managed to woo her to his way of thinking.

But Mercedes had fixed a few of his more unpopular styles, and in the process, gained customers that were fiercely loyal to her and wary of him. For that reason, she and Keegan kept their stations at opposite ends of the salon.

Regardless, he evoked strong feeling, and he was good for business. Mercedes was fairly certain that she was the only person at Maven—besides Gloria Maven herself—who hadn't slept with Keegan. Keegan had even asked her once, playful, pouting, why they hadn't slept together.

"Because if I slept with you, Keegan, I would eventually hate you, and you wouldn't respect me," she'd responded.

"I would worship you!" he had protested.

"For about ten minutes. And then it would ruin this antagonism we've got going."

Keegan would laugh, and the flirtation would continue. Mercedes had thought it was harmless. She'd thought they were friends. She was even fond of him.

"I need to ask you something, Keegan," Mercedes said. "And I need you to tell me the truth."

There must have been something in her voice, because he looked up in surprise.

"Did you and Cora Andelin have an affair?" she blurted.

He laughed, sputtering, and closed the register. "Holy shit, Mercedes. Where did that come from?"

"I just need to know, Keegan," she pressed quietly.

"Why? Why in the world do you need to know now . . . after all this time?"

"You did." *Dios mío. He did. They did.*

"I wouldn't call it an affair. It was more like a handful of one-night stands," he said, shrugging. He seemed uncomfortable but not overly distressed. "I think she knew I liked you, Mercedes." He cocked a hip against the counter and smirked at her, pursing his pretty lips.

"Cut the crap, Keegan. I'm not into you. Especially now."

He laughed as though he didn't believe her.

"Well, Cora was exactly the opposite," he teased. "Once she knew I was into *you*, she was into *me*. And Cora was beautiful. It wasn't hard to change my focus from you to her."

"Yeah. She was beautiful. And she was also married."

"Oh, come on, Sadie. Who do you think you're kidding? We all know how it is with you and Noah Andelin."

"What are you talking about?" Mercedes snapped. She had no tolerance for nasty gossip that made everyone feel better about themselves for the five seconds it took to shred someone else.

"You two have so much chemistry, it's like watching porn through the blinds of someone else's house."

"Do you do that a lot, Keegan? Watch porn through people's blinds?" she growled.

"You two aren't fooling anyone," he shot back. It was all Mercedes could do not to slap his face.

"Well, apparently we are. Noah and I are friends. We have never been more than that."

"Cora thought you were."

"No, she didn't," Mercedes gasped. "She did not, Keegan Tate. That's a lie."

Keegan shrugged. "It bothered her, the way he called you Mer. The way you laughed together. The fact that he always came here to have you cut his hair. You two were tight."

"We've been tight since we were eight years old. But never the way you mean. Never. And Cora knew it."

"It didn't last very long, Sadie," he whined. He didn't seem to like that she was mad at him. "I cut her hair that once, remember? She was cool. And so pretty. Being with her was like . . . being with a mythical princess. That sounds stupid. But she was . . ."

"Ethereal," Mercedes filled in the blank. "I get it."

"Yeah. Ethereal." He seemed to be stewing over the word like he was just learning what it meant. "I cut her hair and she left her number just sitting there on my work station. No name. But I knew it was hers. I shouldn't have called her, but I did."

Mercedes nodded, trying not to judge, wanting to kill him, wanting to kill Cora.

"She grew tired of me pretty quick." He shrugged again.

"Did you grow tired of her?"

"She was married. Sneaking around was kind of fun—kinda hot—for about ten seconds. We'd meet up, have sex, and she would bolt. Then she told me we were done, and that was that. I didn't miss her."

"And what did you think when you found out she was pregnant?" Mercedes whispered, her nerves so tight they were humming a desperate tune.

Keegan swallowed, an indication that he had, indeed, thought about it.

"I always used protection, and I wasn't the only one she was having sex with. She was married, remember? The timing was right, but Noah was deployed right around the time when we were still seeing each other. I thought his deployment might mean we hooked back up, but we never did. Maybe she felt guilty. I don't know. But when she didn't say anything to me, I assumed it was Noah's, and I kept my mouth shut."

"Thank God for that."

"Does he know? The good doctor?" Keegan asked. "Is that what this is about? Did he tell you? He's always been jealous of me."

"I don't know if he knows, Keegan. He wouldn't tell me something like that. And why do you call him that?"

"He's just a little too good to be true," Keegan muttered.

"And you don't measure up."

"Cora thought I did."

"No. She didn't. Otherwise she would have left him for you," Mercedes snapped.

"You sure you're not sleeping with him?"

"You're a pig, Keegan."

He shrugged. "You've always liked me well enough."

"I don't anymore."

"Oh, come on, Mercedes. Don't say that. You're acting like I cheated on *you*. Maybe you like me more than you want to admit," he cajoled, trying to tease her into smiling at him. She couldn't even look at him. And she didn't know how she was going to face Noah, knowing for certain what Cora had done.

"Who else knows?" she whispered.

Keegan shook his head. "Nobody."

She nodded. "Good. Because I don't ever want to talk about this again."

"Mercedes, Cuddy is at the back door again, wanting his freebie," Keegan greeted when Mercedes walked into Maven Friday morning. He didn't look at her as he spoke. Things had been awkward between them for the last week. Even Gloria had noticed.

Mercedes sighed. Cuddy didn't come by very often, and he was harmless and sweet. But he scared off the regular customers, so she'd told him if he needed a cut, he had to be there first thing on Fridays—nine a.m. sharp—and she would take care of him before the salon opened at ten. He was always so grateful, closing his eyes when she washed his hair, fat tears squeezing out the sides. It broke her heart a little every time.

A few years back, about six months before Noah was deployed to Afghanistan, Hill Air Force Base sponsored a community service day, focusing on the homeless problem in Salt Lake City. A good number of the homeless and the mentally ill were veterans, and Hill was partnering with the Governor's office to bring awareness and make basic services available to those who were so often forgotten and ignored. Noah and Cora were passionate about the project, Cora because of her father's military background, Noah because his own mother had been a homeless teenager when he was born, and they recruited Mercedes to take part.

For two days, under a huge tent that covered an entire city block, the community lured the homeless in with free food, beds, and services—

medical services, dental services, counseling, educational opportunities, even haircuts and clothing. Noah got people plugged into AA meetings and provided mental health evaluations, Cora made people aware of educational opportunities and coordinated with a staffing company to get people back to work, and Mercedes did her best to make people feel beautiful again.

She'd participated in the event every year, but there were a few people, like Cuddy, who she saw on a more regular basis. She had strict rules about loitering in front of the salon, hassling the staff, or panhandling in the vicinity, but if they followed those rules, she never turned anyone away. Cuddy was her most regular non-paying customer.

"It's not his fault I'm running late," Mercedes groused. "I'll just have to work fast today. Go let him in, will you, Keegan? And get him settled at one of the sinks."

"You are an angel, Mercedes Lopez. I wouldn't touch that man's head with a ten-foot pole," Keegan said under his breath, but he headed toward the back, snagging a white stylist robe to cover his pristine clothes.

"Be nice to him, Keegan," Mercedes called after him. "Cuddy has powers. He'll put a spell on you."

He would too. Poor Cuddy didn't have all his mental faculties anymore, if he ever had. But he had an uncanny ability to see who was friend and who was foe.

Mercedes rushed to clock in and stash her purse beneath the counter before tying on an apron and heading back to tend to Cuddy's hair.

He was reclining in a chair at the sinks, his long duster coat pulled around him, his eyes closed. His legs were twitching, his knees jumping up and down. He was always a jittery mess until she started washing his hair. Then, like she untightened something in his head, his limbs stilled, and he grew loose and relaxed beneath her hands.

"Good morning, Cuddy."

"Good morning, Miss Lopez."

"Call me Mercedes, Cuddy. You know Miss Lopez makes me feel like a school teacher."

She searched his hair surreptitiously for lice—so far, he'd never brought any with him—and turned on the water, getting it warm before she ran it over his thick hair. He had a mop of it, and he'd gone almost completely grey. She didn't know how old he was—sadly, the homeless all appeared ancient—but from the thickness of his hair, she'd guess he was about fifty. He was tall and wiry—skinny, even—though it was hard to see his body beneath the long coat he always wore, rain or shine. In the summer months, he smelled ripe, and Mercedes often convinced him to make use of the shower in the employee locker room. He wouldn't have time to shower today. Luckily, he didn't smell too bad. A little smoky, a little sweaty, but not too bad.

"It's going to be a beautiful day, Cuddy. Feels like Spring, huh? Now how does that water feel?"

"It feels just fine, Miss Lopez." His eyes stayed closed, but the tears were starting to seep out the sides.

She took more time than she had, washing his hair, rinsing it, and washing it again. She handed him a hot wash cloth and softly urged him to scrub his face and get behind his ears. He obeyed, wiping away the tears that hadn't stopped. It was their routine. He pretended her kindness and the human contact didn't make him cry, and she pretended not to notice.

She wrapped a clean towel around his hair and dried it briskly before leading him to her chair.

"Have a seat, Cuddy. Are we doing the same thing? Or do you want to try something new?" She always said that, and it always made him smile.

"Could you cut it good and short? It lasts longer that way."

He couldn't make eye contact. His eyes never stayed in one place long enough. It made her dizzy when she tried to talk to him. She was grateful he kept them closed while she trimmed and clipped, trying to work fast while still giving him a good cut.

"Miss Cora . . . I haven't seen her in a while," he said suddenly. "She wasn't at the community fair last November. I didn't see Dr. Noah either. Are you coming next month?"

Cuddy knew Cora for the same reason he knew Mercedes. He'd met them through their homeless outreach.

"I'll be there. I don't know if Noah will be. Cora passed away about a year ago, Cuddy," Mercedes murmured. "She was killed in a car accident. It's been a hard year for him, but I know he'll do his best to attend. It's something he cares a lot about."

"Oh, no," Cuddy moaned softly, blinking wildly, shaking his head from side to side in denial. "Oh, no. Not Miss Cora. I was afraid of that."

"What do you mean . . . you were afraid of that? Did Cora say something to you?"

"I saw her just the other day. I hoped I was wrong."

"I don't understand, Cuddy." Cora had been gone for a year, and even Cuddy could blend that many days together.

"I thought I saw her. I thought I did," he mumbled, wiping his eyes. "Cora was so sweet. She was nice to me."

"I'm sorry, Cuddy. I thought you knew," Mercedes said, swallowing the lump in her own throat.

Mercedes finished cutting while Cuddy cried, doing her best to comfort him and hold him still. In the end, she just took her clippers to his curls, and watched as the grey clumps fell to the floor.

He didn't seem to notice she'd taken more than usual, and when she was done, he stood and dug in his pocket. She knew he wasn't searching for cash. This was part of their routine too. Most people paid with money. Cuddy paid with rocks.

"I've been saving that one for you. It's pretty and dark. Like your eyes," he whispered, laying a smooth stone on her workstation table. He laid a few more beside it. "This one's for Cora. This one's for Noah. This one's for their little girl. Will you give these to them, Miss Lopez?"

"I will. I'll put them on Cora's grave. She would like that."

He nodded, staring down at the four stones. Then he reached into his pocket and pulled out another. "Five smooth stones," he whispered. "David killed Goliath with five smooth stones. Don't put them on her grave. You might need them."

NINE

1989

"You didn't get the part," Noah said. It wasn't a question. He'd obviously heard.

"No. It's probably better. Rehearsals would have taken up a lot of time, and I can't afford to miss work," Mercedes said, shrugging.

He was silent, sitting beside Mercedes on the low, block wall, his long legs swinging. Mercedes watched his shoelaces dangle, dirty and torn, and with a sigh, she jumped down and tied them.

"What are you doing?" he asked.

"You're going to trip and fall, and you wear them out when you step on them," Mercedes muttered as she hoisted herself back up beside him. She was wearing a new skirt she'd found at the Goodwill, and it wasn't easy to climb in it and maintain her dignity. But she managed.

"Ah, Mer. You're always taking care of everyone."

"Look who's talking. You've practically raised yourself," Mercedes retorted.

He stiffened, and she sighed again. Noah didn't like it when she insinuated that his mother wasn't responsible. He changed the subject.

"Are you mad at Cora?" he asked.

"No." Mercedes shook her head.

"She only tried out for the play because you were trying out."

"I know."

"And she got the part you wanted," he continued.

"Yep."

"But you're not mad?" Noah asked, his tone gentle. He wasn't trying to stir the crap or stab Cora in the back. He really wanted to know. He wanted to make sure there was peace in their kingdom of three.

"How could I be mad? Cora was amazing. She's a natural. And she's a better fit for the part." Mercedes wondered, in the recesses of her heart, if the way she looked was the deciding factor. Eliza Doolittle was an English shop girl, and Mercedes was the wrong ethnicity, and everybody knew it.

"I watched the auditions. You were good too." Noah was trying so hard to make her feel better, but he'd had to know how this would end. Mercedes had known. But it still hurt when she saw Cora's name beside Eliza Doolittle's and her own name beside a bit part at the bottom of the page.

"I've got fire, and I commit. But let's face it, my cockney accent sucked," Mercedes admitted.

He tried not to, but Mercedes saw a ghost of a smile flit over his mouth. "It was a little too—"

"It was too western," she finished for him.

"Yeah. Think John Wayne does Doolittle."

They laughed together, but her laughter faded when she thought about the way Cora looked, standing under the spotlight, saying her lines. She'd wanted to be angry. Cora had known how much Mercedes wanted the part, and she auditioned for the same role and got it. But how could Mercedes be angry when Cora was so tragic? And so convincing?

"Cora said when she was on the stage, she felt free, Noah. She said she didn't have to be Cora anymore. She was so good, I hardly recognized her up there."

"She wasn't acting. She was escaping."

"Yeah," Mercedes breathed. "And maybe that's why I didn't get the part. I was acting, and I never forgot, not for one second, who I was. I was Mercedes Lopez. Not Eliza Doolittle."

"That's a good thing, Mer."

"It is?"

"I think so. I like Mercedes Lopez. She's smart and funny and fierce. She's loyal and tough and can dribble the ball and shoot free throws better than any girl I know. She's beautiful—inside and out. Why would you want to be anyone else?"

The answer resonated in her skull, almost like someone had spoken the words directly in her ear.

"You know what? I wouldn't. I wouldn't want to be anyone else," Mercedes said, reassured. Noah Andelin was her best friend, and that made being Mercedes Lopez pretty damn amazing.

"It may be a small part, but you'll kill it," Noah promised. *"I know you will. Sometimes it's the smallest part that steals the show."*

Gia turned two on March 22, a Tuesday, two weeks before the one-year anniversary of Cora's death. Noah ordered a dozen cupcakes with pink frosting and a huge bouquet of balloons and wrestled them into his Subaru while trying to buckle Gia into her car seat. She wanted to hold one of the balloons, and it popped in her arms, making Noah swear and making Gia cry.

Noah was trying to potty-train her—two seemed old enough to learn —and they stopped at Walmart to pick out some new underwear in hopes that she wouldn't want to pee on pretty princesses. Gia insisted on wearing them immediately. He purchased them, took her into the Walmart re-stroom, took off her pull-up, put on the new underwear, redressed her, and she peed in them on the way home, soaking Sleeping Beauty, her car seat, and making herself wet and miserable. Two more helium balloons popped before they made it into the house.

Gia wasn't interested in any of the presents he bought, but she cried when there was nothing left to unwrap. He ended up wrapping everything in her toy box so she could pull the paper off, which kept her happy for about half an hour.

Heather was out of town, Alma and Mer had to work, and Gia covered her ears and cried when Noah sang her the birthday song all by himself.

"No scawy (scary) song, Daddy!" she sobbed.

He took the obligatory picture with the cupcake and candles, but Gia wasn't impressed by any of it, and scowled at the camera, fat tears rolling down her cheeks.

It was a lousy birthday, and it only got worse when Mer showed up at eight that night, wearing a long, bright pink coat, cheetah print heels, and a look on her face that spelled trouble. Gia was stripped down to her Cinderellas, clutching a balloon by its string, and demanding Noah carry her everywhere. Bed time could not come soon enough, and Noah still had to work the night shift.

"Happy Birthday, Gia Bug!" Mer crooned, leaning in for a kiss, which Gia happily gave her. Mercedes was trying to hide her excitement. She was hiding something in the deep V of her trench coat, and when a small mewl escaped, Gia gasped, and Noah groaned.

"Oh, Mer. What have you done?"

He knew exactly what she'd done. She'd bought Gia a kitten for her birthday.

"He'll be a good mouser," Mercedes said.

"I don't have mice," Noah retorted.

"But you have ants!"

"You're never going to let that go, are you? My house was a mess one time last July, and you're never going to let me forget it," he complained.

"I will. I will never mention ants again . . . if you'll keep an open mind about Oscar," she promised.

"You named a . . . cat . . . after your dad?"

Mercedes nodded enthusiastically and withdrew a small, black kitten from inside her coat.

"He's a little boy cat, and he has black hair and a gentle personality. Just like Papi. He will be a perfect playmate for Gia. Having a pet will be good for her. You'll see. And he's litter-box trained. I bought all the supplies. You won't have to worry about a thing. I bought him a bed, a litter box, a huge container of kitty litter, and one of those fifty-pound bags of cat food. It'll last a year. You won't even know Oscar is here, except that he'll keep Gia entertained so you can get something done."

Noah groaned again. He didn't want anyone or anything else to take care of, but Gia had grown still in his arms. She stared at the tiny, black cat, her little jaw dropping, her blue eyes so big Noah bit his lip so he wouldn't laugh.

"Kitty," she whispered reverently.

Mercedes put the kitten down on the kitchen floor and Noah released Gia as well, setting her on her sturdy little legs and stepping back.

"Hi, Kitty," she squeaked, extending her chubby fingers to touch the black ball of fluff quivering before her.

Mercedes looked at Noah with shining eyes, and Noah sighed and scrubbed at his beard with both hands, knowing he was screwed.

"He had his first vaccination yesterday. He'll need another one in four weeks and another when he's sixteen weeks. But I'll take care of it. Don't worry. And I got him one of those scratching pole thingies so he won't rip up the furniture," Mercedes reassured.

Noah groaned again. "Mer . . . I really wish you hadn't done this."

"I am prepared to bring Oscar back to my house if you really don't want him. But look at Gia, Noah. She loves him."

Gia was on her knees, her bottom in the air, her cheek to the floor so she was as close to the kitten as possible. The kitten was sniffing her face suspiciously.

"I don't want cat hair all over everything," Noah grumbled.

"I'll vacuum the furniture and all the floors every Monday when I'm here."

"You do that already."

"You're right. I do. I totally deserve this, Noah. Come on, please?" Mercedes wheedled, hands clasped beneath her chin, staring up at him mournfully with her heavily-lashed, brown eyes.

"If *you* deserve it, why is it living at *my* house?"

"Because I'm here more than I'm at home. And I bought him for Gia."

"You *are* here an awful lot. Why is that?" he teased. "Go home, woman."

She rolled her eyes. "You need me. That's why." Then she smiled, teeth flashing, dimples framing her pink lips. "You're going to let her keep him, aren't you?"

"You know I am. Was there ever any question? You always get your way, Mer."

She rolled her eyes again. "Ha! When? I can't think of very many times when Mercedes Lopez got what she wanted just because she wanted it. I *can* think of all the times I worked my ass off and made something happen," she huffed.

Noah leaned over and kissed her forehead. "Thank you for the kitten that I didn't want."

"You're welcome. Now where are those cupcakes?"

Noah straightened the kitchen—and set out a cupcake for Mer—while Mercedes and Gia got the kitten situated. Gia was carrying Oscar under one arm, telling him all the words she knew, which was a considerable amount for a two-year-old. Noah didn't know what was normal, but his daughter seemed to be especially verbal for her age. Mercedes had kicked off her stilettos and was pouring kitty litter into a box, explaining to both Gia and Oscar what it was for. Then she took Oscar from Gia and set him in the box.

"Go potty, Oscar," she ordered.

The kitten sniffed around for three seconds before his little tail rose obediently, and he squatted to do his business. Even the cat couldn't say no to Mercedes, Noah thought to himself. Mercedes clapped as Oscar buried his very small pile of poop—Gia clapped too—and they proceeded to fill the cat bowls with water and kitten kibble.

When Gia chased Oscar into the family room, Noah and Mercedes followed, sinking down onto the couch to watch them play. Noah found himself watching Mercedes eat her cupcake instead, grateful that she'd saved Gia's birthday from being a total bomb, even if it meant he was now the unhappy owner of a cat.

"You always know what to do," he said. "That's a talent. You show up and make everything better."

"Really?" He'd pleased her.

"Yes. Today was a total fail. You saved the day," he admitted.

"I stole the scene." She stood up and took a bow before plopping back down beside him and licking the frosting from her fingers.

"You sure did. Tell me something, Mer. How long have you wanted a cat?"

She laughed. "I've wanted a cat since I was ten."

"I thought so. Remember those kittens they were giving away in front of Albertson's Grocery Store that one time?" he asked.

"There was only one left. He was grey and fluffy. Cora and I were in love, and you weren't interested."

"My load was heavy, even then. I didn't want any more responsibility than I already had. I haven't changed much."

"I wanted that kitten, but I knew I would have to ask Mami. I had to wait for her to get home from work."

"But Cora beat you to it."

"Yep. Cora didn't ask her mom. She just brought the kitten home. She named him Popeye, and he disappeared about a month later."

They were both silent for a moment, remembering.

"Didn't you ever notice that whatever you wanted or whatever you set out to do, Cora wanted to do it too?" Noah asked.

"She wasn't like that."

"She was, Mer. And it's okay to admit it. One of the hardest things about Cora dying is that everyone wants to erase her—the real Cora. They talk about her as though she were perfect. She wasn't. 'Don't talk ill of the dead,' people say. But if we aren't truthful about who our loved ones were, then we aren't really remembering *them*. We're creating someone who didn't exist. Cora loved you. She loved me. But what she did was not okay. And I'm pissed off about it."

Mercedes reeled back, stunned. "Geez, Noah. Tell me how you really feel. She still deserves our compassion," she rebuked.

He nodded. "Everyone deserves compassion. And I know suicide isn't always a conscious act. Most of the time it's sheer desperation. It's a moment of weakness that we can't come back from. But regardless of illness or weakness, if we don't own our actions and don't demand that others own theirs, then what's the point? We might as well give up now. We *have* to expect better of ourselves. We *have* to. I expect more of my patients, and when I expect more—lovingly, patiently—they tend to rise to that expectation. Maybe not all the way up, but they rise. They improve because I believe they can, and I believe they must. My mom was sick. But she didn't try hard enough to get better. She found a way to cope—and that's important—but she never varied from it. Life has to be more than coping. It has to be."

Mercedes nodded slowly, her eyes clinging to his impassioned face. She'd struck a nerve, and he wasn't finished.

"I know it's not something we're supposed to say. We're supposed to be all-loving and all-compassionate all the time. But sometimes the things we aren't supposed to say are the truths that keep us sane, that tether us to reality, that help us move the hell on! I know some of my colleagues would be shocked to hear it. But pressure—whether it's the pressure of society, or the pressure of responsibility, or the pressure that comes with being loved and being needed—isn't always a bad thing. You've heard the cliché about pressure and diamonds. It's a cliché because it's true. Pressure sometimes begets beautiful things."

Mercedes was silent, studying his handsome face, his tight shoulders, and his clenched fists. He was weary, that much was obvious, but he wasn't wrong.

"Begets?" she asked, a twinkle in her eye.

He rolled his eyes. "You know damn well what beget means."

"In the Bible, beget means to give birth to. I wouldn't mind giving birth to a diamond," she mused.

"You ruin all my best lectures."

There was silence from the kitchen. Silence was not good.

"Gia?" Noah called.

"What, Daddy?" she answered sweetly.

"Are you pooping in your new princess panties?"

"No. Poopin' in box."

"What box?" His voice rose in horror.

"Kitty box."

Noah was on his feet, racing toward the kitchen. Mercedes followed.

Gia was naked—her Cinderella panties abandoned in the middle of the floor—and perched above the new litter box.

"No!" Noah roared in horror, scooping her up and marching to the toilet.

"Maybe it won't be a turd, Noah. Maybe Gia will beget a diamond," Mercedes chirped, trying not to laugh.

"I blame you, Mer!" he called from the bathroom. "She was almost potty-trained, and now she wants to be a cat!"

A guilty conscience and a kitten that was more up to date on his shots than his two-year-old, had Noah making an appointment for a well-child check with Gia's pediatrician. Noah had looked through the filing cabinet and found Gia's immunization record—she'd had a well-check exactly one year before—and bundled her up, feeling compassion for his wife, who'd gone to every checkup without him and cried her heart out over the pain she'd inflected on their daughter.

Cora had been worried about side effects and had monitored Gia zealously in the days after her immunizations, calling Noah at work several times a day for reassurance. Noah had decided she worried enough for both of them, and hadn't worried about the vaccinations at all.

He was nervous now. Maybe it was the fact that he felt so unprepared and awkward. He'd never taken Gia to the pediatrician. When she'd had an ear infection, he brought her to the Emergency Instacare at Uni, and they had him in and out with a prescription for antibiotics in ten minutes flat. It paid to know people. He didn't know what to expect or how to act at a well-child check. Or maybe he was just nervous because inevitably questions would be asked. They always were.

"Where's her mother? Are you on duty for the day? What a good daddy to give Mommy a break!"

He would have to tell someone—the receptionist, the nurse, the doctor—that Cora was gone, and he would have to endure the mournful eyes and sincere condolences as the word spread through the office.

His dread was unfounded. Everyone was nice, and everyone already knew, which was a relief. He'd told Mer once that a hospital was like a small town, and gossip spread faster than germs. Apparently, that extended beyond the walls of the hospital to the entire medical community. This time he was grateful for the lack of privacy. He didn't have to explain himself or ask for things to be explained to him. They just assumed he was clueless.

They weighed and measured Gia, who had managed to stay dry in her Little Mermaid underwear, though Noah asked her every ten minutes if she needed to go potty. They measured her head circumference, tested her motor skills, and asked her a few questions, which she responded to in full sentences, surprising the nurse and making her laugh. The nurse asked Noah some questions too—any allergies, any concerns, any recent colds, when was the last time she was on an antibiotic—and he was able to answer them all. Dr. Layton came in and listened to Gia's heart and lungs, checked her ears—Gia hated that—and looked at her teeth and her throat. Gia hated that even worse and began climbing Noah like Oscar (Mercedes had lied about the furniture) climbed the living room curtains. The doctor laughed and pronounced Gia perfect.

"Do you have any questions for me, Dr. Andelin?" she asked Noah.

Only a million. But he settled on two. "I know Gia had her one-year immunizations, but she didn't have her 18-month visit. Life was a little crazy, and it got away from me. What shots do we need to do today?" Noah asked.

Dr. Jill Layton was a pretty woman in her early fifties. Noah knew her name and her reputation, but he'd never met her before. She was well liked and respected, and she was comfortable with both him and Gia, which he appreciated.

"She needs a DTaP, her second hepatitis A, and the varicella today. I'll have a nurse come back in and administer those last."

Noah nodded. Three shots wasn't too bad.

"I feel like I'm playing catch up . . . I *am* playing catch up," he confessed. "I was in Afghanistan when Gia was born, and I'm afraid there are things I should know that I don't. And my wife isn't here to tell me." He cleared his throat. "Just looking at Gia's file, can you give me a rundown on her history? Is there anything I should be aware of?"

Dr. Layton smiled, her eyes kind, and she opened the file in front of her once more.

"Well, let's see." She turned a page and read silently for a minute, nodding. "She was a good size at birth—eight pounds, twenty-one inches long. She was jaundiced, but nothing serious."

"That was due to the Rh incompatibility, correct?" He remembered Cora mentioning it.

"Probably, but not necessarily. Jaundice is fairly common. We put Gia under the lights and monitored her. With first babies, the Rh incompatibility is usually not as severe—it's a little like someone with an allergy to bee stings. It's not until they get stung the second time that there's a problem. Cora's second pregnancy would have been at much higher risk."

"I remember the basics," Noah said, nodding.

"Because of Cora's blood type—O Negative—we tested Gia right after she was born. Gia is A Positive. One benefit of the testing is that you now have that information. Most parents don't know their child's blood type."

"What?"

"Knowing your daughter's blood type could be helpful," the doctor explained patiently, as if he hadn't heard her.

"I agree, but what type did you say Gia was?"

"She's A Positive."

"She can't be," Noah countered calmly.

"She is," the doctor retorted.

"I'm O Positive. Cora was O Negative. Two O's can only make another O."

Dr. Layton looked down at the record and back up at Noah. A deep crimson flush was climbing up her neck, but her eyes were steady on his.

"You're sure you're O?" she asked.

Noah pulled his dog tags from beneath his shirt. Old habits die hard, and he always wore his tags. "Positive." It was there, stamped beside his name and his religion on the little metal plate, still warm from lying against his skin. The doctor peered at the tag longer than was necessary. Oddly enough, the obvious answer had not occurred to Noah. His heart wasn't pounding. His thoughts weren't racing. He just wanted to correct the medical record. Gia was O Positive—she had to be—and a mistake had been made, which alarmed the clinician in him. Mistakes like that could be dangerous.

"We'll retest. It's easy enough, and your insurance will pay. It wouldn't be a bad idea for you to retest too, Dr. Andelin. The military can make mistakes." She began scribbling an order for lab work, not looking up at him.

"I've been tested twice. Once in high school and once when I enlisted," Noah said quietly.

"Okay. Well." She finished writing and handed him the lab order.

"Gia is a perfectly healthy, beautiful two-year-old girl. You're doing just fine, Dad. I'll send the nurse in to catch her up on those shots. Tylenol or Motrin every four hours if she needs it." She reached out and took his hand, shaking it firmly. "It was so nice to meet you, Dr. Andelin. And I'm very sorry about your wife."

She practically ran from the room.

TEN

1989

"Put some alcohol on the cotton ball. Take the lancelet and prick your finger. If you don't want to prick your own finger, your partner can help you," Mr. Ward droned.

"Two students threw up already today," Noah told Cora cheerfully. "One of them was in Mer's class. She said it was awful."

"Once you have pricked your finger, and have a good-sized droplet of blood, press your finger down on the glass in three separate places, so you have three separate drops of blood on the slide," Mr. Ward explained.

"No one's listening," Noah said, annoyed. "They're all going to screw it up."

"I will be coming around to apply a dropperful of the monoclonal antibodies to your slide. You will mix each antibody—Anti A, Anti B, and Monoclonal D—with one drop of your blood on your glass slide. Make sure you use a different toothpick to mix each one. Once your blood is mixed with the antigen, look at your worksheet to determine what is happening with your samples. That will tell you which blood type you are."

"I can't prick my finger, Noah," Cora whispered. Her eyes were squeezed shut and her face was so pale, her freckles looked like ink blots.

"Are you afraid it will hurt?" Noah asked gently.

"No. I don't want to see the blood," she whispered, jaw clenched.

"Okay. I'll do it. Don't worry."

She didn't flinch when he stuck her finger, but her hands were clammy and her fingers rigid.

"You good?" he murmured.

"Fine."

He pressed her finger along the slide, three perfect dots of deep red, and then proceeded with his own slide. Cora sat beside him, her eyes still closed. He wondered if she would stay like that all hour. She shouldn't have come to class. Noah could have explained to Mr. Ward. He would have understood. Since her dad died, Cora and blood were a no go. She had fainted last week when Noah got hit in the face with the basketball and his nose bled.

Mr. Ward applied the antibodies to the slides, nervously eyeing Cora. "If you feel sick, you can go, Miss McKinney."

"I'm fine as long as my eyes are closed. Noah can tell me which blood type I am." It kind of defeated the purpose of the lab, sitting blind while your partner did all the work, but Noah didn't mind. He watched as the blood on the two slides reacted to the antibodies.

"You're O, Corey. So am I," he said after a moment.

"We're the same?" she breathed.

"Almost. But I'm O Positive, and you're O Negative."

"Is O Negative . . . bad?"

"It's blood, Corey. It can't be bad or good. It's definitely rarer than O Positive. According to this chart, in one hundred donors, only seven are typically O Negative."

"What was Sadie? Did she tell you?"

"She was A Positive. Very common. She was disappointed." He laughed. "I think she was hoping to discover a whole new type."

"I would think Sadie would have the rarest type," Cora said.

"Why?"

Cora shrugged. "Because she's so . . ."

"Original?" Noah supplied.

"Yeah. I wish I was more like her. She's not afraid of anything."

"Everybody is afraid of something," Noah argued. "Even Mer."

"Is anyone still . . . bleeding?" Cora whispered.

"Nah. Everybody's done. I think you're safe."

"I'm not safe, Noah. I've never been safe. Nobody is safe."

They were the same words crazy John David Cutler had said to him years ago. Noah froze, stunned, and slowly turned his head to look at his partner. Cora still sat, hands over her face, refusing to look around her.

Noah clutched Gia to his chest as she cried in outrage at being repeatedly stabbed while her father stood by and allowed it. The nurse said something to him and handed him Gia's updated shot record. He thought he nodded and mumbled something in return. He wasn't sure. There was a numbness in his head that was plugging his ears and fogging up his thoughts. It crept down his throat, through his chest, and pooled in his hands.

He slipped Gia's pink shirt over her head and pulled her pants on, covering the three Tweety Bird Band-Aids on her stubby legs before putting on her pink boots and buttoning her coat with fingers he couldn't feel. Then he picked her up again, his thoughts screaming while he consoled her with soft words.

He didn't go to the lab.

He walked through the clinic on wooden legs, his eyes straight forward. It was the day Cora died all over again. He had the same sense of being outside of himself, of watching his life unfold from a two-way mirror. He crossed the parking lot and unlocked the Subaru without remembering a single step. He buckled Gia into her seat the way he'd done the day her mother left them. Mer had run to the store and purchased one, so he didn't have to drive home without Gia buckled in. Gia's other car seat had still been upside down in the creek in Emigration Canyon.

Gia's seat faced forward now, and her legs were longer. He'd buckled her in hundreds of times since that day. He'd kissed her cheeks a thousand more times than that. He kissed her now, an automatic response to her tears, and she grabbed his beard, curling tiny fingers into his face to keep him close.

"Dee-uh sad," she cried. *Gia's sad.*

"I know, Bug. I'm sad too," he choked. And suddenly he was. Terribly, terribly sad. Distraught. Dismayed. Devastated. The grief blew through his disbelief and seared the fog in his head, in his heart, and in his limbs. He clenched his teeth at the sudden, ferocious return of sensation.

"Daddy sad?" Gia asked, still clutching his face.

"Yeah. Daddy's sad."

"Daddy cwy?"

His face was wet. His eyes were streaming. The flames continued to grow, and the heat continued to gather, and it was all he could do to extricate himself from Gia's little hands so he wouldn't scorch her too.

He hurried to the driver-side door and climbed in, shaking and sick, afraid to drive, afraid to sit still. He thought of calling Mercedes. She would make him feel better. She would look after Gia while he burned. But he couldn't run to Mer every time life got hard. He was Gia's father, and she was his responsibility, not Mer's.

"I'm Gia's father," he choked, and realized he'd spoken out loud. *Was he?*

He couldn't call Mercedes. Then he would have to tell her what had happened. He would have to explain. He would have to face a terrible possibility.

"Daddy go?" Gia asked from the backseat, her shots clearly forgotten. She didn't understand why they sat in a cold car. She didn't understand why he cried. She didn't know his world was on fire.

"Daddy?"

"Yeah, Bug?" he whispered.

"Dee-Uh hungy."

He turned and looked at her, sitting so patiently in her car seat, the tears still drying on her cheeks.

"Gia's hungry?" he asked.

She nodded and then smiled, showing him her small white teeth.

Feed, clothe, comfort. He could do that. He *would* do that. He pulled his seatbelt on and turned the key.

"Noah?" Mercedes called, shutting the door behind her.

His house was silent and thankfully tidy, but no one answered her when she called. Noah's Subaru was in the garage. His wallet, his phone, and his keys were still in the middle of the kitchen table beside the container of soup she'd left him yesterday. The soup hadn't been touched.

She climbed the stairs and cracked his bedroom door. He was sprawled across his bed, shirtless, wearing the same sweats he'd been wearing when she'd checked on him the day before.

Heather had called her at work Saturday morning, Gia babbling in the background. "Mercedes? Noah just brought Gia over. She had a doctor's appointment yesterday. Had her shots, poor baby. But she seems fine . . . not even sore. Something's wrong with Noah, though. He looked bad, Mercedes. He said he'd called in sick to work, but he still wanted me to watch Gia. I told him I would keep her tomorrow too, and he agreed. He never does that! I asked him if something else was wrong, and he said he's just tired, but I don't believe him. The anniversary's coming up." Her voice broke. "Do you think it's that?"

Mercedes had promised Heather she would check in on him, and slipped over on her lunch hour Saturday afternoon. Noah was in bed asleep, and she didn't bother him. She left a note and a quart of chicken soup from the deli down the street. He hadn't called back, but she hadn't been too worried. Until now. Now she was back again, twenty-four hours later, and he didn't appear to have left his room.

"Noah?"

He pulled a pillow over his head but he didn't greet her.

"Good. You're awake. Are you okay?"

"No." The sound was muffled, but she heard it.

"Are you sick?"

"No."

"Are you . . . sad?"

He didn't answer, and she walked around to his window and opened the blinds, letting the weak afternoon light into the room. She cracked the window and breathed deeply, sensing rain in the air. The room was stuffy and smelled of musky man and fabric softener, an odd combination, indicating Noah's face-plant was sudden and not a slow decline.

"You haven't left this room in two days. You've been asleep since yesterday morning. Do you want to tell me what's going on?" she asked, turning back toward the bed.

Noah pulled the pillow off his face and stared at her mulishly. His hair was messy, his eyes bloodshot, and if he'd actually slept, he hadn't slept well. Dark circles rimmed his eyes.

"I don't want company right now, Mer."

"Why?"

"I'm tired."

"Why?"

He groaned, clearly annoyed by her questions, but a moment later he tried to explain. "What did Abuela used to say . . . about the three things? The three things that matter?"

"Only three things matter. Who He is. Who you are. And who your friends are," Mercedes parroted.

"Yeah. Well, I don't know the answer to any of those things right now."

"Um, hello?" Mercedes said, incredulous. She stomped over to the bed and sat down beside him, making the mattress bounce. "I'm right here. Say that to my face."

"I don't know who Cora was, Mer. I thought I did. I was sure I did. But I didn't know her."

"What happened, Noah?" she asked, trepidation churning in her belly.

"She told me once that nobody is safe. Is that true, Mer? Is nobody safe? I tried so hard to make her feel safe."

Grief swelled and swam in Mercedes's eyes, but Noah simply shut his and shook his head, as if he didn't know the answers anymore. For a moment they were quiet, both lost in their own thoughts.

"It'll be a year on the fifth," he whispered.

"Yeah. It will." Mercedes felt a sliver of relief. Maybe Noah was still coming to terms with the way Cora died. Maybe that was all this was.

"I'm just going to sleep a little longer. Okay?" Noah rolled away from her, and for a minute Mercedes considered letting him have his way.

"No. You need to get up now," she said softly.

"I'm tired."

"No, you aren't. But you do stink. You need a shower, and you need food, and you need to go get your daughter from Heather's. She's worried about you, and I want to see Gia."

"You go get her. I'll sleep," he mumbled.

Mercedes threw the blanket from his legs and wrapped her arms around him, trying to hoist him up. He was all warm skin and stale breath and shuttered eyes that made her heart quake and her stomach clench.

"Damnit, Mer."

"How long has it been since you had something to eat?" she asked. "I'm not leaving until you're washed and fed."

He didn't reply, but he relented and stood, letting her herd him into the bathroom. She put toothpaste on his brush and wetted it beneath the faucet, talking to him like he was five years old, and she was his mother.

"Brush," she demanded. He obeyed, scrubbing listlessly at his teeth.

"Get your tongue too," she bossed.

He just shook his head and bumped her out of the way so he could spit and repeat. She filled up a capful of mouthwash and held it out to him as he finished.

"Gargle. And then get in the shower."

"Get out, Mer," he whispered.

"No," she snapped.

He gargled loudly, swishing the minty antiseptic—guaranteed to make a dog's breath smell fresh—around his teeth before spitting it into the sink and shoving Mercedes toward the door.

"Go," he rasped.

"I don't trust you. You'll lock me out and stay in here until I leave."

"I need to take a piss."

"Go right ahead. I'll turn my back and plug my nose, so I don't have to smell your urine."

"Mer, I'm not a child," he sighed. "Go."

"I know you're not a child. So grow up and do your business. I'm not leaving." She folded her arms and stared him down. Or up. Even in her four-inch heels, she only came to his chin. His hair, bristled and standing on end from sleep and neglect, made him even taller.

"I can't pee with you listening," he argued.

Mercedes stepped around him and turned on the water in the shower, adjusting the knobs so it would warm up.

"I can't hear you now. It's all just water flowing. Pee," she insisted.

He moved away from the sink, and she heard the toilet seat clank against the porcelain back. She kept her back turned as promised. She didn't want to humiliate him. She really didn't. But she knew him too well, and there was something in his face that reminded her of Cora's dad the day before he shot himself. It was the look her mother had in her eyes after Papi's funeral. It was the quiet, awful realization that life would never be the same and the growing temptation to leave it all behind.

He was scaring her. She could endure many things. She *had* endured many things, but life without Noah wasn't one of them. His despondence made her frantic. Her heart was pounding and her palms were hot, her fingers numb. She curled her hands into fists, willing them to cooperate, willing Noah to cooperate.

"I'll wait right here while you wash," she demanded, but her voice wobbled, and she winced and cleared her throat. But she didn't step down. "Then I'm going to make sure you get dressed and brush your hair and put on deodorant and maybe scrub your teeth again for good measure. Then I'm going to make you breakfast and hold your damn hand while you walk out the door. Then we're going to go for a walk. A long walk. And we're going to sweat and breathe the fresh air, and you are going to stop thinking about how much life sucks."

"Are you going to watch me undress?" he said, his voice flat.

"If I have to." She knew she was being completely unreasonable, but the severely depressed were not trustworthy. "You're already half naked."

"Not the half that matters."

The toilet flushed behind her, and she stepped away from the bathtub, moving toward the door, happy to give him space but unwilling to leave. The bathroom was arranged with the sink and the shower facing each other, the toilet tucked back in the corner.

After several moments of silence—no sounds of splashing or the shower curtain being pushed aside—she turned around and found him facing her, his sweatpants still clinging to his lean hips. His naked chest was rising and falling rapidly, as though he was hanging over a precipice, as though he was holding on for dear life. Steam began to billow from above the cheery yellow shower curtain, but he made no move toward it.

"Noah," she urged, her voice a frantic call for action. He didn't even lift his head.

"Noah!"

"Just go, Mer," be begged.

"No. I won't. You have to take care of yourself. You have to keep moving. Remember numb? Numb is better than dead. You are not dead! So quit acting like you are."

He turned his back on her.

She rushed him, slapping at his lean back and broad shoulders, pummeling him, desperate to make him react. There was no weight behind her blows, no power. There was only fear and frustration and a refusal to let him be. He turned, his right arm rising to ward her off.

"Stop it," he roared. "Can't you leave me alone for five seconds? Just leave!"

"It's not going to happen! I will never leave you alone, do you understand? I will never leave you alone," she shouted.

He grabbed at the towel rack above the toilet so vehemently it came loose in his hand, bits of plaster and a tiny screw winging through the air. He slammed it against the vanity above the sink, cracking the mirror in a jagged web. His rage filled her with relief.

He threw the towel rack aside, and hit the mirror again with both fists. The cracks continued to scurry, rushing away from his rage, distorting his reflection, making her flinch. He swore in time with his blows, each curse punctuated by bits of falling glass. His hands were bleeding, and Mercedes cried out for him to stop. Instead, he turned and grabbed the yellow curtain, pulling the whole rod down on top of him. He howled in outrage, shoving it aside before he came at her, his intentions clear. She refused to leave, so he was going to make her leave. She was about to be bodily removed from the bathroom.

With no thought other than to force him to follow her beneath the spray, she stepped into the shower fully-clothed, heels, hoops, updo, and all.

Noah stared at her in stunned outrage as water soaked her blouse. It was silk, and it would be ruined, but she didn't care. She stepped out of her heels and handed them to him. He flung them aside, and they clattered against the door.

"Let me help you."

"You would be a terrible therapist," he rasped.

"That's why I'm not one. But I'm a damn good best friend. Now get your ass in here and wash it."

"This is not what I need, Mercedes. This won't fix anything," he groaned, his anger spent as quickly as it had come. His shoulders drooped and his hands fell to his sides, the blood dripping down over his fingers.

"It will fix one thing," she said quietly. "You'll be clean."

With a sigh of submission, he stepped beneath the nozzle without removing his sweatpants, blocking her from the pounding spray. The water sluiced over his unkempt hair and down his face, and he dropped his chin to his chest, leaning toward her, hunching beneath the warmth.

His blood dripped and swirled around their feet, and she picked up his hands, examining them.

"You're going to feel this tomorrow," she breathed. It pained her, seeing his shredded knuckles, physical proof of his despair. She held his hands under the water, looking for bits of glass. He winced but allowed her to mother him for a minute before he withdrew his hands from hers.

"They're fine, Mer."

She pushed his hair back from his forehead, willing him to meet her gaze, looking up into his beloved, bereft face, and wishing with all her might that she could take his pain away. She would take it all if she could. Taking his pain would ease her own.

"What do you need, Noah? Tell me how to fix it. And I'll do my best to give it to you," she murmured, stroking his bowed head. This brand of comfort was universal. The soothing, the stroking. He pulled in a ragged breath and let it out again, as if giving himself permission to accept it.

His hands rose to her hips, tentative. Then his fingers splayed, gripping her, his hands circling her waist, kneading and desperate, and he groaned with such pent-up sorrow and despair that she stepped into him, wrapping her arms around him to buoy him up.

They stood in a loose embrace, their eyes closed against the water that streamed over their heads and down their clothes. Her hands continued moving over him in a steady caress, soothing and comforting, desperate to wipe his despair away, to slough it off and watch it swirl around the drain with his blood. She pressed her mouth to his chest to quiet his troubled heart, and felt her own pulse quicken instead.

All at once, collective sorrow and shared solace became something else.

Something new.

Something old.

Sympathy morphed into empathy and became a physical response. The heat around her became heat inside her. It bubbled and simmered, licking at the small of her back and the pit of her stomach. It climbed up the length of her legs and curled around her breasts, growing in her chest and billowing out her lips. And she was not alone. She felt a new tension beneath Noah's skin, a change in the rhythm of his heart, an awareness in his touch.

His hands found their way under the edge of her blouse to the skin beneath, and she raised her face to his, offering herself up without hesitation. His jaw was no longer clenched, and his countenance was lit with unexpected fire, his lips parted, his breathing rapid. For a moment their eyes clashed and clung, and an inaudible series of clicks—left, right, left, unlock—echoed in her head and reverberated in her chest. It was a lethal combination, and they were opening the safe.

They didn't speak at all. Didn't say each other's names. Didn't ask permission or test boundaries. It was simply there, between them, the knowledge that they weren't going to stop or step back. And they knew exactly what they were doing.

Then Noah kissed her, anxious and harsh, his mouth colliding with hers in old emotion and fresh defiance, as though he expected her to retreat or wrench her face away. When she did neither, his mouth softened, his tempo slowed, and a tremor shook him, shaking them both free of their senses. He unzipped her drenched skirt and pushed it down her hips until it slapped against her bare feet. He yanked her blouse over her head, dislodging the pins from her streaming hair so it fell in reluctant coils around her shoulders.

His mouth was as insistent as his hands, searching and clinging, looking for an answer she was only too willing to provide. Her consciousness —all of it—was riveted on the moment, centered on their mouths, fixated on their wet skin, intent on the scrape of his beard and the soft slide of his tongue. There was no past or future, no consideration or deliberation. There was now.

Here I am, her thoughts screamed. *Here you are. Here we are. This is us.*

But she did not know this Noah.

She did not know this side of him, the way his breath caught when she stood naked before him, curved and full-bodied, warm-skinned and round-hipped. The way he moved his hands around her thighs and lifted her, pulling her legs around his waist, one arm beneath her, one arm behind her, cradling her head from the cool tiles at her back. The way he gasped when he entered her, like he'd never been with a woman before. The way he moved against her, lost in the rhythm and the gathering storm.

She did not know this Noah.

She was making love to a stranger, and her eyes were wide, her heart pounding with curiosity, her body warbling with inquisitive wonder.

She didn't expect to feel so much. She didn't expect to come undone. She was so engrossed in him, so awed by the dreamlike cast of each elongated second, that the sensation caught her off guard, sweeping up through her in a sudden gust, and she pulled her mouth free from his, desperate for air, for escape from the intensity of it all, only to have him sink his hand in her hair and force her mouth's return as he followed her over the edge.

Then the present widened and stretched, reconnecting itself to yesterday and the day before, to tomorrow and all the moments to come. She was no longer riveted on *now*. She was skewered by *then*, by everything that had come before, and she didn't know if she could face what would happen next. *Oh, dear God, what had she done?* She shivered, the wall of the shower clammy against her bare back. She listened as Noah's heart slowed, as his breathing quieted, and when she couldn't avoid him any longer, she gently pushed him away.

Noah released her hesitantly, easing back as her legs slid down his and her feet found the bottom of the tub. She raised her chin, refusing to cower or cover herself. She was beautiful. She liked her body. She liked herself. *You're nothing like Cora,* her insecurity whispered. *Noah loves Cora.* She flinched before shoving the thought away.

"Is that what you needed?" she asked softly, needing to remind him, to remind herself, how they arrived at that moment.

He didn't answer, his lips pursed, his jaw tight. His eyes were so wide and tragic she wanted to cover her body with her hands and beg him to look away. She had not helped him. She'd simply woken him up, and pain lined his face and billowed from him like the steam clinging to the shattered mirror. He wasn't numb anymore.

But she held his gaze.

"You still haven't washed," she continued, donning her sass like an old robe, covering her naked flesh and her bared emotions. "Finish your shower and get dressed. I'll be downstairs getting us something to eat. I'm starving. And don't think for a minute I'm going to let you off the hook. We're going outside. And then we're going to a movie. And tomorrow you're going back to work, and I'm bringing Gia home."

She stooped and picked up her sodden clothes, then stepped out of the tub like she was climbing out of a limousine. She would not be ashamed. She dropped her wet clothes in the sink, wrapped a towel around herself, and left Noah standing under the lukewarm spray.

In the end, they didn't go to a movie or out for a long walk. Mercedes borrowed some shorts and a T-shirt from Noah's drawer, but she couldn't stroll around the neighborhood in baggy boxers and four-inch heels. She whipped up a pan of bean and cheese burritos—refried beans, store-bought shells, and cheddar cheese with some diced onion, cilantro, and tomato to make them taste good—and they huddled around his kitchen table, eating in silence. She wanted to run. God, how she wanted to run. Her pulse thrummed in her throat and her thighs shook beneath the table.

Noah ate half the pan and downed three glasses of milk as if he hadn't eaten in a week. He'd bandaged his knuckles with Minnie Mouse and Donald Duck, and didn't seem to be bothered by his cuts. But he struggled to meet her gaze, and their silence was not the warm space filled with memory and comfort that it usually was.

"Thank you, Mer," he murmured.

"W-what?" she stammered, stunned.

"Thank you for—" he began.

"For the shower sex?" she interrupted. "Any time, big guy. Any time." No one could say she didn't recover quickly.

"Really?" he murmured, raising his eyes to hers. "Any time?"

"No," she muttered, and cleared her throat.

"Then don't say that, Mer. And don't put words in my mouth."

She nodded, chagrined, and took a big gulp of her milk. She didn't like milk. Why had she poured herself a glass of milk? She held the liquid in her mouth, unwilling to swallow.

"Thank you for holding me accountable," he continued quietly. "Thank you for being here. Thank you for making me burritos and making me brush my teeth. I didn't know you wanted to jump me. If I'd known, I wouldn't have asked you to leave, and my favorite sweats would still be dry."

The milk in her mouth shot painfully from her nose.

She stood, choking and laughing, and splashed water on her face, relief flooding her belly and lightening her heart. They were going to laugh about it. Thank God. They were going to laugh like they always did, and they were going to be okay. *He* was going to be okay.

"I didn't know that was going to happen," Mercedes gasped, trying to catch her breath through her giggles.

"The milk coming out of your nose . . . or the sex?" Noah teased, deadpan, and she laughed harder. "I was wrong. You would make a great therapist. I feel much better," Noah continued, still shoveling beans into his mouth. "We could open a clinic together, offer alternative forms of therapy. Your healing powers are remarkable."

"Staaaahp," Mercedes wheezed, unable to catch her breath.

"Hot. It was hot, Mer. Almost as good as your burritos."

ELEVEN

1989

"*W*here's my dad?" *Noah asked.*

Shelly Andelin huddled down inside her blanket and kept her eyes on the television. She loved Night Court *and Judge Harry Stone. Sometimes he would catch her smiling at the screen. She didn't laugh, and she didn't yell, the way he sometimes did when he watched the Jazz. She watched the antics, listened to the canned laugh tracks, and rarely missed an episode.*

He'd asked her before, but she'd always shrugged her shoulders and said she didn't know. He'd asked what his father's name was too, and never got an answer.

"Was his last name Andelin?"

"No. We weren't married. You have my last name."

"What was his last name?"

"Stone. His name was Harry Stone."

"Really?"

"No."

"What was his name, Mom?"

"I'm not sure."

"So you have an idea?"

"No. No idea."

"Why?"

"Because he didn't introduce himself, Noah."

That had shut him up for a long time. He didn't want to know what that meant. But the labs in Mr. Ward's class had him wondering again. Blood. Connections. Belonging. He knew nothing about his father and very little about his mother. Sure, he knew she didn't like to go out. The fact that she'd kept a job in the records department for fifteen years was miraculous. The fact that she worked alone among the accounts of death and disease, slipping out of the hospital in the early-morning hours when everyone else was arriving helped. And he'd helped. That was miraculous too.

He knew her boss—a woman named Carole Stokes—and her coworkers by the shifts they worked and by their competence. He knew who accomplished the most and who skated through the hours, shoving files aside for the night shift to catch up on. Carole was good to his mother. She looked out for her, and by extension, looked out for him.

Carole knew Shelly Andelin's limitations—mainly interaction—and never pressed the issue. She never told her Noah couldn't come to work with her, though it was certainly against hospital policy. Nobody else brought their kid to work. Carole was the one who hooked Noah up with the course on medical transcription when he was fourteen. He listened to a tape recording, typed what he heard, and did the corresponding assignments in the workbook and mailed it in. When he finished the course, Carole hired him—technically she hired his mother—to do transcription work on the side, skirting the fact that he wasn't old enough to be on the payroll. She'd given him the tools to do the job, and do the job he did.

Noah had asked Carole once if they were related. She'd smiled and told him no. She'd met Shelly when she worked in Admitting in the ER. Shelly had been brought in, hugely pregnant, with pre-eclampsia. She almost died. Noah almost died too. When Carole discovered that Shelly had been living under the overpass, she started pulling strings and calling in favors. A bed in a shelter led to a room in a halfway house. The room in the halfway house became a room in a women's group home.

It helped that Shelly didn't have a drug habit—that came later in the form of sleeping pills. It also helped that she was quiet and didn't make trouble. She worked hard and did everything she was told, and when Carole was hired to run the records department, she brought Shelly with her. From the group home, Shelly and Noah moved into the Three Amigos Apartments. It must have felt like an oasis to Shelly, with the space and quiet and privacy she longed for. For the first time, she could stop holding her breath. She could exhale. The problem is, she never inhaled again.

Noah knew all of this about his mother, yet he didn't know her at all. She didn't share her thoughts. Didn't have a philosophy about life. She existed, and he existed with her. But he wanted to know more.

"You said he didn't introduce himself . . . my father. What does that mean?" Noah asked.

"I didn't know him. I didn't want to know him."

Noah swallowed and closed his eyes. He felt sick and scared, but he needed to know, and pretending the world wasn't ugly didn't change its face.

"Were you raped, Mom?" He was fifteen, not five. He knew the basics.

"No. We had an arrangement. It was over pretty quick. He didn't hurt me."

"And you don't know who he was?"

"He was just another homeless man. I found a different place to sleep after that."

Noah wasn't surprised. He'd been unable to imagine a scenario where his mother would have had a relationship that resulted in a pregnancy. It was hard to imagine her in any relationship at all. But knowing his father was a random, homeless man didn't do much for Noah's self-worth. He had no response to the revelation. What could he say? Surprisingly, it was his mother who broke the silence.

"You're a miracle, Noah," she whispered, haltingly.

"What?"

"You're a goddamn miracle."

Her vehemence shocked him, and he stared at her, waiting. She met his gaze before looking back at the TV. The honorable Harry Stone was comforting his bailiff, Bull.

"You made me a believer," she muttered.

"In what?" He willed her to look at him again, afraid she would just stop talking like she so often did.

"In God."

"Why?" he urged. His voice had risen, and she exhaled heavily, like the whole conversation just made her tired.

"I sure as hell didn't create you. That piece of shit who humped me didn't create you. We made your body. But we didn't make your soul. Your soul came from somewhere else, I'm sure of it."

It was the nicest thing his mother had ever said to him. The wisest thing. And maybe because she rarely said anything at all, he believed her.

Noah didn't know what the solution was. On the one hand, he didn't want to know whether Gia was biologically his. On the other, he couldn't ignore the fact that she might not be.

Before Afghanistan, he'd known he and Cora were in trouble. He'd known she wasn't happy. Oddly, he'd never suspected she was cheating on him. Maybe it was his own naivete, maybe he'd thought she loved him more than she did, or maybe it wasn't about love at all. With Cora, it was hard to know. And now Noah would *never* know.

Part of him wondered if what happened with Mercedes over the weekend would have happened had he not been so angry with Cora. The thought worried him. He'd had a psychology professor who used to say, "hurt people hurt people." It was true, but it didn't mean it was okay. He didn't want his hurt and anger harming Mercedes.

Would he have made love to Mercedes had the opportunity presented itself a week ago? Would he have moved so quickly from despondence to desire had he not been feeling so betrayed, had he not wanted to "show" Cora he didn't love her either? The thought made his chest ache and his hands curl in shame. He wanted Mercedes left out of the equation. He wanted his feelings for her, his love for her, kept entirely separate from the ugliness in his head. But the lines had been blurred—the lines had been erased—Sunday night. He needed to fix that.

He'd moved through the stages of grief quickly—denial, anger, bargaining, and depression—before arriving at acceptance. Friday he'd walked out of the pediatrician's office numb with denial. He'd swung between anger and depression Saturday and Sunday. When Mercedes left Sunday night, he'd found himself bargaining with the universe, negotiating and rationalizing. But acceptance came on Tuesday as he fed Gia her breakfast, a ritual that he enjoyed on the days he was home with her in the mornings.

Gia usually woke cheerful, which made waking easier for him. He was never ready to wake. On Tuesdays and Thursdays they ate, babbled, and took their time with life, moving through the morning without haste or hurry. Gia liked to help him clean—*Dee-Uh cween, Daddy*—and handed him clothes from the dryer, wiped everything knee level and down with her little, pink towel, and rode on the vacuum like she was a train conductor. He'd invented that game when Cora was alive, and Gia still got excited when she heard the vacuum whir.

Gia was a happy, little companion, a tiny reminder of all that was good and right in his world. As he watched her that morning, toddling at his heels, mimicking everything he said, and blissfully unaware of his heartbreak, he decided he could face the truth, whatever it was. Gia would not be fatherless. Not like he was. He was her father, and he would *always* be her father. His name was on the birth certificate, and his presence—the minutes, hours, and days—in her life meant more than the blood in her veins.

Commitment didn't require genetics, and he was all in. But he'd never been one to stick his head in the sand. It was too frightening, too dark and gritty, his ass in the wind, his senses dulled. Whatever the truth was, he wanted to know it, if only to better protect his daughter, to better understand his wife, and to better prepare himself. So on Tuesday afternoon he got Gia dressed and prepared himself for the worst.

Gia might be cheerful, but she was also stubborn, and if she looked like a tiny bag lady when they left the house, it was not her daddy's fault. She had a thing for layers, and she hated shoes. Maybe it was because Mer painted her toes every Monday—usually a different color on every toe—and Gia liked the way her toes looked and didn't want to cover them. The only shoes Noah could reliably get her to wear were the pink sparkly snow boots that Heather had given her for Christmas. They were growing too small, and Noah, worried that she would outgrow them before she was ready to part with them, had purchased three pairs in the next three sizes. Pink snow boots in August could be a problem, but he would cross that bridge when he came to it.

Noah was constantly trying to woo Gia with other options, but so far, she was not interested. Mer had found some slippers that looked like Oscar's siblings, and Gia liked those too—Oscar didn't—which wasn't much better. So with a pair of stretchy cotton pants splashed with puppies, a matching sweater featuring the mama dog, the pink snow boots, and a fur-lined cloak that looked fit for the opera, Noah and Gia paid a visit to Montlake.

At reception, Noah greeted Char, who cooed and complimented Gia on her fancy clothes, but he bypassed everyone and everything else but the lab on the first floor. His visit was personal, and he knew that Ronnie Claridge, who ran the lab, would realize in an instant what he was up to, but there was no way around it.

Gia didn't like Ronnie's scrubs or the gloves on his hands. She'd just had her shots and she wasn't excited about the prospect of more. She immediately went into flight mode, and Noah got right to the point before things escalated.

"Ronnie, I took Gia for her two-year checkup a couple of weeks ago."

"Okay," Ronnie nodded. He and Noah had been friendly from the first day, and he clearly wasn't uncomfortable doing him a favor.

"When her pediatrician was reading through her file with me, she mentioned Gia's Rh incompatibility with my late wife. My wife's blood type was 0 negative."

Ronnie continued to nod. "So they kept an eye on her?"

"Yeah. No problems during pregnancy," Noah said. His stomach was churning.

"She hadn't been sensitized," Ronnie supplied.

"From what I understand. But they still tested Gia's blood type when she was born."

"Standard when mother is negative, and father is positive," Ronnie agreed.

"Right. Apparently, Gia is A Positive."

"Okay."

"I just need to verify if that's true," Noah finished quietly.

Ronnie stared at him, puzzled.

"We can test her blood type here, can't we, Ronnie?" Noah asked.

"Sure . . . I can do that."

"Will you test me too, just so Gia isn't scared?"

"I don't understand, Noah."

"My wife was O Negative, Ronnie."

"Okay . . ."

"I'm O Positive."

Ronnie eyed him for a moment, realization dawning. "Okay, Doc."

For all the trouble it was to get Gia to wear shoes, she wasn't excited about parting with her boots so Ronnie could prick her heel. But Ronnie was skilled, and he had what he needed before Gia registered that she was "injured." Plus, she couldn't see the welling drop on the bottom of her foot. Noah slapped a Band-Aid on her heel and pulled her boot back into place, keeping up a steady conversation about ice cream and a trip to Hogle Zoo to see the monkeys when they were through. He hated the zoo, but Gia loved it, so they went often. Season passes and a good stroller made it bearable. The fact that it was five minutes from his house helped too.

Noah offered up his own finger, and Ronnie worked quickly and quietly, his eyes on the droplets.

It took less than five minutes to confirm that Gia was not Noah's biological daughter.

Ronnie was stunned. Embarrassed. Compassionate. But Noah was calm. Acceptance was like that.

"You're sure your wife was O Negative?" Ronnie murmured.

"That's what Gia's file said. That's what a test in health class, freshman year, confirmed. I saw the results with my own eyes."

"What are you going to do?" Ronnie whispered, his empathy and friendship stripping away all pretense.

"Go zoo!" Gia cheered. Noah laughed. The sound was a little choked, but he laughed, and Ronnie smiled too.

"That's what we're going to do, Ronnie. We're going to the zoo," Noah said.

"Doc?" Ronnie ventured.

"Yeah?" Noah responded.

"I was adopted. Blood's important. But to a kid, blood means nothing."

"I know, Ronnie. That's what I keep telling myself," Noah whispered.

Gia and Noah spent the rest of the day—a day that ended up holding more sunshine than showers—visiting the giraffes and the elephants, the kangaroos and the koalas. They stood outside the monkey enclosure, calling and whooping and doing the monkey dance. They strolled slowly past the snakes and the lizards so Gia could growl and hiss at them, half-terrified, half-entranced. They ate corn dogs and stayed too long, but for once Noah didn't mind. The animals had no quarrels or cares. They didn't worry about who they were, where they came from, or what tomorrow would bring, and Noah pledged to do the same.

When all the hurt and the betrayal was stripped away, nothing had changed. His love for Gia was unaltered, her dependence on him was just as great, and in the end, just like Ronnie said, love mattered a whole lot more than blood.

Mercedes was always moving. You would think someone like that would be hard to be around. But Mer wasn't. She wasn't jittery, and she didn't pace or pick at things. She was just always *doing*. She didn't walk fast—she sauntered—but she never sat down. Noah watched her walk through the salon, sky-high heels, hair slicked back from her beautiful face into that long, sleek, ponytail that very few women could pull off. She hadn't noticed him yet, but he took note of her dewy lips, her perfect skin, her dark eyes, and her long lashes. She said they were fake, but they'd been just as long when she was ten years old.

Wherever he looked, the salon reflected her influence. Maven didn't have that new-agey, goth feel like a stereotypical salon. It reminded Noah of lemons in a brown, wicker basket. It was bright, with dark wood floors, buttery walls, and white trim. It even smelled like fruit, like a veranda on a pineapple plantation, complete with icy beverages and soft, ocean breezes.

Everywhere you looked it was pristine and bright, no loud, pulsing music or even Zen mandolins. The music wasn't actually music at all. It was white noise—waves and seagulls and the occasional distant laughter, like kids on a beach. It was nice.

Noah knew if he asked her to, Mercedes would cut his hair at his kitchen table like she'd done the first few months after Cora died. But for some reason, today he needed the salon around him. He needed the safety of eyes and ears. He hadn't seen her since the weekend. Since she'd forced him into the shower. Since he'd kissed her mouth and removed her clothes and had sex with her against the tile wall.

He'd thought about going somewhere else, to the barbershop with the old-fashioned pole just across the street from Montlake. It would have been easier, just this once. But that would wound her. Avoiding her would break her heart. And Noah had no wish to hurt Mercedes. The thought of causing her pain made his heart twist and his arms tighten around Gia, who was asleep against his chest. He could feel a little wet spot where she'd drooled on his shirt.

Mer wasn't easily intimidated, but he saw her shoulders stiffen and the slight double-take when she saw him standing just inside the front door, Gia in his arms. She wore nude heels that made her slim legs look longer, even though the only thing that was "long" on Mer was her hair. Her snug, khaki skirt matched her shoes, and a fitted, white, button-down shirt was tucked into the high waistband. Gold hoops and a slim, gold necklace with a cross, framed by her creamy skin, completed the outfit. The bottom of her shoes, her nails, and her lips were red, and he was guessing her toenails were too. They'd been red on Sunday.

"Today's been crazy. I lost track of time, and I totally forgot today was our day. Go back to the sinks and pick a chair. I'll be with you in five," she said softly, meeting his gaze head-on. "If Gia wakes up, I'll have one of the girls take her and give her a snack."

He nodded and obeyed, walking to the row of inclining chairs and easing himself into one. Gia didn't move at all. Noah caught the lingering gazes of several stylists, including that obnoxious Keegan—Gia had that effect wherever she went—and waited for Mer to arrive. He closed his eyes for half a second, and was surprised when he felt her hands in his hair and liquid heat on his scalp. He kept his eyes closed, letting her take care of him, the way she always had.

She smelled good. Always. Morning, noon, and night. After work, before work, the middle of the night. Sweet and warm with a hint of spice that was uniquely hers. And it made Noah uncomfortable. Even before Sunday, it had made him uncomfortable.

In the last few months, he'd begun to notice things he already knew. He'd known Mercedes for most of his life, and he'd watched her become the adult version of his childhood friend. In that respect, there wasn't much about her that was new. But suddenly he was seeing things that he'd once studiously ignored.

Mercedes's skin had always been her best feature. Clear and unblemished and smoky, like a spoonful of coffee in half a cup of cream. When he was with her, he ached to touch it. He wanted to run a finger over her cheeks and across her hands, down her slim neck and behind her ear. He wanted to rub his thumb along the high arch of her small foot and continue up her calf to the smooth skin at the back of her knees. That made him uncomfortable too.

Mercedes didn't need to wear make-up, but she always did. There were times growing up when she'd worn too much, though with Mer it never seemed like she was attempting to wear a disguise. She was practicing. Experimenting. Learning. He'd let her cut his hair once at sixteen, and resolved to never let her do it again. When she came back two months later, asking for another try, he'd succumbed, and she'd succeeded.

She'd been cutting his hair—minus his stints in boot camp, Kuwait, and Afghanistan—ever since. It was the time they caught up with each other. Their worlds could be running in opposite directions, but they always made time for a haircut. Then they would talk nonstop, trying to catch up in the thirty minutes, once a month, they spent together. Mercedes had spent more time with Cora after they married. They went to lunch and hit the gym together. He joined them sometimes, though he would rather run around the University of Utah campus than do yoga.

Mer said yoga was relaxing as long as you shut your eyes; otherwise, yoga class was just asses in your face, which was not especially calming. When Noah had fallen in love with Cora, he'd made a mental note not to consciously appreciate other women's asses. It wasn't especially hard. He saw a nice ass, he looked away and thought about his wife. Mer had an exceptionally nice ass—another thing he'd noticed—and it hurt to think about his wife, so what was he supposed to do now? He opened his eyes, needing to change his train of thought, and found Mer's face above his.

"I thought you were asleep," she murmured.

"I was. For a minute."

"I can't imagine why. Today is Friday . . . which means you haven't slept since when, Wednesday night?" She smirked and quirked one perfectly-groomed eyebrow.

"I'll sleep tonight."

"Something's gotta give, Boozer."

He smiled at her, as though they were just Stockton and Malone again, playing on the cracked square of concrete at the Three Amigos.

"I'm okay, Stock."

"Last weekend you hit a wall, remember?" she scolded.

"Yes. Uh. In more ways than one. Actually, it was you who hit . . . a wall." He waggled his brows, trying to tease her the way he'd done in his kitchen, making her laugh, restoring the old give and take. But her cheeks pinked, and she turned away, snatching up the conditioner even though she hadn't yet rinsed out the shampoo. Flustered, she set the conditioner down and turned the water on. But the nozzle was facing outward, and she soaked her shirt and missed his head completely.

"Son of a—," she hissed. She adjusted the temperature and rinsed his hair, not meeting his gaze. "Lately, I tend to get wet when you're around." Her eyelids fluttered like she couldn't believe she'd just said what she said, and an expression of complete humiliation crossed her face.

"Mer?"

"Hmm?" She didn't look up.

"I'm sorry. I thought you would laugh."

"I'm going to go change. I have another shirt in the back. Can you hang tight right here? You can close your eyes for another minute." She turned and practically ran through the door that led to the employee break room and the massage rooms beyond. He and Cora had helped Mercedes paint the whole area one spring.

"Well, damn," Noah whispered. His hair was dripping, and his arms were full of sleeping child, but he eased himself up and followed Mercedes through the door marked "Employees Only." He didn't think anyone would stop him.

He should have waited a few minutes. The door to the employee locker room had caught and not completely closed, and he pushed it open with his shoulder. Mercedes was standing near an open locker, her back to him, her wet shirt removed. A pale pink bra strap crisscrossed her caramel skin, and she threw an outraged glance over her shoulder.

He glared back. "The door was open, Mer. Anyone could have just walked in. Keegan could have walked in!" He still hadn't forgiven Keegan for being straight. Noah was the straight best friend. Keegan was going to have to find someone else.

Mer yanked a black T-shirt with Maven written across the front from inside the locker and eased it over her head, careful not to mess her sleek ponytail. She tucked the T-shirt into her skirt, and Noah marveled again at the ease in which she made everything look good, the way she made everything work.

"I thought we were going to laugh about Sunday," he said gently.

"We are." She shot him a bright, fake smile and a cheesy, "Ha ha ha!"

"You're upset."

"I'm having a bad day, Noah. That's all. Homeless Cuddy stopped by this morning. That's twice in the last month. He keeps asking about Cora, and I keep trying to explain. I guess I just don't feel like laughing today."

Noah had never met Homeless Cuddy. Mer and Cora had talked about him often. The name wasn't meant to be derisive. In the beginning, it was simply a way of identifying him, and the name stuck. He'd seen Cuddy lurking from a distance, but he'd never made use of Noah's services. Cuddy had adored Cora, and he got regular haircuts from Mer, but he steered clear of Noah.

"What if . . . we never talk about the shower scene again? Not even jokes," he suggested.

She nodded, swallowing. She wasn't acting like Mer.

"But what if . . . I want . . . to do it again?" she whispered.

She was joking. He was sure she was joking. Almost. He looked for her tell. She turned her head, so he couldn't see her face.

"Do you?" Noah asked.

"Yes. And so . . . it's not actually funny to me."

"You want to have sex in the shower?" His voice sounded a little hoarse.

"Yes. Or on a bed. Or maybe on the kitchen table. Or in front of the TV. Or maybe we could try out the front seat of the Corolla. It's surprisingly spacious."

Noah started feeling lightheaded and looked for a place to sit down. His arms were cramping from being in the same position for the last half hour. He sank down on the long bench centered between the walls of lockers

"I'm kidding, Noah." Mercedes began to cackle and dance around, shooting the air like she was totally killing it. He'd known it. He'd called it. So why couldn't he catch his breath?

"You aren't a nice woman, Mer," he grumbled.

"You should have seen your face. You looked like you were going to faint."

"It was the Corolla that scared me. I don't think it's spacious enough. You know I'm claustrophobic."

"You are not."

"But I *am* a germaphobe. The kitchen table is an absolute no."

Mer laughed and sank down beside him, smoothing a hand over his wet hair. He still needed that haircut. He wondered if he would actually get one today. She pulled her hand away and sighed.

"All kidding aside, I feel very guilty," she muttered, and rubbed the space between her brows. "I keep dreaming of Cora. I don't dream, Noah. You know this. I sleep like the dead." She grimaced. "But I keep dreaming of her. In my dreams, she's alive, but Sunday still happened. And I wake up feeling terrible. I haven't been able to shake that feeling all week. Do you feel guilty?"

He didn't feel guilty at all. Not one whit. But he wondered, in the far recesses of his mind, if he would feel guiltier had he not been so angry with Cora. He was going to have to do something about that anger, something that wouldn't backfire on his best friend.

"Surprisingly . . . no. I don't. I found comfort in a friend, someone I trust. Someone I love. It didn't feel cheap or tawdry," he said.

"It didn't?"

"No, Mercedes. It didn't."

"Good. That's something." She exhaled heavily.

"But I have been worried about you. About us. I need you, Mer. It's obvious, isn't it? I don't want you thinking that I . . . expect . . . what happened last weekend to happen again."

"You don't?"

"No. I don't expect it to happen again." He hoped it would. But he didn't expect it to.

"Huh." Mer bit her lip.

Gia arched her back and came awake in Noah's arms, opening her big, blue eyes and staring up at him blearily.

Noah shifted her again, trying to ease the ache in his biceps, and Gia spotted Mercedes.

"Meh," Gia greeted sleepily.

Mercedes smiled and leaned in to nuzzle Gia's cheek, whispering hello into her soft ear. Noah caught a whiff of roses and bergamot, and his legs went weak, and the back of his neck got hot. He really hoped it happened again.

TWELVE

1989

"*D*o you believe in ghosts?" *Cora whispered. She and Mercedes were lying in a mound of pillows and blankets on Cora's bedroom floor. They were having a sleepover for the first time in a while, and they'd made themselves sick on Oreos and Mountain Dew. They'd watched St. Elmo's Fire and then danced to every music video on MTV for hours, but it was midnight and Mercedes had a pounding headache and a roiling stomach. She thought longingly of her own bed only three doors down, and was jealous of Noah who'd just gone home, Papi's guitar in tow. Alma had given it to him with Mercedes's blessing, and he was teaching himself to play. He wasn't very good—he probably never would be—but he tried hard. He'd danced around with it while the girls sang, all of them pretending they were the Three Amigos version of Tears for Fears, their current favorite.*

Alma and Heather had agreed that now that Mercedes, Cora, and Noah were all in high school, Noah couldn't sleep over. No boys allowed. Mercedes wanted to leave too, but she knew Cora would be disappointed if she did, so she laid back against the pillows and closed her eyes, listening to Cora prattle and responding only when she needed to. Cora's last question had her opening one eye blearily and staring at her friend.

"No. I don't believe in ghosts. Do you?" Mercedes asked.

"Yes. My mom says there are no such thing as ghosts . . . only angels, but I don't think that's true."

"Abuela says Papi's an angel. I like to think of him that way. Maybe he sells shoes to all the little angels at the gates of heaven. Like the song," Mercedes said.

"Will you sing it to me?" Cora asked. *"I love that song, but I can't ever remember the Spanish words. Maybe Noah can learn it on his guitar."*

Mercedes, her eyes closed, sang *"A la Puerta del Cielo"* all the way through, singing the story of the barefoot angels and begging them to sleep. She hoped Cora would sleep too. *"Duérmete niño, duérmete niño, duérmete niño, arrú arrú."*

"Duérmete niño, duérmete niño, duérmete niño, arrú arrú," Cora repeated softly, her accent bad but her voice lovely. *"What's the verse about the mothers who watch?"*

"The children who sleep, God bless them. The mothers who watch, God helps them," Mercedes sang in English. *"Maybe we should change the words to 'the fathers who watch.' We both have fathers who watch over us, don't we?"*

"None of us have fathers. Not me. Not you. Not Noah. We should form a club," Cora answered, her tone bitter. For a long moment, she was quiet, and Mercedes started to drift off, imagining her father smiling while he sold shoes to the angels. Papi would like that. Mercedes may not have a father on earth, but she still had a father.

"Do you think people who kill themselves go to hell?" Cora asked abruptly.

Mercedes jerked and sat up, alarmed.

"Geez, Corey. Why would you say something like that?"

"That girl—Brittney—in history class? She says suicide is a sin. Like murder. And murderers go to Hell."

"Remind me to punch Brittney when I see her again," Mercedes grumbled, lying back down.

"If you believe in God, you have to believe in Hell, don't you?" Cora asked. Her eyes were troubled, and Mercedes groaned. Her belly hurt, and she didn't want to talk about Hell or ghosts or obnoxious Brittney who wouldn't know Hell from a hot tub.

"I don't HAVE to believe anything. I believe in God because Abuela believes in God. And the God Abuela believes in is kind, and He loves all of His children. Especially the ones who need Him the most. Especially the ones who are sad enough that they want to die. He isn't going to send them away to hell or anywhere else. That's what I believe."

"That's a good thing to believe." Cora sighed. "Let's beat up Brittney together."

"Deal. Now can we go to sleep? I feel like barfing, and I'm tired."

"Okay." Cora switched off the light and plopped down beside Mercedes, snuggling down in the blankets. She was quiet for several minutes, and Mercedes was almost asleep when she spoke once more, her voice so soft, Mercedes wasn't even sure she was talking to her.

"There might not be such a thing as Hell," Cora whispered. "But I do believe in ghosts . . . because sometimes I think I see my dad, sitting in his wheelchair in the living room. It's just for a second, and then he's gone. But it's happened more than once. I want to ask him why he left me, but he always disappears."

Mercedes pretended to be asleep and didn't answer. But her heart was pounding, and she was wide awake. She desperately wanted to go home. But there was no way she was walking through Cora's living room now.

Two weeks after the first anniversary of her death, Mercedes accompanied Noah to Cora's grave. Heather had gone on April fifth, and Mercedes told Noah she would stay with Gia whenever he wanted to go, but he shook his head and said nothing more. He was quiet. Reflective. And for a while he seemed resistant to going at all. Whenever Mercedes brought it up, his lips would tighten and his head would bow, as if to say, "There is something I need to say but won't." And he wouldn't. Mercedes didn't even bother trying to wheedle it out of him.

There was a new awareness between them, but it wasn't uncomfortable. It didn't rub in all the wrong places or cause them to constantly check their feet to see how they looked as they walked, like a kid with a new pair of sneakers. It was simply another layer, and it was almost frightening that it didn't feel strange. Maybe it was because *they* didn't change. They still teased each other and bickered like they were twelve. They still behaved exactly the same way. Except for the times Mercedes caught Noah gazing at her with an expression that heated the skin of her throat and tightened the muscles of her lower belly. When she caught that look she remembered how it felt to kiss him, and she desperately wanted to do it again. But they didn't. She didn't. The shower scene, as he'd called it in the salon, had not come up again. Not in innuendo or in real life. It was not forgotten, but it wasn't discussed.

On the eighteenth of April, a Monday, Noah came home from work and suggested they go to the cemetery together. They bundled Gia against the threat of rain and climbed in Noah's car, stopping at the store to purchase flowers. They had several graves to visit. They bought yellow roses —her favorite—for Cora and a sprig of evergreen mixed with baby's breath and a few red roses for Papi. Maybe it was too Christmas-y for April, but Christmas made Mercedes think of ever-faithful, ever-loving Papi. Noah bought a spray of daffodils for his mother. The woman who was afraid of the light deserved a little sunshine. Finally, they bought a small, mixed bouquet to lay on Sergeant Mike McKinney's grave. He wasn't buried near the rest, but in the Veteran's section at the top of the rise. Through the years they'd never forgotten him, though Noah and Mercedes had never really known him. Sergeant McKinney and his missing parts had made a lasting impression. Sadly, not the impression he would have liked, they were sure.

They wove their way to the best access point for the graves they needed to visit, and parked the car. By some unspoken agreement, Cora would be last. They visited the oldest loss first, trekking to Sergeant McKinney's grave and laying the flowers beneath his name. Heather had already been to his grave too. There was a picture of Cora and her father together—it looked like a Xerox copy—in a plastic sleeve to protect against the April rains. Mercedes supposed it was Heather's way of reminding her dead husband that it was his turn to look after their daughter.

"I know what you're thinking, Mer," Noah murmured, his eyes on

Mike McKinney's name.

"What?"

"You've got that damn song in your head."

"Dem Bones?"

"Yep."

"It's completely inappropriate. But ever since we had that talk, I think of it whenever I think of him. How did you know?"

"Because you're tapping your toes in the rhythm of the song . . . and because it's been stuck in my head for a year."

"I'll sing 'Red Red Wine.'"

"Don't you dare."

Mercedes patted the stone, and Noah saluted it. Gia wanted to climb up on it, and Noah swooped her up so they could move on without desecrating Gia's grandfather's resting place.

Papi was next in the rotation. He and Sergeant McKinney had died fourteen months apart. Mercedes got him fourteen more months than Cora got her dad. Cora said it wasn't fair. Mercedes reminded her that loss wasn't a competition, but Mercedes never argued that the way Cora's father died was worse. It was. Papi slipped away as peacefully and as quietly as he'd lived. His family missed him dreadfully, but there was no violence in his death. Only the violence of broken hearts.

Mercedes sang a verse from "A la Puerta del Cielo," the lullaby that made her think of Papi, and touched her fingers to her lips and then to his name before rising. Noah reached out his hand to her, and she took it, walking with him, missing her father but moving on.

"What was that?" Noah asked.

"The song?"

"Yeah. You were singing that to Gia the other day, and Cora sang it too, though she usually just hummed it."

"I taught it to her."

"To Cora?"

"Yeah. A long time ago. It's called A la Puerta del Cielo – At the Gates of Heaven. Papi used to sing it."

"Tell me the words."

"A la puerta del cielo—at the gates of heaven. Venden zapatos—they sell shoes. Para los angelitos—for the little angels. Que andan descalzos—

that go barefoot."

Noah smiled. "Maybe that song is the reason *my* little angel never wants to wear her shoes."

"No sooz!" Gia piped up, right on cue. Mercedes and Noah laughed.

"Dee-Uh walk," Gia insisted.

Noah let her down, telling her to stay close, and they walked in fits and spurts toward Shelly Andelin's grave, coaxing the little girl along.

Shelly's grave was a simple slab with her name and the word *mother* engraved above it. Noah had had no money when she died. What nineteen-year-old kid does? But he'd scraped enough credit together to buy a casket, a plot, and a stone to mark the spot. He'd told Mercedes once that his mother said he was the only thing she'd done well . . . and she hadn't really done much. In Mercedes's opinion, Noah was the best thing about his mother.

"I feel sad when I come here. I don't miss her . . . not the way I should. I'm hard on her. In my head and in my memories, I'm hard on her," Noah said. "Everyone deserves to be mourned, and I didn't mourn her enough."

"You've never been very good at pretending."

"No." He shook his head, and Mercedes could see the conflict in his face, the same conflict he'd been struggling with for weeks, but he shrugged it off again without unburdening himself.

"Gia, come on," he called. Gia was lagging behind, weaving in and out of the stones, putting too much distance between them.

"I coming, Daddy." She tried to run, her feet heavy in her pink snow boots, and Noah watched her with a small smile on his face.

"She's not calling you Noah anymore," Mercedes commented.

"No. She teases me sometimes and calls me Noah. How can a two-year-old child even know the concept of teasing? But she does. At first, I would roar and tickle her. But I realized I was reinforcing it. So now I ignore it completely. If she wants my attention, she has to call me Daddy. Otherwise, I'm blind, deaf, and dumb."

Mercedes laughed. "Very smart."

"I love her so much," he whispered, his tone fierce.

It was such a sudden admission, and so out of the blue, that Mercedes looked up at him, puzzled. But something in his voice and face echoed an inner anguish, and Mercedes was quiet, letting him speak, trying to hear the things he might not say.

"The first year with a new baby is a blur. Dads kinda get shoved to the side. Or maybe we happily shove ourselves to the side. We go to the corner and pray the family survives. But that first year is mom intensive, you know? There's no place for Dad. We're the support, the backup. I obviously didn't do the best job at that, considering my wife . . ." His voice trailed off, and he breathed once, deeply, and let whatever he was going to say dissipate in the breeze.

"The day Cora died, there was a short period of time when I didn't know what happened to Gia. When I called you and you said you had her, and she was safe, I had this visceral, almost transcendent moment of relief. It was like a surge of superpower. That moment has sustained me through this whole year. When I've been at my lowest, I think of how Gia was spared, and it gives me strength. My mother told me once that I'm a miracle. She said she didn't make my soul, and my father didn't make my soul. Someone else did that. That's the way I feel about Gia. I can't take credit for her. I'm just lucky enough to get a front-row seat in her life."

Mercedes couldn't imagine Shelly Andelin uttering those words, but she was touched that she had. She felt a sudden rush of gratitude for the odd, little mouse Noah had called mother, and mentally thanked her for giving him something to hold onto.

When they reached Cora's grave and brushed off the debris left by a long winter, Mercedes handed the roses to Gia so she could lay them on the grave. Gia didn't want to relinquish them, so they let her tromp around with the flowers in her arms, watching as she marched in her private parade.

"I don't know what's going on in her little head half the time, but it looks like fun," Noah murmured.

"It's a party, no doubt." Mercedes laughed. Since the flowers were in use, she dug Cuddy's stones from her purse and studied them before laying them down on Cora's headstone, one at a time.

"What are those for?" Noah asked.

"Cuddy gave them to me. He always leaves me a rock when I cut his hair. His pockets are full of them. I asked him once why he carries rocks. He says they keep him from floating away with the dead."

Noah shook his head. "Cuddy scares me a little, Mer."

"He doesn't scare me."

"Does anything scare you?" There was laughter in his voice, and she didn't respond.

He scared her. Noah scared her. Losing him scared her. It always had, especially after Papi died.

"I like Cuddy. And you know me, Noah. I don't like everyone. I can be a total bitch."

"No, you can't, Mer. You just *think* you can. Big difference."

"Cuddy's been told he's crazy his whole life. And he believes it. He fried his brains with drugs to escape the crazy, and he just made it worse. But there's a sweetness and a gentleness that's constantly pouring out of him. He cries when I wash his hair."

"The Mercedes touch."

She wiggled her fingers. She thought he was kidding, but the way he looked at her said he wasn't.

"Why five rocks?" he asked, clearing his throat.

"He told me one for Gia, one for me, one for you, one for him, and one for Cora herself. He also said David slayed Goliath with five smooth stones. You know, just in case we need to slay someone before we leave today."

"Hmm. Everyone here is already dead."

"Cuddy told me to keep the rocks. But I'm not going to carry them around in my purse. I don't need any help not floating away."

"Plus, your purse weighs twenty pounds without the rocks."

"Exactly."

Amazingly enough, Gia left the rocks alone and was finally coaxed—after one rose was set aside for her—to lay the flowers on her mother's grave. With the sun setting in front of them, the three made their way back toward Noah's Subaru.

"Are you still angry, Mer?" Noah asked, setting Gia on his shoulders.

"Are you?"

He was silent, and Mercedes could feel his indecision billowing like steam from a hot pot. He was stewing in something.

"I asked you first," he said, sounding the way he had when they were ten.

"I'm not angry. Not most of the time. I want to understand, and I'm not sure I ever will."

"No. Me neither. I would give anything to have an hour with her. To talk to her. I have a lot to say," he muttered.

"Do you want to tell me? I've been told I'm a good listener."

"There are some things, some confidences, that shouldn't be taken lightly."

"I'm not taking them lightly, Noah. I never have."

"I know, Mer. That's not what I mean. I don't want to hurt your opinion of Cora with my anger. Does that make sense?"

"Perfect. Mami told me not to tell her when my friends hurt me, because I would forgive them eventually, and she never would."

Noah laughed. "So true. I'm working on forgiving Cora. Forgiving myself. But I don't want to paint her a certain way—a permanent way—because of the way I feel right now."

"Are there things you aren't saying, Noah?" Mercedes asked, wanting to know what he knew but not wanting to reveal her own secrets.

"There are things I'm not saying, Mer," he answered. "Things I may never say."

"Okay," she whispered, wondering for the umpteenth time what was right and what was wrong, what was betrayal and what was love. But if Noah was set on silence, she would be silent too.

"All I know, Noah, is that Cora loved you," Mercedes offered after a long pause.

"How do you know that, Mer?" he asked, so softly, so sadly, that she blanched and waited for him to meet her gaze.

"Because I know who you are, Noah Andelin."

He stared at her, confused.

"You are the best person I know. Always have been. True. Kind. Selfless. Hard-working. Handsome." She winked. "I agree with your mom. You," she poked him in the chest, "are a miracle."

"That's how *you* feel, Mer. Not how Cora felt."

"She was convinced she didn't deserve you, and she did her best to prove herself right. But I know she loved you. She worshipped the ground you walk on. Just like I did."

"Just like you *do*," he teased, ready to leave the serious talk behind them.

"Yes. Just like I do."

"I love you, Mer."

"I love you too, Noah. Now can we please go eat? I'm starving."

"Dee-Uh hungry," Gia piped up from her father's shoulders.

"Gia is always hungry." Noah laughed. "I guess I better feed my girls. Let's eat."

Three days later, at the end of her shift, Keegan was waiting for Mercedes in the parking lot beside Maven, a cigarette between his fingers, propped against his black Volvo like he was posing for a photo shoot.

They hadn't spoken more than a handful of words—always polite, always professional—since the night almost two months ago when he'd admitted the affair. Mercedes had begun to relax in his presence, to even hope that Cora's indiscretion would stay buried with her. Keegan clearly had other plans.

"She looks like me, Sadie," Keegan greeted, grinding out the cigarette with the toe of his pointy black boot. "Cora's little girl. She looks like me." He pushed off the car and approached her Corolla. She had her keys in her hand—she always had her keys ready before leaving the building.

"Don't you think she looks like me, Mercedes?" Keegan pressed.

"I think she looks like Cora," Mercedes said. Her hands had begun to shake, making her keys jangle.

"I hadn't gotten a good look at her before. But when Noah brought her in a couple weeks ago . . . I saw her. I saw her, and she looks like me."

"What are you trying to say, Keegan?" Mercedes's heart was knocking against her breasts, and she wanted to fold her arms over her chest to keep it still. But she steeled herself instead, meeting his gaze.

"What if she's my daughter?" Keegan insisted. "I need to know that, don't I?"

Mercedes stared at him, horrified. His point was imminently reasonable while threatening utter devastation.

"Why?" Mercedes breathed. "Do you suddenly want to be a father?"

"No. Not particularly. But . . . if I am the little girl's dad—"

"Her name is Gia. Gia Mercedes Andelin. She has a name," she hissed.

"Right. Gia. If I am Gia's dad, I want to know. And I want Noah to know."

Again, Mercedes paused, her eyes pouring over his face, trying to understand, to glean motive and malice, to unearth intent. He looked away, clearing his throat and folding his arms.

"Why would you do that to Noah? He's her father. He's been her father since the day she was born. He's done all the work. You haven't. And why would you do that to her? Why would you complicate things this way?"

"Look at her. She looks just like me," he huffed.

Mercedes *had* looked, and Gia did look like him. No one would put it together, but the moment you suspected, it wasn't hard to see.

"Secrets have a way of coming out, Mercedes. It's gonna come out," he warned, shoving his hands into his pockets and taking a few steps toward her.

"So, you're going to go to Noah, and you're going to tell him you think that his daughter is actually *your* daughter? Are you going to sue for parental rights? Force him to fight for his daughter in court? What?" It was all she could do to keep her voice level, to maintain eye contact, to not attack him with clawed fingers and snapping teeth.

"If I have to." He sounded almost apologetic, like he knew what he was saying made him an asshole, but there was no other way to get what he wanted.

"If you have too? You slept with his wife, and now you want to take his child?"

"I think she's mine." He shrugged. "But maybe we can work something out. Me and you," he said, moving so close she had to lift her chin to meet his gaze.

"Work something out?" she asked, her voice flat.

"I need money, Mercedes."

She wasn't following, and her heart was still caught in the horror of his threat.

"W-what?"

"I need . . . cash," he repeated. "I've gotten myself into a little trouble that only money can fix. If you can help me, I'll stay away from Noah and the little girl."

She was reeling, angry, but most of all confused. "You want me to pay you off?"

He had the conscience to look uncomfortable, but he nodded, defiant. "I need money."

"What assurance do I have that you'll stay away once I give you the money? I wasn't born yesterday, Keegan."

"Noah seems like he's a decent guy. I know she's in good hands." Keegan said, magnanimous. "I don't want to hurt anyone."

Mercedes wanted to laugh. As if that was what this was about. Keegan didn't give a shit about the kind of hands Gia was in. He was playing a role. A part. And he wasn't playing it well.

"I need that money, Mercedes. I'll take it, and I'll go."

"You'll go? You'll leave the salon?"

"I'll go to L.A. or New York. I want bigger and better than Salt Lake City, Utah. I made more in one weekend at the Sundance Film Festival than I make in two months here. There's money working for big names. I'll go, and no one will be the wiser."

"How much money are we talking about?"

"Fifteen grand would probably do it."

"Holy shit, Keegan!"

He folded his arms, defensive, but he didn't amend his price.

"Why do you think I have that kind of money?" she asked.

"You live in a dump. You drive a fifteen-year-old car. You shop at Goodwill. But you make good money. You're a saver, Mercedes. I bet you tuck away every last dime." He smiled at her fondly like her frugality was adorable.

"Who are you?" Mercedes said, shaking her head. "I feel like I don't even know you."

He shrugged. "Who am I? I'm kinda thinkin' I'm Gia's daddy."

The words made her shudder, her vision swam.

"We're friends, Mercedes. I like you. You like me. I hate that it's come to this."

"Why has it come to this, Keegan? Nobody's making you do it."

He shifted and looked at her sorrowfully before pursing his lips and tossing his long, blond hair back off his face.

"I'm willing to give her up. But I just think I deserve something in return," he coaxed.

Give her up? Mercedes scoffed so hard she choked. She'd always known Keegan was shallow. Vain. But she'd never been threatened by his faults. Everyone had them, and he was a good stylist. She'd even liked him. She didn't like him anymore. She hated him. And she was afraid he was going to hurt the people she loved most. For the first time, Mercedes considered that Cora hadn't been trying to confess her affair with the paper doll picture. Maybe she'd been trying to warn Mercedes.

"All right, Keegan. I'll pay. I'll pay, and you leave. And I don't ever want to see you again."

THIRTEEN

1990

N oah had been afraid no one would come. Not because Mer wasn't amazing, but because he wasn't sure many people knew just how amazing. Mer did her own thing, and she didn't have a lot of time for a social life. They'd both talked about trying out for the school's basketball teams, but neither had the money or the time. They worked after school and on weekends, squeezing friendship in the cracks. But looking around the crowded room, you would think Mercedes was the most popular girl in school.

Noah pulled at the tie at his throat and straightened the cummerbund at his waist. He'd never worn a suit before, and here he was in the warehouse behind Maven Salon, in a grey tuxedo. Everywhere he looked were high school kids—tuxedos, fluffy dresses, teased hair, and too much eye makeup—just as uncomfortable as Noah. But there was music and platters of food—tamales, tacos, nachos, and churros—making the formal clothing bearable.

Mercedes had told Abuela and Alma a quinceañera wasn't important, but they insisted it was. Mercedes worried about money, and a quinceañera, even one where the venue was free and the food was home-made, wasn't in the budget. Abuela and Alma had pulled off a small miracle, and everything was perfect.

Mercedes was in pink ruffles—she'd found the dress at the Deseret Industries, the local equivalent to Goodwill—and she and Alma had altered it to fit her. Cora was dressed in an off-the-shoulder, deep green sheath that complemented her red hair and made her legs look a mile long, another second-hand find. Heather had taken Noah to a tuxedo shop and helped him rent the penguin suit he found himself in. It had cost him fifty bucks for one night. Mer's present had cost him another $50, but she was worth it. Now he just had to give it to her.

"I have a present for you," he murmured, ducking down so he could speak in her ear. She smelled like pink icing and Exclamation perfume. Mercedes smiled at him, licked her fingers, and set her cupcake down.

"You do?" she squealed.

He shoved the pink shoebox into her arms, relieved that he wouldn't have to carry it any longer. Mercedes's feet didn't show beneath the ruffles of her dress, but he'd heard her wishing for shoes that matched her gown. He'd made it his mission to get her some. They were Cinderella shoes, high-heeled and glittering, the kind of shoes that should disappear at midnight. They looked like they would be extremely uncomfortable, and they were so small he was sure they wouldn't fit. Alma had assured him they would.

Mercedes opened the box, and Noah could tell from her indrawn breath that he'd done well.

"Noah," she breathed. "Oh, my gosh."

"Now you can take off those sneakers," he muttered, pleased that she was pleased, embarrassed because they were pink and sparkly, and he'd purchased them all by himself.

Mercedes was immediately toeing off her stained canvas sneaks and pulling the first shoe out of the box, pushing the tissue paper aside. She balanced herself on his arm as she slid one shoe on and then the other. When she straightened, still clinging to his arm, she was several inches taller.

"I feel so powerful."

Noah started to laugh. She was a tiny, pink toy, like something you'd see on top of a cake—in fact, the cake Alma had created had a figurine that looked just like her.

"I want to wear shoes like this every single day for the rest of my life," Mercedes cried, lifting her skirt so she could stare at her feet, entranced.

"Your feet would fall off if you wore shoes like that every day," Noah replied.

"It would be worth it," she retorted, fierce.

He laughed again.

"Should we try to dance?" he asked, noting the song, remembering it was her current favorite. Madonna's *"Vogue."*

She nodded, ecstatic, and shoved the pink box, her old sneakers inside, under the table.

"This is the best day of my life," she cried, striking a new pose every time Madonna instructed her to.

"Who are all these people?" he asked, trying to keep up with her. His poses were mostly folded arms and a series of bad mimes.

"Cousins mostly. And a few kids from school."

"You have this many cousins?" he marveled. He'd only met Jose and Angel. He had no idea.

"Well . . . not exactly. Word gets around. Mami said not to worry about guests, that she would make sure we had a party. Abuela and Mami have connections, and everyone is related in one way or another. Work, family, heritage." She shrugged. *"Mami told me to invite everyone I knew."*

About fifteen percent of the student body at East High was Latino, and all of them were at Mer's quinceañera. Noah shook his head, marveling.

"Someday I'm going to have a big family," he said, pulling her close as the music changed to Sinead O'Conner singing *"Nothing Compares 2 You."* Another of Mer's favorites. Her heels brought her face closer to his, and he felt that same stirring he always did when he looked at her. She made him feel safe. Happy.

Mercedes smiled up at him.

"Me too," she said.

"Aunts and uncles and cousins and grandparents. It's awesome," he breathed.

"Yeah. I guess it is. We aren't close . . . but in a way, we are. Everyone looks out for each other. After Papi died, we had food for a month. I

didn't know half the people who stopped by."

*Her eyes flickered from his, and she flashed a smile at someone be-
yond his shoulder. He turned his head to see who she was grinning at.
Cora was dancing with a boy who was holding her like she was glass. The
boy looked smitten.*

*"Cora, stay away from Diego. He's bad news," Mercedes barked, and
then winked.*

*"Why are you telling her that? The more trouble they are, the more
she likes them," Noah muttered.*

*Mercedes whispered back, "Don't worry. Diego is the sweetest boy in
the universe. Not a bad bone in his body. She'll be safe with him."*

The money represented years of savings. Fifteen thousand dollars would
pay her rent on the duplex for eighteen months. But Mercedes had approached Keegan and confronted him about something that wasn't technically any of her business, and now she was paying for it. Literally. She'd
made him aware, put ideas in his head, and made herself, Noah, and especially Gia, vulnerable. If she'd just kept her mouth shut, none of this would
be happening. It was her fault, and now she had to fix it.

Paying him to go away wasn't wise, but she didn't know what else to
do, and deep down, she hoped Keegan would have enough shame and self-
ishness that he would take the money and go, never to be seen again. If that
happened, it would be money well spent.

She went to the bank and withdrew the funds, trying to quiet the nervous quake beneath her skin, but she didn't give the money to Keegan right
away. Mercedes wouldn't be giving him a dime until he was officially
gone. She sat silently by as he gave his two-week notice and set the staff at
Maven into a tizzy. No one wanted Keegan to go. For a week, it was all
anyone talked about. Gloria Maven even offered him a raise and ten percent ownership in Maven if he stayed. Mercedes began to see her dreams
of purchasing Maven and turning it into MeLo slipping away.

That night, Keegan was waiting for her in the parking lot again after work, shaking his head and biting his lip. "I don't know, Sadie. Gloria really wants me to stay. She's making it hard for me to leave. I'm thinking fifteen thousand isn't going to cut it, after all."

"And what about your problem that only money can fix? Gloria has sweetened the pot, but not with cash," Mercedes retorted.

"True. Which is why I'm still willing to work with you."

"Work with me?" Mercedes whispered, incredulous.

"Yeah. Make it twenty-five, and I'll leave tomorrow. I'll just go. The two weeks are almost up. A few days won't matter."

"Twenty-five thousand?" Mercedes was going to be sick.

"Take it or leave it. I'm thinking that other little problem will work itself out, and I'd be a fool to walk out on Maven."

"And next week or next month you'll be back saying you need more. That twenty-five isn't enough. So, I'm going to have to pass, Keegan. I don't trust you to keep your end of the bargain." Her back was so tight and her stomach so twisted, she wouldn't have been surprised if her spine suddenly snapped.

She moved to open her car door and Keegan's arm shot out, pushing it closed again. He crowded her, pushing her back against the side of her Corolla.

"Don't do this, Sadie."

"Don't do what? Don't say no to you, Keegan?" she said, shoving him, trying again to get in her car.

"I called a lawyer. I have an appointment for next Wednesday. Twenty-five thousand or Noah Andelin is facing a paternity suit. I don't like the idea of my daughter being raised by another man."

Mercedes froze, and Keegan saw the moment he had her. He put his hands on her shoulders and ducked his lips close to her ear, like a lover saying sweet things.

"Pay up and I'm gone tomorrow, Sadie. Give me the twenty-five, and this is over. You can continue playing house with the doctor and my daughter. I don't really give a shit what you do. But I need that money."

She couldn't breathe. Couldn't think. She just wanted him to go away, to leave her alone. To leave Noah and Gia alone.

"I have twenty, Keegan. I'll give you twenty thousand dollars. That's the best I can do," she relented. Oh, God. Twenty grand. It would take her five years to save that much money again.

Keegan stared down at her, eyes narrowed, and touched her lips with the pad of his thumb, considering. She wrenched her face away and shoved at his chest. He laughed like it was all just foreplay. He didn't step back.

"Twenty isn't enough," he said. "But I'll take it on one condition."

"And what's that, Keegan?" she snapped.

"You bring the twenty, in cash, tomorrow to work. I have to say goodbye to everyone, and I have a couple of clients I need to see in the morning."

"That's the condition?"

"No. I'll take that money tomorrow, but I'll take a kiss now, in exchange for the five thousand I'm leaving on the table. Just so you know what we could have had."

"Is this all just a big joke to you?" Mercedes said, incredulous.

"Come on, Sadie. I want you to like me again." He swooped in, his mouth hot and his hands cold, making her shudder. He clearly misinterpreted her tremor as desire and moaned against her lips, kissing her like he was trying to convince her he was someone else, someone she welcomed and wanted. But she gave him nothing but indifference, knowing indifference would bother him more than anger, and after several attempts to make her respond in the way he liked, he pulled away with a sigh.

"I'll miss you, Mer."

"Don't call me that."

"Ah. That's right. That's what Dr. Noah calls you. I forgot." He grinned again, and winked. He released her and strode away, wiping his mouth as though his lips were still wet from hers. "See you tomorrow, love."

"Keegan doesn't like me," Cuddy muttered as Mercedes led him to the sink. Keegan had passed by, winking at Mercedes but giving Cuddy a wide berth.

"Keegan only really likes himself, Cuddy. But today's his last day. You won't have to see him again."

"I don't like Keegan either," Cuddy mumbled. "He's too pretty. Like a snake."

Mercedes wasn't sure she would ever describe a snake as pretty, but supposed they had their own beauty, if you set aside the ick factor.

"You're pretty too, Miss Lopez."

"Thanks, Cuddy."

"Not like a snake."

"That's good."

"Snakes don't have families," he whispered.

"No . . . I wouldn't guess they do."

"Cora liked to talk to me."

"Well, you're a nice guy, Cuddy."

"I told her about her dad."

"You knew Cora's dad?" Cora had never mentioned it, and Mercedes couldn't imagine her keeping something like that to herself. Cora was obsessed with anything having to do with her father. Daddy issues mixed with abandonment, mixed with the trauma of his terrible death.

"I could see him. Been seeing him for a long time. Now that Cora's gone, I don't see him anymore."

"What?" Mercedes gasped. Cuddy continued rambling as if she hadn't spoken.

"He didn't have any legs. He didn't need 'em anymore, but he still didn't have 'em. Ghosts don't need legs. But he showed himself to me that way . . . maybe so Cora would recognize him."

Mercedes turned the clippers off. Her hands were shaking, and she couldn't get a clean line until they stopped.

"I'm scaring you," he whispered.

He was.

"Why are you telling me this stuff, Cuddy?"

"I don't know." He shook his head. "Sometimes I forget to stay quiet. You make me feel safe, Mercedes. And I say what's in my head." He stuck his hands in his pockets, and Mercedes heard the click and slide of rocks spilling through his fingers. "I need more rocks. I'm floating away."

"Then you keep all your rocks today. I don't need one." She finished with his hair, shaky and uncomfortable, hating that she was afraid of him, hating that she might not feel safe with him again.

"I'm sorry, Mercedes," he whispered. "All my life I've been scaring people away."

She smiled at him, meeting his gaze in the mirror. He had sad eyes. So deep and dark, like the ocean at midnight. So troubled. In that moment, he reminded her of Noah in the eighth grade, his hair shorn too short, his eyes too big in his thin face.

"That's why I give you rocks, you know," he said.

"Why?"

"If you put them in your pocket, you won't float away either. You won't leave us behind."

"Ah, Cuddy. That's sad."

He nodded. "The sadness never floats away. It's heavy. It's like a huge boulder. A mountain."

"Yeah. It is, isn't it? Maybe we can roll it down a hill."

He smiled and suddenly he was laughing, revealing teeth that badly needed dental work.

"Gonna roll my sadness down a hill," he laughed.

"Gonna roll my sadness down a hill, gonna roll my sadness down a hill," Mercedes sang, devising an impromptu tune and clapping, the way they did at Bible Camp when they sang "Dem Bones."

The shop was empty, and she twirled around, unfastening the cape from Cuddy's shoulders and shaking it out in time with her new song. Cuddy reached into his pocket and set a rock on her table.

"Thank you, Miss Lopez."

"See you next time, Cuddy."

He was almost out the door when he turned and walked back sheepishly.

"I saw you arguing with Keegan," he said.

"When? Last night?" The thought that Cuddy had been waiting all night for a haircut made her sad.

He shrugged and rubbed at his face as though the days all ran together.

"A while back. It was dark. I was afraid you'd see me and tell me I was breakin' the rules. I wasn't loitering. I was just walking by." He gulped, and Mercedes knew he wasn't telling the truth.

"And you saw me arguing with Keegan."

He nodded, embarrassed. "Be careful, Miss Lopez. Snakes don't have families."

On Friday, May twentieth, two weeks after Keegan Tate left town, Mercedes came home from work early to find Noah perched on a ladder, attaching a backboard and basketball hoop above her garage door. Mercedes parked on the street behind his Subaru, leaving the driveway clear.

"What is this?" she called, climbing out of her Corolla and shading her eyes to peer up at him. The afternoon was warm—seventy degrees—and beautiful, and Noah was in faded jeans, an old T-shirt, and a backwards ball-cap. His goal had been to have the hoop erected hours ago, but Alma had the day off for Mer's birthday. Alma knew his schedule, knew he'd worked all night, and insisted he have a nap while she watched Gia. He'd slept for five hours, and Alma and Gia had done just fine without him. So the big, red bow around the hoop hadn't happened, and he hadn't showered, but maybe he and Mer could play a quick game of horse for old times' sake.

"This is your birthday present, Mercedes Lopez," Noah said, smiling down at her.

"You remembered!"

"Have I ever forgotten?"

She screwed up her face, considering. "Nope. I don't think you have. But I wouldn't mind forgetting this birthday."

"Feeling old?"

"Yes," she groaned. "I am. Old and depressed. I always hated that you and Cora had birthdays before mine. I hated being the youngest. Not anymore. I never thought I'd actually be thirty. I don't even know how it happened."

"I got you something else too. Something guaranteed to make you feel fourteen again. It's in that bag. I wrapped it, but Gia unwrapped it when I wasn't looking."

Mercedes ran to the bag, pulling out the blue box with the white lettering. "You got me high tops?" she breathed, reverent.

"White, high-top Reeboks with red accents. The basketball shoes you wanted and couldn't afford . . . in 1988." They were about as long as the palm of his hand, but he'd checked the size three times. A woman's size five. Mer's feet weren't much bigger than Gia's.

She squealed and kicked off her obscenely high, red sandals. Not waiting for socks, she shoved her feet into the Reeboks and proceeded to lace them, giggling as she went.

"Do they fit?"

"A little loose, but with socks, they'll be perfect."

"A little loose," he muttered.

"We need a ball," she said, jumping up. Her red dress was a fitted, sleeveless number that hit just above her knees, and the new sneakers— despite the red accents—were all wrong. Yet somehow, she made it look good.

"I bought one. But you're going to have to fight Gia for it. I tried to take it from her, and she morphed from Gizmo into a Gremlin."

"Where is she?"

"She's inside with Alma. She kept chucking the ball out into the street. I convinced her to practice tossing it into the toy box. So far, so good. Although . . . she has been remarkably quiet. She's probably doing something terrible in there."

Mercedes scampered into the duplex and was back moments later, carrying the ball.

"Gia is eating frosting, and she didn't even notice when I took it. Mami made me a birthday cake and tamales. You're staying for dinner, right?"

"I am definitely staying for dinner. I plan on eating half of that cake by myself. You ate half of mine."

"I *made* yours. I earned it."

"True."

"I think that's it," he said, tugging on the net just to make sure. He climbed down and moved the ladder out of the way. "Take a shot, birthday girl."

"I have to get warmed up. It's been at least five years since I shot a basketball. How did that happen?" she moaned. "What have I been doing with my life?" She dribbled around, hiking her dress on her thighs so she could get in a better stance.

Noah played some half-hearted defense, swiping the ball out of her hands and throwing up a fade-away jump shot that managed to find its way through the net.

Mercedes huffed and rebounded his shot. Her ponytail was coming loose, and Noah reached out and tucked a strand of hair behind her small ear. She was so pretty. So precious to him, and the words just slipped out, even though he'd promised himself he wouldn't say anything.

"You got something going with Keegan Tate, Mer?" Noah asked, his voice gentle, his eyes pained.

She stiffened, her eyes flying to his. He'd stayed quiet about what he'd seen for two weeks, knowing Keegan Tate was no longer at Maven, knowing whatever he'd witnessed wasn't his business, and probably wasn't serious. But Mer was his business, and he wasn't going to stand by while someone moved in on his girl. She *was* his girl. Whether they were both ready to admit it or not.

"No." Mer shook her head, her face hardening. "Why?"

He bit his lip and studied her, noting her tight mouth and her wary gaze. "I saw you . . . kissing him . . . the other night. Outside of Maven." He rubbed at his beard, clearly embarrassed. "I swung by, thinking I'd catch you closing up, thinking maybe you'd want to go through the McDonalds drive thru with me. Grab a Coke and a large fry, maybe an ice cream cone if we were feeling crazy. I couldn't get Gia settled down, so I put her in her pajamas and thought I'd just drive around until she gave up. It was nine o'clock when I drove past the back lot. Neither of you even turned your heads as I slowed. I thought for a minute you were upset. But then he kissed you, and I kept driving, glad you hadn't seen me."

"You and Cuddy *both* got an eyeful, it seems."

"Cuddy?"

She shook her head, and waved the question away. "I don't like Keegan Tate, Noah. The kiss was not consensual. And now he's gone, and I hope I never see him again."

Noah felt a surge of rage. "What do you mean, not consensual?"

"I mean I didn't want to kiss him. He got the message. He left. The end."

Noah released his anger with a heavy exhale, and eyed his friend. He hadn't been able to get the image out of his head—Keegan Tate bent over her, his hands on her shoulders, kissing her like she belonged to him. It had worn a hole in his gut, and he'd kept his distance for the last two weeks, noting at the same time that Mer seemed to be keeping hers, beyond Mondays and watching Gia. She'd been quiet. Subdued. And if he didn't know better, she was worried about something.

"Is something wrong, Mer?"

She met his eyes steadily and passed him the ball, a neat bounce pass they'd performed a thousand times over the years. He did an easy lay-up and rebounded the ball before looking back at her.

"You're not yourself. You seem . . . off. You've been off for a while," he pressed.

"Maybe it's just turning thirty." She shrugged. "I'm not where I wanted to be in my life."

"No? Where did you want to be?" he asked quietly, closing the distance between them. She sighed gustily and looked down at her tiny feet in her new Reeboks. Noah wound his hand around her smooth pony tail and tugged gently, forcing her to look up at him. When she spoke, her voice was soft, her eyes shadowed.

"I wanted a place of my own, and I rent. I wanted a business of my own, and I'm still working for someone else, with no end in sight. I wanted a family of my own—a big family—and it's just me and Mami now. I'm getting older . . . and I'm no closer to my dreams than I was when I started. I might even be further away."

He didn't know what to say. Mer had always been as driven as he was. In the last year, his drive had been channeled into daily survival, but he realized he hadn't even thought about what Mercedes's plans were. He'd taken her for granted. Maybe that's why seeing her kissing slimy Keegan Tate was such a shock.

"You look so tired." He rubbed at the crease between her brows. "I've been worried about you," he murmured.

Mer gasped, slapping his hand away. "You never say that to a thirty-year-old woman, Noah Andelin."

"What? I didn't say you looked old. I didn't say you looked ugly. I said you looked tired."

She scowled at him.

"Mer, come on. You always look amazing. Even when you're tired."

"I need specifics, Noah. Or I won't believe you."

"Every part of you is beautiful. The arch of your foot. Your toes. Even your knees are pretty. Your elbows. Your freaking armpits are pretty. Who has pretty armpits? Nobody." He pointed at Mercedes. "But you do, Mercedes Lopez. Even your damn armpits are pretty."

She giggled and raised her right arm, peering at her armpit, her sleeveless red sheath leaving them bare to her view. "They are kind of nice," she agreed.

Noah put the ball in her hands, and Mercedes dribbled past him, squared up, and took a shot. The ball swished, and she wiggled her hips, triumphant. "I've still got it. Thirty years old, and I've still got it." She began doing the moonwalk across her driveway, and Noah snagged the ball before it rolled into the street.

"Tell me more nice things," she demanded. "I still haven't forgiven you. Pretty armpits aren't going to cut it. You're in trouble."

Noah took a shot. "Hmm. Nice things. Okay. You always smell good, and I've never seen you look less than perfect. I remember when you told me you wanted to make people look beautiful, I thought to myself, 'that's because she's beautiful. If anyone knows how to make something beautiful, it's Mer.' You are this little package of perfect. So perfect that sometimes it's intimidating. Cora used to ask me if she was as pretty as you are."

"Cora was beautiful," Mercedes defended, trying to steal the ball as Noah dribbled past.

"Yeah. She was. But she wasn't as good at the presentation. And she knew it."

"She didn't have to be. She was naturally stunning. Hair. Skin. Body. Eyes. It was all just there. I had a mustache when I was nine. It took a little more work for me. I have hips and boobs, and I'm short. I don't have anywhere to store anything extra. Lucky for me, my blood is pure vinegar. It makes for a great metabolism."

Noah laughed. "You never had a mustache. I was there when you were nine, remember? And you have a great metabolism because you never stop moving."

"Will you put that on my headstone?" she asked.

"What?" Noah frowned.

"Here lies a little package of perfect."

"All right. If you promise me one thing."

"Okay."

"Don't talk about your headstone ever again." His voice was pained, and he tossed the ball onto the grass.

"Okay, Boozer. Never again."

He walked to her and scooped her up, red dress, Reeboks, and all, and hugged her tight. She squealed, surprised, but let him hold her, her feet dangling off the ground, his cheek resting against her head.

"You may not be where you want to be in your life, Mer. But I'm so glad you're in *my* life. Your birthday is one of my favorite days, because it means you exist, and I'm so grateful for that," he murmured.

"You can stop saying nice things now. Okay?" There was a tremor in her voice that made Noah swallow his own emotion back. "I forgive you for saying I look tired. I need you to stop being so sweet or I'm going to cry, and then my makeup will come off, and I really *will* look old."

"I meant every word."

"Even about my armpits?"

He began walking toward her front door, still holding her, her legs still dangling. "Especially about your armpits."

FOURTEEN

1990 *

*T*he man was walking along the side of the road when Noah went to pick up his mother at the end of her shift. There was something familiar about the stoop of his thin back and the way he scurried. It was still dark—December mornings were always dark—and hard to make out much, but the man wasn't dressed for the weather. He wore a T-shirt and a pair of drawstring pants, and his beard was frosted with ice. It was hard to see his feet, but Noah didn't think he wore shoes.

He was still walking when Noah returned. Noah hadn't stopped the first time, but he couldn't pass him by twice. As he slowed, pulling up behind the bedraggled character staggering along the road, his mother's eyes snapped to his face and her hand tightened on the door.

"Don't stop, Noah. Don't you do it. He isn't safe," she said, her voice rising in rare passion.

"He's going to die if someone doesn't stop, Mom. Someone has to stop. Might as well be me. Stay here." Noah stopped and threw the car into park, leaving his hazard lights on. He wasn't worried about being pulled over or caught behind the wheel. He finally had a driver's license. He'd been driving for years without one, but now he was legal. If he attracted the attention of the police, all the better. Maybe they would be able to help.

"Hey!" Noah called, running to catch the man who had only increased his speed when Noah stopped. *"Wait up. You're going to freeze to death. Let me give you a ride."*

The man stopped and turned, shaking his head, snowflakes falling from his beard and collecting in the hair on his arms. *"I don't have anywhere to go."*

"Take my coat." Noah unzipped his jacket, the one Mer had given him two Christmases before. He loved the coat, but it was too short in the arms now anyway. Mer would understand.

The man stammered, his eyes on the garment. *"No. I can't do that. You need your coat."* Noah ignored him and slung it over the man's shoulders.

"I don't need it as much as you do. I have a warm car to climb back into." Noah was wearing a sweatshirt, and the T-shirt he wore beneath it rode up on his stomach as he shrugged the sweatshirt over his head. *"Here. Put this on first. Then the coat."*

The man let himself be coaxed into the sweatshirt and coat, shaking so hard Noah had to help him. His arms were long and his shoulders broad, but he was thin to the point of emaciation, and though the sleeves rode up on his wrists, the sweatshirt and coat were roomy on him. Noah zipped up the coat and pulled the hood of the sweatshirt tight over the man's head.

"What size are your feet?" Noah asked.

"Uh. I-I don't know. Big?" the man stammered.

Noah eyed the man's feet. *"We're probably close to the same size. You can have these. I have another pair at home."* It was a lie. He didn't have another pair at home, but he could get some. He'd just gotten paid. He started toeing off his sneakers and pulled off his socks one at a time, balancing like a stork, before placing his bare feet on the road. Damn, that was cold. He handed his socks to the man, who seemed dumbfounded at the offering.

"Do you want to come sit in the car, just so you can put these on?" Noah urged.

"No. No. She wouldn't like that."

"Who? My mom?" Noah glanced back at the car. His mom was watching them, her eyes wide, her hands on her cheeks like she wanted to hide.

"Andy," he muttered.

"Who's Andy?' Noah asked.

The man was staring at him. "You're Andy's boy," he whispered.

"I don't know anybody named Andy. But you should let me take you to the shelter. Let me take you somewhere. It's snowing. And your feet look bad."

Noah pulled off his T-shirt. He was now standing on the side of the road in nothing but a pair of old Levi's. The frigid air on his skin felt like a thousand needles. "Put your hands on my shoulders, and I'll help you balance while we get your feet dry and warm." He used his shirt to dry the man's feet one at a time, pulling on a sock and shoving his foot into a sneaker before moving to the other, so the man's feet wouldn't get wet again. When he'd finished, Noah rose, trying not to shiver. He didn't want the man to know he was cold.

"I have a pair of gloves in the car. Wait just a second." Noah ran to the car and got the gloves he kept in the jockey box for the mornings he had to scrape ice from the windows. He grabbed a ten-dollar bill from his wallet as well and returned to the man, who looked considerably warmer than he had minutes before.

"Here. Put these on. And here's some money for a hot breakfast. McDonald's is open. It's on the corner, about a half a mile down the road. Get some coffee in you. There's a homeless shelter downtown on Rio Grande. Do you know where that is?"

The man nodded.

"I'd be glad to take you there," Noah pressed again.

The man took the money and the gloves and shook his head. He stared at Noah with wet eyes.

"I'm no good, Noah. You should go now."

Noah gaped. "How do you know my name?"

"I met you once before. Remember? I asked you when the flood was coming, and you told me I was safe."

Noah stared and then took a step back, afraid. He remembered now. The man looked so different with a beard, and his eyes weren't nearly as wild. Now his eyes were just old and tired. Sad.

"Thank you, Noah," John Davis Cutler whispered. "Now go. You're going to freeze to death, and Andy will be all alone."

The downpour came on suddenly, pounding the streets and the roofs with pent-up fury. Normally Mercedes would have loved it, maybe even danced in it. A good rainstorm in dry Utah was usually celebrated. But Gia was asleep in her car seat, and Mercedes needed gas. The fuel light in her Corolla had been on for too long. Mercedes was frugal, but she wasn't foolish. She never would have let it get so low, but somehow, she always managed to need gas when she had Gia, and errands with a two-year-old were significantly harder than errands without a two-year-old. She rolled to a stop at the pumps just across the street from the salon and eyed the skies impatiently.

After ten minutes beneath the paltry overhang, eyeing her watch, Mercedes cursed and braced herself to get drenched. The rain wasn't letting up, Noah would be home from work by now, waiting at the house, and she was just sitting there, afraid of getting wet. Grabbing her wallet from her purse, she stepped out of the Corolla and rounded her car at a run. She was soaked before she stopped in front of the pump. Clutching her wallet to her chest, she tried to use her card, only to have it decline and the pump ask her to "see attendant."

"You've got to be kidding me," she cried. She tried the card again. No luck. She pushed the button to call the attendant, and he confirmed that she would need to bring her card inside.

Mercedes swore beneath her breath and swiped at her wet face. She wasn't going to get Gia out of the car in this rain just to run inside for ten seconds. There wasn't another car in the lot and she could see her car from inside the store. She would just run in, have the attendant swipe her card for preapproval, and run back out. Her decision made, she raced, wallet in hand, for the gas station. Her clothes were completely soaked, her hair plastered to her neck, and when she yanked open the door and stepped inside, she glanced back at the Corolla, just to make sure it hadn't floated away. Reassured, she stepped inside and handed her card to the attendant, a kid who didn't look old enough to pop his own zits, let alone sell alcohol.

"Twenty bucks on pump two," she said, shivering.

"Sorry about that. They get glitchy in the rain." He pushed a few buttons and ran her card. "Uh, pump two?" he asked, looking over her head out the window.

"Yes."

"You sure? Looks like your car has other ideas."

Mercedes flipped around, only to see the Corolla pulling away from the pump.

"Call the police!" she shrieked, racing for the door. "Call 911. There's a baby in that car!"

"You want your card?" he called behind her, as she threw herself through the doors.

"Call the police!"

She felt the strap on her flip flop snap and felt a moment's gratitude that she wasn't in heels. She ran, sliding and careening through the wet lot and out onto the street, doing her best to keep the car in sight. Someone blared at her, someone else honked, and she ran, screaming for help, eyes clinging to the brake lights that flickered on as the Corolla careened around a corner and out of sight.

"You okay, lady?" someone yelled, pulling up beside her in their car.

"Help me! Someone stole my car, and my little girl is in the back seat!"

The woman behind the wheel waved her inside, and Mercedes jumped into her front seat, pointing the way to the road where she'd last seen the car disappear. She thought she heard a siren wail, and the woman, a white lady with fluffy, blonde hair and a little dog in her lap, pushed her foot down hard.

"Turn on the next street!" Mercedes cried. "Right!"

"Your foot's bleeding, sweetheart," the lady gasped.

"I'm okay, please, just drive." Mercedes was too afraid to cry, too afraid to blink, for fear she'd miss something.

The woman obeyed, taking the corner with considerable skill. Mercedes scanned the street ahead for the Corolla. A row of cars was stopped at the next light, but her car was not among them.

"There!" The Corolla was abandoned in the middle of a Wendy's parking lot, the driver's side door hanging open. "That's my car!" Mercedes shrieked. "The lot on your right."

The woman flew across two lanes and took the turn into the parking lot fast enough to make her little dog yelp and fly up from her arms. Mercedes had her door open before the woman came to a shuddering stop only feet away from the abandoned Corolla.

Mercedes could hear Gia screaming.

Her legs buckled as she scrambled for Gia's door, desperate to reach the little girl, weak with relief that she was restored, terrified that she'd been harmed. The rain was billowing back through the open, driver's side door into Gia's face, and she was wet and frightened, her eyes wild and her face slick with tears and rain, but she was still buckled in her seat, safe and unharmed.

Mercedes loosened the straps on Gia's seat and pulled the little girl into her shaking arms.

"Shh. We're okay. We're okay, Gia Bug. Mer's got you."

"Daddy!" Gia howled.

"Yeah. We need Daddy." Mercedes murmured, her terror turning to tears. She fumbled for her phone, realizing her purse was still sitting, untouched, on the passenger seat. The car was in park but still running, as if the Corolla had just decided to take a joy ride on its own and changed its mind minutes later.

"Honey, do you want me to call someone for you?" Mercedes's blonde savior peered through the open door, huddled against the rain, her little dog yipping wildly from her car.

"No. No, I have my phone. But I need your name. I can't thank you enough for what you did," Mercedes cried.

The woman's name was Mary Jane Fryer, and she gave Mercedes her number and promised that she would come to Maven for a free cut and color the next time she was in need, but insisted on sticking around until the police arrived. She pulled a blanket from the trunk of her car and wrapped it around Mer and Gia, who sat wet and trembling in the back of the Corolla. Then she climbed in the front seat to get out of the rain.

"You need to get that foot looked at, sweetie."

Mercedes nodded, thanking her again, but her foot was the furthest thing from her thoughts. Noah answered on the first ring, concern in his voice. When she heard him, it was all she could do not to break down. Instead, she gritted her teeth and closed her eyes, willing herself to remain calm so she wouldn't scare him to death.

"Mer? What's wrong?"

"I'm okay, Noah. Gia's okay. But I need you."

Mercedes needed twelve stitches across the ball of her foot. She must have stepped on a piece of glass when she was running down the road. She said she hadn't felt it and didn't know the moment it happened. It started to hurt about ten minutes after the police arrived, after the adrenaline waned and the shock wore off.

Noah arrived minutes after the police—the attendant at the gas station had come through—and Mary Jane Fryer had waited around as well, giving her own account to the police. The police took Mercedes's statement, counseling her to "never leave a child alone in a car, even for a few seconds." Fortunately, they didn't belabor the point. One word of censure and Mercedes hung her head and cried into Gia's pale curls, and Noah got angry.

"She isn't the one you should be chastising, Officer," he snapped.

"Meh cwy?" Gia asked, her lip sticking out so far, the policeman offered her a sucker, and Mercedes did her best to control the tears that wouldn't stop.

"You're the babysitter?" the officer asked Mercedes.

"She's the godmother," Noah interrupted.

"I watch her every Monday," Mercedes added.

The officer nodded and made a few notes. "It looks to me like someone saw an opportunity to steal your car, but when they saw the child in the back, they thought better of it. Stealing a car is one thing. Kidnapping is another."

"But . . . they didn't take anything," Mercedes argued.

"You said you had your wallet. Was there anything else of value in your purse?"

"My phone. Not much else. But it didn't even look rifled through."

"He sees the kid in the back seat, he's spooked. He runs. Not that hard to figure."

Mercedes nodded. It made sense.

"We'll dust the car for prints—there's a big dirty handprint on the steering wheel—and run them through the system and see if we can get a hit. We'll also see if there is any footage from the security cameras at the gas station."

Noah bundled Mercedes and Gia into his Subaru, leaving the Corolla to be processed by the police, and dropped Gia off with Heather so he could go with Mercedes to the emergency room to get her foot looked at.

He was remarkably calm, considering his daughter had been temporarily kidnapped. It was Mercedes who couldn't seem to get a hold of herself. She was the one who had seen it all unfold. She was the one who'd been catapulted into hell before being miraculously pardoned. He was grim. Quiet. And he'd approached the situation with the same steadiness that had accompanied him all his life, but inside he was sick and shaking.

He held Mer's hand as the gash on her foot was stitched, reassuring her over and over again that she'd done nothing wrong, that all was well, and that it wasn't her fault.

The doctor told her she would have to relinquish her heels for a few days.

When she balked, Noah rolled his eyes. "Gia won't wear anything but her pink snow boots, and you won't wear anything but four-inch heels. I blame you for her neurosis."

"I have a great new pair of Reeboks I wear all the time," she grumbled.

"Well, you're going to want to wear a slipper or, even better, stay off your foot completely for the next few days. You'll pull the stitches out if you walk on them," the doctor replied.

"I could get one of those little scooter things you kneel on. Then I could go to work, no problem," Mercedes mused.

"Three days. Just stay off it for three days. Then wrap it up good and tight and wear your sneakers to work, and you'll be fine," the doctor urged.

"A few days off so your foot can heal won't kill you, Mer," Noah said as the doctor excused himself and promised to send an orderly with a wheelchair to push Mercedes out of the hospital.

Mercedes gnawed at her lip, the same worry he'd sensed earlier flickering across her face.

"What's wrong?" Noah asked. "Is there something else going on at work?"

"You know me. It's just hard for me to sit still." She shook her head, dismissing his question with a wave of her hand.

At that moment, the orderly returned with a wheelchair, and Noah lifted Mercedes off the table and set her in it. She grumbled that a wheelchair was ridiculous, and Noah let her gripe, but when he insisted she come home with him so he could take care of her, she nodded, and from the droop of her shoulders and the lack of argument, he could see the day's events had finally caught up with her. They'd caught up with him too. He was almost dizzy with exhaustion. That happened when you only slept every other day. He'd worked Sunday night and been up all day. In the last thirty-six hours, he'd had a two-hour long nap at dawn between shifts. But his little family was safe, and his gratitude far exceeded his exhaustion.

They swung past Heather's house, and Noah retrieved a grumpy Gia from her grandmother. It was ten o'clock, and she was ready for bed, but she perked up when she saw Mer waiting in the front seat of the car.

"Meh," Gia greeted, grinning as Noah buckled her in. Mercedes grinned right back, then immediately burst into tears.

"Hey," Noah soothed, sliding back behind the wheel. "She's okay, Mer. She's fine. It's over."

Mercedes nodded and did her best to stem the tide. At the house, Noah carried Mer into the guest room, took Gia to the bathroom, got her a glass of milk, and put her in her pajamas while Mer hobbled around and got ready for bed. Mercedes kept a pair of pajamas and a few things at his house for the Sunday nights she stayed over, and when he went in to check on her after he put Gia to bed, she was huddled beneath the covers, her eyes closed, the bedside lamp on.

When he moved to turn it off, her eyes snapped open.

"Don't. Please. I need it," she whispered.

He sat on the bed beside her, looking down at her tired, troubled face.

"I have never been so scared, Noah. If something had happened to Gia . . . if today had ended differently," she shook her head, unable to finish, and her mouth began to tremble again.

"I know. But it didn't. She's safe. You're both safe. And we're all here together."

"Will you stay with me?" she asked. "I don't want to be alone."

Noah nodded. "Give me a minute to grab a shower and change my clothes. I'll be back."

She closed her eyes and exhaled heavily. He returned a few minutes later with the pillow from his bed, wearing sweats and a T-shirt, his hair wet from a quick shower.

He climbed in beside her, plumped his pillow, and pulled her into his arms. She came willingly, eagerly, and pressed her face to his throat.

"Noah?"

"Yeah?"

"I'm so sorry. I messed up. I shouldn't have left Gia alone in the car, not even for a second."

Noah lifted her chin, and without a word, pressed his mouth to hers, giving her his forgiveness, absolving her in the only way he thought would penetrate her guilt. She kissed him back, lips soft and anxious, needy and sweet, and he forgot that he'd only meant to calm and reassure. Instead, he kissed her with growing ardor, and before too long, their bodies were pressed together, breaths harsh, lips clinging, hands grasping.

Noah wanted to keep kissing her. He wanted to pull her beneath him and make love to her. But not like this. Not when they were both exhausted and scared. Not when they were running on empty and hungry for reassurance. So he dragged his lips from hers, turned off the lamp, and tucked her head beneath his chin, holding her close while he held her at bay. He felt her shudder once, felt her hands tighten in his T-shirt, and finally, felt her muscles loosen as sleep dragged her under. With a sigh and a soft goodnight, he let sleep take him too.

They spent the next day puttering around the house, napping when Gia napped, eating when Gia ate, playing when Gia wanted to play. Mercedes's foot was sore, but the injury wasn't serious, and the stitches were across the ball of her foot, so she walked on her heel, ignoring Noah whenever he insisted she sit down and let him wait on her. He took comfort in the fact that at least she wasn't wearing stilettos, and her stitches seemed to be holding.

Noah left Mercedes and Gia together Tuesday night when he worked his graveyard shift, and Mercedes took Wednesday off, per the doctor's orders, staying with Gia while Noah slept for a few hours in the morning. When Detective Zabriskie called her on her cell phone Wednesday afternoon, they were sitting around Noah's kitchen table having a late lunch.

"Those prints came back, Miss Lopez. I'm still sure it was a crime of opportunity, but we got a hit. The prints belonged to a John Davis Cutler. Does that name ring any bells?"

"John Davis Cutler?" she asked. "No. I don't think so."

Noah's head snapped around.

"What did you say?" he gasped.

"The prints . . . they think the man that carjacked the Corolla was a man named John Davis Cutler," she mouthed, but the officer was talking again, and she turned her attention to what he was saying.

"He has a record, been in and out of mental institutions most of his adult life. He spent a stint in prison, escaped once, and was released after some new evidence cleared him a few years ago. He's been quiet, and until now, stayed out of trouble since he was released," Detective Zabriskie reported.

"I don't know anyone by that name." Mercedes was staring at a pale, white-knuckled Noah.

"His case worker calls him Cuddy—short for Cutler."

"Cuddy?" Mercedes gasped.

"You know a Cuddy?" the detective asked.

"I do," Mercedes stammered. "He's a homeless man. I cut his hair every now and again. I have for years."

"Well, for whatever reason, John Davis Cutler—aka Cuddy—was the one who took your car and Gia Andelin for a joyride the other day, unless he had some other reason for being in your car and can explain his prints on your steering wheel?"

"No. Cuddy's never been in my car before. Not that I know of, at least. So what do we do now?" Mercedes asked.

"We bring him in for questioning. If he comes in for a haircut, you give us a call, and we'll put out an APB." Detective Zabriskie signed off after arranging for her to come down and make an additional statement.

Mercedes set her phone down and met Noah's gaze.

"What, Noah? You look like you've seen a ghost," she said.

"Cuddy was the one who carjacked you. The homeless guy. The guy who leaves rocks?" he asked quietly.

"Yeah. They think so."

Noah stood abruptly, his sandwich half eaten. He stroked his beard, tension radiating from him. "They said Cuddy is a nickname?"

"Yes. For John Davis Cutler," she answered.

"I met a man named John Davis Cutler when I was a kid, Mer. It was right after Cora's dad died. He was in the psych ward at Uni, but he had a knack for escaping. He supposedly killed a woman because he thought she was 'already dead.'" He raised his hands and made quotes around the words.

"Maybe it's not the same John Davis Cutler," Mercedes said, hopeful. "Detective Zabriskie said he was paroled after new evidence exonerated him."

"And he's been hanging around you and Cora?"

"He wasn't hanging around us, Noah. You know how we met him. I cut his hair every few months. I have for years. He's never harmed anyone. He's sweet. A little loopy, but sweet. I wouldn't call that hanging around. And he said he knew Cora's dad."

"Knew him how?"

"He said he . . . sees him. Maybe . . . he's like Moses."

"Oh, my God," Noah groaned. "It's got to be the same guy. And he's not like Moses," Noah said, shaking his head, adamant.

"Why? Because he smells bad and took drugs and was incarcerated for a crime he apparently didn't commit?"

Noah stared at her, incredulous, his hands on his hips.

"Moses has people who *believe* him. And maybe he has a strong mind and a handsome face and an amazing gift that make it easier to accept what he says. Cuddy doesn't have a whole hell of a lot, but who's to say he doesn't see what he says he sees?" Mercedes insisted.

"That still doesn't explain why he climbed into your car and drove away with my daughter," Noah whispered. "If he's harmless, why would he do something like that?"

It was Mercedes's turn to be flummoxed. She met his gaze, shrugging helplessly. "I have no idea."

"Is this the Cuddy who comes into your salon?" Detective Zabriskie asked, pointing at a picture of a much younger, much wilder looking Cuddy. Noah and Mercedes were sitting at his desk in the busy police station, Gia on Noah's lap, their eyes trained on the photo in front of them.

"Yes . . . I think so. He looks so different now," Mercedes murmured.

Noah just stared.

"Do you recognize him, Dr. Andelin?" Detective Zabriskie asked.

"Yeah, I do. I met him years ago—sixteen years ago, to be exact. But I would be hard pressed to forget him." Noah proceeded to give an account of the first time he saw John Davis Cutler at University of Utah hospital, crouched beside a set of swinging doors.

"And you haven't seen him since?" the detective pressed.

Noah was still, thinking. "I saw him one other time. He was walking along the side of the road. It was snowing, and he was half dressed. I gave him what I could. My shoes. My coat. The sweatshirt I was wearing. Even my socks. I think I probably aided and abetted a fugitive. But I had no idea. He was in a bad way, so I helped him."

"You gave your coat to Cuddy?" Mercedes gasped. "I remember you telling me about it. But I don't remember you saying the guy's name. How weird is that?"

"But you haven't seen him since then?" Detective Zabriskie interrupted-ed.

"No. Apparently, my wife befriended him. Mercedes too. But I didn't know Cuddy and John Davis Cutler were the same guy. I had no idea."

"Well, it's good we've made a positive ID. Here are your keys, Miss

Lopez. If John Davis Cutler shows up at the salon, you give us a call. And it might be a good idea to be extra careful for the time being."

Mercedes nodded and stood, taking her keys from the detective's outstretched hand. Noah stood beside her, and together they followed Detective Zabriskie to the lot where the Corolla was parked. A thin film covered the seats and dashboard where they'd dusted the inside for prints, and on the floor, directly below the steering wheel, were three small rocks. She hadn't driven her car since before it was stolen, and other than plucking her purse from the passenger seat, she hadn't been in the front seat at all. But Mercedes had no doubt about what the rocks meant. Cuddy had left her a peace offering.

FIFTEEN

1992

From the hill just behind The Three Amigos Apartments, they could see the fireworks display better than if they had tickets to the Fourth of July celebration at Rice Stadium where the Running Utes played. Cora was still at work, so Noah and Mercedes went without her, expecting her to show up when she could. They dragged a cooler up the hill and brought a ratty quilt to lay on. Noah brought his boombox, and they listened to Bon Jovi and Aerosmith and ate Doritos and drank Dr. Pepper while they waited for night to fall and the show to begin. They weren't the only ones who used the hill to see the display, but they always climbed the highest and stayed the longest.

"We'll be seniors next year, Mer. Next summer, we may not even be here on the Fourth of July," Noah mused, stretched out beside her on the blanket.

"Where would we be?" Mer asked, her eyes on the darkening sky. They'd watched the fireworks together every year since the summer before third grade.

"I've got to get out of here," he said softly. "I'm suffocating."

Mer sat up and looked down at Noah, her heart in her throat.

"Where would you go?"

He must have seen her dismay, because he sat up too, looping his *arms around his knees and meeting her gaze. Reaching over, he rubbed out the scowl between her brows with his thumb.*

"I don't know yet," he said softly. "Maybe I'll join the army. Maybe the Air Force. You don't have to actually fly planes to be in the Air Force. Did you know that? Maybe I'd be stationed at Hill Air Force Base, so I'd be close. Or maybe I'll just go to Alaska and work on one of those commercial fishing boats for a few months. But I'm going. I have to."

"I don't like the sound of any of that."

"How am I going to learn how to be a man if I spend all my time with women?" Noah asked.

"Helloooo up there!" Cora called, interrupting them. She was waving a flashlight, making a wide arc in the dusk. "Is that you? Why do you two always climb so high? I hate hiking in the dark."

"Get up here!" Noah called. "It's not even dark yet, you dork."

"Yeah, but what if it was? How would I have found you?" Cora grumbled. She climbed the remaining distance and collapsed onto the blanket, wiggling into the small space between them even though there was sufficient room on either side. They laughed and parted for her, shoving at her long legs and arms that were sprawled across them. She rolled to her back and crossed her arms beneath her head, and Noah and Mercedes relaxed beside her, their eyes upward, their conversation forgotten.

"I brought beer," Cora said, satisfaction ringing in her voice. "Cold. Delicious. Beer."

"Beer is not delicious," Mercedes retorted. "It smells terrible. But hand me one."

Cora dug a cold can from her knapsack, popped the tab, and they passed it between the three of them, waiting for the show to start.

In ten minutes, they'd finished two cans and opened another. It tasted better the more they drank. Mercedes had never had the desire to drink before. Angel and Jose had shown up at the apartment once, completely wasted, and Angel had thrown up all over the living room carpet. It had taken a month of scrubbing to get the smell out. The smell of alcohol made Mercedes think of vomit. But she kept thinking of Noah saying he wanted to leave. Mercedes didn't think she could survive if Noah left. Drinking the beer was a good distraction.

When the first colors lit the sky, cracking and shuddering, they'd worked their way through the six pack, and Mercedes began to see why people drank. She couldn't feel her fear. One color bled into another, gold and green, red and blue, the smell of heat and smoke and summertime filling her senses as the beer dissolved her walls.

"De colores," she sang softly. "Y por eso los grandes amores, de muchos colores me gustan a mí."

Cora hummed along with her, unable to sing the words but recognizing the tune.

All the colors. All the colors. All the bright colors made her heart cry.

When they were finished, Cora started a new song, merging one song about colors into another.

"I see your true colors, shining through," Cora crooned. Cora sang "True Colors" even better than Cyndi Lauper, and "De Colores" was forgotten as Noah joined her, his low voice a soft rumble, barely discernible beneath Cora's full-bodied belting.

But Mercedes had stopped singing. Instead, she was crying. Her heart was crying too, just like the words to the song. It was the beer's fault. She sat up and began feeling around for the flashlight. She needed to go home, and she didn't want to walk in the dark.

"Mercedes," Cora said. "What's wrong?"

"I'm going home. I have to pee." Suddenly she did. She had to pee so bad her teeth were floating.

"But you're crying," Cora protested.

"I'm crying because if I don't cry, I'll pee my pants. And Noah is leaving."

"What?" Cora gasped.

"Ah, Mer. I'm not going anywhere yet," Noah said.

Cora looked at Noah in horror, Mercedes's tears forgotten.

"Where are you going, Noah?" Cora cried.

"Nowhere. I'm not going anywhere. Not yet. Mer's just drunk. I don't think someone so small should drink that much beer."

Mercedes started walking, not caring that her friends would have to carry everything down without her. She heard them call her name and tell her to wait, but she didn't stop. For once, they would have to get by without her.

Noah stared up at his ceiling in the dark. He'd read for a while after putting Gia to bed, his eyes continually rising to watch Mer as she played with Oscar, stroking him and whispering to him in Spanish—Noah understood about half of what she said—before she crawled over to Noah, dropped a kiss on his head, and bid him a sleepy goodnight. It was Sunday night, and she was staying in Noah's guest room again—the way she did almost every Sunday night—so she could watch Gia the next day. She'd made it back to the salon on Thursday and Friday and even donned her heels for work on Saturday, just to prove she could. She'd limped around all Sunday because of it, and Noah had bit his tongue so he wouldn't chastise her for her vanity.

She'd slept in his guest room that week more than she'd slept at home, and Noah wondered when they were going to admit to each other that their relationship had changed. The kiss they'd shared Monday night was just one of the indications. Of course, they hadn't talked about it, and they hadn't repeated it.

They were good at that, being vulnerable and honest and real with each other except when it involved romance or their mutual attraction. Then they studiously ignored the fact that they were closer than most married couples. They religiously pretended the love they felt for each other was purely platonic. They fell back into comfortable patterns—bickering like siblings and donning their twelve-year-old selves so they wouldn't have to face the fact that they were all grown up with very grown-up feelings. They relied on each other, took care of each other, freely admitted they loved each other, and whether Mercedes wanted to admit it or not, they weren't simply best friends. To pretend otherwise was to lie, and like Mer said, he'd never been very good at pretending. He could be patient, but at some point, Mercedes was going to have to stop fighting the inevitable. And they *were* inevitable. He believed that.

He'd never forgotten what Abuela had told him before he left for basic training. She didn't speak English very well, and their relationship had been more about hugs and unspoken understanding, more about shared affection than long conversation. But she'd told him, quite clearly, that just because something is meant to be, doesn't mean it's meant to be right now. He'd thought she was talking about his education, about his studies, about his life in general, but her words had come to mind more than once in the last year, and he'd begun to wonder if she hadn't been talking about him and Mercedes all along. She'd been one of those people who just knew things, and he'd believed her then. He believed her now, and he was convinced the timing was finally right.

He closed his eyes and tried to sleep, tried to think of something other than his complicated feelings and his stubborn best friend. He was just drifting off when the baby monitor on his nightstand began talking to him.

He groaned. Gia had an aggravating way of waking up just as he was falling asleep, and it was hell getting her back down. He heard her toss a little, and Noah held his breath, hoping she was just talking in her sleep.

"De kuh wo ways," she said again, and he groaned, but he didn't get up. It kind of sounded like she was singing. She babbled a few more words —words Noah couldn't decipher—and a clear melody emerged. It was familiar, but not overly so, and Noah concentrated on her little voice, singing sleepily in the dark.

It was the cutest thing he'd ever heard.

He pushed back the blanket and grabbed the monitor, wanting to share it with Mer, hoping she wasn't too deeply asleep to appreciate being serenaded by a two-year-old.

Her bedside lamp was still on, the burnished light so soft and low it wasn't much brighter than a candle, but Mer's eyes were closed, and Noah wondered briefly if she was still too afraid after Monday's scare to be alone in the dark. He closed her door and padded to her bed, whispering her name. Her eyes fluttered open immediately.

"Mer, you need to hear something."

"Is everything okay?" she said, sitting up, fully awake.

"Yeah. Yeah. Just . . . I want you to hear this," he soothed. She sank back down on her pillow, and Noah sat down on the bed beside her and turned the monitor up as loud as it would go. For a moment there was simply charged silence, the purring sound of Gia breathing, and an occasional rustle of blankets and the squeak of crib springs. Then Gia started to hum, adding words here and there. Her small voice was like a trail of pearls as she moved through her song.

"She's singing," Noah whispered, as though speaking any louder would cause Gia to stop.

"Yeah. She is," Mercedes responded, delighted.

"I don't know the song. . . but it sounds familiar."

"'De Colores.' She's singing 'De Colores.'" Mercedes looked as though she wanted to laugh, but wanted to listen more, and held the mirth in her chest, her hand pressed to her heart, her ears straining for the Spanish words that were more sounds and suggestions. But the tune, now that she'd identified it, was unmistakable.

"Canta el gallo, canta el gallo," Mercedes sang, matching her voice to Gia's. "Con el quiri, quiri, quiri, quiri, quiri."

"What are the words?" Noah whispered.

"I taught her that verse because the sounds of the rooster, the hen, and the chicks repeat. La gallina, la gallina, con el cara, cara, cara, cara, cara. Los pollitos, los pollitos con el pío, pío, pío, pío, pí," she sang.

"She's right on tune," Noah whispered. "Two years old, and she already has better pitch than I do."

"I wish Cora could hear her," Mercedes said softly, and Noah sighed. He wished Cora could hear her too. He wished Cora peace and rest and forgiveness. But he didn't want to think about Cora.

"Maybe she can," Mercedes mused. "If we believe in Moses . . . and crazy Cuddy, I suppose we have to believe that Cora still exists, somewhere."

"I guess so," Noah whispered, still listening. Gia was losing steam, her little voice quieting, her song slipping into silence. "I knew I remembered that song. I just couldn't place it," he added.

"It was another one of Papi's favorites. I've been teaching it to Gia," Mercedes smiled.

"I never heard him sing it. But I heard *you* sing it. Remember the night of the fireworks? You had too much beer and rolled down the hill behind The Three Amigos."

"It was the fastest way down, and I had to pee." She giggled, remembering.

"You were crying, and your knees were all scraped up. And I felt terrible because it was my fault."

"You told me all of us women were suffocating you," Mercedes pouted.

"I don't think I said it quite like that. But I remember feeling desperate. I didn't have a dad. My best friends were girls. Everywhere I looked, I was surrounded by women. Don't get me wrong. You, Abuela, Alma . . . I had some amazing women in my life. Heather and Cora too. I had no complaints. But I needed a father figure. I recognized it in myself. I was hungry for it. Remember when that Air Force recruiter came to the school junior year?"

"You looked like you'd stuck your finger in a light socket." Mercedes giggled again.

"Yeah. I probably did. He talked to me for a good hour. Gave me his undivided attention. I went home and cried I was so excited."

"I never could figure out why you wanted to go. You had good grades and you could have gotten grants and scholarships and student aid. It just seemed dangerous and unnecessary."

"It felt vital. Like . . . if I didn't go, I was going to explode."

"I always thought you were running away. I was mad at you for a while."

"I wasn't running away. I was running toward," he said, a wry smile on his lips. "I was running for my life."

"I just knew nothing would ever be the same. And I was right. You came back, and you were in love with Cora the way she'd always been in love with you," Mercedes whispered. Her eyes were soft and sad, her dark hair spread across the pillows, and in the ruddy glow of the little lamp, she was so beautiful he could hardly breathe.

"She always needed me. You made it very clear that you didn't."

"Love and need aren't the same thing, Noah."

He nodded, staring down at her. The silence grew and swelled between them, fat with all the things they felt and weren't brave enough to say. He leaned over her, hands on either side of her head, and her breath caught as he lowered his mouth.

He just wanted to kiss her. That was all. Just kiss her, like he had on New Year's Eve, like he had Monday night. Like he had twelve years ago before their paths diverged. But he took one kiss and then he needed another. Soft lips, soft hands, soft sighs, and he knew this time he wasn't going to be able to stop himself from taking more.

The room was shadowed and still, a quiet co-conspirator, keeping the world at bay, and for the first time they weren't laughing or teasing or even comforting one another. Nobody was crying or scared. Nobody was saying goodbye. Nobody was pulling away. And Noah's heart began to pound with hope.

But when Mercedes rose up suddenly and turned off the lamp, Noah realized she wasn't yet ready to see the truth. She pulled his mouth back to hers, urged his body down beside her on the bed, but she was still pretending. She was pretending that what was between them wasn't love. She was "giving him what he needed," like she had the day she'd coaxed him into the shower, all the while denying he was what she wanted.

Noah knew her too well. Even in the dark, he saw her clearly. He saw her with his hands and his mouth. He smelled her skin, heard her thoughts, and felt her touch, and in his head, there was no pretense at all. She moaned against his lips, anxious, needy, pulling at his clothes and urging his body to settle into hers, but he refused to let her set the tempo.

Mer wanted a frenzied dance, so she didn't have to feel too much for too long. Noah understood. But he *needed* to feel. He needed it so badly that his eyes teared up and his hands shook. He didn't want to tease. He wanted to taste. He didn't want to rush, he wanted to relish. Going slow would hurt, because caring hurt. And he cared about Mercedes. He cared deeply.

There was too much history, too much shared joy and agony not to care. But he welcomed it. He wanted it. He told her after they'd made love in the shower that he'd found comfort in a friend. It was true, but it had been more than that. She knew it, he knew it, and he was ready to admit it. Noah didn't want comfort from Mer. Not anymore. This time, he needed it to be real. He loved Mercedes, and he wanted to make love to her. Making love demanded time, and if they raced through the act, Mer could claim it wasn't love at all. She could flit away into the realm of friendship, where love was about safety and consistency, and no one got hurt.

"Slow down, Mer," he whispered, withdrawing, and she stilled, her eyes coming open. Mercedes had beautiful eyes, and in the moonlit darkness they gleamed, questioning and cautious. Her head was framed between his forearms, her hair a black swath across the pale spread. Noah leaned in, inch by inch, his eyes on hers, demanding she pay attention, and he kissed her again.

"Breathe," he commanded. She was frozen, her lips parted, her eyes wide. Her careful exhale fluttered past his lips and warmed his skin. He brushed his lips over hers—never increasing the pressure or the intensity—until her eyes closed and her body softened beneath him. Her hands rose to his face, reverent fingers exploring, savoring, as she opened her mouth and quietly bid him enter.

For a long time, Noah just kissed her. He kept his weight above her, kept his hands in her hair, kept his mouth on hers. Kissing is a thousand times more intimate than sex. He knew some people would disagree, but the first thing that goes when a marriage is coming apart is not the sex. It's the kissing.

Mer's hands were beneath his shirt, hovering at his waistband, pulling and pushing, and even as their clothes fell away, Noah didn't stop kissing her. He didn't neglect her mouth when her hands were rapacious and roving, pleading and punishing. He captured her wrists, urging patience, and when he finally began to touch her, it was not a means to an end. He caressed her because he loved the way her skin felt beneath his fingertips, the silken slopes, the soft swells, the warm scent of private places yet unexplored.

"Noah, please. Noah," she begged, her hips rising, her hands escaping his hold to clutch and coax. He capitulated slowly, mouth to mouth as he sank into her, and was so overcome with emotion, he had to pause. He was Atlas, holding the weight of the world on his shoulders, suspended above her, reveling in the exquisite agony of servitude.

Mercedes yanked at his hair and dug her nails into his back, scoring it, pulling his hips into hers, trying to make him move, to lose control. But he murmured her name and kissed her breasts, lingering over the hollow of her throat and the soft skin behind her ears. It was then that he realized she was crying, tears running from the corners of her eyes and soaking her hair and the sheet beneath her head.

He pressed his lips to the corners of her eyes and sipped at the salt on her cheeks, tasting the feelings she tried so hard to keep from him. He didn't ask her why she cried. He didn't beg her to stop. He understood her pain, and he knew he was hurting her. Tenderly, gently, carefully . . . hurting her. For a moment she was with him, lost in the sweetness of surrender, sobbing his name against his lips. He rocked against her, lazy and slow, a porch swing on a summer evening, just the two of them with nowhere to go. Then she was fighting him again, tugging his lower lip between her teeth, nipping and biting, drawing blood before taking his tongue into her mouth, desperate to distract him, to distract herself, from the unraveling of her defenses.

His pulse pounded, and his body raged, wanting to succumb, to give her passion instead of patience, lust instead of longsuffering. But the anguish of adoration would heal them—he believed that—and he wasn't willing to settle for less, to give *her* less, and he took the punishment, even as her body trembled and quaked around him, even as she begged him to release her, to hold her, to let her go, and to never leave.

"I'm right here, Mer. I'm right here with you," Noah promised, his lungs raw, his chest tight, his will weakening. "And I'm not going to let you go. I'm going to follow you over the edge. Whenever you're ready, honey, I'll be right behind you."

"Damn you, Noah," she whispered, lips trembling, hands fisted in his hair, but her breath caught, her eyes found his, and for a moment they were together on the precipice, caught between falling and flying. Then her chin rose, her eyes closed, and her arms tightened around him. He watched as she fell, tear-stained cheeks and swollen lips, taking him with her into the inky afterward, where sensation peaked and pulsed, slowed, and finally, slid away.

He felt the moment she came back to herself. She stiffened in his arms, uncomfortable and uncertain, and her hands fluttered at his waist, anxious to put him back in his place. He rolled to his back, taking her with him—his reluctant best friend with silky limbs and tousled hair. He ran his hand from the top of her head to the base of her spine, stroking her back, smoothing her ruffled pride, and calming her troubled thoughts, until time tipped them over and they fell again, this time into sleep.

He didn't let himself rest for long, the dawn was coming, and duty called. He came awake about an hour later, easing his arm from beneath Mer's cheek, and carefully sliding away. He stood beside the bed, looking down at her. Mercedes in motion was beautiful to behold, but Mercedes in quiet slumber was like the Timpanogos peaks, peaceful and lovely, the same yesterday and today, outliving them all. She had that quality, as if the waves of the world could crash against her and she would hold steady. If Cora was wind, Mer was rock. Noah didn't know what that made him, but he'd been changed by both.

He didn't touch Mer again—he didn't want her to wake and re-arm— but slipped soundlessly from the room, stepping into the sweats he'd discarded near the bed. *He'd only wanted to kiss her.* The thought made him smile. He'd wanted to kiss her. And he'd wanted everything that came after those kisses too.

He stopped in Gia's room and padded to her crib, pulling her blankets back over her tiny shoulders. She would kick them off again. She always did. He worried about her getting cold, but she never seemed to. Her bow-shaped lips were parted in sleep, and her lashes swept the swell of her cheeks. Freckles were starting to form. Noah ran a hand over her soft hair, wanting to touch her, to tell her he loved her, even if he was the only one to hear. Her hair had grown in thick and smooth, just like Mer had promised it would. It wasn't the flaxen fuzz she'd been born with, but silky and substantive, and shot with a definite strawberry hue. She was going to be a redhead like her mother.

"I've got to go to work, Bug. But Mer's here," Noah whispered. "Look after her, okay? She's going to try to run away from your old man. But she won't run away from you. It isn't in her. She's a forever kind of girl. Once she's claimed you, you're hers. You're hers, Bug. We've just got to convince her that she's ours."

Gia woke her. The monitor Noah left behind was turned all the way up, and her little voice penetrated Mer's dreams, pulling her from fragmented scenes and disjointed sequences to streaming sunlight and Noah's spare bedroom.

"De colores," Gia sang. "De colores." The way she said colores sounded more like cuh wo ways—but her *de* was spot on. "Quiri, quiri,

quiri, quiri, quiri," she chirped, like she was calling Oscar. Kitty, kitty, kitty, kitty. No rolled *r*, but it was unmistakable.

Mercedes lifted Gia from her crib—a big girl bed was in order—and plopped her on her potty while Mercedes brushed her teeth, avoiding her fresh-scrubbed face—she never went to bed with makeup on—and her tangled hair. Noah had combed it with his fingers, and she didn't want to see the result.

He'd run his hands through her hair, and he'd loved her so slowly. So patiently. And she'd cried. *Oh God, she cried.* He'd kissed her so sweetly. He'd kissed her so long and so thoroughly that she'd forgotten that she shouldn't love him, and that it was best if he didn't love her either.

Damn him. He was going to ruin everything.

"All done," Gia said, rising from her tiny throne to see how much liquid she'd produced. She clapped for herself. "Yay, Dee-Uh!" she crowed.

Mercedes wiped her tiny bum, emptied her winnings into the toilet, and set her on the sink so they could both wash their hands.

They'd done this same routine, in some variation, many times. But that morning, with their faces side by side, Gia talking to her reflection, Mercedes suddenly noticed the difference in their skin and their hair, in the color of their eyes, and she had the fleeting thought that no one would ever mistake her for Gia's mother. Women who looked like Mercedes rarely had babies who looked like Gia, regardless of their fathers. It wasn't a *bad* thing. It was simply genetics. But Mercedes *wanted* to be Gia's mother. She *wanted* people to assume Gia was hers. Her musing caused immediate remorse.

"I'm sorry, Cora," she said, and realized she'd spoken out loud.

"I sowwy, Cowa," Gia parroted, and Mercedes laughed, but her heart hurt, and her eyes filled. She turned away from their reflections, scooping Gia off the counter and dressing her for the day.

Mercedes spent the day in frenzied activity, and Gia kept up, for the most part. They cleaned and went to the grocery store and made sure the cupboards were stocked and the refrigerator was full, though Noah was always irritated when she did this, insisting on receipts and payment and compensation. She ignored his wishes and his irritation. She would clean if she wanted to. She would purchase what she pleased, and if what she bought ended up in Gia's drawers or in Noah's cupboards, that was her prerogative as Noah's best friend and Gia's godmother.

Noah's best friend who cried in his arms and came undone in a very *unfriendly* way the night before. Mercedes didn't know how she was going to face him when he got home. Would he laugh again and ask her for burritos? Would he want to hold her and kiss her slowly like he'd done in the dark? Mercedes didn't think she could handle either of those things. She *knew* she couldn't.

"I'm sorry, Cora," Mercedes moaned, and wondered again, like she had the night before, if Cora was listening.

"I sowwy, Cowa," Gia repeated.

"Damn it," Mercedes whispered.

"Damn it," Gia whispered.

Mercedes painted Gia's toenails and then painted her own while Gia turned the pages of the picture books Mer had read so many times she had them memorized. Mercedes made three casseroles and put two in the freezer in single serve portions. She balanced her checkbook, then balanced Gia on her shoulders while she did a hundred squats. When her legs and her nerves were shot, she called Heather to see if she'd sit with Gia for the last half hour until Noah got home. Mercedes couldn't do it.

Heather couldn't do it either.

Heather apologized profusely, trying to come up with a solution to Mercedes's problem, a problem Mercedes wasn't about to explain to Heather. *Well, Heather, I slept with your son-in-law last night. Again. And I'm feeling a wee bit awkward. Can you cover for me?*

"Has something come up? Is it an emergency?" Heather asked, worried.

"No, no. Um, just . . . an appointment. Nothing big. I'll just reschedule."

"Are you sure? Maybe you could take Gia with you?"

Mercedes considered it for a moment, taking Gia to her non-existent appointment so she could avoid Noah for another half hour. Or she could pretend she was running late for her fake appointment and scoot right out the door the minute he walked through it. That would work.

"I'll see if I can move it back a bit," she prattled to Heather, lying like the lying liar she was.

"Noah will be disappointed you can't stay." Heather sighed. "He called me too, wanting me to watch Gia. I think he wanted to surprise you tonight. Just a thank you, he said. He has tickets to a Jazz play-off game. You should go and take Gia! She might love it. And kiddos under three don't need tickets."

Mercedes's chest got hot and then cold, and sweat popped out on her top lip like condensation on a cold glass of lemonade in July.

Sure enough, Noah called Mercedes at 4:30, an hour before he was supposed to be home, to see if she was "game" for a night out. Apparently Mami had agreed to watch Gia.

Mercedes was prepared for his call and had already concocted the most convincing excuse she could come up with—a mandatory staff meeting at six o'clock. That way she could bustle out the door, and he wouldn't detain her. She also told Noah he should go without her—bring a coworker —and Mami could still watch Gia. Mami would be angry if Mercedes robbed her of a night with Gia.

Noah declined. He would give the tickets away; they'd been complimentary anyway.

"Come back after your meeting. We'll watch it on TV, and I'll grill some steaks," he suggested.

"Gloria is taking us all to dinner. Food makes listening to the boss a little easier to bear." Another prepared line. She would be eating alone in her room so Mami didn't pepper her with questions about Gia and Noah and why she wasn't at the game.

"You sound . . . manic, Mer," Noah said.

"What?" she cried, and winced. She did sound manic.

"Are you okay?"

"A little stressed. Nothing I can't handle. I'll see you at five thirty, okay?"

When he walked through the door at five twenty-five, she was prepared. His dinner was in the oven with the timer set, Gia was in her arms, and when he leaned in to kiss her, she purposely misinterpreted his body language and handed Gia to him, grabbing her purse and pressing her lips to his cheek.

"I'm sorry. I've got to go."

"I sowwy, Cowa," Gia babbled. Mercedes winced. She'd been saying that all day.

Noah blanched and looked down at his daughter.

"She just went potty—no accidents today—but it's been a while since she's eaten. She's hungry. Food is in the oven, so you don't have to fuss with dinner. Oh, and she didn't nap. She should go down early."

Noah watched her hurry away, standing on the front step of his narrow, two-story townhouse with the red door and the big tree, looking out over his tidy lawn with his squirming toddler in his arms.

"Bye-bye, Meh," Gia called. Mercedes waved and smiled, pretending to be in a terrible rush. Then she climbed into her car, pulled out of Noah's drive, and made it a block down the street before she burst into tears.

SIXTEEN

1993

C ora was waiting for Noah on the top step. Her hair hung around her shoulders, as vivid as the red leaves on the trees that warmed the hill behind The Three Amigos. When he'd flown in, the mountains below him had been alive with color. The mountains were alive, and his mother was dead.

Carole Stokes found her. Noah was grateful it hadn't been Mer or Alma. He knew Mer checked in on her, but Shelly Andelin wasn't an invalid. She was only thirty-eight years old. She didn't want Mer stopping by, and Mer had respected that. But when Shelly hadn't shown up for work two nights in a row, Carole had gone to the apartment to find her. Mer had let her in, but it was Carole who walked back into the bedroom and found Shelly huddled beneath the blankets, dead. She'd taken too many sleeping pills and they'd finally done their job. She'd gone to her eternal rest. Whatever that meant.

Noah had graduated from Basic Training at Lackland Air Force Base, lined up with hundreds of airmen all in blue with their perky flight caps. Everyone around him had someone there to congratulate him. Noah had no one, but at least his mother had waited for him to finish boot camp. He appreciated that. Perfect timing. She died in the one week he could handle the funeral arrangements and clear her belongings out of her apartment.

Their belongings. Their apartment. He would have to find a storage unit. Something small, though they didn't have much worth storing. And he would have to pay for her burial. Someone had suggested cremation, but Noah couldn't do it. His mother had hardly existed. He needed to give her a stone, if only to prove she'd lived. Maybe he did it for himself, but Shelly Andelin deserved something more permanent than ash.

"You look different," Cora said, smiling as he climbed the steps to the second-floor apartments. He'd climbed the steps thousands of times, but as he walked toward her, he found himself wishing he wouldn't reach the top. He wasn't ready.

"They fed us constantly. I exercised, and I ate. I gained twenty-five pounds." He had muscles on his muscles. He hardly recognized himself.

"You have pecs and your hair is gone."

Noah stopped on the step below her, and without hesitation, Cora wrapped her arms around him and held him tight.

He felt the grief rise, a sudden, surprising tsunami, taking him unaware. He should have known. The signs had all been there—he'd been drawing the tide into himself, quaking and rumbling, trying to come apart where no one would notice, where no one would see. But like an earthquake in the ocean, the waves had to hit landfall eventually. He'd expected Mer to be waiting. He'd wanted Mer. But Cora held him tight, her arms strong, her words soft, and when his tears threatened to wash him away, she kept him tethered to her, keeping him from drowning. When his tears slowed, she spoke again.

"Alma and Sadie cleaned the apartment. Everything is packed up and labeled. There's not much left for you to do."

"Where is she?"

"Sadie? She's at work. I told her I'd call the salon when you showed up. Do you want to go inside?"

He didn't. He wanted to walk back down the stairs. Or better yet, go find Abuela and put his head in her lap and let her tell him all about God and purpose and Heaven and Hell. All the things he didn't believe but still found comfort in, because Abuela believed enough for all of them. If Abuela said his mother was in God's arms, he wouldn't argue.

Cora took his hand, leading him forward, and she waited as he fished out his key.

Just as she'd said, the rooms were immaculate, the boxes stacked, the furniture worn and terribly forlorn. It wasn't worth saving. He walked on shaky limbs to his mother's room and stood in the doorway. Her bed had been stripped. The mattress was missing—he didn't want to contemplate why—and the box springs remained beside the nightstand where a little, wind-up alarm clock had once sat. His mother hadn't ever decorated. The walls had always been bare, and the apartment didn't feel much different than it had when she'd been in it.

He turned away from her room, unable to contemplate the emptiness a moment more. He walked toward his own room and stepped inside, feeling like a stranger in his own home. He'd left his room in good order, but he could see Mer had been there too. His sheets had been washed and his pillow plumped. The old carpet had been cleaned too. The ammo box he'd purchased a few years ago at an army surplus store remained on his dresser, but everything else was packed up. He walked to the ammo box and opened it. A few of his treasures remained inside. A valentine Mer made for him when he was nine years old, a dog-eared copy of Man's Search for Meaning, *a handful of pictures, and half of a geode from a rock mining expedition freshman year to Utah's west desert. The geode didn't look like much on the outside, but when he'd broken it in half, it was deep purple inside, and the coolest thing he'd ever seen. He'd had both halves once but had misplaced one somewhere.*

The ammo box was the only thing Noah wanted from his room. Everything else was cleared out, as if Mer had known he would need a place to sleep, but had wanted to relieve him of everything else.

"What now?" Cora said, sitting on his bed. Noah sat down beside her, the geode clutched in his hand. The edges were jagged and bit into his palm.

What now indeed.

"I go to New Mexico for Tech School. I'm on emergency leave right now. Maybe I'll be deployed. There's talk. The rent is paid through the end of the month. I'll stay here until after the funeral, and then I'll go." Carole Stokes had promised to handle the service itself, which was a relief to him. It would be a grave-side service—prayer, a few words, a song. He wondered if he could play the theme song to Night Court *on his guitar. It was a little too funky. And it needed horns. He laughed at the ridiculous train of*

his thoughts, but the laugh broke on a choked sob, and he ran a hand over his face. He wasn't going to cry again.

"There's nothing holding me here anymore. I guess I can go wherever I want," he whispered.

"You'll always have me . . . and Sadie. We love you. My mom, Alma, and Abuela love you too. We're your home. We'll always be home, whenever you need us," Cora said, and her voice was choked too. "Just . . . please . . . don't leave and never come back. Please don't do that."

He didn't know if he could promise to leave and never come back. At the moment, it was all he wanted to do. So he sat in silence for far too long, considering her request. When he finally spoke, he offered the only guarantee he could.

"I love your letters, Cora. Don't stop writing, okay? If you write, I'll always write back, and we'll stay connected. I look forward to your letters. You . . . surprise me."

"I do? Why?"

"You're different in your letters."

"Nah. I'm just me without restraints," she replied.

"You without restraints. What does that mean?"

"Words are like souls. Soundless, even shapeless. But full of substance. You are getting all substance and none of the distraction in a letter."

"See? That surprises me," he murmured. Her letters had been like that. Insightful. Illuminating. Even intoxicating.

She smiled at him, and he noticed again how pretty she was.

"You're lucky," she said.

"I am?" he asked, his voice wry. "How do you figure?"

"When my dad died, I wanted to move. I didn't want to stay in the apartment where he died. We left for a week, remember? The apartment was painted and recarpeted. Mom bought a new couch to make it feel like a different place. Dad's wheelchair was taken away, and all his things were cleared out. But it was hard living there, seeing him, even though I knew he was gone. You won't have to stay in this apartment, seeing your mother whenever you close your eyes. It will be good to leave it behind. I've never been able to leave my dad behind."

"I'm sorry, Cora." He'd never considered how hard it must have *been for her to live where her father had died.*

*She sighed. "I've made this about me. I'm good at that. I'm sorry."
She reached up and touched his face.*

"What I'm trying to say is, I'm glad you can leave this apartment behind. But don't leave us behind. Okay? Don't leave . . . me . . . behind."

He stared at her too long, the deep red of her lips, the clear blue of her eyes. Cora was all contrast while Mer was a warm blend. Then Cora leaned forward and placed her mouth on his, and all comparisons slid away for another time.

He didn't hear Mercedes slip quietly out of the apartment, as silently as she'd entered, leaving her two best friends sitting side by side on Noah's bed, her chest aching, her eyes wide open, her path set.

Mercedes avoided Noah all week. She didn't return his calls. Didn't respond to his messages. Didn't reach out at all. If he had done the same to her, she would have hunted him down and sliced off his fingers. She wouldn't have let him get away with it, and she knew eventually he would come looking for her. But by then he would realize what she was trying to tell him, and she wouldn't have to say the words.

She was ashamed of her cowardice. She cursed herself and called herself ugly names in both Spanish and English. But she didn't know what to do. At times, she would find herself lost in daydreams of wedding bells and cohabitation, only to shudder and cross herself for thinking it could work. And if it couldn't work, she wouldn't risk it. She needed to find her way back to the way it was before, to the Mer that Noah loved but didn't make love to, to the Mer that he needed, but didn't need too much. She wanted to be the Mer that would grow old beside him, platonic and persistent, the kind of friend he never outgrew.

He caught her between appointments at lunchtime on Friday, walking up to the counter at Maven, terse and tight-lipped, his timing impeccable. Grim face notwithstanding, he looked good. His pale blue dress shirt was tucked into fitted grey slacks, and he'd rolled the sleeves to his elbows and pulled off his tie. The color lightened his blue-black eyes and contrasted with his dark hair. The counter separated them, but she could smell him, clean and warm, like pine cones and peppermints—and her thoughts tiptoed back to the way he kissed and the way he felt and the way he made *her* feel, even when she was afraid. Remorse for avoiding him grew in her chest and climbed in her throat.

"Hey," she said weakly.

"Hey." He didn't smile, but he didn't scold. Not yet.

"I have an appointment at one o'clock. I don't have much time," she said.

"I'm your appointment."

Mercedes scowled down at the ledger, looking for his name.

"We can talk in the back, or we can talk with me in your chair, but we're going to talk, Mer," he murmured.

"Your name isn't on the schedule," she argued, still evading him.

"I was afraid if I used my name, I'd be pawned off to another stylist, and you wouldn't be here." She deserved that, but she shot him a glare anyway.

He regarded her patiently. "Are we going to do this here?"

"Let's go in the back," she relented, the knot factory in her stomach going into overdrive. She didn't want to talk to him on the open floor with ten stylists and their clients pretending they weren't listening in. He followed her at a comfortable distance, but she could feel his eyes on her back and his mouth in her memory, and she wondered if she could kiss him once more before she told him they should never kiss again.

But when they walked into the employee changing room, he didn't crowd her or try to take her in his arms. He sat down on the long bench and met her gaze.

Mercedes didn't sit. She was too unnerved. And disappointed.

"Do I need to find someone else to watch Gia on Mondays?" Noah asked. His voice was level and kind, and Mercedes imagined it was the voice he used with his patients, never getting ruffled, never losing his cool. She knew his patients yelled and screamed sometimes. She knew they cried, and she could picture Noah sitting with them, his face compassionate, his hands folded, looking at them the way he was looking at her.

"What? Why?" Mercedes said, remembering suddenly that he'd asked her a question.

"Because you're obviously avoiding me. You won't be able to continue to avoid me if you watch Gia on Mondays."

"Are you threatening me?" she asked, desperate to turn the conversation away from her own crappy behavior.

"Mer." He sighed. "Seriously?"

She began to pace. "Don't you get it? This—right here—is the reason why s-sleeping together was a t-terrible idea. Now you want to replace me! It's awkward, and you want a new babysitter. I knew this would happen. It's the reason I fought you so hard."

"You fought me so hard?" his voice rose mildly.

"Don't use that tone with me, Noah Andelin. I see right through you. So calm and kind. Well, I'm not falling for it."

"Falling for what, Mer?" No anger. No mockery.

"Falling for you!"

He stared up at her, eyes gentle, face calm. "It's too late. Isn't that what this is about? We've fallen for each other. And you don't know if that's what you want . . . if *I'm* what you want. And you don't know how to tell me."

Mercedes wanted him. She did. She wanted him so much. She folded her arms and unfolded them. She sat down and rose again, and he watched her, clearly waiting for her to confirm or counter his point. He sat with his legs slightly spread, elbows to knees, his chin resting on his clasped hands. Where did he find the confidence to just lay it all out there like that? Where did he find the courage?

"Remember when you had a few bad days? I came over and bossed you around. And you told me that . . . showering . . . was not what you needed?" Mercedes asked, grasping, trying to find the right thing to say to make him understand. The shower scene was a tricky one to navigate.

"Yes. And you informed me it was exactly what I needed. You were right."

"I was wrong," she argued.

"No, you weren't. I stunk. I hadn't showered or eaten in three days, and I was depressed. You were right."

"I was wrong because I didn't respect your boundaries," she countered, wagging her finger at him even though she was criticizing herself.

"My boundaries?"

"Yes," she said, firm.

"What boundaries? We've been best friends since we were eight years old. There *are* no boundaries. You just wanted what was best for me."

"But that's just it, Noah. Nobody gets to decide what's best for you, but *you*," Mercedes said, enunciating each word, loud and clear. "I decide what's best for me, you decide what's best for you, and if we don't respect that, then we have no relationship at all."

"You're so full of shit, Mer," he said quietly. If he'd snapped at her, the way she'd snapped at him, it would have been easier to take, but he said the words with such authority, such soft assurance, that it stung more than it otherwise would have.

"I have boundaries," Mercedes hissed. "You didn't respect them last week."

"You wanted to have sex with me, and I wanted to make love to you. Is that what you're talking about?"

"Yes! You make *love* to a girlfriend . . . or your wife. I'm not your wife!"

"I don't have a wife, Mer. I've come to terms with that. Have you?" He hadn't raised his voice, but his eyes gleamed.

"Yes. I have. But it's irrelevant. I am not your wife. Gia is not my daughter. And that is not our relationship. I need *you* to respect my boundaries, okay?"

He shook his head, incredulous, and unclasped his hands so he could stroke his beard the way he always did when he needed time to regroup or a moment to think. He stood abruptly, and for a minute she thought he was going to walk out. He didn't. He just stood with his back to her, his head down, his hands in his pockets.

His silence was so loud Mercedes wanted to scream at him to shut up. Her heart was pounding, and her palms were damp. She rubbed them on her skirt and headed for the door, desperate to move, to keep up with her pulse.

"I'll be at your house Monday morning. Early. As usual. No more Sunday sleepovers unless it's a double shift and you're gone. Also, your hair is getting long, and your beard needs a trim," she ordered, desperate to find her equilibrium and to help him find his. "We won't have time today. Text me, and I'll squeeze you in on Wednesday. And bring Gia. Her bangs are starting to fall in her eyes."

"So this is how it has to be?" he murmured, turning back toward her. The gleam was gone.

"Yes. This is how it has to be." She would re-establish Noah and Mer if it killed her.

He nodded slowly. "And if I'm not on board?"

"What does that mean?"

"What if I don't agree? What then? We do it your way or no way at all?"

Mercedes shrugged helplessly. "But . . . it'll be the way it's always been, like it was before." She heard the pleading in her voice and hated it. She shouldn't have to beg him to be her friend.

He nodded again, but he wasn't agreeing with her. He was nodding to let her know he heard. "The way it was before. Got it," he said, monotone.

"So we're good?" she asked, tentative.

He sighed and shook his head, resisting, but he said the words she wanted to hear, and she ignored the mixed message. "We're good, Mer."

"Yeah?" She felt a shiver of relief.

"Yeah." He didn't smile, and his eyes were bleak, but they weren't arguing, and he wasn't threatening to walk out of her life and take Gia with him. Mercedes could work with an unhappy Noah. It was no Noah at all that she couldn't bear. He would see. In the end, they would both be better off. Everything would be all right. She would make it all right.

Mercedes didn't have any early appointments on Wednesday, and Gloria was opening—she'd been opening since Keegan had left two months before. Mercedes walked into Maven at noon and was greeted by a beaming Gloria.

"He's back, Mercedes. He's back!"

Mercedes could only stare, her face blank, her breath trapped.

"What?"

"Keegan didn't like LA, and until he has something substantial lined up, he's promised to stay. This place has been buzzing all day. Word has spread, and we've had an endless stream of walk-ins and phone calls, all hoping to get on his schedule."

Mercedes began to cough on her rising dismay.

Gloria made a concerned face and patted her back. "Are you okay?"

Mercedes nodded and smiled numbly before rounding the reception area and walking back to the long row of gleaming stations. The place was packed, and Keegan was in her spot. His old spot had been absorbed in a new layout, and she'd been the only stylist not working that morning. It made sense that Gloria would put him in her station temporarily.

He was smiling and making suggestions, turning his client this way and that, but when he saw Mercedes, his smile slipped a fraction and he winked at the woman in his chair—in Mer's chair—and excused himself, snapping his fingers at one of the trainees and asking her to wash his client's hair and bring her back when she was done.

Mercedes strode past him and felt him fall in behind her. She was breathing, but not deeply enough, because her lungs were burning and her exhalations were hot.

"You're back," she said, pushing her way into the locker room.

"I am."

"That's not what you agreed to."

"Well, I have to make a living."

When she stared at him, dumbfounded, he ran his hands through his hair and tried again. "Look, Mercedes. I just . . . can't . . . I just . . . I don't want to go. My life is here. I'm happy here. People like me. I have clients and I make damn good money."

"Yeah . . . okay. Which brings us to the crux of the matter. You took twenty thousand dollars from me. Are you going to give it back?"

"I can't. I'm sorry. It's gone. I told you . . . I had a problem only money could fix."

"And Gia?"

He stared at her blankly for a heartbeat before his expression cleared. He hadn't known who she was talking about.

"I haven't decided," he lied.

"I see. And when will you decide?" She was so angry her voice was trembling, but she kept her eyes steady on his.

"I don't know, Mercedes. And it's really not any of your business. You inserted yourself into this, and I'm not going to be run out of town by you or anyone else," he snapped, as if she had done him wrong and not the other way around. "You want to talk terms, I'm all ears. But unless you're willing to part with some serious cash and some side benefits, I think I'll keep my options open."

Mercedes turned and strode from the room. Someone said her name, but she kept walking, her heels clacking, her stride long. She stopped in front of Gloria, who looked at her in surprise. There must have been something in her face, something in her eyes, because Gloria's face paled before she even began to speak.

"I've worked here since I was fourteen years old," Mercedes said quietly. "I've given Maven my heart and soul. I've given you my loyalty and my energy, Gloria, and you've always treated me well and made me believe I had a future here. But I won't work here with Keegan Tate. Either he goes, or I go."

"Mercedes," Gloria said, stunned. "Why?"

"He's a snake. He's a cheat. He's a liar."

"Oh, no. Did you sleep with him, honey?" Gloria whispered, reaching for her hand. Mercedes stepped back. "No. I have more self-respect than that. I'm smarter than that too. But I *did* trust him, and I paid pretty dearly for that trust. It won't happen again."

"Mercedes, come on." Keegan was standing in the arched opening between the style floor and reception. He'd apparently heard most of what she'd said.

"Keegan? What's this about?" Gloria said to him, her eyes wide. "What did you do?"

"Mercedes is the one with the issue. I'm just here to work and glad to be back," he answered mildly, folding his arms.

"Mercedes? Can you be more specific?"

Mercedes considered spilling the whole sordid story for all of five seconds, long enough for Keegan to pale and her protective instincts to kick in. She wouldn't be telling a single soul that Keegan Tate might be

Gia's biological father.

"I don't think Keegan would appreciate specifics, Gloria. He knows what he did. I know what he did. That will have to be enough."

"Mercedes, I-I can't just fire Keegan because you say so," Gloria stammered.

"All right. Then consider this my two-weeks' notice, Gloria," Mercedes said flatly. She turned and brushed past Keegan, who was smart enough to step out of her way.

"Oh, and I've got an appointment in five minutes, and I need Keegan out of my work station and as far away from me as possible. Otherwise, today will be my last, and don't think I won't tell all my clients that he's the reason I'm leaving."

For several days Mercedes swam in an eddy of outrage and despair only to find herself at outrage again. By the following Friday, four days from her final shift at Maven, she'd escaped the whirlpool only to be thrust headlong into quicksand. Her fear was a soul-sucking hole that worsened every time she made a move. And worst of all, she couldn't call for help. She hadn't told anyone what had happened. Her coworkers knew she was leaving, but none of them knew why. Her clients knew she was leaving—they'd all been given a card, and she had their contact information—but she hadn't filled them in either.

She'd quit her job. Her savings were severely depleted, and she had no immediate prospects. She'd never worked anywhere else but Maven, and she'd always had a plan. She didn't anymore. For the first time in her life, she had no idea what she was going to do.

She didn't want to work for someone else. She wanted to open her own place. Her clientele was huge, but many would not follow her to a new salon, simply because humans are creatures of habit. Many of her ladies would continue their patronage of Maven simply because it was what they'd always done. And if Mercedes didn't have a place to bring them, one that was comfortable and accommodating, she would lose even more. She couldn't take months to resettle. It had to be immediate. Seamless. And she had no prospects.

She'd been looking at retail spaces, crunching numbers, and making calls, but even amid her fears for her future, her thoughts had been filled with Noah. She missed him terribly, and for the first time in her life, she couldn't confide in him. She didn't know how. The story involved too many moving parts, too many secret pieces, and too much pain. Her story would cause *him* pain, and she couldn't tell it, not even to save herself.

Noah had said they were good, but they weren't good. She'd done what she'd promised herself she'd never do, she'd done what she'd intuitively known not to do. She'd slept with him, and she'd lost him. Maybe not forever. Maybe not completely. But their relationship was battered and bent, and at the moment, she didn't have the focus or the fortitude to smooth it out.

Her life was a mess, and opening the salon on Friday morning and seeing Cuddy hovering at the back entrance, waiting for her, just added another layer of chaos. She cried out, startled to see him, and immediately raised her hand in warning.

"I don't think you should come here anymore, Cuddy," she said, knowing she should run inside and lock the door behind her. But even as she considered it, her eyes traveled over his gangly form and his battered clothing, lingering on his grey head and his sorrowful blue eyes, and she couldn't find it in herself to be afraid.

"W-why not?" he stammered. "Aren't we friends anymore, Miss Lopez?"

"I'm not going to be working here much longer, Cuddy. Next Wednesday is my last day at Maven."

"Oh, no!" Cuddy cried. "Why? Where are you going?"

"I don't know. I haven't decided yet."

"Can you still give me a haircut?" he pleaded.

"Not today, Cuddy. It's only been a month since your last cut, and you and I need to talk." She pointed at the low wall that edged the rear parking lot, and motioned for him to sit. She perched beside him and took a deep breath, ready to begin her interrogation, but Cuddy spoke first.

"I'm worried about you, Miss Lopez."

"W-Why?" she stammered, surprised.

"Because . . . because Miss Cora is worried about you. That's why I . . ." his voice faltered.

"That's why you took my car?" she asked softly. He scrubbed at his cheeks and blinked rapidly several times before nodding, his shoulders drooping with his confession.

"But I didn't really take it. I was just . . . moving it."

"Cora's little girl was inside. You drove away and scared me to death. I was so scared, Cuddy. What you did was very wrong."

"It didn't feel wrong," he whispered. "It felt scary. But not wrong."

Mercedes shook her head. "Why did you do that, Cuddy?"

"I keep seeing her. I keep seeing Miss Cora. She's afraid for her daughter. She's afraid for you and Noah. I thought she wanted me to."

"Why did you leave the rocks? You had to know I would think of you."

"I wanted to tell you I was sorry. I didn't mean to scare you or the little girl. Sometimes I don't know what to do. I try . . . but I make the wrong choice."

"It was definitely the wrong choice."

"It didn't feel wrong," he whispered again. "And I left you my best rocks. One for you, one for Gia, and one for Noah. I'm sorry for Noah, most of all."

"Have you been following me, Cuddy?"

"No . . . not really. You've got a car. I've only got my two feet." He held up one of his boots, the soles held on with duct tape, and Mercedes sighed.

"We need to get you a new pair of shoes, Cuddy. Those ones are dead."

"Yep. They done give up the ghost," Cuddy agreed. "Noah gave me his shoes once. Did you know that, Miss Lopez?"

"He told me," Mercedes said. "Noah doesn't like to see people suffer."

"Noah is a good boy. A good man," Cuddy corrected himself. "He gave me his sweatshirt and his socks and shoes. He gave me his coat. He even gave me my first rock. After that . . . I started collecting them because they made me feel safe. Kept me from floating . . . you know."

"He gave you your first rock?" Mercedes couldn't help but smile. Sometimes Cuddy was so child-like, and something about him pulled at her. It always had.

"Yeah. It was in his coat pocket. I've kept it ever since." Cuddy dug into the pocket of his worn jeans and pulled out half of a broken geode, it's purple crystals peeking out like a tiny fairy castle encased in a globe of stone.

"I was there when he found that," Mercedes said, oddly moved. "It looked like a regular grey rock. Then he hit it with the pick, and it cracked open. Noah was thrilled."

"Should I give it back to him?" Cuddy held out his hand, the geode sitting on his palm. "Maybe he didn't mean to give it to me."

"Why don't you ask him yourself? He knows who you are," Mercedes said. "He knows your real name."

"He does?" Cuddy stammered. "I always s-stayed away from him because I thought it would scare him if he recognized me. People said I did some bad things."

"Taking my car was a bad thing. The police told me to call them if you came back here."

Cuddy nodded slowly, but he stood and began to inch away, as if preparing to run. "I understand."

"I'm not going to do that, Cuddy. I'm not going to call the police."

He stopped short. "You're not?"

"No. I'm not. But I need you to promise me you won't do something like that again. It might not feel wrong, but it is wrong. Do you understand why?"

"I scared you."

"It was the worst moment of my life."

"Worse than when Miss Cora died?"

"Worse than that, Cuddy."

"I'm sorry, Miss Lopez. See . . . I've been staying close to the salon because Miss Cora wants me to. I saw you pull into the gas station across the street." His mouth twisted with emotion, and he rubbed his face again, clearly anxious. "He was watching you too. He was sitting in his car in front of the salon, watching you. I was afraid he was going to take the baby."

"Who?" Mercedes asked, flummoxed.

"Keegan."

"Keegan was watching me?"

"Yeah. He was watching you . . . and I was watching him. He's weak, Miss Lopez. He's weak like I am."

"What do you mean, Cuddy?" Mercedes was reeling, trying to keep up with Cuddy's train of thought while processing his revelations.

"People like Keegan . . . people like me . . . we don't know how to handle our shit." He grimaced. "Sorry, Miss Lopez. We take pills to forget and pills to hide and pills to feel better. I don't take them anymore. But he does," Cuddy accused. "Keegan does. And he sells them too."

SEVENTEEN

1993

*T*hey didn't cry for Shelly Andelin. They didn't know her well enough. They cried for Noah, standing beside her grave in his dress blues, his cap in his hands, as he did his best to eulogize her. He gave a brief life history—born, lived, worked, died—while trying to humanize and personalize a woman who had withheld herself from almost everyone and everything.

Carole Stokes had praised Shelly's steadiness and her work ethic, her reliability, and her loyalty. Carole became emotional when recounting how she met young Shelly Andelin, heavily pregnant, without a friend in the world and nowhere to go, and how her son now stood, fully-grown, a credit to her and a blessing to everyone who knew him. If our children are the gauge of a successful life, Carole said, Shelly had done just fine.

When Carole was finished, Noah looked to Mercedes, his throat working, and Mercedes stepped forward like she'd promised she would, the box of coffee mugs in her arms. It was silly, but it was something. She'd had the idea when she was packing up Shelly Andelin's things, and Noah had embraced it, even smiling when she made the suggestion.

"Shelly Andelin never had much to say, and for a woman of few words, I found her penchant for motivational coffee mugs . . . endearing," Mercedes said, struggling to say the right thing. "You are all the people who cared about her. Noah and I think she would want you to have something that was hers . . . a small part of her life . . . something to remember her by. She wasn't good at conversation, and maybe you never had the opportunity to have a cup of coffee with Shelly. But now . . . we'll all have a cup together . . . and remember her fondly."

Mercedes began passing Shelly's mugs, one at a time, to the group huddled around the open grave. Alma and Abuela followed behind, filling each cup with coffee from two large thermoses. There were mugs of every color, but it wasn't the varied shades that made them remarkable. Each mug was stamped with a different quote. They weren't cute and pithy or even funny, nor were they the rag-tag assortment everyone tends to accumulate over time. It was a very specific collection, as though Shelly had chosen each message carefully.

The sayings printed on the ceramic mugs were the kind you'd find on sappy greeting cards, the kind most people skimmed over if they read them at all. They were flowery phrases full of hope and poetic wisdom, and Mercedes had read each one as she'd washed and boxed them up, her wonder growing at Shelly Andelin's selections. The sentiments on the mugs weren't repeated or reflected anywhere else in Shelly's life. Not on the walls of her home, or the words that she spoke, or the shows that she watched. She hadn't kept a journal or read the Bible; the only books in the apartment were in Noah's room, stacked against his wall. But Shelly's mugs each gave a small sermon, as if her daily coffee was the closest she got to religion, and Mercedes had been fascinated by them.

Mercedes handed a mug to Noah, to Cora, and finally to Mami and Abuela, who filled their own cups and then filled the cup Mercedes had kept for herself. She wouldn't be parting with it. It had been the last mug in the cupboard, and Mercedes had gasped, thinking Abuela's words of wisdom had somehow become commercialized. But the quote on Shelly's mug wasn't the same as Abuela's at all. It said: "In the end, only three things matter: How much you loved, how gently you lived, and how gracefully you let go of things not meant for you."

Mercedes had stared at the powder blue mug with its melancholy quote, and she'd pondered why Shelly had chosen it. How much had Shelly Andelin really loved? She'd lived so gently she'd barely lived at all. And Mercedes didn't know if it was grace or fear, but Shelly had clearly let go *of everything in her life but Noah. In the end, she'd released him too. May-be she'd believed there was nothing meant for her.*

When every cup was filled, Mercedes raised her mug. "To Shelly An-delin. You will be missed."

"To Shelly," they all agreed. The mugs were lifted in unison, and the mourners sipped, quietly sharing a cup with the woman who usually drank alone.

"Dr. Noah, it's Moses Wright." His voice was an uncomfortable rumble, and Noah would have known it even if he hadn't identified himself.

"Moses, how are you?" Noah was thrilled to hear from him. He'd worried about him and wondered how he was faring.

"I'm alive, Doc. Tag's alive, though he has a tendency to find trou-ble."

"Where are you? Can I help you with something?"

"We're in France. And safe . . . at least for now."

None of us are safe. The words trembled in Noah's mind, an odd memory rising from years past. He pushed it away, needing to focus on Moses and the reason he was calling.

"France?"

"France. We've been to London, Ireland—Belfast and Tag didn't mix —and tomorrow we're heading to Spain. Tag has this desire to run with the bulls."

Noah groaned.

"Yeah. That's what I told him," Moses quipped. He sounded good. Light. And then he got to the purpose of his call, and the heaviness re-turned to his young voice.

"So, Doc. Cora . . . I'm seeing her again, all of a sudden."

Noah braced himself. Lately, every sentence that started with Cora's name brought him grief. He rubbed at his beard.

"What do you mean, Moses?"

"She keeps showing me Lopez."

"Mercedes?" Noah gasped.

"Yeah. Your little friend."

Noah almost laughed out loud. He pictured Al Pacino in Scarface saying, "Say hello to my little friend," as he wielded a grenade launcher. Somehow, the comparison of Mer to a grenade launcher wasn't too far off the mark. But Moses wasn't laughing.

"Did Lopez show you the pictures I drew the day she came to see me at Montlake, Doc?"

"Yeah. She did."

Moses cursed, his relief evident across two continents and an ocean. "Good. I didn't know how . . . shit."

"Moses?"

"The paper dolls. You saw those?" Moses pressed.

Noah thought about the drawings, the connected figures. Him, Mer, and Cora. Him, Mer and Gia. Almost like Cora was giving them her blessing. The thought eased something inside of him. He hadn't allowed himself to interpret the picture that way. But maybe . . . now he could.

"The man in the one picture? Cora keeps showing me that man." Moses interrupted Noah's thoughts.

"The man?" Noah didn't understand.

"Yeah. Uh, you know. The paper dolls. The picture I drew with Cora, the little girl, and the man. Together. Cora keeps showing me his face. Do you . . . know who he is?" Moses asked, his words so constricted it made Noah's throat tight.

"Cora's showing you images of Mer with a man?" Noah asked.

"Yeah, but not . . . together. I think Lopez is in trouble."

Noah was silent, thoughts whirling. Moses hadn't ever called him. He wouldn't have called him unless he was seriously concerned.

"Doc, I gotta go. I'll try to call tomorrow. But no promises. We'll be on the train for most of the day. If I don't see her again, then that's the best I got. I can't tell you anything more. But I'll call when I can . . . just to make sure everything is okay. Tell Lopez hello."

"Thank you, Moses," Noah said, but the line was already dead.

It took Noah ten minutes to get out the door. It was bedtime, but he couldn't wait for morning. Gia's clothes needed to be changed, she pulled off one sock before he could put on the other, and she squalled when he tried to make her wear shoes.

"We're going for a ride, Gia Bug. Come on, help Daddy," he begged.

"No wide," she grumbled. "No sooz."

"We're going to see Mer, and you have to wear shoes if you want to walk."

"Meh!"

"Meh," he whispered. He didn't know whether to be angry or afraid. He settled on both.

He didn't tell Mer they were coming, and she was surprised to see them. Happy to see them. Her teeth flashed, and her right cheek dimpled, and the weariness he saw in her face lifted. Her pleasure hurt Noah's chest and made him even angrier. She was holding a cup of coffee, and she stepped back from the door to let them in and reached for Gia, who reached right back. Noah brushed past her and set Gia down in the middle of her living room instead. He was there for a reason, and he didn't want either of them getting comfortable, though Gia had plopped down and was already tugging at her shoes.

"Is there a reason you're being a baby hog, Boozer?" Mer asked, surprise underlining her teasing. Noah moved in on her immediately.

"I need to see the pictures Moses gave you at Montlake. All of them." If he'd had any doubt she'd kept something from him, he didn't have any now. Mer's eyes widened, and her mouth tightened. Her poker face snapped into place a second later, but he'd seen enough. She pivoted obediently, walking to the china cabinet in her dining room. Noah followed on her heels. Setting her coffee cup aside on the dining room table, she opened a drawer in the cabinet and withdrew a thin folder. Noah yanked it from her hands.

"Noah!" she cried. Blood welled up in a long, thin line across her fingers. He'd pulled the folder too hard and sliced her finger. He set the folder down and took her hand in his, pulling her toward the kitchen sink. He ran her fingers under the cold water, still angry, still confused, but disgusted with himself. She was bleeding, and it was his fault.

"It's a paper cut. I'll survive," she clipped, but he could hear the fire beneath the ice.

"You didn't show me all the drawings, Mercedes." He turned off the water and tugged a dish towel from the rack. The towel was red and wouldn't stain. He wrapped it around her hand and moved to her medicine cabinet to the left of the fridge where he knew she kept her Band-Aids.

"So you come in here, stomping and barking and withholding baby hugs?" she snapped.

As if on cue, Gia strolled in, shoeless. "Meh!" she squealed.

"Mercedes," Noah said, feeling the walls closing in. "I need to see those pictures."

"Suit yourself." She pointed to the dining table where he'd set the folder and stooped to pick up Gia.

He walked back to the folder, Mercedes snuggling Gia like none of it mattered. Maybe she held her too tight or maybe it was just the attention span of a toddler, but Mercedes radiated a tension Gia wasn't used to, and Gia squawked and demanded to be released. Mercedes complied, and Gia scampered off, most likely to unload the basket of toys Mer kept for her visits. Mercedes approached him, her arms folded defensively, waiting for him to find what she'd hidden.

The picture was on the bottom of the small stack of drawings, like she'd tried to bury it and forget about it. It had the same flavor and flow as the other paper doll drawings, but it was not Noah's face or form attached to his tiny family. He stared at it in horror, recognition dawning.

"Do you know what this means?" he whispered, raising his eyes to Mercedes.

Her eyes were wet and wide, her teeth clenched to keep her mouth from trembling. When she spoke, her voice was soft, but she made no excuses for herself and gave no apology.

"When Moses drew that picture, I knew . . . I knew it couldn't mean anything good. Not for Cora, or you, or Gia. So I put it in that drawer, and I haven't looked at it again. I can't help Cora anymore. But I can protect you and Gia."

"You can protect me?" Noah scoffed.

"I can try."

"Moses drew this picture months ago. And you kept it from me. All this time."

"Yes. I did," she said, defiant.

"Why?"

"Why?" she repeated, incredulous. She laughed, but the laugh broke and shuddered like a sob. "You've been through hell. Cora didn't just *die*. That's hard enough. There's a good chance she killed herself. That's a thousand times harder. And just when I was starting to come to terms with it—when *you* were coming to terms with it—she gives you that?" She pointed at the picture. "Cora wasn't ever cruel. But that is cruel, and I didn't want any part of it. If she had a confession to make, too bad. She missed her chance, and I was not going to make it for her. Not this time. Not ever again."

Tears were streaming down her face, and she swiped at them, frustrated. Mercedes had never been prone to tears. Anger, passion, laughter, but rarely tears. In the twenty-two years he'd known her, he'd seen her cry only a handful of times. That had changed with Cora's death. In the last year, she'd cried more than all the other years combined. And more often than not, they were tears for him.

"Mer . . . you can't make those kinds of choices for me. How am I supposed to trust you?" he rasped.

"Trust me?" She pressed her hand to her chest. "Me?" she cried. "I would do just about anything for you, Noah. Haven't you figured that out yet?"

"This is Keegan Tate. This is a picture of Keegan Tate with *my* wife and daughter." Noah shook the paper in her face, so incensed he could only stare, trembling, at the innocent rendering. "You should have told me."

"Told you what? That your wife had an affair with Keegan Tate? Why would I do that?" she asked again.

"Because I deserve to know!"

"You're right. You did deserve to know. But I didn't want to be the one to tell you."

"Who else was going to tell me, Mer?" he choked.

"After I saw that picture, I went to Keegan, and I asked him if he had an affair with Cora. He admitted to . . . to sleeping with her . . . a few times. He said the relationship was short. Not serious. And she broke it off with him before you left for Afghanistan."

"I see. So you went to Keegan, but you didn't come to me." Noah was so upset he was shaking, and he set the picture down, unable to face it any longer.

"I couldn't . . . protect you . . . or Gia . . . if I didn't know what I was dealing with. I had to know."

"You didn't protect me! You betrayed my trust. I feel like a fool, like everything between us is pretense. I don't need you to take care of me, Mer. Okay? I need you to love me enough to tell me the truth, even when it's ugly."

She stared at him numbly, tears dripping from her chin. She shuddered and turned away, a sob escaping from her lips. When she spoke, her voice shook and her words were strangled.

"You knew she was unfaithful, Noah. Don't pretend you didn't. It was the thing you wouldn't say in the cemetery. And I respected that. I understood it. And I left it alone."

"I didn't know it was Keegan Tate! Hell, I don't even know if Keegan was the only one. I found out at Gia's well-check last March that Gia couldn't be mine. Our blood types don't jive. Did you know that, Mer? Did you know Gia isn't my daughter?" He was crying now too, and Mercedes spun to face him.

"Oh, Noah," Mercedes moaned, reaching for him. "Why didn't you tell me?"

"Why didn't I tell *you*?" he gasped. "Because it was none of your business! I wasn't withholding information about *you*."

She dropped her hand immediately and stepped back. "Okay. I see. So that weekend, when I came over and you were in a bad way, that was just after you found out. And everything that happened next—everything that has happened since—was about you getting back at Cora. You were mad at Cora, so you had sex with me."

"This is not about you!"

"Then why are you so angry with me?" she shouted back. "What have I ever done to you but love you? My entire life, I have loved you and Cora. And now I love your daughter as if she were my own. So don't you dare tell me this is not about me!"

Noah was too upset to think rationally, too distraught and dismayed not to say more words he didn't mean. He swiped at the powder blue coffee cup sitting on the table, and watched as it clattered to the floor, shattering as it struck the colorful tiles Mercedes had laid herself. Then he strode to Gia, swung her up in his arms, and pushed his way out of Mercedes's front door, not even stopping to locate Gia's shoes or find her sweater, not looking back at his best friend who had made no move to stop him from leaving.

Noah wanted to kill him. He drove aimlessly, Gia asleep in her seat, the night soothing, the radio soft. His anger billowed and blasted and slowly dissipated out the open window into the night air. June in Utah was beautiful. Not too hot. Not too cold. He let the breeze caress him and whisper reassurances.

Keegan Tate. Gia's father was Keegan Tate.

Cora could really pick 'em.

Oddly, as Noah's anger ebbed—he'd never been particularly good at holding onto it—his relief grew. Now he knew. Part of the agony was the faceless threat. Someone suddenly appearing out of the blue, and threatening his daughter—threatening him—with a custody suit. It was a relief to know what he was dealing with. Keegan Tate was no threat. If he suspected Gia was his—and he would have, knowing the timeline and his own involvement—he'd never said a word or so much as blinked in her direction.

Mercedes hadn't done anything wrong.

He was angry because he felt like a fool. He was embarrassed. He was in love with Mer, and she'd kept something very important from him. Something that she should have showed him. Something their relationship demanded she reveal.

But Mer had been trying to protect him, to protect Gia, and she had seen no point in stomping on Cora's memory. Hadn't he said the very same thing at the cemetery? The truth is, they were both still trying to take care of Cora. Maybe it was time they stopped.

He hadn't told Mercedes about the day at the pediatrician. He'd kept that from her, and regardless of what he'd said, it worked both ways. Mer had been given a picture, drawn by a psych patient who claimed to commune with the dead. It wasn't a whole hell of a lot to go on, to destroy someone's reputation over, or to break his heart with. He probably would have done the same in her shoes.

Thoughts of Moses brought back the conversation that had started it all.

I think Lopez is in trouble.

"Damn it!" Noah said out loud, realizing he'd driven away from Mer's house in such a snit, he'd forgotten why he'd gone in the first place.

"Damn it," a little voice said from the back seat, and Noah sighed heavily. He had completely failed at life today. He'd thought Gia was asleep. He looked in his rearview mirror, and she smiled and kicked her bare feet. He was half an hour from home, driving aimlessly, and Mercedes might be in trouble.

"Let's go find Mer," he said, turning the car around.

"Go Meh!" Gia clapped.

Noah called Mercedes and waited as her phone rang and rang and eventually went to voice mail. No Mer. He'd left her house two hours ago. It was now midnight. She was probably in bed. Where he should be. Where Gia should be. He'd rolled up the window and turned down the radio and Gia had fallen asleep in her car seat once more. But Noah had a nervous prickling in his gut, and his mind wouldn't settle. He didn't want to leave things the way they were. He also needed to make sure she was okay. Moses Wright wouldn't have called him for nothing. He drove to her house and sat, staring at her darkened windows, feeling like an idiot. He climbed out and lifted Gia from her seat. She lay limply against his shoulder and didn't stir when he knocked on Mer's door.

He knocked for several minutes but no one answered. He tried her phone again. Several times. He didn't know what to do. He knocked harder and rang the bell. Alma came to the door, bleary eyed, wielding a broom like a bludgeon. She put it down when she saw him.

"Alma, I'm sorry. Mercedes and I argued. I'm worried about her."

She stared at him wearily. "You made her cry, Noah."

"I know."

"It's very late."

"I know that too. I'm tired. Gia's tired. But I need to see Mercedes. Will you let me in?"

"She's not here."

"Are you lying to me, Alma? Did Mer tell you to lie? Because I'm worried. I need to know if she's all right. If she's in her room, angry with me, that's fine. But if she's not, then I need to find her."

"You love her," Alma said.

"Yes. I do."

"She loves you."

"I know."

"So marry her!" she snapped. "Marry her, and give Gia a mother. Give me a grandchild!"

"I would marry Mercedes tomorrow if she would have me."

"Sí?" Alma gasped.

"Yes. But she . . ." Noah wasn't sure if he could explain. He didn't understand it himself, why Mer was fighting him so hard, why she resisted the obvious.

"She is stubborn," Alma supplied.

"Yes."

"And afraid."

"Yes. I think so," he sighed.

"She's not here, Noah."

"Okay. Then I need to find her."

"You leave the bebe. Go find my daughter."

He sighed. He eased Gia into Alma's arms, knowing she would be better off in a bed than driving around with him.

"Do you have any idea where she went?" he asked

"She said something about Keegan and the salon," Alma murmured, kissing Gia's soft head.

"Keegan?" The nervous flutter in his stomach became an angry swarm. "I thought Keegan Tate had left Maven."

"He did. But he's back, and Mercedes is looking for a new job. She wouldn't tell me what happened, but she's been upset."

"Damn it, Alma. Why hasn't she called me? Why hasn't she told me any of this?"

"She needs to be strong. She needs to fix things. She's good at loving, but she's not very good at being loved. You will have to convince her, Noah."

EIGHTEEN

1995

"*N*oah?"

The man turned, scooping up the ball as he did, and Mercedes let out a whoop that ricocheted throughout the whole complex.

"*Noah!*" *she shrieked. The exhaustion she'd felt only minutes before was replaced with heady euphoria. He was home. He was home! Then she was running, not caring that she might break a heel—or her ankle—flying across the grass between the parking lot and the concrete court where he stood beneath the paltry lights, waiting for her.*

"*The girl can still move! Slow down, Mer,*" *Noah said laughing, closing the last few steps and swinging her up into his arms, squeezing her tight as she buried her face in his shoulder and prayed he'd never let go. She wrapped her legs around him so he couldn't release her, making him laugh harder, and rained kisses on his scruffy cheeks.*

"*What is this fuzz you're growing on your face?*" *she crowed.*

"*I haven't shaved since we left Kuwait. I'm not shaving again until I absolutely have to.*"

"*I like it,*" *Mercedes declared.*

"*Me too.*" *He pulled back but didn't set her down and gazed into her beaming face.*

"I missed you so damn much," Noah said.

"I missed you too, you big, dumb idiot," she whispered, trying not to get emotional, calling him names to keep her tears at bay. "Why didn't you tell me you were going to be back today? I was expecting you next week. I had big plans for a welcome home fiesta with food, folks, and fireworks."

"That's why I didn't tell you." He laughed again. "I didn't want a big shindig. I wanted to surprise you. Plus, this right here? This is the best welcome home you could have given me. Although I gotta say," he bounced her in his arms like she was a fussy child, "you're a little heavier than I remember. What are you up to now? One oh five, soaking wet?"

"It's the shoes," she said, giggling. "They weigh five pounds apiece. But I look amazing in them."

"Let me see," he said, and set her on her feet. She stepped back, releasing him, and twirled.

"Yep. Amazing. But can you play ball in them?" Noah leaned down and grabbed the ball, bouncing it expertly between his legs before he tossed it to her. She strutted like Ru Paul on the runway, dribbling as she went, before stopping, posing, and throwing the ball up like she'd practiced the move a thousand times. The ball dropped through the hoop, and Noah crowed, and they were immediately enmeshed in a game of HORSE. It soon became a game of TRUTH. Instead of gaining a letter when you failed to make a shot, you had to admit a truth. They'd been playing the game for as long as they'd known each other, but still managed a few new confessions. Being apart for the last year provided some new fodder.

"'Fess up, Noah," Mercedes taunted after Noah missed a shot she'd banked in." Truth? I got here two hours ago, Abuela made me dinner, and I ate everything. Even the part she told me to save for you."

Mercedes gasped in mock horror. "But I'm starving!"

"Abuela also told me if I waited out here, I would be able to see you coming. Still driving the Corolla, I see."

"If it ain't broke," Mercedes quipped. "That Corolla and I are going to grow old together. She's given me her best years, and I'm not going to abandon her just because she's ugly."

"Loyal to a fault," Noah said, taking several steps back so he was in three-point range.

"Always. You're ugly. And I've never turned my back on you."

"This game is called TRUTH, Mer. Truth. And I am a beautiful man. However, you haven't ever turned your back on me. That part's true enough." He let the ball go, and it flew home, nothing but net.

Mercedes tried to make the same shot and missed. It was her turn to supply a truth.

"Truth," she said. *"I didn't really have a shindig planned. Food, yes. Fireworks, possibly. But no folks. I didn't want to share you."*

Noah stopped dribbling and approached her with a soft smile. She smiled back, and tried to steal the ball. He gave it to her instead.

"You never change, Mer," Noah said quietly. *"That's one of the things I love about you. While I was waiting, I worried that maybe things would be awkward or that things wouldn't be the same. But they are. You are. And I can't tell you how happy that makes me."*

"Truth? I love you more than any Caucasian male on this planet. That won't ever change. Even though you ate my dinner," Mercedes said.

"What about Hispanic males? Or Asian males? Or African males? Is there something you aren't telling me? Have you fallen in love with someone while I was gone?" He waggled his eyebrows expectantly, but there was an odd look on his face.

"Truth?" she asked.

"Truth," he replied.

"I'm never going to fall in love. It's too messy."

Noah nodded slowly, his eyes narrowed, and Mercedes turned and put up another shot. But somewhere between truth and flat-out lies, the game had suddenly come to an end. She fetched her own rebound and tossed the ball to Noah. He bounced it right back.

"It's yours. I took it from the top shelf in your closet. Talk about messy."

Mercedes scoffed. Her closet—her whole room—was pristine.

"You want to come inside?" she asked. *"Or maybe we could hit Taco Bell for some sixty-nine cent burritos. You owe me dinner."*

"And the final truth of the night . . . I've got to go. Heather knows I'm in town. I called her to get Cora's schedule. She had a late class, but she should be home now."

"Okay. I'll put dinner on your tab," Mercedes teased.

"Come with me," he urged.

"No. I'll see you tomorrow. Or Sunday. I've had my turn. Go see Cora."

"Is everything okay between you two? You both wrote faithfully, but neither of you talked about the other. I started wondering if maybe there was something up."

"We don't see each other as much as we used to. Since she and Heather moved out of The Three Amigos, it's not as easy to just drop by. Cora's in school. I'm working." Mercedes shrugged. "But we talk at least once a week."

He seemed reluctant to leave. "Come with me," he repeated. "It will be like old times. Just the three of us."

"It won't be like old times," she hedged. "Some things haven't changed . . . but other things have."

He searched her eyes, waiting for her to elaborate.

"You and Cora?" she pressed. He had to know she knew. Cora hadn't kept it a secret.

He nodded slowly, though Mercedes wasn't sure if he was confirming the new relationship or just letting her know he heard.

"You won't change your mind?" he asked quietly.

"No. You go," she insisted.

He nodded again, and something rippled across his features and was gone.

"Tomorrow?" she asked.

"Always," he answered. He gave her a quick, hard hug, and loped away, leaving her standing alone beneath the streetlamp, holding her ball.

Mercedes cried when Noah left. Maybe it was the coffee mug he broke, the mug she'd saved from his mother's collection, the mug with the words that had become a bit of a mantra in the last ten years. *In the end, only three things matter. How much you loved, how gently you lived, and how gracefully you let go of things not meant for you.*

The irony of the quote was not lost on her now.

Mercedes had loved hard, she'd lived the best way she knew how, and she'd never taken something that wasn't hers. And look where it got her. She picked up the broken pieces of the mug, hoping it could be saved, and cried harder when she realized it could not.

Maybe her tears were not for the old coffee cup. Maybe it was the weeks—the months—of strain, the intense emotions, the loss of everything she'd worked for, and the change in her relationship with Noah. Whatever the reason, she sank to the sofa in her aging duplex, a thousand square feet that housed everything she owned and nothing—besides Mami—that she couldn't leave behind. This was her life, and she was overwhelmed with the emptiness of it all. Used, re-used, shined up, fixed and refashioned. It was all clean. All bright. She'd done her best with the space, and it reflected her taste and her knack for making something out of nothing. But looking around through tear-filled eyes, through sobs that wracked her chest and left her drained, she felt nothing but despair.

She turned her face into the couch cushions, shutting it all out. She should go to bed. She should sleep. Maybe then she wouldn't see Noah's shattered expression and re-hash their argument over and over in her head. But she didn't think she would be able to sleep. She needed to move, to work, to do something—anything—to take her mind from her troubles. She heard Mami come in from work and tiptoe to the couch where she was huddled.

"Estás durmiendo?" Mami whispered, touching her back.

"No," Mercedes muttered, turning her face a little so her mother could hear her. "I'm not sleeping."

"Qué pasa?"

"I'm fine, Mami," Mercedes lied. "Just tired. Just a little emotional. I think I'm going to go to Maven tonight and do the inventory. I don't have to do it. It's Keegan's job now . . . but it's been my job for so long, my pride won't let me leave it undone. And I don't think I'm going to be able to sleep anytime soon."

"Were Noah and the bebé here?" Gia's boots were sitting in the middle of the floor where she'd pulled them off. Seeing them made Mercedes's heart ache and her eyes shimmer. She turned her face back into the couch cushions so her mother wouldn't see.

"Yes. They were. But they left."

"Without shoes?"

"It's July, Mami. Gia will survive without her snow boots."

Alma patted her back and said nothing more, climbing the stairs to her room with a tired, "Te amo, Mercedes."

"Te amo, Mami," Mercedes whispered, and even saying the words she'd said a million times hurt. Everything hurt. *Enough of that.* She pulled herself from the couch, stepped over Gia's little boots, and headed for the kitchen. She needed coffee, and then she would head to Maven and work until she was too tired to feel hopeless.

The pictures Moses had drawn were scattered across the table. Had she done that or had Noah? They'd both been so upset. The picture of Keegan, Cora, and Gia was crumpled in the corner where Noah had clutched it in his fist. Mercedes reached for it, smoothing out the angry wrinkles. She considered destroying it, ripping it into tiny pieces, and then she sighed, knowing she wouldn't. It would be like burning a Picasso because she didn't care for his paintings. It was art, drawn by a remarkable artist, and she couldn't find it in herself to destroy it, even if she hated what it represented.

She tucked the drawing into the folder, thumbing through the other pictures as she stacked them. She wished she could frame the picture Moses had drawn of the three amigos. She would hang it along with the picture of Noah, Mercedes, and Gia, in full view, so no one had to hide. So no one had to wonder where they fit. Maybe then they could all be a family without questioning if it was okay, if it was all right.

Her eyes filled again. She picked up the picture of the flag draped coffin, so detailed and so tragic, the dog tags framing the scene. That picture, more than any other, symbolized the event Cora could never get beyond. Maybe showing Moses those images was Cora's way of explaining a lifetime of struggle.

"We knew, Cora. We always knew. You don't have to explain," Mercedes murmured, talking to her friend the way she found herself doing from time to time. She moved on to the next picture—simplistic by comparison—of the five stones. At the time, Mercedes had interpreted them as river rocks, smooth and unassuming, piled innocently atop one another. She'd seen the rocks and imagined the river where Cora's car had landed in

Emigration Canyon.

Looking at them now, she thought of Cuddy and his pockets full of gravel. She thought of the five smooth stones he'd given her as payment the day she'd told him Cora was gone, the rocks she'd then placed on Cora's grave. One rock for each of them—Cora, Noah, Gia, Mercedes . . . and Cuddy. As if they were all connected.

But they weren't connected.

And maybe that was the reason she cried. If anything they were all as shattered, disconnected, and broken as Shelly Andelin's old coffee mug.

Mercedes shoved the drawings back in the drawer, unwilling to dwell on them a minute longer. She grabbed her purse, shoved her feet into a pair of cheetah print wedges, and stopped in front of the mirror to fix what was left of her makeup. Five minutes later she was pulling out of her driveway. She had work to do.

Mercedes didn't want to park in the employee lot. It felt too vulnerable, like she was broadcasting to everyone that she was inside. She'd been jittery and uptight since Keegan had returned, afraid in a way that wasn't normal for her, afraid in a way that made her do things like park one block over so he wouldn't see her car and walk to the salon, letting herself in through the front door and locking it behind her while she disabled the alarm.

These days she was consumed by "last-time-itis." *This is the last time I'll close shop. This is the last time I'll open. This is the last time I'll cut so and so's hair or go to lunch with my coworkers.* Tonight would be the last time she logged in the inventory and made an order for the upcoming month. There was no part of running a salon/spa that she wasn't familiar with. That was something she could be proud of. From payroll to pedicures, she'd done it all, and the thought suddenly infused her with calm. She had a skill set. She would be okay. Even after Maven.

She walked through the darkened space, not bothering to illuminate anything other than the back hall that led to the storage room. The warehouse just right of the employee parking lot was now being rented out as a Cross-fit gym. Mercedes had brokered the deal for Gloria Maven, convincing her that gyms and spas go hand in hand. The space had been mostly unused for years—Mercedes's Quinceañera at fifteen had been the most action the warehouse had seen in decades—and the rental had been a boon to Maven's business and to her bottom line. Mercedes clicked on the light in the stock room and got to work. About an hour into her duties, she thought she heard voices. She frowned, cocking an ear.

Keegan was the only male stylist. Maven employed two male massage therapists and the Cross-fit gym was riddled with testosterone. But no one had a reason to be inside the salon this late on a Saturday night. She listened, straining to make out the voices, wondering if she needed to investigate, or at least make her presence known, when the voices got louder, and Mercedes identified Keegan as one of them.

Gloria had apparently given him back his keys. Bitterness welled in Mer's chest, but she shook her head and released it. She couldn't blame Gloria for the things she didn't know. But it might not be a bad idea, now that she was leaving and now that Noah knew the truth about Keegan, to have a very frank conversation with Gloria about her favorite stylist. Or maybe not. The thought of telling anyone that Noah wasn't Gia's biological father stuck in her throat. She wasn't sure they were words she would ever willingly say, even as a courtesy to her longtime boss.

The voices approached, and Mercedes scrambled for the light, instinct making her hide, though she wasn't the one in a place she shouldn't be.

"Anybody here?" Keegan called, and her heart tripped and slipped to her stomach. She didn't answer.

"The alarm wasn't on. It should have been on," he said, and there was a nervous quiver in his voice that made her wonder who he was with. She raced for the door and locked it seconds before the handle turned.

"You don't have a key?" the unknown voice inquired.

"I've never needed one. It's usually open."

"Well usually isn't gonna cut it, is it?"

"Hold on . . . let me see what I've got here," Keegan grumbled. The soft jangle of keys accompanied the slide of a key in the lock. "That's not it," Keegan muttered.

Mercedes scrambled for a place to hide. Snagging her purse, she crawled beneath the nearest row of shelves as the lock released and the door swung open. She could hear Keegan feeling around for the switch, and suddenly light bloomed.

Shit, shit, shit, shit, Mercedes chanted silently. She could feel her purse vibrating against her chest. Someone was calling her. The setting was almost inaudible but not quite. She squeezed her eyes shut and willed her phone to cease. The two sets of feet stopped in front of her face.

"It's in the towel bins."

What was in the towel bins?

Keegan had waltzed in earlier in the week, carting bins overflowing with white towels, like he was delivering food to poor, starving children.

"We won't need to buy new towels this year, Gloria," he had bragged. "A local hotel chain was having a close-out. I got these for next to nothing. Solid white, just like we use here. They look brand new. There are close to one hundred towels in these bins."

Gloria had clapped and congratulated him on his resourcefulness, even offering to pay him what the towels cost, plus a finder's fee. He'd declined, magnanimous.

"This is my contribution to Maven and my thanks for hiring me back on." Keegan had opened one of the bins to show everyone the quality. But he hadn't opened all of them. He'd stacked them in the storage room, one on top of the other, in the space next to the door where they would be out of the way until they were needed.

"So all these bins, huh?" the stranger asked.

"Just the bottom two. The top two are just towels."

"You got ten kilos hidden beneath towels?"

"Twenty. And it's hidden inside the towels. All cut, mixed, and bagged. All we have to do is deliver it, and you'll get the money I owe you, plus interest, just like I promised. Let's get 'em and go. That alarm should have been on," Keegan worried.

Mercedes didn't dare reach into her purse or pull out her phone, but it continued to vibrate against her chest, threatening to expose her. She needed proof. Something that she could take to the police. Something that would ensure that Keegan Tate wouldn't be in any position to threaten Noah for custody. She had the suspicions of a homeless man and a conversation about kilos and towels. It would be nice if she had more. She listened, hardly breathing, as the two men moved the two top bins, brimming with towels, to the side and positioned the two bottom bins on a dolly.

"Is that your phone that keeps buzzing?" the man asked Keegan.

Mercedes stopped breathing.

"Nah. It's not mine. I thought it was yours," Keegan grunted.

"Check it," the man insisted, and from her vantage point, she could tell when Keegan released the handle on the dolly, lowering the platform, to search for his phone. She couldn't see their faces, couldn't see anything but their feet, but she could imagine how it must have unfolded.

Keegan reached for his phone, looking down as he did. The other man reached inside his jacket, ostensibly to check his phone as well. Instead, he pulled out a gun, and without hesitation or second thought, he pulled the trigger.

The sound in the small space was deafening, and had Mercedes been a different type of girl, one who is prone to squeaks or squeals, she would have given herself away.

Instead, she stared, dumbstruck, into the sightless eyes of Keegan Tate who had fallen to the floor mere feet from where she was wedged, cheek against the linoleum, a paltry, plywood shelf separating her from a stone-cold killer. Keegan had died without pain or protest, a hole in his forehead and blood seeping through his golden locks like he'd suddenly decided to go red. Alive one moment. Gone the next.

The man with the gun leaned down and picked up Keegan's phone. It had clattered to the ground when he fell, skittering away from his body toward the door. Mer caught a brief glimpse of dark hair and a brown leather jacket before the man straightened again. Then he propped open the stockroom door, pushed the loaded dolly from the stock area, and shut the light off behind him. No snide one-liner or cackling laugh like you see in the movies. He simply shot a man, shut off the light—*gotta save electricity* —and trundled off with his bins of cocaine.

Mercedes lay in stunned horror, afraid to move. In the darkness, she could smell the blood. It had found her hiding place, and when it touched her face, warm and wet, expanding in an ever-widening pool, she hugged the wall next to her and pressed a hand over her nose and mouth.

Maybe the man was simply quiet as he made his getaway, or maybe her ears were permanently damaged from the gun being fired in close quarters, but Mercedes couldn't hear anything. Not her pounding heart or her labored breaths. And that scared her most of all. If she couldn't hear, she wouldn't know if he was gone. She wouldn't know if she'd given herself away. She wouldn't know if she moved silently.

But she did know one thing. If the man found her, if he heard her or saw her, she would die. So she laid in Keegan's blood and begged Lady Guadalupe, Abuela, and Cora—whoever could hear her—for protection. Then she began inching forward beneath the shelves, trying to put some space between her body and Keegan's blood, desperate not to make a sound, but knowing if she didn't move, she would lose her mind.

She'd almost worked her way to the far wall, a good five feet from Keegan's body when the door swung open again and light filled the room once more. He was back.

She froze again, praying she was still hidden, and closed her eyes so she wouldn't see the moment he discovered her.

He began pulling items from the shelves, stepping over Keegan's body like it didn't bother him at all. He upended a box of commercial toilet paper over Keegan's body, the rolls individually wrapped in paper bouncing merrily over the dead man. One rolled beneath the shelf where Mer was huddled, and came to a stop. She prayed he wouldn't care enough to retrieve it. He didn't. He ripped open a ream of scratchy paper towels, the kind that stack inside a wall dispenser, and let them flutter over Keegan's inert form. He emptied several packages, burying the body in paper products. Mercedes heard a snick and the smell of aerosol hairspray filled the air with an accompanying whoosh. Her hearing was coming back, but her eyes stayed glued to his feet, willing him to leave again. If he kept pulling things from the shelves, he would eventually find her.

He liked the hairspray. He doused the towering pile of paper products in a long, steady stream, emptying one can and tossing it aside before opening another. Mer's throat started to tickle, and her eyes began to burn.

Don't sneeze. Don't cough. Don't even breathe.

She didn't see him pull out his lighter, but she saw the moment he dropped the burning ream of paper towels, and the whole pile whooshed into flames, a funeral pyre on the stockroom floor. Through the flames she watched him leave, flipping off the light once more, and pulling the door closed behind him.

NINETEEN

1997

*C*arole Stokes had a green thumb, and when she wasn't running the records department, she was digging in the dirt. Her yard was beautifully landscaped and big enough for a handful of guests, and she wanted to contribute to the wedding in some way. Everyone did. Carole was providing the location, Alma and Abuela were in charge of the food, Heather had hired a minister and a DJ, and Mercedes had done hair and makeup for everyone in the bridal party.

"You should wear your hair down," Mercedes insisted. "I'll weave the sides into the curls, but your hair beneath that veil is stunning, and Noah likes it down."

The salon was quiet around them. Noah and Cora had chosen a Sunday afternoon to marry, and everyone else had already left to make final arrangements, leaving Cora in Mercedes's capable hands. Cora had been jittery—teary even—most of the morning, and Mercedes had already redone her makeup once. They'd moved on to hair, but Mercedes would have to hurry if she was going to have time to get ready herself.

"I know I can't make a better choice than Noah," Cora said suddenly. "I'm lucky. He chose me . . . and I know how lucky I am."

Mercedes met Cora's eyes in the mirror and asked the question she'd asked three times already that day. "Cora, what's wrong?"

"He will be a good husband. A good father too. The best. And I know him. That's so important, to truly know who you are marrying, don't you think? I know him," Cora babbled, avoiding the question.

"And he knows you," Mercedes said, her hands moving almost automatically while her eyes clung to Cora's face. Cora nodded slowly, and Mercedes moved the curling iron up and down with the motion of her head.

"He does. But . . . how well do we ever really know someone, Sadie? Have you ever been in a dark room . . . a room so dark that you can't see your hand when it's right in front of your face?"

"Yeah," Mercedes said, trying to follow along.

"Sometimes . . . I feel like I'm in a huge, dark room. There's this space, endless space, all around me. I'm there, but no one could possibly see me. Not the real me. Because there's so much . . . darkness and distance all around me. I'm a black speck on a black canvas. And only I know who and where I am."

Mercedes had stopped curling Cora's hair and was staring at her friend. *"What's going on, Cora? What's wrong?"* she repeated. *"Do you want to postpone the wedding? Do you need more time?"*

"You would like that, wouldn't you?" Cora shot back, and her eyes filled with tears once more.

When Mercedes didn't respond to the accusation but kept her gaze steady on Cora's, Cora wilted.

"I'm sorry, Sadie," she murmured.

"Don't apologize to me. Apologize to Noah. If you're going to cower in the dark and worry about existentialism while an amazing human is waiting at the end of the aisle, ready to promise his life to you, ready to stand beside you, to be a light in your darkness, then have the decency to tell him. Otherwise, I better see some rejoicing. I better see you smile. I better hear some hallelujahs and some celebrating. Because this is a good day."

"But . . . what if . . . I'm not enough?" Cora whispered.

And there it was. At the heart of everything, Cora was still the little girl whose dad had chosen death over her, and nothing would ever convince her otherwise.

"You're the only one holding a yardstick," Mercedes said.

"What?"

"You decide if you're enough. Noah already thinks you're enough. He chose you. Just like you said. But he can't change the way you feel about yourself. That's up to you, Cora."

Cora shook her head, resistant.

"Do you want to marry Noah?" Mercedes pressed.

"Yes."

"Then do. And be happy. That's your only job. Because if you are happy . . . he'll be happy too."

Two fat tears fell from Cora's eyes and slid down her powdered cheeks.

Mercedes groaned. *"You're killin' me, Smalls."*

"Quit quoting The Sandlot. *This isn't a baseball game,"* Cora huffed, reaching for another tissue.

"There's no crying in baseball!" Mercedes yelled, quoting yet another favorite film.

Cora giggled and blew her nose.

"Promise me you'll give him your very best," Mercedes implored. *"Take care of him. Love him. He hasn't had a lot of love, Cora. You know that. He might be the easiest man in the universe to love, because he expects so little. He expects nothing and is grateful for everything. With a man like that, how could you worry about being enough?"*

For a moment Cora was quiet, deep in thought, and Mercedes continued to fix her hair in silence.

"Do you hate me, Mer?" Cora asked. It was Noah's nickname, and Mercedes wondered if it was intentional.

"Cora, I've loved you from the first minute I saw you, twirling around and playing pretend all by yourself at The Three Amigos," Mercedes reminded her.

Cora smiled, but her lips trembled, and her eyes swam.

"I remember that day. I was playing alone. Then you and Noah showed up . . . and you made everything better," Cora whispered.

"We always do," Mer teased.

"You always do," Cora agreed. She was quiet again, and Mercedes thought maybe—finally—her nerves had settled.

"You're in love with him, and I took him from you," Cora said softly, sadly, raising her eyes to Mercedes's in the mirror. *"Deep down, I guess*

I've always known it, and I didn't want to admit it."

"No. I love him. That's not the same thing," Mercedes insisted, her gaze unflinching.

"I think it is, Mer," Cora said, shaking her head. *"In your case, I think it is. And I hope someday you'll be able to forgive me."*

Mercedes's Corolla wasn't parked in front of Maven, and it wasn't in the employee lot in back either. The business was dark, and when Noah tried the front door it was locked. Two cars were tucked next to the curb in front of the boutique a few doors down, and beyond that a car here or there dotted the mostly deserted thoroughfare. Noah climbed back in his Subaru and pulled into the gas station across the street, sliding into a parking spot beside a seasonal snow cone shack. Three festive tables clustered around the tiny establishment, and the row of empty parking spaces served both businesses.

Mercedes obviously wasn't at the salon, but he didn't know where else to look. Maybe he'd just missed her. Maybe she'd gone looking for him.

He doubted it.

Mer had a soft heart but a good chin. He'd dealt her some blows, and she'd still been standing. She wouldn't be the one to come looking for forgiveness. He'd stormed out. He would have to storm back in. Her phone rang and rang.

"Come on, Mer," he whispered. "Pick up. Don't ignore me."

A tapping on his window had him flinging the phone across the front seat.

"Shit!" he cursed, startled. A grizzled face peered at him through the window, palm pressed to the glass, a tentative smile revealing broken teeth.

"Noah?" the man said. "Please don't be afraid. I'm worried about Miss Lopez."

"Cuddy?" Noah said, his voice calm despite his galloping heart.

THE SMALLEST PART | 241

The man nodded eagerly. Noah eased his car door open and stepped out, facing the man across the roof of his Subaru. He liked having the distance between them. Plus, the passenger side doors were locked.

"Do you want to be called Cuddy . . . or should I call you something else?"

"Like what?" the man stammered.

"John? Mr. Cutler?"

"Oh." The man seemed disappointed in the alternatives.

"Isn't that your name? John Davis Cutler?"

"Yeah. It is. But you can call me Cuddy."

"You said you were worried about Miss Lopez. Why?"

"She went inside." He pointed at the salon. "I know she works there. But it's late. And Miss Cora keeps showing me towels."

"Towels?" Noah stammered. It was easier to question the towels than the mention of his dead wife.

"It doesn't make sense. I know. But every time I try to rest—I got a spot in the grass back behind the carwash there. Nobody says a word as long as I clear out before the sun comes up."

"You try to rest—" Noah prodded.

"Yeah. Every time I try to rest, Miss Cora won't let me. I close my eyes and all I see are stacks of white towels. I wish I had some," he said sadly. "Whenever Miss Lopez wraps my head in a towel, it makes me feel better."

"Cuddy?" Noah pressed, trying to be patient even as his pulse jangled.

"Miss Lopez is nice to me," Cuddy whispered. "I'm worried about her."

"Why would she—Cora—show you towels? And why would that make you worry?" Noah asked.

"The dead don't speak. Not to me, at least. They show me pictures," Cuddy said, apologetic.

Noah grunted. It was exactly what Moses had said.

"They aren't very good at communicating—or maybe I'm just not good at understanding," Cuddy muttered.

"You saw Mercedes go in the salon? When?"

"I'm not good with time, Noah."

"Tonight? She went in tonight?"

"Yes. Tonight," Cuddy affirmed.

"Before I came?"

"Yeah. She parked somewhere else. She walked from somewhere and went inside. A little while later, you drove by."

As Noah watched, a dark truck pulled up in front of the salon, and Cuddy started to back away, obscuring himself in the shadows.

"You don't want to let that one see you, Noah," Cuddy warned. "Get back in your car."

The pumps in front of the gas station were well lit, but the corner where the snow cone shack stood was dark and partially obscured by two tall pines. Noah's car was dark, and his lights were off, but sensing Cuddy's distress, he slid back behind the wheel of his car and watched as Keegan Tate and another man stepped out of the truck and scanned the street as they approached Maven's entrance. Keegan unlocked the front door and looked around like he was uncomfortable about something. The man with him urged him inside and the door swung closed behind them.

Cuddy rapped on the passenger side window. Noah flipped the locks and Cuddy, not missing the subtle invitation, slid into the seat beside him. His knees crowded the glove compartment, and he was unable to recline because of the bulging pack he wore on his back.

"That was Doze," Cuddy muttered. "I don't like Doze."

"Doze?" Noah questioned.

"The guy with Keegan. Everyone's afraid of him. He never opens his eyes all the way. Looks like he's half-asleep. People call him Doze."

"Why would he be with Keegan?"

"Drugs," Cuddy answered.

"Keegan Tate has a drug problem?"

"Lots of drug problems," Cuddy muttered. "His biggest drug problem is Doze."

A few minutes later the front door opened and the man—Doze—exited Maven pushing three Rubbermaid containers, one stacked on top of the other, on a dolly. He didn't look around, didn't slow, but continued at a leisurely pace to the truck parked in front of the boutique. Noah watched as he hoisted the bins into the back of the vehicle and then returned to the salon, leaving the dolly sitting on the sidewalk.

"Do you think I could have that dolly?" Cuddy asked after they'd waited several more minutes. "I would like that."

"Are you sure you saw Mercedes go inside?" Noah pressed. The thought of Mer being inside Maven with Keegan and Doze wasn't sitting well with him.

"I think so," Cuddy hedged, worrying his lip.

A few minutes later Doze was back, jangling a set of keys. He opened the driver's side door of the truck and climbed in. Noah expected to see Keegan exit Maven as well, but Doze wasn't waiting. He started Keegan's truck, and without a second look, pulled away from the curb and headed south down the street.

"That's Keegan's truck. Where's Keegan?" Cuddy said. "And why didn't Doze put that dolly back?"

Noah waited a few minutes more, his eyes glued to the front door. No lights. No Keegan. No Mer. Maybe she wasn't inside. Poor Cuddy wasn't giving him much confidence with his talk of towels and his innocent coveting of the abandoned dolly.

"If you call the police . . . will they take me away?" Cuddy said abruptly.

"Why—" he stopped, sniffing the air. "Do you smell smoke?" Noah hissed.

Cuddy sniffed the air too, and then sniffed at his clothes. "I always smell like smoke."

Noah was out of the Subaru and running across the street before Cuddy even managed to entangle himself from the front seat. Noah wrenched on the door of the salon, but it was locked. He pushed his face to the glass, peering into the gloom, trying to see what was happening inside.

Cuddy was suddenly there beside him, his face pressed to the window, hands framing his eyes.

"Miss Cora is here," Cuddy wailed, making the hair stand up on Noah's neck. "I can see her inside."

"What the hell?" Noah hissed. His instincts were screaming, and a red glow had begun to glimmer from deep in the store. It was on fire, and Keegan Tate had gone inside and he had not come out. That much Noah knew.

"I need a rock. Lots of rocks. Or maybe just a really big rock. Yeah, a really big rock," Cuddy mumbled, shrugging out of his black backpack.

Noah eyed the enormous rock Cuddy pulled from the depths. "I've been feeling extra floaty lately," he explained, self-conscious. Without warning, he heaved it through the glass.

"Was that wrong, Noah? It didn't feel wrong," Cuddy worried.

Noah picked up Cuddy's backpack, still brimming with an assortment of rocks, and zipped it closed. He swung it at the window, clearing away the shards. Smoke billowed out around them. Handing Cuddy the backpack, he grabbed the man by his shoulders.

"I need you to go back to my car, find my phone, and call 911. Tell them there's a fire at Maven Salon. I need your help, Cuddy."

"But . . . I can't talk to the police," Cuddy stammered. "I moved the car. I moved the car so Keegan wouldn't take the baby. But they won't believe me."

"None of that matters now. I need you to call the police, and then wait for them. Wait for me. Don't go inside the salon!"

"But Mercedes is in there. I know it. Miss Cora is with her, but it's hard to breathe," Cuddy wailed.

Noah didn't want to believe him. He wanted to put a hand over Cuddy's mouth and tell him to shut up, to stop scaring the shit out of him.

But he did believe him.

And that belief meant Mercedes was inside a burning building and Keegan Tate was unaccounted for.

"Call 911, Cuddy!" Noah demanded, and without waiting to see if Cuddy obeyed him, stepped through the gaping hole they'd made in the glass.

The smoke was so thick he pulled his T-shirt up over his nose and mouth and ran forward, looking for signs of life. The building was old, but the surfaces were stone and glass and faux wood floors. Ceramic sinks and metal chairs were all less flammable than the ceilings, and the flames had traveled upward, licking up the more incendiary surfaces. Noah felt for the row of sinks he knew should be just to his right and found the nozzled end of a long hose. Turning the water on full he doused the area around him, soaking himself and everything within range.

"Mercedes!" he roared. The back wall was on fire, and the flames had climbed to the ceiling tiles. On the other side of the wall was the stockroom—the stockroom would be full of accelerants—and beyond that, the rear exit that led to the employee parking on one side and the warehouse/Cross-fit gym on the other. The locker room and a row of smaller rooms for waxing, facials, and massage were to the right, just across the hall from the stockroom.

"Mercedes," he shouted again. He could smell hairspray and something else. He'd smelled it in the hospital in Kabul. Burnt flesh.

"Oh no," he groaned, choking. "Mercedes! Where are you?"

He stumbled forward several steps, trying to see through the roiling waves. He would never find her. She could be lying five feet away, and he would never see her.

Suddenly smoke became form, the flames to his right becoming the streaming hair of his late wife.

"Cora?" he whispered, and for a moment he considered that he was already too late, that he'd slipped from one dimension to the next without even realizing it. She beckoned him forward and he followed. She glimmered and shifted, and he took several more steps, tripping over something —someone—crumpled in his path. He sank to his hands and knees, the air clearer closer to the floor, and found Mercedes, her hair lank and soaked in blood, her white blouse black with it. With a cry of both horror and relief, he scooped her up in his arms and turned toward the front of the salon, moving as fast as his oxygen-starved lungs would allow, begging Mercedes to hold on even as he choked and clutched her still form to his chest. He staggered through the smoke, the distance to the entrance feeling like a city block. He fell against the front doors, only to have them wrenched open by a fireman on the other side.

"Anyone else inside?" the fireman shouted, reaching for Mercedes. Noah clutched her, unwilling to release her, as he turned his head and peered through the gloom, looking for Cora.

"Anyone else?" the fireman repeated.

"I don't know," Noah said. "I don't know."

"We're going to get you and the lady to a hospital, okay?" the fireman said. "Can you tell me your name?"

"I need to stay with her," Noah rasped.

"We'll do our best, okay?"

Then ambulance workers were running toward him, a gurney between them, and Noah relinquished Mercedes to the professionals. She was breathing on her own and her pulse was steady—he heard that much—but she was unconscious. They slid an oxygen mask over her head, and before Noah knew it, they were slipping one over his head as well.

"It's for the smoke inhalation. We treat it with oxygen. Just breathe deep, man. You can sit up here by the lady. We're going to get you guys to the hospital."

Noah lifted the mask, needing to check on Cuddy. "There was another man here. Did you see him?"

"We got him. He tried to go inside—he was the one who told us you were there—but we kept him back. There's another ambulance pulling up now. We'll make sure he gets checked out. Now put the mask back on."

Mer was intubated en route, and Noah closed his eyes, gripped her hand, and prayed that she wouldn't leave him. She didn't appear burned—miraculously—and her color was rapidly improving, and as they pulled into the emergency room entrance, she opened her eyes and looked at him.

Noah was treated for smoke inhalation in the ER at the University of Utah, and released hours later with medicine to ease his raw throat and his pounding head. Mercedes had been immediately admitted and undergone a series of tests and treatments. He'd called Alma and Heather, who'd come at once, with Gia in tow. Alma had stayed with Mercedes, Heather, upon seeing that he would be just fine, took poor Gia back home, and Noah, still grimy, his clothes foul with smoke, found his way to Mercedes's bedside. She opened her eyes and lifted her hand in greeting. They'd removed the tube from her throat, but when she tried to speak, Alma shushed her.

"Doctor says no, Mercedes. Your throat needs to heal."

Mercedes kept her hand extended, and Noah sank into a chair beside her bed, taking it and pressing his lips to her palm, needing to tell her how sorry he was, how much he loved her, and how scared he'd been. Alma stood, rounding the bed to reach him. She ran a hand over his filthy hair, kissed his cheeks like he was precious to her, and whispered her gratitude.

"You found her, Noah. You saved her. How will I ever repay you?"

Noah could only shake his head, guilt and grief making him resistant to her praise. Alma told him she would be back with coffee and fresh clothes for him to change into, and left them alone, pressing a kiss to her daughter's forehead. Mer waited for her to leave before she disregarded the doctor's orders.

"I saw her," Mercedes whispered, her eyes steady on his. They were red-rimmed and bloodshot, and two dark circles were forming beneath them. His had looked the same when he'd encountered his reflection in the bathroom mirror.

"Who?"

"Cora." Mer blinked rapidly, trying to hold back the tears, but they escaped and slid down her cheeks and hid in her dark hair. Someone had washed it, and it lay damp against the white pillows.

"I froze," she continued, her voice rough. "I was in that room, terrified that if I moved he would hear me and come back, but knowing I had to get out or I would burn."

"Mer," he moaned, wanting to beg her to stop, but her words kept coming, washing him in horror.

"Keegan was there with someone. A man. I couldn't see him. But he killed Keegan. Shot him right in the head. And then he made a bonfire. I was hiding under the shelves," she rushed. "I managed to slide out, and I called 911, but I couldn't wait for help, and I couldn't go out the door without walking through the fire. So I went up."

"Up?"

"I climbed the shelves, and I pushed out a ceiling tile and crawled out on one of the rafters. There was so much smoke, and I was coughing. I was afraid I'd fall. Then I saw her. I kept crawling toward her. I shouldn't have been able to see her. I couldn't see anything else."

"She was part of the smoke," he said, overcome.

"Yeah. She was," Mercedes agreed tearfully. But she continued, not asking him how he knew. "Once I was up, I had to get back down. I slipped. One minute there was a beam beneath me, the next minute there wasn't. I remember falling right through the ceiling tiles, but nothing after that. They think I hit my head and knocked myself out. But I know what I saw." She was quiet for a moment, her eyes fierce, her lips trembling.

"I saw her too, Mer."

Their eyes met and held, and for several heartbeats, they said nothing and everything without exchanging a word.

"I didn't know for sure you were even inside. But I saw her . . . and she helped me find you," Noah said. "I didn't save you . . . Cora did."

"Of course she did." Mercedes whispered. "We always save each other, remember? It's what we do."

For a moment they clung to each other, their emotion making conversation impossible. But after several minutes, Noah pulled back, anxious to speak.

"I'm sorry, Mer, for all the things I said," Noah choked out. "I was angry. Hurt. Embarrassed. But none of this was your fault."

"I made such a mess of things," she said. "I was trying to fix something that I couldn't fix, and I made everything worse."

"We save each other, remember? It's what we do," he repeated, but this time his voice was wry. "But we can't save Cora from this."

"What do you mean?"

"I've spent my whole life not having a clue who my dad is. I don't want that for Gia. Someday I'm going to have to have a conversation with her and explain things like infidelity and use words like 'bio dad.' I hate that. I am her father, but I will have to strip that from her, I will have to take that from her. The comfort, the sense of self, her place in the world. It will all be shaken. Even if she's the most confident, well-adjusted kid in the world, even if I love her as hard as I can, she's going to be hurt by that revelation. Cora put me in a position where I have to harm my daughter, and that just sucks so bad. The betrayal—the fact that she messed around on me—that was the easiest thing to face. But she robbed Gia. And that's going to take me a while to get over."

"She robbed you both."

"Yeah. She did. And yet . . . I'm still trying to protect her. *You're* still trying to protect her."

"Old habits."

"Yeah. So you didn't tell me what you knew. And I didn't tell you what I knew. We just suffered and worried," he said gently. "We can't do that anymore."

"Okay," she whispered.

"Okay?"

She nodded slowly, her throat working. "Mami said the police want to talk to me."

"They're going to want to talk to us both. I talked to them a little already," Noah agreed, nodding.

"Do they think I killed Keegan?"

Noah reared back, stunned. "Why would they think that?"

"Because I . . . paid him . . . to leave. And he came back. I had good reason to hate Keegan, and I was there when he died."

"You paid Keegan to leave?" Noah gasped, incredulous.

She nodded, wincing with the movement of her head.

"Mercedes," he breathed. "Why?"

"He promised he would go and leave you and Gia alone."

"How much money did you give him?" Noah pressed, anger billowing up his charred throat.

For a moment Mercedes didn't answer, and Noah raised her chin and made her meet his gaze. Fear and remorse warred in her eyes, and he smoothed the hair back from her face.

"How much, Mer?"

"Twenty grand."

"Mercedes Lopez," Noah whispered. "What the hell were you thinking?"

"I couldn't let him do it. I couldn't let him take Gia," she cried, her face crumpling with the confession.

Noah pulled her into his arms and held her as sobs wracked her small body. Mer cried like she'd been holding it all in for decades.

Noah wanted to cry with her, but he was too stunned. Too humbled. He'd known Mercedes for twenty-two years, and she never ceased to blow him away.

TWENTY

2003

"*D*em bones, dem bones, gonna walk around,*" Mercedes sang softly, touching the tiny newborn, lying in her arms. Her ears, her hands, her feet, her nose. She was so perfect. So peaceful. So sweet.*

"The foot bone connected to the leg bone,
The leg bone connected to the knee bone,
The knee bone connected to the thigh bone,
Oh, hear the word of the Lord!

"Don't sing that one," Cora whispered from the bed nearby. *"You'll give her nightmares."*

"I thought you were asleep, Mama," Mercedes crooned, still looking down at the sleeping baby. Cora had labored for almost twenty-four hours to bring Gia into the world. She needed to rest while she could.

Mercedes had been beside her for most of those twenty-four hours. She was exhausted too, but mostly she was relieved. Heather would be coming back soon to stay with Cora and the baby through the night.

"Sing something else," Cora murmured. *"Sing the one about the angels with no shoes."*

Mercedes complied, singing about the gates of heaven and the bare-foot angels, asking God to bless the children who sleep and the mothers who watch over them.

"Cora, what's wrong, honey? Why are you crying?" Mercedes asked, abandoning the lullaby when she saw her friend's tears.

"I'm not sure. Happy. Glad it's over. Glad she's here," Cora said, her lips trembling. Mercedes decided she had every right to cry. It had been a grueling nine months and an emotional delivery. Cora had weakened as the end neared, informing Mercedes that she couldn't possibly give birth.

"I can't do this," Cora had groaned. "I don't want to do this. I changed my mind."

Mercedes had laughed, but swallowed her mirth as Cora leveled her with a look so venomous she'd checked her reflection in the mirror above the bed to make sure her eyelashes weren't singed off.

They had walked, up and down the halls, Cora leaning on Mercedes when a bad wave hit, and it was then that Cora revealed the names she'd chosen.

"If it's a boy, I want him to be called Noah. Noah Michael. Michael for my dad. If it's a girl, Gia Mercedes Andelin. Gia was my dad's mother. She was Italian and Grandpa was Irish. Dad and I got his genes, but at least Gia can have Grandma's name," Cora had panted.

Mercedes had been peppering Cora with names from the moment she'd heard the news, but Cora had refused to tell her what she was considering. She wanted it to be a surprise. She'd also refused to find out the baby's sex. Mercedes had considered bribing the ultrasound technician to give her the information on the down low so she could be prepared. Unfortunately, the tech was honorable—the doctor too—and nobody would tell her what the baby's gender was. She'd suffered and seethed for seven interminable months, culling the Goodwill for the best items in impossibly boring neutrals. She'd wheedled and begged, but Cora hadn't budged, until now.

"I'm telling you in case something happens to me," Cora had groaned.

"Stop. Nothing is going to happen to you. You're in a hospital surrounded by medical personnel. You're perfectly healthy. Your best friend is

a force of nature—"

"That's true."

"—And you are about to have a little girl who needs her mother."

Cora had emitted a tortured moan, clinging to Mercedes, who wobbled in her heels but planted her feet and held tight until Cora's contraction waned.

"You said little girl," Cora had panted. *"Do you know something I don't?"*

"Just a feeling. And my gut is rarely wrong. You know this. Plus . . . I need a namesake."

Her gut hadn't been wrong.

Two hours later, Gia Mercedes Andelin came into the world, and Mercedes had been poised to catch her and lay her on her mother's breast. Now, washed and weighed, poked and pricked, tiny Gia Andelin was swaddled and sleeping, and Mercedes was enjoying every second.

"Duérmete niño, duérmete niño, duérmete niño, arrú arrú," she sang while Cora listened, still silently weeping.

"Noah was happy," Cora whispered, tears trailing down her cheeks. She closed her eyes and brushed at her wet cheeks wearily.

"I've never seen him so happy," Mercedes answered, touching Gia's tiny fingers, and smiling as the infant instinctively wrapped Mer's finger in her fist.

"I thought maybe he would want a boy," Cora sighed.

"Noah? The man whose best friends growing up were girls? He wouldn't know what to do with a boy."

When the connection was made and Noah was patched through via Skype, he was indeed thrilled. He'd looked weary—almost like the wait and worry had been its own form of labor. When Mer had lifted Gia up so he could see her, he'd greeted her warmly, but his eyes were glued to his daughter's pale hair, her round cheeks, and her rosebud mouth.

"Look what you did, Corey," he had breathed. *"Look at that beautiful little girl. Look at our baby girl."*

When they'd signed off, he'd been beaming.

"He already loves her," Cora murmured, her voice so soft, Mercedes considered not responding. Cora was almost asleep, her tears drying on her cheeks.

"Of course he does," Mercedes whispered, but her eyes were on Gia. "One look is all it took. One look, Gia Mercedes, and it was all over. You've got your daddy wrapped around your tiny finger."

"Just pray he never lets go," Cora murmured. "Gia needs a daddy. Every girl needs a daddy."

They found Keegan Tate's body amid the burned wreckage of the salon. The fire had caused significant damage and Mercedes was no longer the only stylist at Maven out of work. Gloria Maven had begged her to come back when the restoration was complete, making big promises and dangling incentives. Mercedes hadn't agreed to anything yet. She had a new goal—or an old dream—in mind.

The police questioned Noah and Mercedes extensively, both together and separately, adding Cuddy's scattered testimony to the picture, and they were eventually cleared of all suspicion. Two days after the fire, Doze had been apprehended, and they would all be testifying against him when his trial began. Keegan Tate had gotten involved with the wrong people. And it had gotten him killed.

Detective Zabriskie said charges would be pressed against Cuddy for the joyride in Mercedes's car, but when Noah intervened on his behalf, he was released from police custody as well, cautioning them to keep an eye on him.

"He's got a bad history. Don't let your guard down." Detective Zabriskie warned, processing Cuddy's release with a wariness Cuddy probably deserved, but Cuddy's countenance fell and his shoulder hunched in shame, even as Noah explained what would happen next.

"You know I work at a special hospital, right Cuddy?" Noah asked, waiting for Cuddy's eyes to rise to his.

"Montlake," Cuddy muttered.

"Yeah. Montlake. The authorities don't want to let you go to wander the streets. They want you admitted or incarcerated. They're afraid you're going to hurt yourself or someone else . . . even if it's unintentional."

"I don't hurt people, Noah."

"I believe you, Cuddy. But the car incident, combined with your record, doesn't make them feel very confident. And there have been some complaints from businesses around Maven."

"No one ever said anything. I didn't think they even saw me," Cuddy said.

Noah nodded. It was a sad truth. But people saw the homeless and the indigent. The problem was, they didn't *want* to see.

"We have some programs at Montlake—I think I could get some state funding for you to stay there for ninety days. You could get some treatment. You would be clean. Fed. Looked after. And we could talk. Every day. And we could figure out how to make you feel better."

"At Montlake?" Cuddy asked, awestruck.

"At Montlake," Noah replied.

"And you'll be my doctor?"

"If that's what you want. We have lots of good therapists and doctors at Montlake."

"What about my rocks?"

"You can't take your rocks to Montlake. But I'll keep them for you. All of them. And when you're through the treatment plan, you can have them back if you still want them."

"Why wouldn't I want them?" Cuddy asked, his brows lowering.

"Well . . . if you start feeling better, maybe you won't need rocks to keep you grounded."

"I won't need them to keep me from floating away?"

"Yeah."

"Okay. But I love rocks. I especially love the one you gave me. Did Miss Lopez tell you? I'll give it back if you want me to."

"I have one just like it. You keep it," Noah insisted.

"Noah?"

"Yeah?"

"I'll go to your hospital."

"Good. I think that's a good choice. And I can take you there now."

Cuddy shifted nervously, his backpack hanging low around his shoulders. "Now?"

"Do you have somewhere else you want to go first?"

"No. I don't have anywhere to go," Cuddy whispered.

Noah nodded once, and together they left the police station, side by side, eyes fixed ahead. It wasn't until they were pulling into the parking garage of Montlake Clinic, that Cuddy spoke again.

"I'll try hard, Noah. I'll try hard to get better. But . . . the medicine doesn't make the ghosts go away. I've tried medicine. It just makes me itch. Some of it makes me crazy. Even crazier than I am," Cuddy said, a note of desperation coloring his words.

"I don't think you're crazy, Cuddy.'

"You don't?"

"No. I think you might just need a little help knowing what's . . . spiritual and what's real."

"It's all real to me," Cuddy said, his eyes apologetic.

"I know. And just because everyone can't see it, doesn't make it less real."

Cuddy grinned, the corners of his mouth rising slowly until they peaked and the smile touched his eyes. "You're a good doctor, aren't you, Noah?"

Cuddy was a model patient. He fell into the routine at Montlake with a touching determination to exorcise old demons, though Noah tried not to think about demons or ghosts, or spirits of any kind. It wasn't until two weeks after Cuddy's admittance that Noah arrived at work to reports that Cuddy was agitated and emotional, and he'd been asking to see him.

Noah found him in his room staring out the window, his hands cupping his lean cheeks, his eyes troubled. He didn't wait for Noah to pull up a chair before he began to pace.

"I need to tell you something, Dr. Andelin. Do you want me to call you Dr. Andelin? I would rather call you Noah."

"You laughed when I told you my name the first time . . . remember?"

Noah asked softly.

Cuddy got a distant look in his eyes, and he tipped his head as if to jostle his memory, to slide his thoughts back into his mind.

"I laughed?"

"You asked me when the flood was coming."

"The flood?"

"I think you were referring to Noah and his ark. That flood."

"Noah was a prophet . . . everyone laughed at him. No one believed the flood was coming," Cuddy said, nodding his head slowly as if it was all coming back to him.

"Are you a prophet, Cuddy?"

"No," Cuddy said, adamant. "God doesn't tell me things. But I need to tell you something, Noah," he insisted again.

"All right," Noah said.

"You might laugh. It's okay if you do. Or you might be sad. Very, very sad." Cuddy brought a hand to his face again, anxious, scrubbing at his cheeks as though the motion comforted him. Noah did the same thing when he was agitated, and he waited patiently for Cuddy to speak again, confident he would, eventually.

"I wish I had my rocks," Cuddy whispered.

"Do you want to hold my hand?" Noah asked. "Would that help?"

"I would like that . . . yes," Cuddy murmured. "But I don't think I should."

"Why?"

"Because I need to tell you something. And it might make you very sad. And you might not want to be holding my hand when I tell you."

"Have you seen something that scares you Cuddy?"

"No. I *know* something. And it doesn't scare me. It makes me happy. But it might scare you."

Noah controlled his expression, nodding with a neutral face. But he was surprised. "Why don't you tell me, and we'll talk about it."

"I knew your mother."

"You did?"

"Yes. I called her . . . Andy."

"Are you sure it was . . . my mother?"

"Yes. I'm sure. I called her Andy . . . short for Andelin. She called me

Cuddy—"

"Short for Cutler," Noah said, putting it together.

"Yeah. We were just kids."

Noah stiffened. "You knew my mother when she was . . . a kid?"

"I knew her when she didn't have a home," Cuddy whispered. "Neither of us did."

The rigidity in Noah's limbs spread to his chest, trapping his breath and seizing his heart.

"Why don't you sit down, Cuddy. Then you can tell me about her," Noah said. His words sounded strangled and odd, even to his own ears. Cuddy nodded eagerly and rushed to obey.

"I never knew her real name. Not all of it. Everyone had nicknames. Nobody uses their real names. It's like that on the street. None of us know much about each other. Nobody wants to talk about where they came from or the fact that they have nowhere to go."

Noah nodded, urging him on.

"I thought she liked me. I liked her. She was quiet. She didn't yell or swear. But I . . . took too many drugs then. I thought it would make the ghosts go away," Cuddy explained.

"Did it?"

Cuddy shook his head. "For a while it did . . . and then I started seeing a different kind of ghost. Not like Cora or . . . or the angels. The dead I started to see were . . . dark. Scary. They wanted me to let them in. They wanted my . . . home."

"Your home? They wanted . . . your body?" Noah kept his tone warm, but his hands were cold.

Cuddy nodded. "They hadn't ever had bodies. They weren't the dead. They were ghosts who'd never lived. And they wanted to."

Noah was silent, waiting, not wanting to rush the tale or take Cuddy down a path he wasn't ready to go.

"I was afraid," Cuddy whispered. "And Andy was afraid too. I was no good, Noah. No good. One day, she wasn't beside me when I woke up. When I finally found her she told me to go. She told me she didn't want to be found. She told me she couldn't be around . . . me . . . with a baby in her belly."

Noah made himself breathe. *In and out. In and out.* And he held Cuddy's gaze.

"Andy said the baby wasn't mine. But I knew it was. Andy wouldn't let . . . anyone else touch her. She didn't like to be touched."

Noah could only nod, overcome. No. His mother hadn't especially liked to be touched.

"I never saw her again. Not until you found me on the side of the road, and I saw her sitting there in your car. I thought for a minute I was seeing her ghost. I thought maybe she was dead. Thought maybe I was dead. Then . . . I realized she was . . . yours. And you were hers. You were . . . hers. Which meant . . . you were *mine*. I know that's not . . . something you might want to hear. But . . . I . . . I think . . . I'm your dad, Noah."

Noah was too stunned to speak. He clutched his clipboard, needing to hold on to something, anything, that gave him purpose and presence of mind. He suddenly understood what Cuddy had meant by floating away, and longed for rocks.

"I saw Andy . . . sitting in the car. She saw me too, Noah."

Noah nodded. She *had* seen him. And she'd been afraid. Noah had assumed it was simply the fear of a stranger. The fear of the downtrodden. Of the unknown.

"She didn't tell you . . . who I was?" Cuddy asked.

"No. She didn't tell me," Noah whispered.

"That's good," Cuddy murmured, his voice forgiving. "It would have been a hard thing for you to hear. You woulda tried to take care of me then like you're doing now, and you were just a boy. You didn't need that."

Noah could only stare at Cuddy, drinking him in, absorbing his tale, seeing him for the first time.

"They put me back in prison for a while. I'm good at slipping away. Like a ghost." He laughed softly. "I guess they've taught me a few things."

"I have your eyes," Noah said abruptly. "And your hands. The way you rub your face. I do that too."

He felt ridiculous. Unnerved and dizzy. He wrote his name several times across the blank page on his clipboard, just to remind himself who he was, who he'd been ten minutes ago when he was fatherless and self-assured. In the back of his mind, a little voice argued that it might not be true. But that voice was denial, and denial often lied. Noah knew it was true. He had no doubt.

"I saw you at the Homeless Fair," Cuddy continued. "After all those years. I recognized you. And I was so happy. Then I met sweet Cora. And Miss Lopez. And I got to see how you turned out, and what a good man you are. I was so proud." His voice broke and he wiped his eyes.

"Why didn't you tell me?" Noah whispered. "I would have believed you."

"I didn't want to . . . scare you away. I couldn't risk it. Just seeing you . . . was enough for me."

"Did Cora know . . . or Mercedes?" *Had she kept that from him too?*

"No," Cuddy whispered. "I never told anyone. Not until now."

"Why now?"

Cuddy swallowed and wrung his hands, and Noah resisted the need to explain himself or apologize.

"Because you deserve to know."

Noah felt the sorrow rise. He'd said the same thing to Mercedes. But he knew better. Life wasn't about getting what you deserved. It was about enduring what you didn't and not letting it destroy you.

"Andy and I . . . we were so broken. But you! You are p-perfect and wh-whole," Cuddy stammered, his voice almost reverent. "I don't know how it happened. But . . . you are a miracle, Noah."

Noah laid down his pencil and his pad and buried his face in his hands. For many long moments, he fought tears. He wanted to get up and leave the room, to take a minute to collect himself, but Cuddy had shown courage. Faith even. And Noah didn't want to reject his offering, even if it meant fighting his emotions in full view of his patient. He was going to need to get Cuddy a new therapist.

"Was I wrong to tell you?" Cuddy whispered. "It didn't feel wrong. Scary. But not wrong."

Noah smiled through his tears. Cuddy's need to self-examine was endearing. "No. You weren't wrong to tell me," he choked. "It's just that . . . my mother said the same thing."

"Are you sad?" Cuddy pressed.

"I'm shocked. But not sad," Noah reassured, wiping at his eyes.

"My blood isn't blue," Cuddy confessed sadly. "My blood is tainted."

"Someone told me once, Cuddy, that blood's important, but to a kid, blood doesn't matter at all. It doesn't matter to me."

"You know what I mean. I'm trash. I'm not smart. I'm messed up in the head. I've wasted my life. Been in jail. Never had my own place. Never done one good thing."

"That's not true. Because of you, Mercedes is alive. You watched out for her, and you saved her life, Cuddy. When you saved her life, you saved mine. I don't think I can live without Mercedes. I don't *want* to live without Mercedes."

"But . . . I didn't save Miss Cora."

Noah shook his head, wondering how many people would bear that cross. "No. None of us did. But you cared about her."

"I did." Cuddy nodded emphatically.

"Sometimes that's all we can do," Noah said gently.

"I care about you and Miss Lopez. I care about little Gia too. And I cared about . . . Andy."

"Not many people cared about my mother," Noah whispered. "I'm glad you did. It makes me feel better knowing that you did."

"I let her down. I was messed up for a long, long time. I'm still kinda messed up, Noah. I wish I was a better man. Someone you could be proud of."

"I've never had a dad, Cuddy. I've always wanted one. I've always needed one. So much. And I still do."

Cuddy began to smile and nod, his eyes shimmering with emotion.

"I feel like I'm going to float away, Noah. But it feels good this time," Cuddy said, gripping the sides of his chair with both hands.

"I know what you mean," Noah said, smiling through his own tears. This session had not gone at all as planned—not even close—and Noah took a few deep breaths and looked down at the clipboard in front of him. There would be time for treatment plans and coping strategies soon enough. For now, they both probably needed some time to let their emotions settle.

"What next?" Cuddy whispered, clearly feeling as unsure as Noah. "I want to get better so I can be a real dad."

"I need you to talk to me. I need you to be patient with yourself. And I need you to tell me when something isn't working. And I promise you I'll do my best to help you get better."

"Gonna roll my sadness down a hill, gonna roll my sadness down a hill," Cuddy sang. "Miss Lopez taught me that."

Noah laughed. He could almost hear Mercedes singing it, shaking her hips and tapping her toes like she did. She'd taught him a few things too.

Dem bones, dem bones, dem dry bones.
The thigh bone connected to the back bone,
The back bone connected to the neck bone,
The neck bone connected to the head bone,
Oh, hear the word of the Lord!

Funny. For the first time in his life, all the little pieces and all the small parts were coming together. Noah felt strangely whole. He stood, and Cuddy rose with him, his face hopeful.

"Just keep singing, Cuddy. That's not a bad place to start. Miss Lopez has a knack for making life beautiful."

"Is Lopez okay?" Moses greeted, not even saying hello.

"Lopez is okay," Noah replied, a smile in his voice. "Thank you, Moses."

He grunted, uncomfortable. But he didn't sign off the way Noah expected him to.

"I don't like worrying about people," Moses said, his tone accusatory. "I've been worried for the last two weeks. Decided I better call."

"Are you still seeing Cora?" Noah asked.

"No. Thank God. I was glad to see her go," Moses said, unapologetic. His irreverence and disregard made Noah laugh. Noah's laughter made Moses sputter.

"Holy shit, Doc. What I just said was mean as hell. And you're laughing."

"I'm laughing because you're so transparent," Noah shot back.

"Nah. I'm not transparent. But your wife is." If that was Moses's version of a "Yo Mama" joke, it could use some work.

"The fact that you can't see her anymore is a relief, Moses. I'm hoping it means Mercedes isn't about to get herself killed. Again."

"Your wife was playing guardian angel," Moses stated.

"Yeah. I guess so. We've always looked out for each other. Why quit now?"

"I can't say I understand it. But I got the feeling Cora loved Lopez."

"She did," Noah murmured. "They loved each other."

"You three are all tangled up like . . . like a ball of string, or some shit. I can't say I understand it. But I felt it."

"History is like that. Messy. Involved. And we have a lot of history."

Moses was silent, but he remained on the line, like he wasn't ready to let Noah go quite yet.

"I found my dad, Moses." Noah blurted, surprising himself.

Moses said nothing for so long, Noah wondered if the connection was lost.

"How do you feel about that, Doc?" Moses asked hesitantly. For a moment they were both silent, their roles reversed, and then they started to laugh.

"How do I feel? Hmm . . . well, he's a recovering drug addict who sees dead people."

Silence again.

"You messin' with me, Doc?" Moses asked softly, a shadow of hurt in his question.

"I would never mess with you, Moses. I tried that once. You made me bleed."

Moses scoffed, but the hurt was gone. "A recovering drug addict who sees dead people," Moses mused. "Hmm. Sounds like you found *my* dad. You sure we ain't brothers?"

Noah laughed again. "He's the wrong color. He's a pasty white guy. Actually . . . he looks like me. I didn't see it. Not at first. But I can see it now."

"Isn't that the way of things? Once we know, it all seems obvious."

"Yeah. But even when we know . . . it isn't always easy to accept," Noah replied.

"Ain't that the truth," Moses grunted. "I still can't accept what I know." He cleared his throat and changed the subject. "So you found your dad. What next, Doc?"

"I have to make Mercedes Lopez accept something *she* already knows."

TWENTY-ONE

1984

"*I don't have any valentines,*" *Noah worried, staring down at the list his fourth-grade teacher had passed out just before the bell rang. "Mrs. Hayes told us we had to give a valentine to everyone in the class. I don't know what to do. Last year, I pretended I was sick and went to the nurse during the party because I didn't have anything to pass out. Is your class making valentines?" he asked Mercedes.*

"*The whole fourth grade is celebrating Valentine's Day, silly. The whole school is,*" *Mercedes laughed. "But don't worry. I have some paper. All colors. We'll make hearts. I know a good trick.*"

They dropped their coats by the door of Mercedes's apartment, and Mercedes dug her class list from her backpack and assembled the supplies they needed on the kitchen table.

"*All right, Noah. Watch,*" *she demanded. Mercedes folded a piece of pink paper in half, and with a skill that belied her nine years, cut out half a heart. Unfolding it, she presented it to Noah with a satisfied smile. "See? Perfect.*"

Noah nodded, impressed, and watched as she cut out several more.

"*You cut the hearts, and I'll write the names on them,*" *Noah suggested. "I write pretty good.*"

"*That's a lot of hearts,*" *Mercedes warned. "Twenty-five for my class.*

Twenty-five for yours."

"We can do it," he said, confident and more than a little relieved. They worked quietly for several minutes, concentrating on their assignments, Noah carefully crossing out the names on the lists and making two different piles, one for each class. When they were done, they sat back and stared at what they had accomplished.

"They're kind of plain," Mercedes said, wrinkling her nose. "They need glitter or something. I wish we had some stickers."

"We could write something nice on the other side, like . . . a Valentine's message," Noah suggested.

"So they look like those candy hearts!" Mercedes clapped. "We'll write Kiss Me, Hug Me, Love Ya. *Stuff like that."*

Noah grimaced and shook his head. "We could just say You're Nice *or* You're Cool. *I don't want to write* Kiss Me *on any of them."*

Mercedes snickered, and together they started writing short messages on the back of each heart.

"This one says my name," Mercedes said, holding up a yellow heart from his stack. "I don't need to give one to myself."

Noah took it from her hand. "It's from me, goofball."

Mercedes stared at him, her brows lowered. Then she cut out one more heart from her scraps of paper. "Okay then. This one's to you from me. A pink one. Your favorite color."

"Pink's not my favorite color."

She giggled, and he realized she was teasing him. She wrote his name on one side and then turned it over.

"What else are you going to write on it?" he asked.

"It's a surprise."

Noah frowned and looked down at the yellow heart he'd made for Mercedes. Yellow wasn't her favorite color either. He turned it over and thought about what he should write. There were so many things he could say. He could say I Love you. *It was Valentine's Day, after all. But that seemed weird, and Mer would laugh and think he wanted to be her boyfriend. He could write that she was funny and cute and nice. She was all of those things. He thought for a minute longer and then picked up a pencil and wrote* THANK YOU *in bold across the back. He stared down at the words. They seemed so simple, but he was grateful for his friend. Every day he was so grateful.*

"Can I have that now?" Mer asked, trying to see what he had written.

"Maybe. Can I have that?" Noah indicated the pink heart with his name on it.

She pursed her lips, considering. Then she handed it to him. He pushed the yellow heart toward her, suddenly shy.

She'd written two words on the back. YOUR MINE. *He knew she'd spelled you're wrong, but he didn't tell her. He traced the words with his eyes. She made him smile. You're mine. Not Be Mine. You're mine.*

"You're welcome," Mercedes said, and Noah looked up in surprise.

"You wrote thank you. You're welcome," she said again. "But thank you for what?"

"For being my best friend," he said, shrugging.

She grinned, revealing her two missing teeth. "And you're never gettin' rid of me. I'm yours." She pointed at the pink paper heart in his hand. "And you're mine."

Mercedes found the mugs on her kitchen table with a note from Noah, apologizing for the one he'd smashed. Eight mugs, all powder blue, just like the one he'd broken. But that's where the similarity ended. Each mug had a pink heart on the side with the words YOUR MINE written across it. You're was misspelled.

"What the hell?" she mused. That was going to drive her nuts. She stared at the misspelled word, puzzled, and then a memory niggled, and she began to laugh.

She called Noah, and he picked up on the first ring.

"Hey, Mer."

"Hey, Boozer. I came home and found some weird coffee mugs on my table. You misspelled you're."

"No . . . *you* misspelled you're."

"I can't believe you remember that! Geez. You're a freaking elephant."

"I still have that valentine in my ammo box. I found it last week when I was cleaning Cora's things out of the closet."

Mercedes's heart lurched painfully. "You should have called me. I would have helped," she said quietly. "I was going to do it for you. But I didn't think it was my place."

"I should have done it a long time ago. I just . . . never got around to it. It was time." He cleared his throat and changed the subject. "How's work?"

She was at a new salon—she'd needed somewhere to take her clients —and the adjustment had been grueling. She'd managed to keep her Mondays open for Gia, but hadn't carved out a place for Noah, and the time apart had created an uncomfortable expectancy. She knew she'd been quieter than usual. Subdued even, and in typical Noah fashion, he'd given her all the space and patience he thought she needed.

"Work's fine," she sighed. "How's Cuddy?" She'd been as shocked as Noah when he told her Cuddy's confession. The last month had been fraught with change and new beginnings, but she and Noah were still tiptoeing around each other, not sure where to start.

"Cuddy's pretty damn . . . amazing," he whispered. "I like him."

"I do too. Always have."

"Mer?"

"Yeah?"

"I hope you don't care that the mugs are a little . . . different . . . than the one I broke."

"I miss my old mug," she teased. "It spoke to me."

He grunted. "I hated that mug. I never knew why you chose that specific one."

"You hated it?" she said, surprised.

"Yeah. I didn't like the 'letting go of things not meant for you' part. It pissed me off."

"That was the part that spoke to me."

He grunted. "I'm sure that's the part that spoke to my mom too. She was good at letting go. But what about fighting for the things and people who mattered? Every time she used that mug, I wanted to throw it against the wall."

Mercedes laughed, incredulous. "Well, I guess you finally did."

"Yeah. I guess I finally did."

Silence grew between them, and Mercedes knew she should end the call. But she missed him. He'd come to her house to tell her about Cuddy, about the revelation that had rocked his world, and she'd been shocked and attentive, holding him while he talked. But when he'd tried to kiss her, she'd stiffened in his arms, and he'd immediately pulled back, not pressing her. She hadn't meant to stiffen. She'd been nervous. Scared. And he'd backed off.

"I love you, Mer. I miss you," he said quietly, pulling her back to the present. "How can I make your life easier?"

"I love you too, but unless you can cut hair and wax bikini lines, I think you're just going to have to support from afar." She'd meant to be funny, but instead she sounded like she was brushing him off. *Damn.*

He sighed. "Will you call me tomorrow?"

"I'll call you tomorrow," she promised. And with a soft goodbye, he hung up.

Noah had a staff meeting Monday night and didn't get home until seven. Mercedes had a client who insisted on seeing her before she went on vacation, and the only time Mercedes could fit her in was Monday evening, so Alma took Gia until Noah could come by and grab her, and another week went by without them seeing each other at all.

When the weekend rolled around, Heather called Mercedes, concerned about Noah.

"He asked me to take Gia, and he didn't tell me where he was going or what he was doing. He had all of Cora's things packed up in the back of the car. I know everything's probably fine . . ." Heather's voice faded off.

The last time Noah had dropped Gia off for a long weekend with her grandmother, Mercedes had had to drag him from his bed, and the shower scene ensued. Even then, he hadn't told her what was bothering him. Mercedes didn't have a lot of faith he would tell her now.

Mercedes promised Heather she'd check on Noah, and Saturday night, when she finished her last client, she drove to his townhome only to find it dark and empty. She let herself in, took off her shoes, and sat down to wait for him. She tried calling him a few times, but he didn't pick up. She waited for an hour. She made coffee and washed and dried the dishes in the sink. She waited for another hour. She called Montlake, but he wasn't at work. She called him again. His phone went straight to voicemail. By the time she heard his key in the lock a little after ten, she was almost frantic with worry.

"Where have you been?" she gasped when he greeted her with a smile. He didn't look strung out. He looked good. He smelled good. He gave her a quick hug and walked into the kitchen.

"I've called you a dozen times," she complained, trailing after him.

"My phone was dead, and something's wrong with the charger in my car," he said easily, seeing the coffee and pouring himself a cup.

"Noah?"

"Yeah?"

"I was worried. Where were you?"

"I had a date," he said easily, throwing the words over his shoulder as he reached into the fridge for the milk.

"A d-date?" she stammered, the words penetrating like a slice from a sharp knife. First the cut, then the realization, then the pain.

"Yes. A nurse from Uni. We've been friends for a while. She's divorced, and . . . she's nice. And I'm . . . single. I . . . just thought . . . maybe . . . we could," he stopped, shrugging.

Mercedes turned away, so humiliated, so stunned and raw she couldn't breathe. And she definitely couldn't stay.

"Okay. Cool. Well, I'll be here on Monday for Gia," she bit out, searching for her shoes.

"Mercedes?"

"See you on Monday, Noah."

"You're upset." He almost sounded pleased.

"I didn't know where you were. I was scared!" she snapped. She stormed toward the front door. She had to get out.

"I'm thirty years old, Mer. I don't have a curfew," he said, and she could hear the smile in his voice. He was so stupid. Such a freaking idiot.

She was going to cry.

She pushed her feet into her heels and grabbed her purse, not looking at him, not looking at anything but the door through which she needed to escape.

She felt him behind her, but she didn't slow. She dug her keys from her purse as she walked and slid behind the wheel without looking at him again. He'd followed her from the house. He was a dark shadow to her left, lurking several feet from her car. She turned the key, backed out, and drove away, leaving him framed in her rearview mirror.

Since Cora died, Noah had never dated. He hadn't spent time with any woman. Besides her. At least . . . not that Mercedes knew of. Going out on a date was not a betrayal, not of Cora. Not even of Mercedes. She'd told him in no uncertain terms that they were only friends. But that was before the fire. That was . . . then. She thought he knew how she felt. *Didn't he know how she felt?* Cora was gone, and he deserved to move on with his life. And now he was. So why was she crying? Why was she howling in pain, driving through the streets toward home?

When she pulled into her driveway and slowed to a stop, she kept the car running, needing the warmth and the rumble of the engine to cover her anguish. Her duplex was dark and empty, and she didn't want to be alone. She searched her glove compartment for a napkin and found a crumpled handful. She blew her nose and tried to fix her makeup in her visor mirror, only to give up as her tears continued to fall. Lights swung into her driveway and Noah's Subaru boxed her in.

She should have known he would come. Maybe she *had* known. Maybe that was why she was sitting in her driveway, trying to make herself look pretty, even as she cried her eyes out.

She watched him step out, shut his door, and approach her car. He leaned down and peered at her through the driver's side window.

"Do you want me to get in, or are you getting out?" he asked, raising his voice above the Corolla's purr.

She turned the key, surreptitiously wiped her eyes, and pulled on her pride. Noah stepped back so she could open her door, and she climbed out, head high, slicking gloss on her mouth and offering him the other half of her slice of gum, the way she always did. The burst of icy flavor helped clear her head. She just hoped the darkness provided sufficient cover for her red eyes and trembling lips.

"Are you crying for Cora, Mer?" His voice was low. "Or are you crying for me?"

Clearly it provided no cover at all.

"I'm crying for me," she confessed, angry that it was true.

"Why?"

"Because—because." She ground her teeth. She couldn't admit it. She couldn't tell him. But she couldn't be the other girl in his life. Not anymore. Not again. If she had to move aside and let someone else take his time and his energy, his words and his affection, it would destroy her. It would destroy them.

"Do you love me, Mer?" he asked softly.

"You know I do."

"Yeah. I know you do. But that's not what I'm asking. Not the way a girl loves her best friend. Do you love me the way a woman loves a man?"

She was silent.

So was he.

They stared at each other, considering, wary, watchful. The need to run trembled in her legs. The pull to stay was stronger. She was strong enough to hold her position, but she wasn't brave enough to speak.

"You have been pushing me away your whole life," Noah whispered. "I don't know how to read you right now, so you're going to have to tell me how you feel."

"What are you talking about?" Mercedes gasped. "How have I pushed you away?"

"You are too honest, and we've known each other for too long for you to pretend you don't know what I'm talking about." Noah's voice was soft, but his eyes were steely as he looked down at her.

"I have always been there for you. Always. I've never let you down, Noah. I've tried harder with you than with anyone in my life. I'm proud of who I am with you. I've been a damn good friend. Don't you dare accuse me of anything else." Her anger was hot in her belly, and it felt good, cleansing. It burned away her cowardice and put words on her tongue. She could work with anger.

"I'm not accusing you, Mercedes. I'm trying to understand you."

"Well, understand this. I am not your sister or your nanny or your maid or your . . . your one-night-stand . . . or your . . . your—" The tears were gathering again, and she wanted to scream. She wanted to hit him and hurt him. She wanted to hurt herself. She wanted to hurt herself so that she would remember this moment—this pain—and never repeat it.

Then he was there, wrapping his arms around her, holding her so tight the scream died in her chest. She fought him for a moment, arching her back and pressing against his shoulders with the palms of her hands.

"You're still pushing me away," he rasped. "Why?"

She froze, realizing she'd proven his point, and she slowly wilted against him. She let him hold her, and after a moment, she raised her arms and looped them around his waist, releasing her pent-up breath and laying her cheek against his chest.

He pulled away slightly, his arms still locked around her back, and looked down into her face. In the pallid light from the street lamps, his blue eyes were as colorless as the dark, July sky.

"When I was a kid, I always thought it would be me and you. I was sure we were soulmates," he said.

"When did you stop?" she asked, her voice low, sidestepping his confession.

"What?" He tipped his head to the side, confusion playing across his features.

"When did you stop thinking it would always be me and you?" she clarified. He gazed at her, thoughtful, his lips pursed, his eyes solemn.

"Maybe . . . I never did," he confessed. "I just assumed you would always be there. I've taken you for granted, haven't I?"

"That's what friends are for. Taking each other for granted and not keeping score," she said, trying not to cry all over again.

"Yeah." He nodded. "Exactly. And do you know what a gift that is? To feel so safe and so certain of a person that you are able—*able*—to take them for granted? Most people go their whole lives afraid to be who they are, afraid to be real and vulnerable and human, because they are sure the people they care about will walk away. And that fear becomes a self-fulfilling prophecy. In an effort to be perfect, to be loved, they hold it all in. And when they finally lose control—as they inevitably will—they self-destruct. They overdose. They cut themselves. They lash out and physically hurt someone else. Their response is magnified a hundred times because they are dealing with a well of suppressed reactions."

"You sound like a psychologist," she whispered, teasing, trying to release some of the pressure on her heart and failing miserably.

"That's because I am one. But right now, I'm not speaking as Dr. Andelin. I'm Noah, Mer's best friend, and you need to listen to me."

She nodded, and he took a deep breath.

"I never feel that way with you. I never feel like I'm holding it all in, and that when you discover the real Noah you'll cut me out of your life. You know me. I know you. There's always been a place in my heart that was exclusively yours. A small, private corner . . . all yours. You've never let me down, Mer. Never. You're right. You have been my safe place. My constant. All my life, you've cultivated and cared for that little part, that little piece of me that was yours. And I think—I hope—I've done the same for you. For more than twenty years, Noah and Mercedes—our friendship —has endured."

"Things are different now," she said, aching.

"Yes. They are," he breathed, and he lifted her chin, pressing his forehead to hers. "If I kiss you, will I lose you?" he whispered, and she groaned, inexplicably angry.

"Why are you asking me? Why don't you just take what you want? Why don't you just kiss me? Why do I have to give you permission and guarantees and sign a freaking form before you—" Her rant was swept aside by the brush of his lips. He was gentle and tentative, holding her face in his hands, pulling her shuddering breath into his throat, and giving it back to her. For several heartbeats, his mouth moved with hers, no urgency, no pressure, no pain.

In the sweetness of his kiss she remembered the boy he'd been, the girl *she'd* been, and the tears and the years began to flood her mind and spill from her eyes. His kiss was an extension of the man—kind and careful, giving without thought of gain, and she gloried in the sensation, even as her heart raged, wanting more from him. She had always wanted *more* from him, and it was time she admitted it. It was time she took it.

"You're crying again. Why are you crying, Mer?" he murmured against her mouth, and she could taste his frustration. She liked the flavor. It was sharp and tangy, and she licked his lower lip, tugging it between her teeth, hungry for it. She wrapped her hands in his lapels and jerked him against her, desperate to make him understand.

His response was immediate, burying his hands in her hair and taking her darting tongue into his mouth like he'd been waiting all day to taste her. Then he wrapped his arms around her waist, pulling her up and into his body until her feet left the ground and her heart was pressed against his, beating in perfect time. The roof of her mouth tingled, her breasts swelled, and her lips grew deliciously raw from the scrape of his beard and the fervor of his response. He kissed her like he wanted more too. He kissed her like it wasn't enough to just hold her anymore, like it wasn't enough to just laugh anymore, to just talk anymore, to just be friends anymore. And it gave her courage.

She freed her mouth and braced her hands on either side of his face, breathless, but needing to confess her feelings before her nerve failed her.

"I haven't pushed you away. I've been holding on for dear life! I don't know how to show you how I feel. I don't know how to tell you that I need you. That I want you. That I want you to want *me*. I don't want to just be your best friend anymore, Noah. I want to be your lover. Your partner. I want it all. Not the small part or the private corner. I want the whole damn thing, all of you. And I want to give you all of me."

"Thank God," he breathed, his eyes clinging to hers. Then he was kissing her again, whispering against her lips. "How long? How long have you felt this way?"

"All of my life," she answered, each word punctuated with a press of her lips. Noah drew back, surprised.

"Come on, Mer," he scoffed. "You were interested in every guy *but* me."

"That's funny, Noah. Very funny. I was never interested in anyone else *but* you."

He didn't gasp, but she felt it. She felt his disbelief, his surprise. And his eyes screamed his skepticism. She pushed against his shoulders, and he set her on her feet.

"You were my Noah. Mine." She thumped her chest, so adamant that he reached out to steady her as she wobbled on her too-tall heels. "You were my best friend. And I wasn't going to mess us up. You were the most important part of my life, and I was my best self when I was with you. But Cora loved you too . . . and when I held back, she stepped forward. She staked her claim. So I shut it off—all those feelings—and I locked them up tight."

"Before I left for basic training, I tried to tell you how I felt. I tried to show you how I felt. But you . . . you didn't act like you wanted the same thing," Noah stammered, still disbelieving.

"I never wanted anyone else, Noah. But you loved me because I was strong. I was steady. And having your love and your affection was too important to ruin it with sex and jealousy and childish love triangles. I knew that if I gave up all claim on your body, I could keep your heart. That was the part that mattered most to me."

His eyes were bright, and he swallowed like the words in his throat were too big to say. He hugged her fiercely, lifting her off her feet once more, the way he always had, the way she hoped he always would. "You are so wise. How did you get to be so wise?" he whispered.

"I'm an idiot," she whispered back. "And a coward. I have been so afraid to lose you that I almost let you go. Again."

"You are the smartest woman I know. The very best woman I know. And I do love you because you're strong and you're steady. But those aren't the only reasons. Those were never the only reasons."

He brushed his lips over hers, convincing and caressing, and her eyes fluttered closed.

"Mer?"

"Yeah?" She didn't want to talk anymore. She wanted to kiss him.

"I didn't have a date. I lied. I was trying to make you jealous."

"What?" she gasped, but his mouth returned, kissing her with all the frantic devotion she was feeling, and she forgave him immediately.

"Do you love me, Noah?" she panted.

"You know I do," he murmured against her mouth.

Frustrated laughter bubbled up from her chest, and she pinched him, pulling back slightly so she could clarify.

"Are you *in love* with me, Noah?"

"I'm in love with you, Mer. Madly. Deeply. Head over heels in love with you."

"I'm in love with you too," she whispered, freed. Ebullient. "I always have been. I always will be."

EPILOGUE

L oving Mercedes wasn't like falling off a cliff. It wasn't even the heart-clench of a missed step. It wasn't a jerk or a jostle. It wasn't tripping or tumbling at all. It was the slow climb of a lifetime of moments, the line upon line, day after day kind of love. And it was deeper and more durable for it. You would think with a love like that there wouldn't be passion, there wouldn't be heat, but there was. It sizzled and crackled between them like a sparkler in July, constantly surprising him.

Once Mercedes was in, she was all in, just like he knew she would be. One weekend, toward the end of August, they left Gia with Heather for a few days and boarded a plane. They didn't tell anyone where they were going or what they had planned. No invitations or announcements were sent out. They were married on a beach in Mexico—a place neither of them had ever been, despite Mercedes's heritage. It was just the two of them, barefoot and hand in hand, making promises to each other and looking to the future. He'd teased Mercedes about being a barefoot angel, and she'd started singing "A la Puerta del Cielo" and dancing in the surf, kicking up the water in her white dress, her dark hair streaming behind her.

Alma had been shocked when they told her. Hurt. She had wanted to see her only child get married. She'd wanted their ceremony to be in a church with a priest. She'd wanted to give them a huge celebration.

"You deserve it, Mercedes! Why start your marriage this way, running off like you are ashamed? Like you need to hide? Gia should have been there, at the very least."

Mercedes had put her arms around her mother and, in a language Noah didn't speak, told her the love story of two old friends who needed a chance to look ahead without the distractions of the past

"We needed it to be about Noah and Mercedes, Mami. Not the three amigos," Mercedes explained. "Entiendes?"

Alma shook her head. "No. No entiendo," she whispered.

"We needed it to be about the future. Not the past. Our lives have always revolved around everyone else. And that's okay. But I wanted our wedding day to be about us. I didn't want to think about Cora, or Shelly, or Abuela or even Papi—though I felt their presence. I didn't want my wedding day to be a reminder of what had come before. For once, I needed it to be about the two of us—me and Noah—and nothing else."

Mercedes and Alma had cried, and Noah had cried too. He didn't understand the language but he knew the reasons, and he'd felt every word.

Mercedes and Alma moved into the townhome with him and Gia, but he'd immediately put it up for sale. They needed a house where they could start fresh, a home big enough for Alma and Cuddy and Heather too when she wanted to visit. A home with room to grow.

Noah found empty office space not far from Montlake with a 5000 square foot loft situated above it, and he took Mercedes with him to look it over. He suggested they purchase the office space and turn it into a salon and day spa—MeLo—and live in the loft.

"It's so much money . . . and we'd have to totally remodel it, top to bottom. Right now it's just open space," Mercedes had sputtered.

"Then that's what we'll do," he answered calmly. "It will be perfect."

"We can't—I can't afford that Noah, even if we could get the financing," Mercedes said, but her eyes were wide with the possibility.

"We can."

"What? How?"

"Cora's life insurance policy paid out. There's a suicide clause, but their findings were inconclusive." Noah took a deep breath and held her gaze. "Bottom line, none of us will ever know what really happened that day. The insurance company closed the inquiry, and a few days ago . . . they sent me a check." He reached into his pocket, pulled it out, and handed it to Mercedes.

Mercedes began to shake her head, resisting. He kept his hand extended until she took it. Noah knew exactly how she felt, and he'd been struggling with it since he'd received the news. Then he'd thought about Mer, and how she'd happily emptied her bank account to keep Gia safe and to protect him, and he knew what to do.

"You've been walking around with this in your pocket?" Mercedes gasped, her eyes widening at the amount.

"I'll tuck some away for Gia, for college and a rainy day. But if Cora were here, she'd tell you to take it, Mer. She was there when the dream began, and I think she'd like to see it come true."

It had taken them eight months to make the loft a home and turn the space below into a spa, but they'd moved in the day after Mercedes's thirty-first birthday, and MeLo had its grand opening three weeks later.

They'd worked hard, but that was nothing new, and Mercedes was tireless. Cuddy had turned out to be quite handy, and he'd framed up all the walls, hung the drywall, and did all the painting. When Noah told him one of the rooms was his, he'd cried. He cried a lot. He still cried when Mer cut his hair, and when Noah slipped and called him dad, he'd wept for an hour. Noah had been calling him Dad ever since, and Cuddy had adjusted. He promised Noah the flood would eventually end, but Noah had simply hugged him and told him not to worry; everywhere he looked there were rainbows.

They had a great deal in common. The difference between Cuddy and Noah was that Noah had had people who loved him. Cuddy hadn't. But now he did.

They celebrated the Fourth of July at their new home. Since finishing the interior, Cuddy had moved his efforts to the roof. It was endless and flat with a three foot wall around the sides, making it ideal for a green space. Cuddy had performed wonders in three months, hanging lanterns and building raised planter boxes. There were vegetables in some and flowers in the others, and they were overflowing and blooming in riotous color. He'd asked if he could make a rock garden too, and he and Gia had spent hours making fairy houses to place among the stones.

Noah bought a canopied table and some deck chairs, and they grilled burgers and listened to eighties songs on the boombox for old times' sake. Alma and Mercedes made paper stars with long streamers while they waited for the fireworks to start. The view of the sky above the stadium was almost as good as the view from the hill behind The Three Amigos.

"You fold the paper this way, back and forth, back and forth," Mercedes told Gia, helping her turn the paper, pressing and folding and folding again. They'd left the stars to Alma and were using perforated computer paper to make a chain of dolls long enough to include the whole family.

When they were done folding the paper, Mercedes began to snip and cut, wielding the scissors like the professional she was. Gia sat at her feet, the white paper clippings fluttering around her strawberry locks like snowflakes on Christmas morning. She laughed and closed her eyes, squealing for more.

She called Mer Mami now. No one had coached her. One day Meh became Meh-Meh. Meh-Meh became Mama, and Mama morphed into Mami. No one said a word. Not even Heather, who had taken it all in stride, even going so far as to say it was "meant to be."

Heather was Grammy, Alma was Abuela, and Cuddy was Papa. Of course Cuddy had cried with joy the first time Gia had laid that nickname on him. Three years old, and she had a mind of her own. He was Papa, and no one argued with her.

Mercedes finished snipping and carefully unfolded the paper chain.

"There's Daddy." Gia pointed to the first figure.

"Okay," Mercedes said, nodding.

"Daddy, Mami, Gia"—she said her name perfectly now—"Papa, Abuela, and Grammy. And one more."

"Yep, one more," Mercedes agreed. "We have a big family."

"Cora," Gia supplied, touching the final figure.

"That's right. We can't forget her."

Gia smiled, wrinkling her little nose, and picking up the paper dolls, skipped off to involve them in some secret game only she was privy to. They streamed behind her like a lacy kite, and Noah and Mercedes watched her go.

Want more?

Turn the pages to read an excerpt from
The Law of Moses by Amy Harmon

ACKNOWLEDGEMENTS

S uicide affects everyone. My own son attempted suicide twice in his teen years. His second attempt resulted in a long hospitalization, and it is a subject I take seriously, and an experience you never fully recover from. Every year, I donate a portion of my profits in the month of May to the AFSP.org through the Keith Milano Memorial Fund, a fund started by a book blogger, Denise Milano Sprung, after the death of her brother. You can contribute to Denise's efforts at www.keithmilano.org

Veterans are some of the most frequently affected by suicide, and *The Smallest Part* gives you a glimpse into this tragedy. Whether you are a vet or simply someone who needs a listening ear, you can call **1-800-273-8255**.

If you are a mom struggling with postpartum depression, there are resources out there for you too. If you need more information, please visit https://theemilyeffect.org/—a great website put together by a local family after they lost their mother to postpartum depression and anxiety. You are not alone.

This book was in my head for a long time. Ever since I wrote *The Law of Moses*, Dr. Noah Andelin's story has been in my head. It took me three years, but I finally wrote it down. I hope you love Mercedes and Noah as much as I do.

The Song of David is David "Tag" Taggert's story, a companion novel to *The Law of Moses*, and it is now available at your favorite online vendor as well.

Big thanks go to my assistant and dear friend, Tamara Debbaut. Without her, I couldn't function. Thank you, Tamara. My gratitude on this project extends to Nicole Karlson, whose enthusiasm for my books makes writing a pleasure. Thanks to Cristina Bon and Ashley Ruiz for reading The Smallest Part early and making sure I correctly represented the Hispanic culture.

To my agent, Jane Dystel and her team, including Lauren Abramo and many others, thank you for taking such good care of me.

Continued thanks to Karey White and Courtney Cole for editing and advising on this novel. A good editor is something to cherish. Thank you Hang Le for the beautiful cover and for capturing the spirit of the book. To Julie Titus of JT Formatting for always making time for me and for doing such beautiful work on the interior files for my books.

To all the bloggers who read and review for the love of it, thank you too. Authors can't do it without you. I'm thankful for every single one of you.

And finally, I'm so grateful for my readers. I know how fickle the market is, I know how fandoms come and go, and I know that there are always a million books to choose from. Thank you for reading mine.

The following is an excerpt from THE LAW OF MOSES,
available at your favorite online retailer!

THEY FOUND MOSES in a laundry basket at the Quick Wash, wrapped in a towel, a few hours old and close to death. A woman heard him cry and picked him up, putting him against her skin and wrapping them both in her coat until she could get help. She didn't know who his mother was or if she was coming back, she only knew that he wasn't wanted, that he was dying, and that if she didn't get him to a hospital soon, it would be too late.

They called him a crack baby. My mom told me crack babies are what they call babies who are born addicted to cocaine because their mothers do drugs while they are pregnant. Crack babies are usually smaller than other babies because most of them are born too early to unhealthy moms. The cocaine alters their brain chemistry and they suffer from things like ADHD and impulse control. Sometimes they suffer from seizures and mental disorders. Sometimes they suffer from hallucinations and hyper sensitivity. It was believed that Moses would suffer from some of these things, maybe all of these things.

They shared his story on the ten o'clock news. It was a great story, a human interest piece—a little baby left in a basket at a dingy laundromat in a bad neighborhood in West Valley City. My mom says she remembers the story well, the pathetic shots of the baby in the hospital, hanging onto life, a feeding tube in his stomach and a little blue hat on his tiny head. They found the mother three days later, not that anyone wanted to hand the baby over. But they didn't have to. She was dead. The woman who had abandoned her baby in a laundromat was pronounced dead on arrival from an apparent overdose at the very same hospital where her baby lay struggling for life, several floors above her. Somebody had found her too, though not in a laundromat.

The roommate, arrested that same evening for prostitution and possession, told the police what she knew about the woman and her abandoned baby in hopes of getting a little leniency. An autopsy of the woman's body showed she had, indeed, given birth very recently. And later, DNA testing proved that the baby was hers. What a lucky little guy.

He was "the baby in the basket" in news reports, and the hospital staff dubbed him baby Moses. But baby Moses wasn't found by the daughter of the Pharaoh like the biblical Moses. He wasn't raised in a palace. He didn't have a sister watching from the reeds, making sure his basket was pulled from the Nile. But he did have some family—Mom said the whole town was a buzz when it was discovered that baby Moses's deceased mother was sort of a local girl, a girl named Jennifer Wright who had spent summers with her grandmother, who lived just down the street from our house. The grandmother was still in the area, Jennifer's parents lived in a neighboring town, and a couple of her siblings, who had moved away, were still well-known by many as well. So little Moses had some family after all, not that any of them wanted a sick baby who was predicted to have all sorts of problems. Jennifer Wright had broken their hearts and left her family tired and shattered. Mom told me drugs do that. So the fact that she left them with a crack baby didn't seem especially surprising. My mom said she'd just been a regular girl when she was younger. Pretty, nice, smart, even. But not smart enough to stay away from meth, cocaine, and whatever else she became a slave to. I imagined the crack baby, Moses, having a giant crack that ran down his body, like he'd been broken at birth. I knew that wasn't what the term meant. But the image stuck in my mind. Maybe the fact that he was broken drew me to him from the start.

My mom said the whole town followed the story of baby Moses Wright when it happened, watching the reports, pretending like they had the inside scoop, and making up what they didn't know, just to feel important. But I never knew baby Moses, because baby Moses grew up to be just plain Moses, juggled between Jennifer Wright's family members, passed around when he became too much to take, transferred to another sibling or parent who then put up with him for a while before making someone else step in and take their turn. It all happened before I was born, and by the time I met him and my mom told me about him in an effort to help me "understand him and be kind," the story was old news and nobody wanted anything to do with him. People love babies, even sick babies. Even crack babies. But babies grow up to be kids. Nobody really wants messed up kids.

And Moses was messed up.

I knew all about messed up kids by the time I met Moses. My parents were foster parents to lots of messed up kids. They'd been taking in kids all my life. I had two older sisters and an older brother who were out of the house by the time I was six. I'd been kind of an oops, and I ended up being raised with kids who weren't my siblings and who came in and out of my life in stages and revolving doors. Maybe that was why my parents and Kathleen Wright, Jennifer Wright's grandma and Moses's great-grandma, had several conversations about Moses sitting at our kitchen table. I heard a lot of things I probably had no business knowing. Especially that summer.

The old lady was taking Moses in for good. He would be eighteen in a month and everyone else was ready to wash their hands of him. He'd spent time with her every summer since he was little, and she was confident they would do well together if everyone would just butt out and let her do her thing. She didn't seem concerned about the fact that the month Moses turned eighteen she would turn eighty.

I knew who he was and remembered him from summer to summer, though I'd never spent any time with him. It was a small town and kids notice each other. Kathleen Wright would bring him to church for the few Sundays he was in town. He was in my Sunday school class, and we all enjoyed staring at him while the teacher tried to coax him into participating. He never did. He just sat in his little metal folding chair like he'd been heavily bribed to do so, his oddly-colored eyes roving here and there, his hands twisting in his lap. And when it was over he would race for the door and out into the sunshine, heading straight for home without waiting for his great-grandma. I would try to race him, but he always managed to get out of his seat and out the door faster than I could. Even then I was chasing him.

Sometimes, Moses and his grandma would go for bike rides and walks, and she would haul him into the pool in Nephi almost every day, which had always made me so jealous. I was lucky if I got to go to the pool more than a few times all summer. When I was desperate for a swim, I'd ride my bike to a fishing hole up Chicken Creek canyon. My parents had forbidden me to swim there because it was so cold and deep and murky— dangerous even. But drowning was preferable to never swimming at all, and I'd managed not to drown so far.

As Moses got older, there were some summers when he didn't come to Levan at all. It had been two years since he'd been back, though Kathleen had been pushing for him to come stay with her permanently for a long time. The family told her he would be too much for her to handle. They told her he was "too emotional, too explosive, too temperamental." But apparently, they were all exhausted and they gave in. So Moses moved to Levan.

We were both entering our senior year, though I was young for my grade and he was a full year older. We both had summer birthdays—Moses turned eighteen July 2nd and I turned seventeen August 28th. But Moses didn't look eighteen. In the two years since I'd seen him last, he'd grown into his feet and his eyes. He was tall with broad shoulders and clearly-defined, ropy muscles that covered his lean frame, and his light eyes, strong cheekbones, and angled jaw made him look more like an Egyptian prince than a gang banger, which rumors claimed he was.

Moses struggled with his school work and had difficulty concentrating and holding still. His family even claimed he had seizures and hallucinations, which they attempted to control with various medications. I heard his grandma telling my mom that he could be moody and irritable, that he had difficulty sleeping, and that he zoned out a lot. She said he was extremely intelligent, brilliant even, and he could paint like nothing and no one she'd ever seen before. But all the medication they had him on to help him focus and sit still in school made him slow and sluggish and made his art dark and frightening. Kathleen Wright told my mother she was taking him off all the pills.

"They turn him into a zombie," I heard her say. "I'm willing to take my chances with a kid who can't hold still and can't stop painting. In my day, that wasn't a bad thing."

I thought a zombie sounded a little safer. For all his beauty, Moses Wright was scary looking. With his tapered body covered in bronze skin, and those funky-colored, light eyes, he reminded me of a jungle cat. Sleek, dangerous, silent. At least a zombie moves slowly. Jungle cats pounce. Being around Moses Wright was like befriending a panther, and I admired the old lady for taking him on. In fact, she had more courage than anyone I knew.

Being one of only three girls my age in the whole town made me a loner more often than I liked, especially considering neither of the other girls liked horses and rodeo the way I did. We were friendly enough to say hello and sit by each other in church, but not friendly enough to spend time together or pass the boring summer days in each other's company.

It was an especially hot summer. I remember that well. We'd had the driest spring ever recorded, which led to summer wildfires popping up all over the west. Farmers were praying for rain and the sizzling nerves and sky-rocketing temperatures made tempers short and self-control shorter. There'd also been a rash of disappearances throughout the clustered counties of central Utah. A couple of girls had gone missing in two different counties, though one was thought to have run away with her boyfriend and the other was almost eighteen and her home life was bad. People assumed they were okay, but there had been a few similar disappearances in the last ten or fifteen years that had never been resolved, and it made parents edgy and a little more watchful, and my parents were no exception.

I'd grown restless and resentful, itchy in my own skin, eager to be done with school and on with life. I was a barrel racer and I wanted to hitch the horse trailer to my truck and follow the rodeo circuit, seeking freedom with only my horses, my projected rodeo winnings, and the open road. I wanted that so badly. But at seventeen, with disappearing females in the forefront of their minds, my parents wouldn't let me go on my own, and they weren't in any position to take me. They promised me we'd figure something out when I graduated and turned eighteen. But graduation was so far away, and summer stretched out in front of me like a dry, empty desert. I was so thirsty for something else. Maybe that was it. Maybe that was the reason I waded in too far, the reason I got in way over my head.

Whatever it was, when Moses came to Levan, he was like water—cold, deep, unpredictable, and, like the pond up the canyon, dangerous, because you could never see what was beneath the surface. And just like I'd done all my life, I jumped in head first, even though I'd been forbidden. But this time, I drowned.

Read THE LAW OF MOSES now!

ABOUT THE AUTHOR

Amy Harmon is a *Wall Street Journal, USA Today,* and *New York Times* Bestselling author. Her books have been published in eighteen languages, truly a dream come true for a little country girl from Utah.

Amy Harmon has written thirteen novels, including the *USA Today* Bestsellers, *Making Faces* and *Running Barefoot,* and the Amazon #1 Bestseller, *From Sand and Ash.* Her novel, *A Different Blue,* is a *New York Times* Bestseller. Her recent release, *The Bird and the Sword,* is a Goodreads Best Book of 2016 nominee. For updates on upcoming book releases, author posts, and more, join Amy at www.authoramyharmon.com.

Website: http://www.authoramyharmon.com/

Facebook: https://www.facebook.com/authoramyharmon

Twitter: https://twitter.com/aharmon_author

Instagram: https://www.instagram.com/amy.harmon2/

Newsletter: http://eepurl.com/46ciz

Pinterest: https://pinterest.com/authoramyharmon/

BookBub: https://www.bookbub.com/authors/amy-harmon

OTHER TITLES

Young Adult and Paranormal Romance

Slow Dance in Purgatory
Prom Night in Purgatory

Inspirational Romance

A Different Blue
Running Barefoot
Making Faces
Infinity + One
The Law of Moses
The Song of David

Historical Fiction

From Sand and Ash

Romantic Fantasy

The Bird and The Sword
The Queen and the Cure